THE SPITHEAD
NYMPH

Historical Fiction Published by McBooks Press

THE SPITHEAD

NYMPH

by

JAN NEEDLE

THE SEA OFFICER
WILLIAM BENTLEY NOVELS, NO. 3

McBooks Press, Inc.
Ithaca, New York

For Terry Gardner,
With love and thanks

Published by McBooks Press 2004
Copyright © 2003 by Jan Needle

Cover painting by Paul Wright

Library of Congress Cataloging-in-Publication Data

Needle, Jan.
  The spithead nymph / by Jan Needle.
    p. cm. — (The sea officer William Bentley novels ; #3)
  ISBN 1-59013-077-4
  1. Bentley, William (Fictitious character)—Fiction. 2. Great
Britain—History, Naval—18th century—Fiction. 3. Great Britain. Royal
Navy—Fiction. I. Title.
  PR6064.E414S65 2004
  823'.914—dc22

                              2003025064

Distributed to the trade by National Book Network, Inc.,
15200 NBN Way, Blue Ridge Summit, PA 17214
800-462-6420

Additional copies of this book may be ordered from any bookstore or directly from McBooks Press, Inc., ID Booth Building, 520 North Meadow St., Ithaca, NY 14850. Please include $4.00 postage and handling with mail orders. New York State residents must add sales tax to total remittance (books & shipping). All McBooks Press publications can also be ordered by calling toll-free 1-888-BOOKS11 (1-888-266-5711).

Please call to request a free catalog.

Visit the McBooks Press website at www.mcbooks.com.

9 8 7 6 5 4 3 2 1

AUTHOR'S NOTE

One of the great enduring myths of naval storytelling is the innate rightness, even goodness, of the protagonists, high and low. Given that for several hundred years the sailor was looked upon with a combination of fear and horror by "ordinary" people (those who lived on land), that is all the more surprising. Portrayed in modern books as bluff, brave, loyal, deferential, and perhaps a little stupid, most common seamen were, in fact, rootless, homeless, desperate men, who lived by the bottle and the knife. Their contact with women was almost exclusively in the "sailor towns" of every port, and the "doxies" were not the sort they would have introduced to mother, had they had one. Their lives, to borrow from the great philosopher, were nasty, brutish, and short.

In some ways, naturally, the officers were different. With few exceptions they rose not from the "lower orders," but from a class-base that provided at least a minimum of financial security. Some were, indeed, very rich, and there was tradition too—for many, the navy was a family thing, steeped in expectation of success. Some of these men became great heroes, and contemporary records of their unbelievable courage and daring do exist. It should be borne in mind, however, that many of these accounts of skill and heroism were written by the protagonists themselves, or their agents, as were the accounts of other career officers who might have had an axe to grind. Even William Bligh, a man with not one but two famous mutinies to his name, considered himself a hero, sadly misunderstood, and wrote a chronicle of the events on board the *Bounty* that is startling in its lack of insight.

Bligh, much hated by his men, believed in punishment, of course, as did Nelson, who was quite clearly held in reverence and awe by his. In fact, the "people" of every naval ship—many of them brought on board against their will, all of them virtual prisoners for years at a time—were kept under control by a combination of brutal discipline, exhausting work, inadequate food, and terrifying quantities of liquor. Some commanders clearly understood the psychology of this— and some spectacularly did not. Hugh Pigott, of the *Hermione*, in the name of smartness and efficiency, chose to flog the last man down from every sail change or adjustment, as a matter of course. When the men rose up and butchered him and his officers, the Admiralty spent years and a fortune tracking them down and hanging them—the same Admiralty that then shot Admiral Byng for using his imagination. Like Pigott, they did it "to encourage the others," as Voltaire put it dryly. Discipline was the watchword.

The other great myth fostered by historic books is that of justness, fairness, necessity—war forced upon our protagonists by the greed or viciousness of the other side. During the seventeenth, eighteenth, and nineteenth centuries, Britain fought naval wars with Holland, France, Spain, America, and almost any combination of the four, and every one was a "just war," against a foe prepared to plumb the depths of savagery. Last year's bitter enemy, however, was quite possibly this year's loyal friend, and each war, inevitably, was fought with God on our side and not on theirs. Tragedies sometimes befell the foe—massacres, sackings, starvation—but war crimes weren't invented until the last century, and of course, by unstated definition, only the losers in any conflict can commit those.

In the period of this novel, the innate crime level in any war was nearer the surface than it is nowadays. Put at its simplest, it was the naked struggle of emerging states to carve for themselves a "fair" proportion of the wealth existing in the discovered world. Portugal, then Holland, rushed to the east, Portugal and Spain rushed to the west, then the French and British put in their bids. New sources of wealth included precious stones and metals, spices and cotton and textiles, then sugar. Wealth extraction required more than indigenous labour, and there sat Africa—wild, enormous, and with newly found populations to subject to slavery. The Iberian lands, then Holland, Britain, France, and Scandinavia joined the stampede. The natives of the Caribbean islands were exterminated or displaced, Spain and Portugal raped Central America, and the French and British drove the native tribes of America and Canada ("New France") towards the western wilderness.

There is little point, to my mind, in trying to apply modern ideas of blame to these events. The men who did the fighting and the raping were treated almost as brutally as the people they brutalised, while even the general populations of most European countries and emerging states lived in a form of slavery. Atlantic slaving was a business, and Britain benefited enormously from the trade, then deftly sought to take the moral prize by fighting for its abolition. The Jamaican planters like those in this story treated their slaves with a viciousness and cruelty that strikes one as almost medieval (none of the punishments described was abnormal by the standards of the time and place), but most of them genuinely believed that they acted from necessity, that it was somehow for the slaves' own good, and that in any case they "bore the mark of Cain." Some slaves ran away to become "Maroons," and visited atrocities to match those of their oppressors, not just on them, but on other Africans as well. Racism as it is understood today is *possibly* a product of all this, not a cause; history is too blunt a tool to let us judge, I think.

What is unarguable is that life for many black people in that time, as for many white, was bleak to the edges of belief. Deborah, a poor and hopeful runaway from the Stockport hatting trade, became a whore to live, and (almost) hoped to be kept in (almost) comfort as a demure mistress. Poor Black Bob, for reasons way beyond his comprehension, became a rich man's toy. This was not unusual in those days. Even Samuel Pepys, the "saviour of the British Navy" and by no one's standards a villain or a thug, quite liked the idea of a small black human "pet." And to the men of the *Biter*—the normal sailors of the era, torn from homes, families, or the gutter to go and die by violence or disease—Bob was merely a curiosity, a luckless victim, then the target in a drunken spree. No one thought much worse of him for it. Or even them. Such was life . . .

This, then, is a brutal book, but I can not apologise for that. The era of fighting sail was a great one in our perception, which is shot through inevitably with our romantic notions of the sea. Will Bentley and his friends and enemies are on a voyage of discovery, and I'm going to have to follow them, I'm afraid. The waters are uncharted, and I'm not sure at all what I am bound to meet. All I can hope to do is report back honestly.

ONE

Lieutenant Peter Coppiner was not a bitter man. At sixty-some years old and still lieutenant, why should he be, indeed? Not that his age was known to anyone save him, least of all the clerks at Admiralty, however hard they'd probed and searched the records. Indeed, Lieutenant Coppiner did not know himself exactly, now that his old mother had been dead eleven years. It was expunged, wiped clean, forgotten, totally denied. All he knew was that he was lieutenant still, and would take that signal lack of honour to his grave. He was not a bitter man: he was filled with active rage, and hatred.

The stench on board his place of work this night was something worse than usual. The weather in the Thames had been exceeding hot and still for days, and his last big intake, from off a spice ship inward from the East, had been running with the stomach fluxes and a spot of scurvy for good luck. Most of them had left his tender care by now—many, indeed, had eaten food grace of His Majesty then died, in sight and sound and smell of loved ones and their hearths—leaving naught but paperwork for him, and little chance of bounty for the taking of them. Paperwork and ridding of the corpses, and the vomit, shit, and smells. Lieutenant Coppiner was not a bitter man. He was murderous.

Outside his cabin—"great," once called, when the receiving hulk had been a man-of-war—he could hear men approaching. There was a sentry of marines to guard his door, a most necessary item in his hated trade, and the lieutenant had an understanding with this soldier. If the caller was known, and his business had been stated well beforehand, he would be made to wait. If he was further known to be a man particularly hated by Lieutenant Coppiner, the delay would be prolonged, acutely. As the voices sounded, first mild, polite, then with a rising note of exasperation, a smile homed in upon the deep-lined face. Coppiner ran long fingers through his patch-white hair. This was one to relish.

In the passage, in the reeking gloom, the scene took on an air of studied farce. The Navy officer, whose name was Richard Kaye, was a young, stoutish, florid man, whose colour rose from red to brick as he stoked his fury up. He was flanked by two silent, stolid seamen, one of whom, Tom Tilley, was a giant. He was stooped uncomfortably, even in the high 'tween-decks of the former 90-gunner, and he looked as if his ham-hands itched to break the soldier's neck. The other, boatswain Jem Taylor, small and tough and Irish-looking (although he had an England accent) was indifferent. His eyes dwelt on the unmoving face of a little black boy in a velvet suit, attached to the officer's belt by a whited lanyard looped round his neck. The black boy's suit was also black, as were his large, soft eyes. As black as jet—and suffering.

"Well, you can tell Lieutenant Coppiner," roared the officer, "that I am here on business that cannot be delayed! My intentions were communicated two days ago, and the process is severe. I have the ship, I have the stores, I have instructions from the highest in the Board! Rouse him out, damn you! That is an order! I shall not be delayed!"

At his enormous table, groaning under piles of paperwork, Coppiner allowed his smile to reassemble as a sneer. You jumped-up popinjay, he thought. Has promotion rendered you more pompous yet? But no, not possible, you were ever a poltroon. You may fool their lordships, any man of interest can do that, but you surely can't fool me. I am lieutenant still, and you are post, I hear. Well then—you shall wait!

"I beg your pardon, sir," said the marine soldier. "I have my orders, sir, and I cannot take them different from another man, I beg your honour's pardon. Lieutenant Coppiner cannot be disturbed. He is desperate busy, sir."

Coppiner was getting pleasure out of this, great pleasure. Some of the soldiery were too dim to milk a situation, but not this young skinny redcoat. He would be rewarded for his pains.

"I know your officer!" the Navy captain bawled. "And although *you* may not recognise the marks of rank I bear, I am his superior!"

"Sir?" said the marine. "The lieutenant is my officer, beg your pardon, and his orders were quite clear. I cannot disobey, sir, rank notwithstanding. That I understand."

"Rank notwithstanding? Do you know who I am?"

This was too rich to be borne. Coppiner, galvanic, uncoiled his long body and sloped across the deck to snatch the door back with a bang. Kaye goggled at him.

"Indeed I do, sir," said Coppiner. His voice was hearty. "Lieutenant Kaye, well met! Lieutenant Kaye!"

Kaye's nut-brown eyes bulged dangerously. His face was dark with anger.

"I am *Captain* Kaye," he hissed. "I am *captain,* Coppiner, and very well you know it!"

"And I am a lieutenant," responded the lieutenant, calmly. "I would ask you to address me by my rank, sir, in front of commonality. And indeed, sir, by the by, I was not aware their lordships had confirmed. Are you yet a captain? Or is it *acting* Captain Kaye?"

All the "commonality" were as stony as the grave. However much they might appreciate this struggle, they knew to the last bone that they must not make commentary, by word or look or gesture. Even the tiny black boy's eyes were glazed expressionless. Indeed, his body had gone rigid when the shouting had begun; beneath soft velvet was a hardened knot of fear. Coppiner, a master of the slanted insult, moved it on.

"Of course," he added reasonably. "I know you are a hero now, which is why they made you up. So I am prepared to hail you prematurely, if it pleases you. Never let it be noised about that Coppiner despises heroes, eh? I must indeed congratulate you, Lieuten—Oh! Captain Kaye, sir. Come—may I shake you by the hand?"

As he extended it, and Kaye, defeated, shook, three men and a boy most visibly relaxed. Tom Tilley looked at Taylor, and their eyes agreed: Coppiner was a bastard, a right royal one. From their acting captain, there arose a smell of sweat.

"Now, sir," said Coppiner, briskly. "Forgive me for recalcitrance, but I ha' not forgot. You are come to me today, to my most humble kingdom, to top off your company. Remind me if I err, but it is the Indies, ain't it? You are filling up to go and save the planters from their fear of blacks. The natives are revolting, they do say. As to the planters . . . well. But you must go and hold their hands, and tuck them up in their distressful beds o' nights. That is correct, sir? Have I remembered right?"

Still sore, the tubby captain decided to let it lie. Coppiner was insolent, but then he always had been. At least it looked as if some men would be forthcoming. So often in the past, that had not been so. He shrugged.

"You have the right of it in part," he said. "We are headed for Jamaica, true, because there is Maroon activity. There was a revolt on another island some time past, and the Squadron has the whole Carib to patrol, as well as looking out for Johnny Frenchman. The Jamaica planters fear they're left too open to attack."

The old lieutenant nodded. It was like a pleasant conversation, Kaye felt. He was beginning to relax.

"Aye, I remember it," said Coppiner. "When the black men rose and terrorised the white, their masters." He fixed a steely eye on the little velvet boy. "I hope you have no such vicious schemes afoot," he told him sternly. "You would not cut your master's throat, would you, while he lay sleeping near?" He smiled at Kaye. "Antigua, was it? Where the throats were cut?"

Coppiner's suggestiveness was subtle this time, although the boy, Black Bob, stiffened as if in fear of retribution. Strangely, perhaps because in theory he had little English, hardly none at all, and was anyway assumed half-witted.

Kaye's nascent relaxation congealed back into hatred of this twisted man.

"You're well informed, sir, for a prester," he responded insultingly. "But I have little time for banter, Coppiner. I—"

"*Lieutenant* Coppiner. I thought we had agreed?"

Kaye's grip was getting tenuous. The soldier's eyelid had begun a twitch. When officers fell out it was the men who suffered, everybody knew. Even Taylor, the coolest of cool men, had licked his lips.

"Lieutenant Coppiner," Kaye gritted. "And I am—"

"Captain Kaye. Yes, for a courtesy. And I have a little sickener for you, Captain, because—I have no men. I am sorry for it, but there it lies. Despite my best efforts, the coop is empty, I have none. You must grant me pardon."

There must be an explosion soon. Tilley stirred his mighty shoulders, letting out a tiny sigh. He wondered if he could get away with killing Coppiner, or breaking some few bones at least. He thought maybe he might soon, and be lauded for it. He might also get to stuff the soldier's musket up his arse.

"No men? But you had warning yesterday. Indeed, the word was put out at the Rondy near a week ago. The Office—"

"Is full of jumped-up little clerks! I am a receiver, Captain Kaye. I do not collect the men myself, do I? When you were on the Impress, did you not leave me dry sometimes, or am I wrong in memory? If I get men delivered, I have men to place; if not, I don't! I receive, sir! That is all I do—receive."

Kaye gritted out the words.

"You had men yesterday, and the day before. You knew my needs; you knew the timing of my orders. I was frank with you, Coppiner. Too frank."

"It is your memory that's at fault, not mine," said Coppiner, quite mildly. "*Lieutenant* Coppiner, remember?"

"Lieutenant then!" said Kaye. It came out as a splutter, half a shout. "And you had men, did you not? I was told it at the rendezvous. You had half a dozen for me, according to the clerk! This mission is important, sir! Their lordships are behind it to the full! My vessel has been half-rebuilt. We are taken off the Impress; there is heavy work afoot! You had men for me, and I need them still. Now! I need them now!"

What little light there had been in the passageway was fading fast. The reeking air was still, and, in the pauses of the argument, it was extremely silent. None of the creaks and groans of a living ship, no sounds of wind and cordage from the outer world. The sailors were sick of the bickering; Black Bob, uncomfortable, seemed prone to tears. And the prester, who had a rhythm all his own, made a decisive move. He slammed his cabin door behind him, produced a key and locked it up, turned abruptly, and shouldered through without a by-your-leave. The others, save the soldier-guard, followed him—there was no other choice. As he passed a lantern, guttering in a recess, Coppiner picked it up. He curled a lip at Captain Kaye, neither smile nor scowl but impertinence.

"They died," he said. "I thought I'd told you. I have a handful still, three or four left over from a different source, but I fear you will not relish them. Indeed, sir, they are almost diabolical, not fit to scrub your heads. But it's all you're getting because it's all I've got. I wish you joy of 'em."

He knew his hulk; he knew each stinking passageway, each hatch and opening. The lantern threw a blur of light that left the others blundering, but Coppiner's pace was sure. He walked a hundred feet to a descender, and as he clattered down they had no choice but to follow his dying glow. Kaye stayed closest to him, being a clumsy man in most need of guidance, and there were squeaks of pain from Bob as the lanyard round his neck was jerked and hauled upon. Tilley and Taylor, seamen born, kept up with practised ease. In terms of space, to them, this sad old ruin of a ship was prodigal. But Christ— both thought—she stank.

Two decks down they reached the main holding area. By this time their eyes had grown accustomed more, and there were dim smoking lights at intervals along the sides. They revealed a vast expanse of dirty planking, clearer than a ship's deck cleared for action, not a mess bench, not a gun. It was like a courtyard, or a crypt. The only furniture was mounds of rusty chain and ring-bolts. It was a prison, where lived the hopefuls, old and young, the scourings of the Press, before Lieutenant Coppiner sent them to the Navy ships he chose— most carefully—for them. He was proud of his ability, was Coppiner, to match such men to ships. To mismatch, rather. His pride was in mismatching. Mayhem for captains, and no blame to him. He revelled in it.

"You see," he said to Kaye, holding his lantern high. "Nobody. The bastards died like flies. There are your men, down there. The only good thing, they are just in from the Indies. That should joy them, should it not, to be shipped straight back again? Ah, 'tis a noble thing, a sailor's life!"

Kaye made no comment, although the news excited him. So Coppiner had been holding out, as he had thought. He'd said the men were diabolical, no good for him, and now they turned out to be West Indies hardened. That in itself was wonderful, given the rate of death among new Caribbean hands. He had heard it said that six out of ten might die if they were unlucky with the fever-rate prevailing. Clearly, Mr Vinegar had planned to keep them from him, and had failed.

However, he still could not see "his men." Then he caught a movement in the gloom, in a corner of the 'tween decks, at one end. The grim lieutenant gave a grunt.

"Aye, that's them. Captain Kaye, I am a fair man, as you know. I would not advise them, sir, you would be better off with rats. They strike me as vicious, sir. Leave them here to rot awhile; I'll foist them off on some poor unsuspecter without your perspication. Away, sir, they are not fit!"

Kaye did not even grace that with a reply. Transparent oaf, he thought. Prime seamen, clearly, and inured to the malodours and the fluxes of the West. And he would try to keep them from him, would he? He strode across the decking with clear purpose.

"How many?" was all he said. "What are their names; what were their ships? They're Englishmen, of course?"

There were three of them together, and one not far apart. The huddled three were lightly bearded, pale-skinned, pale-haired, and curly. As Kaye and Coppiner got nearer, followed at a short distance by the seamen and the boy on lanyard, they turned a gaze upon them that was like the odd gaze of an animal, three pairs of eyes but singular. Although of slightly different ages, the men were virtually identical, peas from one pod, a creature with three faces but one look. Their bodies were close-touching also; in the gloom one could not sort or separate. Three faces like sharp axes, long, angled noses; high bones underneath the eyes; pale eyes of the lightest grey; thin, hard, unforgiving lips, tight compressed.

"Not English. Scotchmen," Coppiner responded. "From Aberdeen, someone has told me. Not them; they tell me nothing, do you, boys? They're Scotch, from Aberdeen. First fisher folk, then slavers. Ain't that so, boys? Ain't it?"

"And they are brothers?" said Kaye, a note of wonder in his voice. Coppiner laughed, dryly, as if to call him fool for statement of the obvious. Indeed, the sharp axe faces were so clearly of one mother borne, the wonder was that she herself could have told them apart. Their clear eyes gazed at Kaye without apparent animosity.

"Scotchmen, eh?" he said, heartily. "Well I have been to Scotland, boys, and fine seamen you will be, I'm sure of it. You will like my ship, the *Biter*. The cook is from those parts, Geoff Somebody his name. Do you know him?"

Coppiner's lined face twisted to a grin of bare-concealed derision. Tilley coughed into his hand. Even Bosun Taylor smiled. He was relaxed, though, as if his captain's comment was the soul of sense.

"Raper," Taylor murmured. Then, louder, "Geoff Raper, of Buckie, I believe. No insides, one leg. If you've ever met him, you'll not have forgotten, that's for certainty." The Scotsmen's eyes did not even flicker. They were self-contained, indifferent. "She's a good ship," Taylor ended lamely. "Man could do worse than ship with us."

"They have no choice," said Coppiner, concisely. "Captain—an' you want them, they are yours. Let it be remembered for the record, though, that I've vouchsafed my opinion. They are the lowest scum. I'd only have them on my ship in irons. It is my fairest warning."

"You make a meal of it," Kaye said dismissively. "I'll wager you I have lower scum on board my ship than these McTavishes." He paused, as if he'd just remembered something. "Christ, talking of Geoff Raper, can they speak English? Our peg leg cook cannot, hardly. It is like a bag of porridge, with a voice. You, sir—speak me some words. What is your real name? Not McTavish, I'll be bound?"

Whichever one he had spoken to, not one of them replied. There was a silence for a moment, then strangely, Coppiner stepped in.

"Not McTavish but Lamont," he said. "Captain Kaye, my time is getting short, I must move on, and getting these grim brothers to converse is something you'll do easier with a rattan in your hand. They are Scotch and they are painful. If you want one other man I have an Irish, and he is worse. He came off the same returning fleet as them, and they were fighting when they were took. Like them, he knows the waters, though. He claims he shipped out as a freeman planter, then fell down on his luck."

"A dirty Irish, eh?" said Kaye. "There'll be no truth in that shit then. The Irish are not freemen ever, are they? Not in their nature. Where is the dog?"

The man had been in sight the while, although in a dim corner, leaning on a grown-oak knee. His dark and hairy face turned on them now, and he raised a hand in mock salute. He spoke words that sounded like a greeting, but they were not English, or if so were no wise comprehensible.

"You, sir," snapped Kaye. "You are in England now; I command that you speak our language. Can you speak it? Can you?"

"Sir, I can," he said. "And I can sing in it, as well. Can you speak Irish? Now that's a question."

"Ah, Christ, an imbecile," said Kaye. He turned to Coppiner. "All right, Lieutenant Prester. Three good men, one bad and imbecile. It is a fair crack, in this day and age. Let us go aft and sign the papers. I must to the Rondy, then the Office."

The Irishman, arms wide, had started singing. His voice was deep and mellifluous, although the words could not easily be caught. The standing men, and the small black boy, caught off their guard, were listening. The voice rose powerfully, filling the reeking gloom. The last lines throbbed with a sort of irony.

Leave old England, westward go
Sail for the Indies—
Where golden grass doth grow.

For a moment when he'd finished there was silence. Who would speak first, Kaye or Coppiner? Who was aggrieved the most?

The man spoke, himself.

"It is a West Indies song," he said. "We sing it still." His voice was sombre. "Men go there with high hopes, and are betrayed by them. There is no golden grass. I was two years finding out, three years escaping. Now you will take me back. I curse you for it, Captain. I curse you for it."

. . .

Later that night, talking to the mirror with a bottle in his hand, Lieutenant Coppiner was lavish with self-praise.

"I played him for a booby and I won," he said. He took a giant quaff of wine, sweet, heavy, red, and watched it running down his chin. He took another quaff, and laughed. "They bring me men who should be hanged," he said. "They land me with their rogues, their rats, their scum, their dregs, and tell me I must set them up on ships, which is impossible. And then I get Lieutenant Kaye—a captain, pah!—and play him like a penny violin."

One more mouthful, and self-pity began its cruel blight. He saw it in his mirrored eyes, he opened lips to speak again—but found that he could not. Oh God, they've made him post, he thought. And me they praise up to the skies, I do their filthy work for them, and I will never, ever rise. I rid them of their awful scum, I fill their ships for them, and Captain Booby is their latest captain.

Coppiner, dead drunk as usual once he'd wet his lips, dropped the bottle and lay down beside it. It was his baby, leaking at the neck. Peter Coppiner wept tears for it, gently, because his baby made him ill so very quick, because he could drink so little any more. He could still ease any man into a ship, though, however terrible that man, if he could find a penny violin to play. The three Scotchmen were murderers, it was thought. They had fled from the Carib rather than be hung. Now Richard Kaye would take them back again.

"And he thinks he has a bargain," thought Coppiner. "I would that I could join him in the West to see!"

He pulled the bottle across the planking to his face, placed the neck between his lips, and sucked.

"I wish you joy of them," he mumbled, as the wine leaked down. "Great joy."

TWO

In the months since he had seen her, Will Bentley's ship, the *Biter,* had been transformed. At first, racing towards her in the two-man wherry hired at the bridge, he did not recognise her lying at the Deptford tiers outside the basin. Both topmasts were taller, and her topgallant poles seemed white and willowy. Indeed, the whole ship gleamed, with yellow paint and varnish in overwhelming evidence. Her stern was somehow higher, her sprit more raked. From a standard old ex-coal tub, she had taken on a raffish air. And all her canvas, at the yards, was new and creamy white.

"Is that the *Biter,* then?" he mused, aloud. The boatmen glanced at him but did not bother to reply. It's a fine Navy officer that doesn't know his own ship, they probably were thinking. And also—typical.

But *Biter* had been changed, completely for the better. As they swung round across the ebb and nudged up to the boats tethered at the boom, he could smell fresh linseed, cord and tallow, and discern new cleanliness. Above the waterline, at least, she could have been a new-builder. Below it, though, he noticed quite long fronds, and— obscurely—was comforted. This ship, which he had never thought to see again, still had secrets, dirty ones. As he passed his coins and climbed up the ladder like a gentleman, he wetted dry lips. Ah well, he thought, it was either this or hanging, when all's said.

The first man that he saw when on the deck was the sturdy boatswain, Taylor, who recognised him with frank surprise—but moved with characteristic speed and seamanship to catch Will's sea bag that came flying across the rail from the wherry, unannounced.

"Ho, Jem," said Bentley, with a brittle bonhomie. "I thought that I had come to the wrong ship."

"Perhaps you have, sir," replied Taylor, with a smile. Then he caught himself, and added, almost formally: "Nay, sir, she is the *Biter* still, but a little different. It is more Navy fashion, sir. We are not pirates any longer, nor yet ruffians of the Press. Captain Kaye is a captain; he is Post. We're to say our prayers on Sundays."

Will had liked Jem Taylor in the times before, a liking that was mutual. But the slackness of Kaye's vessel had been notorious and could never have been let to last. Both of them knew it, standing there. They were awkward.

"She is looking fine," he said. "And is Captain Kaye on board, or any other officer?"

"No, sir, it is you so far. How should I call you, sir? It was indicated . . . well, Captain Kaye . . . it's said you are Lieutenant Bentley, now?"

Bentley could feel a reddening. "And you thought"—he would have liked to say—"that I was still in jail." But he did not. He muttered gruffly: "Aye, I am Lieutenant Bentley, Acting. I have not . . . ah, to hell with it!"

The poop-break door was opening, so they were off the hook. A tall, heavy man was stooping out, a man dressed in London finery, a city man or merchant. Behind the silk and ruffles, Will saw to his astonishment that it was a man he knew.

"Ah yes, sir," Taylor breathed. "It is Mr Gunning. He has sold her to their lordships, sir, but he is helping Captain Kaye to work her up. As you can see, sir, he got a noble price!"

John Gunning, full-lipped and curly-haired, was figged up in such finery that Bentley could hardly stop from goggling. He was a London mariner who had somehow got the *Biter* years ago, had owned her lock and stock, and then been hired by the Navy as a tender to the Press when new vessels were rare as teeth in geese because of war. Old and cranky, she had served their lordships well, not least because Gunning had been part of the agreement, and acted as a sailing master and provider of a crew. Now, it seemed, the Navy owned the ship but not the man, who was richer by a good and solid lump. He was bearing down upon them, like a summer storm.

"Mr Bentley!" he said. "Now, well met, sir, well met indeed! And where is your companion, Mr Holt? Not far behind I hope, sir—you are sailing in the morning! Not I this time, though, no, not I! I have had my fill of working for my living, sir! I do the other thing!"

Before Will could reply to this—or even gather thoughts to form denial of the central claim, that they were sailing in the morning—there was a high-pitched flute of laughter, and a clatter at the doorway once again. A garish vision of young loveliness—or at least a Thames-side doxy of the brightest hue—tripped out, controlled herself, then clutched at Gunning's arm for steadiness.

"No longer pirates, eh?" said Will, hardly loud enough for Taylor to pick up. "Well, if this is the Navy Royal, their lordships will have fits!" Jem grinned and they shared a minor pleasure. The maiden though, wide-eyed and rosy-cheeked, was staring at Will, and sway-ing.

"Oh, Jack!" she said to Gunning. "I know him, Jack, I know him! It is my little peach, remember? That night that we and Ellen, was it? And Eddie Campbell!" She reached a hand out for William, who, horrified, stepped back. To his distaste, she gave another high-pitched squawk of laughter.

"You play the virgin still I see, sir! Oh Jack, can I have him, Jack? Will you buy him for me, to be my pet?"

Will, looking round for succour, noticed only that more men had come up on the deck, ostensibly for duty, more likely just to stare. He recognised some of them with another shock. His life had been so strange and circumscribed in the past months that his mind had blanked these sailors out, as if assuming they had died. But *he* had been rotting in a filthy jail, not they; they were not traitors as he had been widely held to be. They stared covertly, but still they stared. If *Biter* was his home once more, it was a fearful homecoming.

For a moment he was tempted to deny the girl—although he did recall her face, if vaguely—then decided that in that direction rocks and sandbanks lay. With a ferocity he did not in the slightest feel, he snarled at the boatswain in front of him to clear the decks of gawpers or to find them useful work to do, on pain of flogging. Jem Taylor got his drift instantly and most heartily concurred, and went bald-headed at the first group with a rope's-end flying in his fist. Bentley turned a grim face onto Gunning.

"Mr Gunning, sir, well met," he said. "I understand you've made a killing with their lordships, and I wish you all benefit of it. How-ever, I am in command of *Biter* as of this instant, and I would ask you what your business is on board."

"Ooh," said the painted lady. "Ooh, Jack, he's stern." But her voice was not half so brazen as before, and Gunning put a hand out to make her quiet. He could be a wise man and a brave one, Bentley knew, when he was not in drink. What were the chances on this sultry afternoon? Good, it would appear.

"Now, Sal," he said, "be quiet or I'll throw you overboard. Mr Bentley here has work to do, and we are in his way." To Will he added, with grave politeness, "I came on board to talk with Captain Kaye. I have been aiding him to get the ship in readiness. You are going very far. Tomorrow. I had come to bid farewell."

Something in his gaze was speaking very plain to Bentley. It occurred to him the "tomorrow" was for the doxy's ears. Whether or no, he did not care to challenge it. He nodded, and the other smiled.

"Captain Kaye will be here later but I cannot say exactly when," said Will. "But there is very much to do, sir, so if I may . . . ?"

"Indeed, sir. Come, Sal—this is Sally Marlor, by the way. She has helped your captain with his . . . with his furnishings. He will not object to Sally having called. And I, sir, I would wish you good voyaging. You have got a perfect ship, at least; she is fit from truck to keel. You have my word on it."

Nods were exchanged, and Sally Marlor, chastened maybe, tried blowing a small kiss, but quite half-heartedly. Gunning took her to the side, whistled up a wherry, then lifted her with facility across the bulwarks down to the waterman's arms. Bentley turned away and stalked towards the cabin. In front of him a man appeared, slinky and obsequious, whom he recognised as Josh Baines, called Rat, or Ratty, who was asking if he might carry any dunnage. His question was ignored because it was his place to carry it, naturally, and Bentley let himself into the after world without another word—but with a shadow. There was more space there now, under the new-raised poop deck, with two not insubstantial shuttered-off cabins on either side for the officers and any other persons of importance the *Biter* might have to accommodate. Baines went to one of them unbidden, as if he knew for certain that it was Bentley's. He put the dunnage down and touched his forelock, but did not dare to speak. Bentley ignored him.

The cabin that he had been allocated—much bigger than any

quarter he had occupied before—was most noticeable for the carriage gun that squatted squarely in the middle of its deck. Of course, when they went into action, his walls would fall, his cot would rise, his cupboard, writing desk, and washstand would be stowed away by keener hands than Baines's (he hoped). This furniture all folded down to very little, and his sea bag and the chest that soon would follow with the carter's men already had their designated place, he guessed. Then his bed and work and thinking room would become a station in a fighting ship, drenched in sweat and smoke and maybe blood, but he would be above it, on the deck. Strange life, he thought: strange bloody life indeed.

"Who else is here?" he asked abruptly. "There are four berths. Are they taken?"

The little rat-faced man adopted the look of acute dishonesty that Will knew so well. The tongue flashed out to dab the lips, so like a rodent it could scarce be borne. His eyes looked up and under from his ginger brows.

"The officer of marines," he said. "He's here. Lootenant Savary. Must have lots of friends though, in our opinion, sir, on account he's young to be a man of power; well . . ." He smiled, not pleasantly. "He's about fifteen, by the look. Only got four sodjers, though, so not no problem, is it?"

"Are they installed on board then? Where are they all?"

"All of 'em on shore, sir. Something about their uniforms, or their guns, or summat. All due back tonight, Jem Taylor says, for what that's worth, sir, beg your pardon. About Jem Taylor, sir. Can I make so bold, sir? Word in your shell-like, like?"

"Where are they installed, I asked you, Baines. They're meant to buffer us from you people, ain't that the scheme? So where are they quartered?"

Baines, rebuffed in his scurrility, merely swallowed.

"Below where we're standing, sir. They slings their 'ammacoes afore the gunroom. That's a laugh, though, ain't it? Four sodjers strung out on a washing line to guard one little snotty, eh?"

Bentley had a jolt of interest. A little snotty, on this most benighted ship?

"What, a midshipman? Are you sure of this? Is he on board?"

Baines smirked, gratified to have stirred real interest. The tongue flicked out once more.

"Ho no, sir, not yet awhiles. But it's truth, not rumour. It's set in iron, cast. Some nephew of the captain, sir, or some such relative." He almost laughed, about to be quite daring. "Poor country cousin, sir, is favoured with the betting men. Some waif he's got to give a place to, you knows the form."

The tongue again, projected by anxiety. The shifty eyes showed fear he might have gone too far in insolence. But Bentley relished such unguarded information. At times, on board a ship, such blatherings could save men's lives.

"I heard a rumour we were set to sail tomorrow," he said casually. "That's set in iron too, say you?"

Baines snorted his contempt.

"That's that big bugger Gunning, ain't it? For to mystify his paint-eyed tart, that Sally-thing. If she thinks we're off tomorrow, she'll stay away from us and leave him be, won't she, for fear his Missus comes along to wave goodbye. Mebbe she's got her dander up, the wife, and he needs Sally clear a while, or maybe there's another tart bespoken for a shag. If he's not dead drunk, he's whoring, is Jack Gunning's lay. His weakness, too. And now he's got the gold, sir. Well, bugger me!"

"But does she think he's going with us, this Sally Marlor? I don't understand. He's not, is he?"

"'Fore God he's not! He's got what he wanted out of the *Biter:* he's got money coming out of every pore. He's took the Office for a pretty penny, a lovely guinea, then a ransom more. They say her bottom's like a pear; when them West Indies worms get teeth to it we'll be learning to be fishies or we'll die."

"Rubbish, man," said Bentley testily. "Their lordships don't disburse so blindly. They'll have had her planking gone through with a fine-tooth comb. Speak sense."

Baines smiled for once with genuine amusement, it would appear. He nodded, with unusual vigour.

"Well, we're all in her so we'd best believe, I guess," said he.

"Although Gunning's friends get everywhere in these parts, most everywhere that deals with ships, in any way. I'd like to know the bottom-feeler's name, sir, if you'll pardon me dooblyentender. But I'd bet my sister's tits some money greased around! You know Gunning, sir. Do you think to understand him in his wiles? And where is Lootenant Holt, sir? Is he still in pris—"

The merry outflow stopped, and a look of terror crossed the rodent face. Baines, in his self-induced excitement at skewering a target he guessed would be acceptable, realised he had strayed into most dangerous waters.

Bentley, who was shorter than most of the *Biter*'s former crew, was, however, on eye level with Josh Baines. He stared into the hot and slippy eyes, his grey ones diamantine.

"If I smacked your face for that, Baines, I would smack it very hard," he said coolly. "You must not forget how I deal with insolence, never. Lieutenant Holt will join us in a day or two. And shortly after that, as I believe, the last of our ship's company, and arms and vittles—everything—will be got in readiness and to perfection."

"And Gunning can spend some time with wife," said Baines, forlornly. An attempt, Will thought, to get out of the mire he had set himself. "Perhaps he'll come for shake-down runs. The sails and rigging is all new, an' all. She'll need at least one man knows how to handle her, that can sail her proper like a . . ."

He tailed off, the look of terror back. Now he would insult their seamanship, would he? But Bentley did not care.

"The last cabin is for the master, I presume? Is he appointed yet?"

"No, sir," Baines said, gratefully. "No master yet, and only half a crew of men. Well, we've got a company, damn near, but half of them are still in irons, till we clear off of London River, like. They look to run, is Captain Kaye's worry, and he's damn right in some of 'em. They had an easy life, did Gunning's lads, and if we took their shackles off they'd be overside like water fleas. Don't blame 'em, neither."

"Gunning's lads? What mean you, Baines? Good God, you don't mean . . . ?" In front of him, Baines dissolved in laughter. "By God, you do! Well, what a demon trick!"

John Gunning, when he'd rented *Biter* to their lordships, had also rented out a good half the company that sailed her. They, naturally, had scorned the proper Navy men, and mocked them into fits of fury sometimes because they, not slaving for the government, drew more pay, got leave ashore at any time (and lived nearby, to boot), and best of all, could never be impressed. Why should they be, indeed, when they were working on an Impress tender? And now, with *Biter* wholly bought, not on a hiring fee, well—what, exactly?

"Let me understand you, Baines. Friend Gunning, having sold his ship to make an easy penny, has betrayed his gallant crew into the bargain? What, all those surly ruffians that used to work the ship with such ill-grace and never lend a hand? He's pressed them on the *Biter?* Well, kiss my arse!"

"It was a pretty bloody little do, sir. Big John and Cap'n Kaye must ha' dreamed it up over a pint of wine or six, then got Tom Tilley and Jem Taylor to put up the other strong-arms for the fun. Billy Mann and Hugg took the London loafers to a Deptford spirit house to give a fond farewell when we was rumoured for the Indies trip, then word was put about that one of Gunning's shag-in nights— if you'll beg my pardon, sir—was on. You can guess the rest."

Will could. He had stumbled onto one of Gunning's "shag-ins" himself, and it was a prime enticement, certainly. He pictured drunken revellers, the thoughtful Taylor waiting, the giant Tilley and the massive Tommy Hugg. With Kaye and Gunning in the wings, perhaps, with pistols, if he knew his bold commander. No, not Gunning though—he'd surely need to keep well out of it. It was a close and tight-knit bunch, East London sailormen.

"Friend Gunning kept well clear?" he said. Rat Baines nodded.

"You know the score on that one, sir," he said. "Naught to do with good old Jackie, oh dear no. 'If you're betrayed, lads,' he would have told 'em, 'it weren't by me, my dears. Blame the King's Navy bastards. And when they lets you out of irons, give them kicks and steel.'"

"But they won't believe it, though? They'll suspect he's lying, surely?"

"Who knows? Someone is, or was, but who's the likeliest? It was us Navy men as took 'em, and gave them broken heads. We'll find out who they blames when we're out-away, at large upon the ocean. Then we'll see. They're still in irons down below. They're ugly, Mr Bentley, sir. Oh yes, indeed."

My God, thought Bentley. Another happy ship for me to sail upon. They'd have to be in irons until the *Biter* sailed, unless Kaye had armed guards in mind on mast and deck. How long was that to be? Not long, said Kaye, not long. But then with Captain Kaye, Slack Dickie as his people knew him . . . Great heavens, it was shaping, it was shaping up.

"They ent the worst, neither," said Josh Baines. "He've brought us some in from the Press. Old Vinegar's palmed off the dregs of the receiving hulk, but Cap'n thinks—"

That panicked look was back, and gone. Interrogation, with Josh Baines, could be rewarding. Will regretted all the months he'd scorned to even give him space to live in, a piece of unconsidered scum.

"Old Vinegar is Coppiner, I presume. And Captain Kaye thinks what? That he's done well?"

He was verging on the dangerous himself. He smiled encouragingly, and Baines responded, caution to the winds.

"Well, 'tis what Jem Taylor told us, leastways," said Rat. "On the pull back from Coppiner's lousy old hulk, says Jem, the captain was cocky hoop because he reckoned Vinegar had tried to keep them from him, these lot, but he'd wheedled and tricked until he'd called his bluff. He reckoned Coppiner was desperate not to let 'em go, probably because he'd promised them to some other captain, for a bribe. I stayed back at Rondy after we'd saw them, so I didn't hear all this. But to me, it looked . . . well, begging your pardon, I'd say Coppiner would have give his mother's life to have got shut of them."

'Fore God, thought Bentley, Kaye had said he wanted pirates. Below decks it sounded as if he'd have more a magazine, already primed to blow.

"How many of them, then? And will they team up with Gunning's lucky crew? It sounds good luck we've got some soldiers this time round, don't it!"

Baines blinked at the joke. Soldiers on board were not good in a sailor's eyes, not ever, for whatever reason. But he could not contradict, could he?

"There's three," he said. "Well, four if you count the Irishman. The Scotch have sworn to kill him though, it seems; they don't like dirty Irish, as who does? He's a Papist and they're not, and he mocks them in a foreign language and it gets them steamed, or so it's said." He smiled briefly. "I steers away from 'em if possible, sir. They seek to catch men as they walk past. They broke two fingers on one of Gunning's men because he sat too close. Tilley tends 'em mostly. He's big enough to kill all three."

So, thought Will. Three Scotsmen and a Hib. And a gang of betrayed Londoners, and all the *Biter*'s old originals, and four soldiers and a man-child officer. No master yet, and Kaye, Slack Dickie Kaye—who was, however, reckoned as a hero! And Sam, who, when he'd seen him last had been still pale and weak and racked with injury and pain. Good God, he thought, there's no one there could even con them down the London River on a summer's day!

"And what of the *Biter*'s Navy lads, then, Baines?" he said. "Now we're no longer on the Press, but must sail across to distant parts and maybe even fight. Aren't they for running while there's still a chance?"

Baines surprised him. He shook his head in vigorous denial.

"No sir, Mr Bentley, sir," he said. "It ain't just there's a war on and we knows our duty, but the Press is tedious, ain't it, always breaking heads and drinking in the London houses, and catching nasties off the London whores. In the Carib they say the sun do shine like silver all year round, and the local brew is rum and there's barrels of it in the street. They make so much of it, it's free to white men, who are masters, and the black girls give you everything because they're slaves. Hugg's been there, sir, and so has Si Ayling, even one-leg cookie, Geoff. It's all true, sir; it's a kind of paradise. We don't want to skip ship, sir, far from it. We want to go."

Inwardly Will was laughing, but his expression did not change. One section of the crew, then, would be happy for a while; they needed it. Rat Baines's head went from shake to nodding.

"The one to watch on running will be the captain's boy," he said. "You know, Black Bob, the little neger. For over there, sir, they're blacker than in Africa. The whole place bursts with them. Black Bob looks out the window, what does he see? His people, beckoning to him at last. Oh yes, sir, Mr Kaye will need infernal vigilance, won't he? The moment we drops hook—Bob's gone."

Not so long, in fact. Black Bob was gone and lost not many days beyond this conversation. Not run though—he was hunted.

THREE

It was not until very late that night that Lieutenant Bentley (Acting) met his captain. Before then he had set himself to rights, made contact with the *Biter*'s people who remembered him, and seen Gunning's sulkers and the four from Coppiner. He had also reviewed another motley bunch of men impressed earlier, which Baines had not even bothered mentioning, and introduced himself to a mild-faced young lieutenant of marines, who had returned just after midnight with but three soldiers, the fourth having been knifed badly in a drunken brawl ashore. Then William had stood on the afterdeck alone, at the far end from the dockyard watchman still deemed as necessary by the Navy Office until the *Biter* should be made officially Captain Kaye's command.

Sweet is the air this night, thought Bentley, trying to call a line of verse from out of memory, but with very small success. The river, on a gentle flood, smelled fresh and warm, and full of aromatic mud reminders, one of his favourite smells. On the ebb, and with a different wind to sweep it down from London, the effect could be much different, he well knew. The stench of smoke and furnaces, molten iron and acidic gas, the city's sewage and the acrid reek of industry and bloated dead. London is big and violent, he thought, and I'm a country man. But what, God help me, will the West Indies bring?

Until a week before, Bentley's life had been constrained by four damp walls, and thoughts of moving air, either sweet or vile, had been the stuff of weary memory. He had been in jail, first on a Portsmouth hulk, then in Petersfield, then somewhere south of London, and he had almost given up hopes of getting out, at least for some long years. Had he not had certain interest, had there not been a flow of letters, lawyers, representations, bribes perhaps—well, God knew what the outcome might have been. In all the months, he had been interrogated by officers of many ranks, men in lawyers' garb, and others who were clearly spies. The most heartening thing had been a letter from his Uncle Daniel Swift, who was out in the Straits "carving my way as ever," as he put it. This letter, which had been opened by the Office and resealed, had exhorted him to take heart, for all would certainly be well. Will could not find his Uncle Swift a comfort normally; more, he was a kind of black beast to him, as the French might say. But this time, he *was* comforted. Stay in jail he might; but if Swift was in the picture, something would be happening. What it was, he could not guess. But he would not be forgotten.

That, as he stared across the black and sliding water of the Thames, he remembered as the worst part of incarceration—the feeling he had slipped off of the edge. True he had come ashore in Langstone Haven as a sort of fugitive, but he had expected rationality, and a hearing. He had landed in an open boat, half dead with cold and tiredness, his friend Sam Holt three-quarters gone from gunshot wounds beside him, and a French girl, called Sally or Céline. Three days later, in a tiny cottage in Langstone village, still uncertain as to what they ought to do, they had been taken by dragoons. Will had seen Sam once in all the time since then, weak and shrunken from his injuries, bronchitic in a Forton jail, and Céline not at all. From no one, neither visitor nor inmate, nor from any correspondent despite his strongest pleas, had he got a word or even hint about her fate. She was French. She was a smuggler or a spy, or even both. She smuggled men, from England into France and vice versa, and she had helped to save his life, and that of Sam. He feared that, in the English way, she had been hanged.

Then, eight days ago, the amazing thing had happened. He had been sitting at his table in his cell, with his mind a dozing blank. It was a state he had been practising for many months, and which he could achieve sometimes with good success, sometimes less so. As he was a Navy officer of some sort his cell was hardly comfortless, and his mother sent good food and wine for consolation of his soul. In front of him he had a pack of playing cards—almost certainly smuggled, he had noted with some gloomy satisfaction—that he shuffled restlessly from time to time, but most of his energy went in keeping his mind clear. Clear of Deborah, clear of Céline, his family, Sam, his enemies. Most painfully and frequently, Deborah refused to go—Deborah whom he loved and he had killed, he feared. But other thoughts pressed in. How had he come into this pass, how to escape, what, in the name of God and Satan, would the future bring, and when? On this occasion he had achieved his sleepy blankness, to be brought back to a present consciousness by the rattle of his jailer's keys.

Bentley had looked up, bored and helpless, at the rough-planked door. There were no lawyers due, no family. Who could it be? There was an enormous weight on him, a weight of dull similitude. His eyelids drooped. A break in the routine, and tiredness was his sole reaction. Oh Christ, he thought, I'll die if I don't get out soon; I'll die. Then the door swung open and his eyes jerked wide on Richard Kaye. Will, on his feet intantly, was almost stammering.

"Sir? Great heavens, I . . . Sir, this is a . . . this is an honour."

In Bentley's sight, it was a Richard Kaye transformed. He was in a coat of shrieking newness, a Navy blue of most expensive cut and style, and his trousers were fresh sprung from under the flat-iron. Still tall and stout, he seemed wider, more expanded, with his face alive with confidence. More, with friendship, which was the big surprise. They had parted on the verge of enmity and suspicion. What, Will wondered, could have wrought the change?

"Indeed an honour, and a pleasure too, I hope," boomed Kaye. "You have heard of my good fortune, I have not a doubt. But did you guess you were to have a part of it?"

Bentley's face made his lack of knowledge clear. To Kaye, though, who thought only of himself, that was incomprehensible. Bentley, he imagined, would have spent his waking hours contemplating Richard Kaye's success.

"I am made captain as you know," he said, "post captain, with both rank and vessel now confirmed. The *Biter's* still in my command, but she is no longer with the Impress, and she has been much improved. Masts taller, poop deck raised, extra guns, extra room for men. Good sakes, Mr Bentley, we might even ship a chaplain to bring the word among the nigger Carib slaves!"

The young midshipman stood there, in his drab and dingy shore-side clothes. He had known that Kaye had risen in their lordships's eyes after the action that had broken him and Sam, but he had not realised how far. The *Biter,* standing off the Goodwin Sands, had saved about sixty souls, in fact, and Slack Dickie's courage had been exemplary. His courage, and John Gunning's seamanship, had projected him from a booby—albeit a rich one and an aristocrat—into a man their lordships could finally accept as a proper naval officer: his life's ambition.

"The Carib, sir?" said Bentley. "A chaplain?"

Kaye's eyes, like polished hazelnuts, shone pale with pleasure. He liked to see sharp Mr Bentley dull and ox-like.

"Aye, the Carib, sir! We are off to the West Indies betimes to do some proper work, not chasing round to dredge up dogs to later mutiny. I am post captain, and I need a good and gallant crew. And officers. You, sir, will be my first!"

The effect was giddying. He was a prisoner, awaiting trial! Moreover, Kaye was not a friend; he never had been. Surely he was not a friend?

"But I am . . . I was . . . but a midshipman, Mr Kaye," he said. "How can I be your officer? And I am in jail."

"Pah! Not for too much longer, that I promise you. The orders are coming down from the Office posthaste, and I was given leave to tell you first. I need officers because there is a war on, Bentley, and I need a certain sort because we're sailing to a wild and foreign part. I have a mission, sir—two missions, although the second part is . . . well, never mind that now—and I need a certain type. Not to mince it, I need men who would be pirates, if they could. You fill that bill!"

The door was still half open from Kaye's entry, but he moved across to swing it closed. The jailer, apparently, had left them to it, clearly told there was no question of escape, but Kaye had grown conspiratorial. Will, however, was still agape.

"A pirate, sir? What can you mean?"

Laughing, Kaye swung his body round to perch a buttock on the flimsy table. It squeaked and shifted, and papers slid onto the floor, which both ignored.

"Oh, butter would not melt!" he said. "But you will not deny, I hope, that as a loyal midshipman you have proved something of a failure? Bentley, a pirate is a man who will, contra orders, naturally, take on a beach full of armed smugglers damn near single-handed and run a cockleshell through hurricanes for no other reason than insubordination. Deny it how you might, you are more a pirate than a King's officer, and I will have you as my first. You will be Lieutenant Bentley. We will rise."

Inside Will there were churnings he could not understand. He was giddy with sensation. To be saved from jail by this man, whose machinations had put him there to start with. To be beholden morally to a man whose morals were, to all intent, non-existent, to a man who was a murderer, probably. And all because he'd fought him tooth and nail. It was absurd. Not possible.

"I cannot be," he said, simply. "I am not a lieutenant; I am a mid. I have taken no examination, nor could I pass one. I cannot even navigate."

Kaye's full lips curled. His disdain was almost palpable.

"Pah, navigation. Boys' tricks. We will have a sailing man, a master, to do all that. You can fight, can't you? That's what they're looking for. Your testing for lieutenant is coming soon, in any way— a week, ten days or so; I have took the liberty. You are expected at the Office on . . . oh, what day was it? I have it writ down, no fear. You will not miss."

The giddiness increased. Had he tried to speak, he would have stuttered. But Kaye did not notice. He was indifferent.

"I am a hero now," he said, casually. "Their lordships had no idea at all of how to handle you, and I put in my oar." He patted a pocket in his smart new coat. "There was a word from Swift, an' all. Your Uncle Dan. He told 'em he'd got wind out in the Straits, even, of your exploit, and demanded you be reassigned to him next time he reached to home. He is a pirate ditto, ain't he? He's ta'en three galleys off Algerie is the word. He's left the Squadron and gone private, and there is hint of gold. I thought to nab you first, to keep you from him! Maybe you will turn out to be another Daniel Swift! That would be a feather for me, would it not?"

"But I cannot be an officer!" said Bentley, passionately. "Whatever you might think, Mr Kaye! My knowledge is so rusty; I have not mugged all the theory, even half of it! I will be a laughingstock! A dunderheaded fool!"

"You will pass with flying colours," said Kaye, all happy smiles. "I will put a wager on it. I'll wager fifty guineas." He stopped, looked round the tiny room, which was cluttered with books. "In any way, you've got a week, ain't you, and you've surely got the library. If you've been shirking, make shift to catching up immediate, but I don't believe it anyhow. I know you, Will Bentley—you ain't been reading the New Testament! You've got ten days or so. So get to it!"

It fell to Will that he should just refuse, point-blank, just cut through the moral knot and free himself. To what end, though? For what? To be a martyr and to watch his family suffer? To continue as an endless money-sink? A further thought slipped in. To be beholden to a rogue like Kaye was one thing, but what if he could use the chance to save another man? He did not choose to think too hard or long, but stepped straight onward.

"And what of Sam?" he said. It came out cool, as if he'd not just thought of it, as if it held the forefront of his mind. "Sam Holt, my friend and fellow. He is the better sailor and the better man, if you seek a first lieutenant. Sam Holt can even navigate. He would pass his tests with colours flying."

Kaye regarded him silently for several seconds, a strange expression on his face. It was quizzical—a kind of smile.

"Sam Holt," he said. "Aye, Sam Holt. Well then, what is he to you?"

"To me, at present, he is nothing, regretfully," Bentley replied. As he spoke the loss became a void. For all he knew, Sam might be dead, he'd been so hurt, so badly cared for, when last he'd seen him in a cell. He steeled himself, put some defiance in his voice and stance.

"But in a fight he is a giant and a tiger, and if it's pirates that you want . . . Sam is an honest man, his honesty is dazzling . . . but he is . . ."

Kaye laughed. Surprisingly, he understood entirely.

"Piratical," he said. "Aye, William, I concur most heartily with that. Piratical—and hungry, I'll be bound. Who pays his wages now, eh, now the Navy don't? But where is he? Is he a cripple, or active still? And surely, if you're accused of derelicting duty, his situation with their lordships must be ten times worse!"

He was mocking, and Will was flushed with sudden anger.

"If Sam comes so do I," he said. "The case is simple. If he does not, sir, then I don't either. We have . . . Sam Holt and me have . . ."

Kaye was nodding, and was smiling still. Will had expected anger at the least, but amusement seemed the order of the day. Post Captain Kaye was less prickly than mere Lieutenant Kaye had been, maybe.

"Well," he said. "I half guessed this might be your reaction, and that's one up to me. Holt is arrogant, with the arrogance of the truly low. But his bravery ain't in question, is it, and with you to keep him under hand, that's good enough for my book. If we can find him, and the matter can be swung, I'll rope him in. Does that meet cases, or have you other orders I must comply with, sir?"

The smile was broader, and Bentley found that he was joining in. Good God, in half an hour he'd come from incarceree to active officer again. A sort of miracle.

"Sir," he said, with genuine humility, "I thank you from my heart, and for Sam too. Will you find him, sir? The Office must surely know. And will . . . can you . . . have you the . . . ?"

"I have the punch at present to do damn nearly anything," said Kaye. "Interest piled on interest piled on punch. Holt himself ain't short of power neither, of a certain sort. There's his uncle, or protector, ain't there, what you will? Sir Arthur, ain't it? Arthur Fisher—one of the old brigade. He can pull some strings, I'll warrant."

"And can you get Sam in for testing, sir?" asked Bentley, boldly. "Put his name down for their lords' examination? If you think I can pass it, he must swim through."

"It's not impossible," said Kaye. "Aye, aye, I guess I can. Good God, who is conductor of this conversation, thee or me? I'll leave you to your books and your inducement. You cannot let yourself be beat now, can you? Sam Holt is low and you are not, sir. Think of the shame if he gets passed lieutenant and you don't!"

Post Captain Kaye had departed then, leaving Bentley with his amazement and his thoughts. For the next few days he had heard nothing more, but had attacked his books and charts with obsessive vigour. It did occur to him that this might be some cruel jest or hoax, but only a time or two. It was so extraordinary, in the end, that he could only believe it and rejoice. Then, one day, the order came and he was released, collected by a Navy Office clerk and taken in a carriage with his sea bag up to Seething Lane. Papers to sign, five guineas in advance given by another clerk (and added, so they said, to the sum already owing to the Navy on his account), no explanations or instructions that were any use. No time to see his parents, scarce time to bespeak some Navy garb to be altered and delivered quick by boat (another charge, on trust of a deposit, that he would have to find, and pay), scarce time to write his mother that a chest be packed and sent. It was the Navy way: he was pushed around and made to sort it out himself. Will was invigorated.

However late he went to sleep at nights, though, however hard he flogged his brain by day, hope for the future was always overlaid. He saw the face of Deborah, in pain and terror, her eyes beseeching him.

FOUR

By the time his captain came on board at last that night, Bentley felt fully a King's officer once more. Despite he'd roved the decks for only a few brief hours, he had a new grip on the ship and people, and a hope that this time round things would be quite different, more like the Navy he'd grown up in, not so desperate slack. Kaye, also, once his boat's crew and Coxswain Sankey were dismissed, expressed a

quiet satisfaction that somehow matched his own about the feeling
on the sleeping brig, the air of clean efficiency and control. Kaye
did not care, it seemed, that more than half the hands were still in
irons lest they ran or—in the Scotsmen's case—indulged in mayhem,
murder, or far worse. Time enough for that when the *Biter,* under
full command at last, became a ship in readiness.

The little black boy, whom he had not seen for many months,
touched Bentley's spirits with cold fingers, though. Bob had not
responded when he'd greeted him, had not even raised his eyes, and
was tethered by a lanyard of fancywork looped round his neck and
the captain's belt. Will hated this, that Kaye still kept him as a pet,
and it made his hopes for new maturity seem hollow. Kaye had other
childish tricks as well, it soon transpired.

"Well, Lieutenant," he said, easily. "She is a good and peaceful
and a proper ship now, ain't she just? What news of anything? Where
is your friend lieutenant? Sam Holt was not so hard to find, and I
expected he'd have joined us ere now. Down below, you'll tell me,
sleeping like a baby?"

"Below, sir? Why, no he's not," said Will, astonished. He'd had no
further news of Holt since meeting Kaye in his prison cell and had
tended not to hope too hard. This was a pleasant shock.

"Nay, I'll warrant not!" crowed Kaye, delighted at his subterfuge.
"I'll warrant he'll be with his whores in Blackfriars! When he learned
he wa'nt to hang, he sprang to life, to horse, and to attention! Now
that, Lieutenant, is what I meant by it—a man piratical!"

Bentley, beneath his belt, was hollowed out. Sam was found, and
that was wonderful—found out and signed up for the brig. But had
he chose to go to Dr Marigold's ere making way to find and talk to
Will? Was friendship then so cheap? And with that thought came
thoughts of Deborah, raw and horrible. It was in the courtyard at
Marigold's gay house that he had abandoned her, crying out and
fighting for her life. Since then he'd feared her dead, in truth, and
borne a weight of sadness and of guilt, a pit of loss and ignorance
he skirted round but could not penetrate. For all enquiries, by word
of mouth and letter, had yielded him no information at all. Nothing,
indeed, had had to be enough.

Sam Holt, at that same moment—but not for Will's imagined reasons—was indeed at Marigold's, in the arms of Thin Annette, his favourite harlot. Pale and gaunt, he had hurried there after Kaye had tracked him down and filled his heart with hope and expectation—and ribald hints that he might find his friend. He had been treated like some welcome ghost by the ostlers, who had seen him always as a lucky common man who'd rose, and not a normal Navy officer, high and mighty.

"Shit and muffins!" said Rich, frankly cock-a-hoop, when Sam had got down from his hack and stretched his bones. "You look like walking dead, sir! I heard they'd stretched you! Are you still alive?"

He reached across and pinched an arm with vigour, then kept his hand there, clasped around the bone.

"Christ," he added, less jovially. "You're bloody scrawny, though. Feel that, Tim!"

"Shot through the neck and through the back, and God knows what else," Sam told them, laughing. "It was Frenchies on a Shoreham beach, and a Frenchie girl that saved my worthless skin, her and an English one or two. Rich—shut your gab. You know who I'm looking for."

Rich thought he did, as did Mrs Putnam also, the fat and comfy keeper of the corridor of whores, who sparkled with clear pleasure when she saw him, and fussed around and felt and prodded, and would not listen to his question, however earnestly he should articulate. Within five minutes, though, he was face to face with *their* guess, Thin Annette, then in her arms. He drank her presence through her lips, while she clung to him with a fervour that Mrs P would have found unseemly, had she been there to witness it. In another minute Annette was naked and undressing him, and tutting and cooing and emitting little frightened cries.

"Oh, Sam, oh, Sam, what have they done to you? Oh, Sam, you're thin. Those scars! Your neck! Your chest! Your—" Brief pause. "Oh, Sam, there's nothing wrong with *that!* Oh, Sam."

When they had done, they lay there like two lovers, not a sailor and a whore, and talked about the weary months since they had done this thing before. Sam made light of his travails and travels, and said that he did not believe his neck was ever due for stretching because he, luckily, had friends. Annette said her life, sadly, had been wearyingly the same since she had kissed him last, but she had heard he'd been a traitor and been hanged and swung on Tyburn tree.

"I went and looked one day," she said. "A day joyout to Execution Dock. Some one of the company pointed out the longest black thing dangling on a gibbet and swore it was you, but I knew it wa' not. Not tall enough." She ran a finger down his white, protruding ribs. "You look more like him now though, although not encased in pitch," she said. "I'm glad you ain't, Sam. I've missed your face. And prick."

It responded to this on the instant, and they made love again. And it was love, too, a sort of love, thought Sam, for his soul had ached with loneliness and want so very long. There was danger, true, in being there if the harlots should reveal his presence to their procurer—he owed the painted whoremaster guineas by the score, but Kaye had given him the chance, now, to pay off debts sometime. Will's part in his rehabilitation—his insistence that Sam must be found—Kaye had, however, not revealed.

"I suppose," Sam asked her wistfully, when they had done, "I suppose none of my friends do come here now? I mean one in particular, I suppose . . ."

She laughed at him, with frank amusement at his reticence.

"You mean Deb's beau!" she said. "Flax-haired William! No, Sam, I ain't seen him at all, but Deb I have, a lot, or rather—"

"Deb?" he interrupted. "What, she's alive still? Good God, Annette, Will was quite certain she was dead! When he last saw her . . . well, he told me, in the jail . . . Well . . ."

"Aye, well indeed. She was stripped naked like a strumpet and was like to have been shagged to death or torn in pieces, except that Marigold saved her and Marge washed the blood off and set her on her way, with kisses and a little bit of money. They killed a man, you know. I bet sweet Willie did not tell you that, did he? He could not have come back here, and that's the reason; they would have tore him off for hanging. 'Fore God, Deb only dared to come herself when she was in a state of terminals. It was the only place she knew."

"And is she here now then?" he said, eagerly. "Christ, Will was mad in love with her, and knowing Will he loves her still! If I could find her, then find him—well—oh fine indeed!"

Annette, lean and hungry as a hunting dog, entwined her limbs with his to get the warmth, and broke the next news gently.

"No, she's not here no longer, not at all. Indeed, if she was anywhere, I'd have thought 'twas with that man you called your uncle to me once, the rich old man in Surrey that looked after her one time. She tried to get there I know, but had to come back here again, and I guess she might have tried another sortie. But if she had got there, would not you have seen her, though? You ha' been living there, I guess?"

Sam demurred, but clearly had no plan to tell her why. Indeed, Sir Arthur had saved him from detention, possibly the gallows even, and Mrs Houghton and her maidens had nursed him back with great solicitude to something like good health. As so many times before, he had returned the kindnesses by leaving Langham Lodge, and that abruptly. As before, he had not been certain what had spurred him—except for money owed, for obligations, for the fact he felt an ever-growing burden to the poor old man, a burden he could not hope to pay for or unload.

"I quit my uncle's some good time ago," he said. "Even if she had got there, I must by then have left. Ah, poor Deborah. Poor Will."

She touched his arm.

"Don't say die, though. If she ain't here she may be there then now, mayn't she? She was a bold survivor, Deb. After Marge Putnam put her out, she got down to Shoreham, so she said, in seeking you and William. Then she got across to Portsmouth."

"We were in Shoreham, briefly . . . Well, on that beach, but . . . but Portsmouth? Why? And how, for that matter?"

Annette laughed.

"The how is easy, for she walked and borrowed lifts on drays and carts to save her cash. The why was to do with smugglers, and Customs men; I don't rightly remember, for she told it kind of bent. But a fat man tried to buy her for a harlot, although he called it by a different name, that Deb found vile. It made it sound like poetry, she said, a nymph of some sort, a—"

"Spithead Nymph," said Sam. "Aye, that's what they call the Navy whores down thereabouts. And she took umbrage, did she? Good for her."

She got up on one elbow, her thin, sharp face severe.

"Ho, Mister Gentleman," she said, pointedly. "Spit and Head don't sound to me like poetry, but what's so terrible to be a whore? I serve you well enough, don't I? I took you for my friend."

"You're not a whore," smiled Sam, and shook her gently by her straight black hair. "You are Annette."

"Ho ain't I, then! What am I? Is whoring a game beneath your dignity so suddenly? Like Deb?"

Sam hunched up quickly to her level and planted a firm kiss on her lips. He wrapped his arms round her and pressed her to his chest. And he was laughing—his saving grace.

"All right, then you're a whore," he said, through lips and teeth entangled. "You are a harlot, and I'm lucky in your arms. I forgot, Annette, you have to earn your board and keep; no one gives you a private yacht to swan it in, like me and all the other Navy officers. But to me you ain't a harlot in the old disgraceful way, and I guess that must be what Deborah meant. What, some fat old lecher tried to gi' her tuppence for a fuck, and she got on her high horse? Well good for her, I say again—and wouldn't you do just the same? You would!"

Annette was mollified. She had to smile, but ruefully.

"It didn't do her any good though, did it? The high horse didn't get her to your uncle's house, although she tried for it, I'm sure. And after that she had to come back here and hope she did not end up swinging from a rope for the murder of the man she did with William." She sighed. "I don't know exactly what scared her off his house, she didn't say, but she was in a bad way when she got to here, though. She was near to bloody starving, and she was ashake with terror case someone give her up to justice. I told her she looked worse than any whore I'd ever seen north of the river, and a Spithead Nymph might be a stepping up." The smile died. "She only cried though," she said, soberly. "She was a poorly little thing that night."

"I can't see Deb crying," Holt said. "She'd don't seem that kind of maid at all."

"She ain't."

There was a pause.

"She'd been a whore before," Annette said. "Of sorts. Funny how it took her this time, but it did. Love, I suppose. A bastardly thing to happen to a maid." She looked at Samuel, levelly. "Starving she may've been when she got back here, but apart from mud and hunger she was as pretty as a painted picture. Marigold would have put her on immediately, but she'd have none of it, she was bound for better things than whoring, Deborah said. I was nearly jealous for a while. Poor little bitch. I hope her body is not rotting in a gutter. Poor hopeful little bitch."

Sam was thinking. He must find Will—he had guessed by now, from Slack Dickie's archness, where he would be—and tell him. They would need to look. He would want to search for her. Good God, thought Sam, she might be at my Uncle A's. Good God.

Her eyes were keen on him, enquiring. Sam noticed.

"I must away, Annette," he said. He crushed her leanness to him, and he kissed her, hard. "But I must shag you first."

"An' you have the silver, master, shag and welcome," she replied, with irony. "I am a whore."

"Silver have I none, fair maid," he quoted. "But I have a long slate still, poor Marigold will vouch for that! Old Marge don't seem to care in any wise; she did not ask for money off a poor young sailor-man."

"And nor will I," Annette laughed. "Your prodder's longer than your slate, and that is good enough for me. Lay on and welcome—for you, sir, it is free."

"I love you for it, maid," said Sam. "I love you."

Sam did find Will, later that night, but it was breakfast time next morning before they could put their plan for seeking Deb to Captain Kaye, and neither had had much sleep to bolster them against a disappointment. Sam had come alongside the *Biter* in a public wherry after three, and had been astonished to find a watchman still awake. He had crept below to indicated quarters, and had woken Will. In some quiet way they had both been overjoyed to see the other, and were rendered emotional by the fact that they could serve together— and at a proper task.

Sam filled his friend in briefly on his past months in the wilderness, but did not mention his news of Miss Tomelty—as Annette had insisted was Deb's proper name—as yet. Will told of his time in prison, of talking to his father about their family's connections with the smuggling that had so nearly brought them to their deaths, and his decision to go along with Kaye when chance was offered.

"We think he is a murderer, a traitor, and a fool, Sam," he said, in the fuggy silent glim 'tween decks. "But I cannot tell what's right or wrong no more. I killed that mountebank damn nearly in cold blood at Marigold's, as Annette has told it to you, and you and me were jailed for what they said was treachery. Add to that, my father convinced me I'm a fool because I could not understand the business of that wicked trade, which he says is free and necessary. So are we rogues or heroes, do *you* know? I'm on the rocks."

In the smoky flare of the cheap-fat candle, Holt was nodding. He had had his own long struggle for understanding, and had drawn a line beneath it, or go mad. It was a line in sand, he knew, but the firmest he was like to get.

"Sir A," he said. "My uncle whom I will admit to treating like a father now, and who lost Charles Yorke in that most vicious way— well, as I understand it, he has interests in the Orient which means he smuggles also, in some sort of way, but to his total satisfaction that everything he earns is for the country's good. I asked what had happened to the smugglers who sheltered us, the smugglers who tried to kill us, the French maid who saved both our lives. He said the Kentish and East Sussex men had paid some price—two hanged, but only humble batmen, not the business crew—and the Hampshire team, Bartram and Mary, Kate, Bob, Joe, and all the boys—well, they were saved and are hard at it still. The tie-up with the eastern lot, the murderers and villains, did not happen, and all the money-men behind the Trade . . . they're free and flourishing. You know one of them is your father, don't you, Will? But that you damn near got hanged, despite? It was a toucher close."

Will nodded, unseen in the dark. His father's explanations, face-to-face in dismal prison rooms, and in letters later glossed passionately by his older sister Lal on her visits, had led him to an understanding that black and white were not shades he could rely on in questions of family and love. Lal had told him that poverty and ruin were skulking in the background always, and their father fought both tooth and claw to keep them well at bay. And then she'd laughed, sunny and self-mocking, in a sprig-muslin dress that made him long for home and carefree times.

"We seek gentility," she'd said. "The new world is on the up and up, Will. We must all rise above the ruck or slide into the mire; it is the coming way. Father might have to take a crooked path, but he is respectable. Next year, perhaps, he will stand for Parliament. Except he has a son in jail, and Mama has had to sell the family silver to pay the lawyer men. La, sir, that's a jest!" Her face stilled, serious. "La, sir, it is not," she added, "not entirely. But never mind, Will, never mind. We shall be strong and strengthen still."

To Sam he replied: "I do know that. I heard that you had got an easy ride, by the same token because Sir A had ears in government. And also, like me no doubt, through expenditure of some poor someone's cash. But you have not made mention of the French maid, Céline. Sally, as you know her. You thought she was a spy behind it all and had betrayed us. She was not, and did not. So did she hang?"

"Know not," said Sam. "I honestly know not. Sir A still wants vengeance for his protégé, for Charles Yorke and his friend Warren, done to death by most dishonest men. If French Sally is dead, I should feel like him, is all. I, too, should want revenge, but on so-called honest ones." He paused. "I am sorry for my doubting, Will," he said. "I am sorry for it."

He told Will then of Annette's tale at Dr Marigold's, and what she'd said of "Deb Tomelty." He hoped that it would lighten up things, and it did. Will, in actual fact, almost exploded with excitement and with joy, and any hope he'd had of convincing anyone—himself included—that Deb was a mere sad memory of the past, dead to *him* at least, if not in fact, melted intantly. Hope had sprung, and it would not be suppressed.

"We must go," he said, and said it over, every two minutes, until Sam could douse him down. "We must talk to Kaye and tell him we must go. Sam. Instanter. Now. What o'clock is it? It must be getting on for dawn. She might be at your uncle's still! Oh heavens, Sam, oh heavens! We must go this moment, instanter!"

"We wake him, do we?" Sam said, ironically. "We barge into his cabin and pluck Black Bob out of his tender arms? Well met, we cry! Your new ship's officers, ready for duty! Except we're going on a jaunt, to hunt some quim! Well, Will . . . shut up, shut eye, and wait till morning. Good God, he has had no sight of me on board yet, and him the captain! Also, he saved our lives!"

They did shut eye and both—as seamen can—seized the chance of sleep, however minimal, though Bentley almost had to drag it down upon himself. But they were up before the lark, got coffee out of one-leg Geoff, washed, dressed, and chafed impatiently in the early warming sun, and watched the *Biter*—still on a shore-bound, half-cock regime—come to life. They watched men they knew, and some whom Sam did not, tumble from the forward hatchway. They watched three soldiers, scrawn and scruff and misery, chivvied from below by an officer who, when fully viewed, struck Sam with frank astonishment.

"Who's that?" he said. "He is a child! Is that our officer of marines?"

"His name is Lieutenant Savary," Will muttered sideways from his mouth. Then shouting started: military orders, morning drill, which filled the sailors with a smug delight. Josh Baines, lurking near the shoreside bulwark, moved his mouth as if to spit into the water, then caught Will's eye, remembering the new regime. He smirked instead, ingratiatingly. Will, his comments masked by the soldiers' racket, added: "He is twenty, I believe. He has four musket men in all, but one of them got stabbed in Deptford. God knows if he'll be ready when we sail."

"Twenty! He looks twelve. Cheeks like a pair of apricots, that curly hair. Christ, Will, Black Bob had need of looking to his laurels. Has not Slack Dickie got the drools for him?"

Lieutenant Savary was beautiful and very like a maid. Will had not conversed with him in any intimacy, but had got the general picture: like himself, a second son or third, no prospects of inheritance, no interest in the church, so therefore bound for army or the sea. Unlike Will, he could not do mathematicals perhaps, or maybe did not relish water. Bad luck, if that were true, bad luck indeed. There was plenty of it, between London and Jamaica.

"You are disgusting, Sam," he said. "We do not even know for certain Kaye has such tendencies, let alone this officer. In formal conversation Savary sounds as manly as the next man, although his voice is somewhat light. You must not let your humour make things hard for him."

Holt grinned, but not repentantly.

"It's true Dick Kaye do like the maids as well," he said, "far as we know it, any way. But this bold redcoat is then a target either road, ain't he—he'll make things hard for him himself! Thinking on, though—Black Bob might thank his lucky star! He might get furlough!"

Black Bob appeared at this point, eyes downcast and meek, barefoot and timid in loose shirt and short slop britches. He moved fast and lightly towards Geoff Raper's chimney pipe to get his master's coffee, but Sam halted him with a call. The small black face rose upwards fearfully, then recognition lit the eyes. He knew Will as a kindly sort, and Sam included, so it would appear. No word, however. He stood silent, a sweet and fragile mite.

"Bob, well met," said Sam. "Talkative as ever, so I see." He smiled, and Bob did not. Sam shrugged. "Ah, well then. Tell the captain, if you please, that I am here. Lieutenant Holt would wish to present himself on board. And Lieutenant Bentley is desirous of a quick word, also."

The boy bobbed like a dipper and hurried off. At the hatch he almost knocked into Jem Taylor, boatswain, who touched him on the shoulder, gently. Will noted with some sort of minor pleasure that

Black Bob allowed the touch and did not spring away in fright. In the past few days, Will had observed, the neger child had displayed blank fear of almost every soul on board.

Taylor came across. He held a hand up, half salute, half greeting. "Sir, sir," he said. "Lieutenant Holt, you've come on board."

"Acting, Jem," replied Sam. "Not got that label yet; we've got to face the old crustaceans, both of us. Who knows, in a few days I might fail so bad I have to call *you* Sir! How goes the *Biter?* She is very clean and smart. If the wherry men ha'nt known her, I'd've shot right past."

Taylor's frank, blunt features became more quizzical, amused but guarded all at once. Grey eyes swept both their faces.

"Easy done, sir. Some might say a wise man would ha' took the opportunity. But aye, she's smart, for which Lieutenant Bentley here can take the credit. Though I must add, sir, that Captain Kaye is much renewed also. He's not so very . . . slack."

Even for a good and trusted man who knew them well, this was bold, thought Will. Slack Dickie was the captain's secret name, but secret from Kaye only, no one else at all. However, though men knew it, it was surely not for bandying around? He said rather stiffly: "I'm glad that you have noticed our regime, Mr Taylor. *Our* regime, not mine, our captain is the *deus* behind this *machina,* if you take my meaning. You are of Rome, as I believe? You know the Latin."

Taylor nodded, twinkling.

"Of Ireland, thus of the Romish faith, though raised in London, sir. But I know the Latin word for God, and can guess the rest, beg pardon. And I will say, if permitted, Mr Holt, sir, that Mr Bentley says it truly. Captain Kaye is a differ—I am proud to serve with Captain Kaye. His conduct of the rescue off the Goodwins, sir, was marvellous. The seamanship and daring brought a tear to many eyes. I do not think we'll get too many runners, sir, before we're clear for sea. The men are looking out to get there. To where the golden grass doth grow."

"Golden grass?" said Sam. "Are you puddled, man? What golden grass doth grow?"

"A song, sir. There is another Irish in the hold, who speaks the

Romish maybe, but our native tongue as well. Black eyes and bruises
and a sense of the ridiculous, I think he is a good man when all's
said. He has a word for everything, and a song. It is what drew men
to the West Indies in the olden days, he says. The story was that even
the grass was pure gold. It ain't, though. He came back a destitute."

Sam eyed him carefully.

"Well, that is pity then, ain't it? Might ha' kept me from a debtor's
prison, to name but one of us. But he hasn't spoiled the story for
his keener shipmates then, you say? They still believe in money for
the picking? Does that make him the captain's friend or theirs, I
wonder, in the scheme of things? And black eyes and bruises also,
did not you say? Wherefrom them?".

Jem Taylor shook his head.

"He's not the only man come back into the arms of Old Vinegar
from the far Carib," he said. "There's three Scotchmen whose talk
makes old Geoff sound sensible. They don't like Mr Ashdown, our
singing Irishman. They dislike him enough to be a threat to his bollocks and his bones. If he goes overside on the voyage, we won't have
far to look, sirs. I'll put down cash on that."

"Do we know why they hate him?" Sam said. "Is it badness or is
there history in it? All from Jamaica, eh? It will be history."

"Did they attack him, then?" asked Bentley. "What, on board of
here? But they're in chains, aren't they? Why was I not informed they
had got out? Now that is slack!"

Black Bob, unseen, had taken drink to Captain Kaye, and then
come out again. He stood at the poop-break watching them, waiting
to be noticed.

"The captain's orders, sir," Taylor said to Bentley, placidly. "He
told me that in the daytimes, when we had soldiers watching, the
new-pressed men were to have the deck for liberty. Two of Jack
Gunning's scarpered overside within ten seconds—the bastards
didn't touch the capping on the rails. The Scotchmen would have
gone an' all, but they saw Ashdown looking for something to float
himself on, and jumped on him instead. He couldn't swim, so they
aimed to ditch him overside, I guess, when they'd bashed his mug a
bit. By the time me and Tom Tilley had got him clear of them,

another Gunning man had jumped, who couldn't swim neither, so nearly drowned, but we fished him out eventually. Tilley's big, sir. We had to lay all three out with a handspike before they would desist. Hence Ashdown's bruises." Small smile. "Captain still thinks chains is not the answer, sir. Beg to disagree."

Kaye, extraordinarily, was standing at the poop door alongside Black Bob. He was in his shirtsleeves—so much for the new regime of order and formality—and his face was open, frank, and smiling. Clearly, he could no longer wait for Bob to pass his order.

One minute later they were in the cabin, and in another five had put their proposition. And Richard Kaye had laughed them both to scorn.

FIVE

The cabin, which might now be reasonably called "great," was transformed as the rest of the sad old coal tub and her men had been. No money had been spared, and it was higher, broader, lighter—and luxurious. The transom was pale paint and scrollwork, the table glowing rosewood, and every chair a minor work of art. There was a writing desk with drawers and doodahs in the high French style—an *escritoire,* Kaye called it proudly—a carved rack that held his spyglass and a brace of gleaming pistols big enough to knock down castle walls, and a lightweight table spread with charts. On them, casually, lay a set of compasses and a rolling rule. As much good to Dickie, Sam thought sardonically, as a cutlass of spun sugar.

"Behind that screen, my sleeping quarters," Kaye said with a smile. "You remember my requirement on the old *Biter?* A bed fit and wide enough for sleeping on, not like the normal shipboard run? Well this one would suit the King! Their lordships demurred, they grumbled like old penny-pinching shrews. So I paid it all myself, and hang the lot of them!"

His hazel eyes were clear and innocent, as if he were a boy. Beside the ornate screen stood Black Bob, eyes down. No separate bed for him that Will could see. Extraordinary.

When Kaye had shown them everything, after effusive greetings to his "new second, the brave pirate Mr Holt," he had let them state their hopes concerning Deborah. He had clearly found them very, very funny.

"Good God, sir," he said to Will, "it is a common strumpet! It was the tittle of the officers at the Lamb! The story of how your own impressers dragged you naked off her at Dr Marigold's . . . well, I have dined off it, and I know I'm not alone! Fine tits, but Debbie is a whore, man. You cannot mean it, what you tell me. Why in hell's name try to get to her again?"

Will had beads of sweat growing on his temples. Outside the big stern windows the Thames was slow-moving, calm. He regarded Kaye's fresh face, so totally uncomplicated, and envied him.

"Sir," he said. "I do not know. But I—"

"Of course he knows, sir," cut in Sam, robustly. "Whore or not, this maiden has a name, a face, and eyes and thoughts. Sir Arthur Fisher has taken her in a time or two before, and succoured her and cared for her. And has again, unless I'm much mistaken. She is good enough for him!"

Sir Arthur Fisher was a name Kaye knew. Sam saw the alteration in his face.

"Aye, Sir A, of Langham Lodge, in Surrey," Sam followed up. "You may know he is my benefactor, and he's exceedingly important. He does not treat Miss Tomelty as a whore."

"Sir Arthur Fisher, eh?" said Kaye. "Mm, an important man indeed. I knew he was your interest in some wise, but I . . . And the maid has got a name, to boot—she's Tomelty, not just plain Deb? Well, but she is still a slattern, ain't she? Maybe he's just a very kindly man. Or maybe he . . . Well, is his wife alive?"

"Sir," said Bentley, stiffly. "Miss Tomelty is . . . it is wrong of all of us to discuss her like a thing. Miss Tomelty is *in extremis,* and I have a duty to her, clear. Whatever my desires might or should be. When last I saw her she was at the point of possible destruction."

"And bollock naked, too!" said Kaye. "Lord, Bentley, I cannot take this serious, however hard I try. And I cannot let you go down there, you know damn well I can't—even if I wanted to, which indeed I don't. This ship is expected daily by their lordships to go to Jamaica to wipe the arses of the whining planters there, and they're breathing down my neck to say that she is ready, which she ain't. Half my pressed men you've allowed to run, half you've clapped in irons, and the other half you say are killing each other for their sport. Well, they're all sprung out today, in half an hour, and that's an end to it. So quit your talk of going for a jaunt and get yourself in readiness, and the ship."

Both Will and Sam attempted argument, but they got short shrift. Kaye was prepared to talk about preparedness, but nothing more. The plan was, he said, to call all hands, to assign the men watches and to stations, and to make the brig a proper fighting ship. Black Bob was sent to get them all a breakfast, which they ate at the grand table, waited on by him. This was much more like the old Kaye they had known: offhand and airy, prepared to make decisions with no care and little thought. On the new people, for instance, and their need to run.

Sam asked: "I've heard we have some dangerous men in the hold, sir, dangerous and in chains. If we release them, we will lose them, surely?"

"What bloody balderdash," the captain answered, smugly. "They have learned their lesson and they will not dare again. I have bespoke a mooring buoy, in any way, and when this shilly-shally talk is over we will ship sweeps, man boats, and move her out into the widest part. Who'll swim then? Not Jolly Jack, for any money. And if a bastard runs, that bastard dies. Bob—clear up this mess, boy. Gentlemen, let's to our work."

They stood as he did, and adjusted their dress while Black Bob helped the captain with white silks and a spanking new blue coat. Kaye then put on a wig, which neither Sam nor Bentley cared to in the normal day-to-day. On deck they could hear shouts and orders, and a whistle call from time to time. Kaye grinned at them.

"You see, boys, there are some changes on this ship. Today or tomorrow we have a surgeon coming on, and a midshipman you can

kick about, and now the boatswain works to times arranged." He
pulled a watch from off his belly and snapped the cover open. "Aye,
Taylor's up to snuff."

"All very well," Sam grinned in turn, "to have a snotty boy to do
our bidding, but not many of the breed can lay a course, can they?
When does the sailing master come, sir? I would be pleased to get
to know him."

Kaye was adjusting his wig in a hand-mirror, and Black Bob
puffed powder on. Kaye grunted.

"You will go for your examinations in a day or so," he said. "When
you are lieutenants true, I'll tell you more, won't I?" The grunt
became a laugh. "Or perhaps I will not bother with a master then!
After all, you will be the very cream of navigation. And surely, the
West Indies can't be hard to find. Columbus did it and he was a
garlic-guzzler!"

Holt and Bentley shared a covert glance. There is no master, their
eyes agreed, and each had stirs of fear. Slack Dickie could not do it,
that was sure. Could *they?* But Kaye was marching on, quite happily. His watch was out once more; he snapped it noisily.

"'Tis time," he said. "All should be mustered and dying for a sight
of us. 'Tis time."

Out on the deck, in a way they scarce could credit given Slack
Dickie's past, it had come about just as he'd said it would. All hands
were mustered, waiting, facing aft, and most of them were clean and
well turned-out. Taylor watched over them, a heavy cane in hand,
and Tilley surveyed the other side with his unsmiling, piggy eyes. He
was a boatswain's mate now, that Will had recommended and Kaye
had signed to, carelessly, as was Tommy Hugg, another "big, hard
bastard" in Taylor's phrase. Tilley held a rattan, that sat oddly in his
massive paw, but Hugg favoured a rope's-end, tarred and unbending,
with a rough-worked monkey's fist that could have felled an elephant.
On the port side of the new-raised poop, still pale and sickly as soldiers always seemed to be, the marine contingent oversaw the rabble,
muskets in hand, with their beauteous commander overseeing them.
The shore was close enough to spit at, almost, but only the greatest

fool would have tried to run. A bullet or smashed skull was readily available indeed.

Clean and well turned-out. Well, most of them, most of them, thought Bentley. But as he crossed towards the ladder to stand in splendour beside his captain, he registered many faces that he knew spelled trouble, in whatever weather. Gunning's men, now pressed, were cleanish but still massively resentful, more so as, until this moment, they had lived in shackles. Then a fair number of more normal "volunteers," sent down from Coppiner's or from the Rondy at the Lamb, who had also been chained up almost constantly. Some of them would warm to the life, no doubt of it, for it was not easy to starve on board a Navy ship, as it was on shore. But half of them had been took as homeward-bounders, probably looking forward to a week or two in bed with missus, and time to calculate the youngest children's ages and conception dates, before they sailed the deep again. There were the usual cripples, too, one of whom, eyes burning in a hollow face, had death hard on him, Will guessed. If Kaye's promised surgeon did indeed exist, he would try to have this fellow intantly discharged. Death from sickness on a crowded ship and early in a voyage was a loathsome thing.

Then, to one side at line end, stood the Scots brothers, called Lamont. They were very clean, which surprised him somehow because he had formed the impression, in his interviews at the shackles in the hold, that they were vicious men, little used to normal human ways. Down there they had gazed at him in the gloom with eyes like knives, the expressions on their hatchet faces of undisguised aggravation. The boatswain, Taylor, privately had told him he would rather see them over side, or run, or gone to hell by handcart than on the muster list. He feared that they were undiluted trouble. After long trying, Bentley had been vouchsafed their names for putting on the articles—Angus, Dod, and Rabbie—but almost nothing else. Today though, their tight-curled strawy hair gleaming in the sunshine, their long, thin faces and their close-cropped beards speaking a class beyond that of the generality, they were more mysterious than the common sailor had a right to be. Will studied them and their eyes stared back without a hint of anger or of threat. He wondered if perhaps he had misjudged.

So where was Ashdown, the Scots' sworn enemy? Further back and at the other side, as far away as possible, it appeared. In the clear air Will could make out bruises on his face still, but no sign at all that he'd been crushed by their ill-treatment. He had volunteered his first name—Jack—and accepted his fate in going back to Jamaica with resigned goodwill. Taylor, again in private, had said the Irishman had claimed great knowledge of the island—and others of the Carib sea—and hinted he could maybe be of help. This, to Will, sounded like ingratiation, and Jem agreed it might be. However, Ashdown had said it quietly, and very little more because the Scotchmen had given him the evil eye. The boatswain thought, in probability, that Ashdown knew a fair amount about them, and surely to their detriment. It was something to be looked to—as was perhaps his safety in their company.

When all was set, Kaye moved forward to the break and looked down across the deck at all his men. Compared with the crew he'd had when *Biter* was a Press tender, it was a multitude, and his shoulders were back with pride, his protruding eyes shining with satisfaction. The men were motley, but the warrants were picked out in blue, as was the coming way, and both his officers looked very much the part. The old *Biter* was dead, long live the *Biter*—it was signalled in his face. He was going to talk to them.

"Men," he said, "my name is Captain Richard Kaye. This ship is the *Biter*, by the grace of God, and in some small way by me. For two years or more she was hired by their lordships, under my command, for the Press service, and we did sterling work, I promise you. Now the war is hotter, the West Indies are much in need of ships, and me and *Biter* and our men have proved ourselves in action furnace-hot. I put it to their lordships I should go, and to indicate approval, they made me post, immediate. When they said they had no ship, I proposed they buy the *Biter*, lock and stock, to save the time, expense, and fag of building one. Or the luck, indeed, involved in buying an existing hull, from God knows what kind of foul filthy rogue, that would sink ten miles off Land's End, even if it got that far. I proposed the *Biter,* a ship I knew like my own hand. And guaranteed her."

He paused, flushed at his own eloquence, blind to the uninterest and stolidity staring up at him. He did not smell the sharp sweat either, produced in Sam Holt's oxters at the amazing arrogance, bordering on blasphemy. The *Biter,* by the grace of God and Dick, thought Sam. Ye gods and pickled turbots! And he wondered at the guarantee. Who'd told him she was sound: her owner? So why, then, was John Gunning staying home?

Kaye chuntered on for five more minutes, exhorting, trying lame jokes, giving threats and promises. He said he'd seen the division of the people into rates, and he approved. He said he'd considered the warranting of the boatswain and his stalwart mates, and he approved. He introduced his two lieutenants with a nod, and warned the sailors that officer Savary was a demon of marines, and his soldiers were . . . well, soldiers. There was another one to come, to make it four (in case they couldn't count, presumably), and there was to be a surgeon, a midshipman, and a sailmaker called Smith. This, he explained "for the new people come on board of us," was to replace the old one, Tennison, who had been a clever man with the twine and needle, but a fool for love. He'd settled down and married, swallowing the killick, and "was probably regretting it e'en now." The laugh from the old *Biter* men was modified by the fact he'd got the name wrong. Peter Tennison had never been in love, except with liquor, and had drunk himself to death quite recently.

Even Kaye could tell the men were getting restive, and even Kaye knew the best and only remedy on shipboard was hard work. Over the next few days, he said, he and his officers had much to do to make the voyage go off with a swing, and he would need to see the Admiralty, the armourers, the vittlers, and God alone knew who else. But if he was away at all on duty, and however long it took for his return, ship's work would continue, morning, noon, and night, and they would be overseen, no question. The boatswain and his mates were vigilant and vicious, Lieutenant Savary would not hesitate to give his men some musket practice, and his officers—who normally would be there when he was not—were denizens of another, crueller world. Lieutenant Bentley, he said, was the nephew of Captain Daniel Swift, of the death ship *Welfare;* need he say more? And Lieutenant Holt had taken on three hundred men and more on Shoreham beach in single combat, and yet stood there before them, sweating, in truth, and hot with embarrassment, like Will—but Kaye did not mention this fact, naturally. He beamed at his two demons, and the common people held their thoughts.

Shortly, the muster was at an end. Orders were passed to Taylor and his mates, calls were made, and the shipboard bustle set about in earnest. Sweeps were extracted from their stowage, shipped through the ports, and readied for the pull out to the buoy. Boat crews were told off to their tugs, mooring lines were singled up, and all made ready. The air was still, the sun warm, the tide slack. *Biter,* smarter and more shipshape than she had ever been, slipped from the tiers and slid across the Thames to pick up the buoy. If anybody looked at the dwindling, friendly shore with deep despair, they dared not show it, and the dockyarders watched their departure with impassivity. Within an hour, the brig lay to her newfound isolation as calm and neat as a resting swan. The hands were called to dinner.

In the great cabin Deborah was mentioned once more, in passing. Kaye said that he had to go ashore—but they could not. He had to dig out Jack Gunning, he revealed, who was due to do a little trip with them, to help shake down the new gear and explain some of the old. He laughed at Sam's idea that Gunning might be murdered out of hand by his former people, whom he had betrayed, but said in any case that "London Jack" would risk it for the money, would risk anything at all. Kaye also had to go and see his father, he said—though not this night—at the family seat in Hertfordshire. "In fact," he added, "I thought—" then stopped. They regarded him. "Well," he went on, "to see one's people is important."

"'Tis true," said Sam. "Sir Arthur Fisher, I am sure, would not be pleased if I were to sail for Jamaica without acknowledgment and a fond farewell. And the young lady . . ."

Kaye laughed.

"Ah, the blessed strumpet! My my, your assiduity knows no bounds, does it? You think she might be there, so . . ."

"So William should come with me," said Sam. "If it were to be possible, sir . . ."

"Well it won't," said Kaye. "The idea is nonsensical. And I don't expect to find you running off, as you have both done in the not too distant past! This time there ain't no good excuse, like catching smugglers. Now sirs—to work. This is a different ship, as you have recognised. I charge that you should keep her so. So shift!"

That night Kaye did go ashore, and the weather being milder, Sam and Bentley loitered on the quarterdeck until the early hours, with wine and conversation.

"I wonder if she is at Langham Lodge," Will said wistfully, before they went to turn in. "Poor Deborah."

"Aye, the blessed strumpet," said Sam, with palpable affection. "Aye, Will. I wonder if she is."

SIX

Deb Tomelty, the blessed strumpet, was not at Sir A's house in the Surrey countryside, but she had been—in or near it—twice in recent months. The first time she was escaping from a Customs officer, as Annette had half remembered, and the second she was saved by one, who wanted her to be his mistress. Both fat, both just as keen to taste of her delights—but two completely different gentlemen.

The first encounter, at Point, in Portsmouth harbour, was the culmination of a long and fearful journey down from London, via the River Adur mouth at Shoreham, where Deb, despite all evidence and common sense, had had some wild hope of meeting William—whom she had last seen being dragged off, roaring, by his own boat's crew at Dr Marigold's the night the man had died. When she'd arrived she had found no one, not him nor yet Sam Holt, her second forlorn hope, but just an empty, storm-swept beach. In her desolation, Deb had approached some fishermen, holding the knife that Marge Putnam had given her well hidden in a pocket, and because she was a maid, they'd helped her. Because she had bruised face, torn skin, and lumps of hair torn out, their women helped her also. For a day or two, at least, Deb Tomelty was safe.

It could not last, no doubt of that. She was put up in a store-shed behind a cottage near the beach, and was listened to with sympathy. Deb, who had no guile or knowledge of the local liveli-hood (beyond the fishery) was open in her desire to know if a young Navy officer had been seen thereabouts in recent days, and if so, where was he now? The men humoured her at first, then questioned her in turn in case she was a spy, which they rapidly concluded she was not. Then her questions about smugglers and her naivete about the trade began to charm them, as did her natural beauty, which soon came shining through the bruises and abuse. As the men got fresher, the women turned to animosity, and her safety slipped almost imperceptibly into another question. Deb was not a fool; she knew she had to go. Her problem now was—where?

It was a little girl called Meg who pointed her to Portsmouth. She came to the shed one evening, after Deb had heard a row inside the house, which she guessed was about herself. The girl was child-ishly direct. There had been a battle on the beach the week before, she said, and she'd heard that a stranger had been rescued by a boat. Word was he was a Navy man, or perhaps was Portsmouth Customs, and in any way the boat most probably had gone down there. The Portsmouth Customs, she vouchsafed proudly, lived in a little creek called Shitty Corner, which was typical of the Hampshire people, who were very low. And then, with clear green eyes full on Deb, she'd added: "Why don't you go there, Miss? You are not welcome here, I promise you."

At two that night a drunk man tried to barge into the store-shed, and at four Deb slipped away. She still had a small amount of Mrs Putnam's money, and it was raining hard, but she chose to walk or beg for rides. Her progress, along the coast from east to west, was adequately fast, but dangerous and unpleasant.

Along the downland road, she caught glimpses of the southern country scenery that reminded her of the northern country she had left—so hopefully—with Cecily, whose remembered death filled her with a dull but sudden pain. The hills, though low, were pleasant, not too dissimilar from the Pennines dropping down to Stockport where the mountain waters met to form the Mersey. The rain was quite familiar also, although she was surprised to see the sea, grey and forbidding, when the cloud banks parted to extend her view. The Isle of Wight, sighted in a clear spell of strong sunshine, backed by a sky of blue, startled her with its beauty. Then it disappeared, as a sharp rain swept across the scrubland horizontal to smack into her face.

Deb crossed the sea at Portsbridge without a horse or cart to ride on, and stumbled through the Lines at Hilsea with a myriad of other grumbling foot passengers fed up with the military building and the wartime clutter. The island of Portsea itself she found depressing, all flat and waterlogged in the misty rain, with a scattering of houses here and there, and yet more forts and white stone ramparts up ahead of her. It took a half an hour to be admitted through the Landport gate despite the fact that it was open and the guards uncaring, while her pleas to be let through the dockyard walls were met with stares. When she asked where the Navy ships were, and how one got to them, they laughed at her.

"On yer back," said one man. "But you'll need to wash it first. And your face and shanks."

They mocked her for her accent, too, and the way she asked directions. The only name she knew was Shitty Corner, and she said it in a way they found exceptional. Unlike little Meg in Sussex, though, they did not find it low to use so blunt a name (perhaps Meg was right, then, about Hampshire people?) and pointed her toward St Thomas's, whose tower she could see in the rainy distance. Once there, they told her, she should keep inside the walls until she reached St James's Gate, then follow Broad Street down.

"If you fall into the water," said the first man, "you'll know you've gone too far. If not, you'll see the Star and Garter on your right, which has its arse resting on the beach of Shitty Corner, and hence the name, I think. Folk stay in the Star and eat and drink and shit, and everything ends up in the harbour, doesn't it? It's a hostelry for whores an' all; the maidens there are Spithead Nymphs, damn nearly every one. Is that your interest, maid? Are you seeking a position?"

"I'm seeking Customs officers," Deb said coldly, "not the Star and Garter. Know you where they are stationed, an' you please?"

"Star and Garter, like I said. They got a shed and jetty on the water's edge, next the Still and West, but they drinks in the Star itself to annoy the Navy men. What business do you have with them, though? Ragged little tart."

Deb, who had had a bellyful of angry men in her time, dodged and shifted in the moving throng and lost this one easily. She hurried on down Broad Street through the city gate in increasing rain, until she saw the rising frontage of the Star and Garter, redbrick and tall-built near the very point. Beyond it the mud road turned back left upon itself, showing her the expanse of Portsmouth harbour, stretching green and choppy right up towards the hill that formed a northern barrier. With the wind coming sharply off the water, the whole place smelled fresh and clean.

It was not, though. Despite her care, Deb stood near ankle-deep in mud, and the houses, dives, and grog shops in her sight were in every part depressing. The road was thronged with dogs and carts and asses, and as she watched, a pair of oxen hitched on to a dray excreted noisily as if to a united signal. The smell of fresh dung acted as a trigger, for when it had faded a reek of rotten, older excrement had overlaid her senses. Scales fell from her eyes, and she saw filth and ugliness.

The place was thronged and bustling, but no one had any time for her. She realised that they were outside the city wall, that Point was a low-lying snout of mud and shingle, presumably where any law in Portsmouth Town had no dominion. To the right, beyond the Star, she could see a muddy creek, with a smaller creeklet, just a mud wallow, running up behind it. The tide was low, and there were banks of green and slimy mud, the bones of long-dead boats, piles of rotting filth and matter—and her, she thought, who hoped to find Sam Holt, or even Will, or Customs men at least, maybe the Royal Navy. There were ships up harbour, what she took for fighting ships, black and yellow, with guns visible at holes cut in the sides of some. Deb was almost overwhelmed with loneliness. Boldness, and a little money in her purse, thank God and Mrs Margery—they were her only hope.

Inside the building things took some long while to get a little better. She slipped in through the front door in trepidation, but need not have feared. There was a long low lobby with doors off of it, some closed, some open, and the normal sounds of tavern life—laughs, shouting, wenches' shrieks. After some minutes a pot-boy passed her, with a tray of tankards and a jug. He glanced, sensed somehow she was at a loss, and cut his freckled face into a smile.

"Maid?"

"Aye," said Deb. "Ah. Could tha maybe tell me—?"

"By! A bloody foreign lass! Art thou French?"

"French! Nay, boy, I come from—"

"Don't tell me! Don't tell! You come from—let me guess! You come from . . . Germany? Holland? Spain? You come from Africa! Why ain't you black?"

Deb Tomelty, completely thrown backwards on herself, just gaped. And the pot-boy, who could have been but twelve or less, curled up with laughing at her. She realised that he was making fun. Somehow or other that relieved her.

"Christ," she said. "If you think I've got a medlar in my mouth, you should've heard me when I first came down from Cheshire. This is lady-talk to me!"

His name was Malcie, and they were quickly friends. He showed her to an alcove, took away his pots and jug, then returned.

"I've got two minutes 'fore they call for me," he said. "If you have come to get a slavey job, you're too good on the eye. If you have come for whoring, speak to Timothy; don't speak to no one else, for Timothy bends the other way, if you get my meaning, and will not hurt or rob you, well, not a lot. If a man with one eye tries to capture you, tell him that you're waiting for your admiral, then hide in the yard till I finds you. What are you here for, anyway? It must be whoring, surely? Must you really be a Spithead Nymph?"

This time he was in earnest, she guessed. She shook her head, though, feeling cold. She explained that she was on the search for someone, an injured Navy officer, maybe a Customs man. She was desperate cold, and wet and tired, and had come exceeding far. But she had money, she was not a whore, and she needed . . . looking after. Now, when Malcie laughed there was no humour in it.

"You don't ask a lot out of life, do you, maid?" he said. Deb blinked; she did not understand. So Malcie sighed.

"Look Deb. This is Point, see, also called Spice Island. The Navy men come here for one thing only, or maybe two or three. Drink is the cheapest, and the best, and men and officers do it together here. It's not the only thing they do together, neither; they do things they could get hanged for on their ships, d'you see? Some also like it for the Spithead Nymphs, who—we boast it proudly-like—are the dirtiest, the cheapest, and the vilest whores of Portsmouth and Portsea, inside or out of walls. The Customs men come in because it's close to their station, because the Navy officers hate them, and because they can shift contraband with the local Free Trade men. In short, maid—it is not the place for thee."

It came upon her, clear and suddenly, that there were lower places on God's earth than Dr Marigold's. It came on further that she was quite alone, and possibly in deadly danger. Her one protector was a little boy.

"I've got some cash," she said, then felt afraid it was the last thing to confess. "I need to find a Navy man called Sam, called Samuel Holt. I think he's been aiding of the Revenue. There may be another one, although I think not, another officer called Bentley, Will. He has yellow hair, and is small and—" She nearly blurted *beautiful,* and she nearly burst into tears. Christ, she thought, I wish I was at home with Ma, in Stockport. Oh Christ, she thought, I'm lost. Malcie was staring at her, and his face was full of pity.

"When it's dark," he said, "the Customs men come in for dinner. Not all of them are on the make, lover. Some of them are honest, and they use this place to seek what's going on between the Navy and the Free Trade men; there is a lot of bad stuff passed from hand to hand. Go you to my quarter. I will guide you there, and you may have a rest and wash yourself. Then, when it's dark, we'll bring you down and see if Sunfield's here, or the other good ones, Teape and Higginson. Pot luck, maybe, but it's all we have. Oh, hide, oh, hide! Duck down behind there!"

He pushed her to a corner and behind a drape as they heard someone approaching to a purpose. Heavy breath, and a shout of "Malcie! Villain! Where are you, little bastard, where?" Deb heard the door wrench open, a grunt, and then a blow.

"Too long away, you bastard! Are you mad? Get back into the lower pot-room. Men are clamouring! What do you here?"

A low reply, another blow, an exhortation to "get back and quick about it," and the door crashed on its jamb once more. Malcie, tears in eyes and red mark across his face, pulled back the curtain and Deb came out.

"That was Geraldo. I have spoke too long. Quick, follow. But if you've any sense, maid, go out now. Find somewhere else to ask your questions." He led across a low, damp room, and clattered up a staircase, then another, then a third, into the roof. "In any way," he panted, at a thin pine door, split and sere, hanging from a single hinge, "in any way, I think you waste your time. This is not the place, Deb. This is a place, truly, only for luckless little whores."

He pushed the door and it dropped inwards, crazily. There was a pallet, a pisspot, and a window with no glass. Also a wash bowl and a large, full jug.

"They keep us clean, though, lover-maid. That way we takes more money, don't we?" He laughed. "Well, off of them as likes their Spitties clean, anyhow. It takes all sorts, don't it? And be silent, girl, till I return!"

That night, roughly washed, roughly tidied, with her hair kempt and pulled across to hide the scars and torn patches, Deb Tomelty went into the dark and noisy parts of the Star and Garter, with Malcie as her covert guide, and tried her luck in finding out the whereabouts of civil men. He had warned her that he could not stick close, and warned her which of the workplace crew she should steer clear of like the plague. Most of all, he'd told her to avoid the doxies, whether whore or matron. Without a reason for her being there, he said, she would be thought an interloper. He feared, from her expression, that she had not understood.

Deb, indeed, while listening, had called up to her mind Margery

and Pam, the two women who had controlled the band of maids
"obtained, sustained, and trained" by Dr Marigold, in his own well-
known expression. Strict they sometimes were, and not above giving
out a slap or two, and pretty sore ones sometimes. But from the way
Malcie went on, you'd have thought these Portsmouth women, by
contrast, demons.

No one had seen her yet. She had not tried to buy a place to stay,
or food, and her pot-boy friend had said she might merge in pretty
well in the dim. The Star and Garter was a busy place, he said,
because—without the city walls—it was not the haunt of "daytime
folk," and the other type were not fond of any form of "painful light."
He also counselled her to seek out Navy officers, or the Revenue,
because their villainy was "better in control than freelance folk's."
What's more, they were what she wanted, were they not?

Deb, in the full crush of a sailors' drinking room, was almost
overwhelmed. The noise was harsh and constant; the shouts and
oaths delivered at the top of every voice. At first she saw no women,
only pushing, drinking, drunken men. There was food there, as at
Marigold's, plates of steaming fish and meat, but it was not carried
round by pretty serving maids with low kerchiefs at their bosoms. It
was piled at tables, attacked, sucked up, knocked over, spat upon the
floor. There were two fat dames behind the serving hatch, one with
a pipe in mouth and spitting. Then dimly, Deb saw a kind of inglenook,
and in it, at a table, two women whose breasts were out and being
fondled by four sailors. As she watched, one of the doxies fumbled at
a breeches front and exposed a stiffened yard.

"Hah!" said a voice behind her. "Your face, maid, is a picture! Six-
pence an' you do the same to me!"

Gasping, Deb spun on her heel to face a man who was certainly
an officer. Not Navy, he was not dressed as the main part of Marigold's
visitors had been, so perhaps a Customs man? He was tall, long-
faced, but kindly with it all. He was laughing at her. She had touched
his funny spot.

"Teape!" he called. "I've got a good one here! A Spithead Nymph
that blushes, as I breathe! Ho, maid, you must come and take a glass
with us!"

"Are you Revenue?" she said. Her blush deepened. "I mean, sir . . . are you, sir? I seek a . . . I am not a Spithead Nymph!"

"No-no! You are not! Heaven forfend, maid, the very thought! Teape! She's not a nymph, hang me, she ain't! Come, lass, come and take a glass. There's Higginson, as well. He knows well how to treat a lady!"

She knew the names and thought she should be glad. Malcie had mentioned them, hadn't he? As the better ones? In any way, she had no choice. The tall man, though kindly looking, had her in a grip that would have bent an arm of metal. If she moved with it, it did not hurt. She moved.

"Sunfield, you dog," said the officer called Teape, "will you never learn your lesson? I came here for a drink, man, not other business." But he smiled at Deborah, to take the sting away. "Sit down and welcome, maid," he added. "But if you are a doxy, then I fear—"

"No, sir! No! I seek a man, not . . . I mean, I am not a whore, God save me from it, I am respectable! Oh please, sir, are you Revenue?"

They were Revenue, but they were, sadly, rather drunk, or very pleased to go that way, and fast. Her accent intrigued them and amused them, and, truth to tell, it was unlikely she could be other than a whore, for only whores came in the Starry, didn't they, and only whores went wandering Spice Island in the night. When the fat Customs man came in and joined them at the table, Deb was close to tears. She knew by then she had not got a prayer of gaining information.

What's more, the other whores—for that is how they saw themselves, and none would disagree—had noticed her, moved in and stared, and muttered filthy words in passing. One, catching Deb's eye, had bared a tongue loaded with a ball of yellow phlegm, rolled it around, and swallowed it. The next one's in your face, her look said bitterly. The next ball is for you, you thieving slut.

The fat man was a different kettle from the other three. They were still trying to understand exactly what this strange wench was wanting when he pushed through to their table, but he put a stop to that. He roared with laughter, reached out one hand for a drink, and the other shot for Deb's bosom, without compromise. Deb squeaked like a maiden girl, jumped up and sideways, and clutched her handkerchief to ensure her breasts stayed hidden. He was like a rampant pig to her, his cheeks fat and purple in her sight, his lips flecked and horrible, eyes bursting with intent. His next lunge pushed her up against a wall, where Sunfield interposed himself, protecting her, his own laugh polite but rather humourless.

"George, George," he said, "contain yourself, at least until you have been introduced. Sit down and drink up like a Christian. This maid is Deb Tomelty and she ain't a whore."

"Not a whore," boomed George, his voice as big as he was, and equally congested. "If she ain't, then what's she doing here, and why's your arm around her?" To Deb he added, leeringly, "Don't trust old Sunny Sunfield, med, just because he says you should. It's always them is worse as looks as if they stirs their tea with it! Come here, I want to feel your lovely little titties."

A serving wench, summoned by Teape or Higginson on the fat man's entrance, arrived at table with a metal jug of ale and a brandy bottle with a glass upturned on its neck. George grabbed the bottle, but disdained to grab at *her,* which she could hardly fail to notice, as he gave a whoop and told her, "Look to your place now, Mary, look to your place. By Christ, you'll lose your living now they've brought in a pretty one!"

Instinct or not, Deb knew she had to get out, and get out fast. She pushed past Sunfield, who tried to stop her with a worried look, then fought through the fat man's flailing arms and open, tongue-filled mouth. She flew past Mary, who was still transfixed, and set a course for the nearest open door. Malcie she needed, needed very bad, but she could not see him and dared not call his name for fear of consequences that would fall on him. It seemed she'd chosen well, for she ended in a wide, low lobby without heat or light, and not any people. For a moment she stood still, listening to the baying roar from the room she had escaped from, then froze as other doors opened, to her front and back. Maids streamed out, boys including Malcie, and the spitting woman with the pipe. Ahead of all was Mary, who flew at her with fangs and claws exposed.

How he did it, Deb never knew, but Malcie accidentally fell, and accidentally tripped poor Mary in full flight. A hand raked Deb's eyes, but the bitten nails, fortuitously, did no damage. She was aware of chants of "whore" and "thief" and "bitch" and a scream of "let me kill her" from the fallen girl, then she was knocked sideways back into the drinking room, and surrounded by laughing men. Foremost was fat George, who jostled Sunfield and Higginson to one side and grabbed her by her wrist and pulled and dragged her clear of the angry women who were trying hard to get at her, and wrapped her in his arms. His mouth was at her ear and he bellowed, all romantically, "A guinea, Spithead Nymph! A guinea and you'll get a bed all night!"

She spat at him. She spat into his face, and pushed him backwards with staccato force, a cry of fury bursting from her mouth. Fat George went over backwards in the manner of a doll or acrobat, his short legs rigid and his feet in air. A table crashed down, then another, and a plate of steaming cutlets hit the flags. In the way that seamen do, the company went bedlam with delight, and ale and punches, then teeth and blood, went flying everywhere. Mr Teape, a riding officer who had suffered silently for very long from his superior, took the presented opportunity to stamp hard (by awful accident) upon his face. Fat George lost the straightness of his nose, and three good teeth.

Deb, five minutes later and without a sign of Malcie or another friendly face, got out into the sharp Spice Island night and picked her way clandestinely up Broad Street to St James's Gate. She walked through the town to Landport, north towards the loom of Portsdown Hill, and found a small inn approaching Hilsea Lines where she was not taken, automatically, to be a hungry whore. She slept in a warm bed with two fat chambermaids, who urged her in the morning to stay with Mrs Tubbs, their mistress, who was a very kindly dame and let them eat for breakfast as much as they could cram. Deb was tempted, but she knew she had to go. North was Surrey. In Surrey was Sam's uncle's place, and maybe safety. Maybe safety, and maybe news of Will. She was sorely tempted, and she knew she had to go.

When she looked back down on Portsea Island from beside the

old George Inn on top of Portsdown Hill, the sadness of her visage won her a lift far up the London Road.

SEVEN

Richard Kaye returned next morning as he had said he would—a big enough surprise—and the gig contained a surgeon and midshipman, as promised. Not a sailmaker called Smith, though, but a fat and sweating purser, Mr Black. Even less expectedly, John Gunning was in the sternsheets, still resplendent in a landsman's long-back coat, and still as sober as a judge. Taylor, without an order being passed, had mustered a receiving party at the gangway and blew a welcome call.

Lines taken, Gunning came up the side before the captain—he had never learned the Navy niceties—as agile as an enormous cat. He smiled at the two young officers, positively grinned, then glanced about the deck proprietorially.

"Slack lanyards there, slack lanyards!" he boomed. "Good God, Capting," (this over the side, to where Kaye still clambered upwards) "the ship has gone to pieces! Those shrouds need setting up immediate! The bloody stick'll come down otherwise!"

Kaye might have been offended, but Sam was secretly amused. Say nothing else for Gunning, he was a seaman born and knew his old ship backwards. Once pointed to, the slackness screamed out loud, and Sam made rueful faces at his friend. What else would Gunning see that we can't, his expression said. God save us in the Western Ocean without a man like him.

As protocol demanded, the captain took them to his cabin first and ordered coffee from Black Bob. He went through introductions with unusual briskness, the lesser mortals getting short shrift. The surgeon was a scrawny misery by the name of Grundy, who shook hands all round distractedly, then went, he claimed, to check his precious chest. The purser, like all pursers, was full of lard and greasy with it, with a greedy, smacking smile. Introduced, he was soon dismissed as not a gentleman (nor yet a successful rogue, like Gunning). Which left the new midshipman, whom Will and Sam examined with the greatest interest. In theory, one day soon, he would turn into them. He was the Navy's hope and future.

"This is Rex, my second cousin's boy," Kaye said. "He is very clever, fourteen years old but thinking forty, and he wants to be an admiral. His family name is Shilling, but we call him Groat. That is a jest, sirs, you may smile."

No one did, however, most clearly not the victim of the crashing humour. Indeed, Rex Shilling, who was exceeding small and pale and ill-fared looking, turned grey eyes on them, which were remarkable only for their coldness.

"I joined the service, sir," he said, "because my father died and my mother has no other funds to raise me. I shall do my duty, sirs, because I have to. I am Rex Shilling, midshipman. The name Groat I do not ever wish to hear."

The second new man doomed to be dismissed immediately. Captain Kaye, blushing with anger, said: "You may go, Midshipman Groat. You are quartered down below in what we call the gunroom. It is your mess. You are alone there. I pray you find it, sir. Ask a common seaman, if you are lost. Ask someone who might know, as you do not. My cousin, your mama, will hear of this. I confide, sir, it will pain her mightily."

Amazingly, Black Bob stepped forward. He had witnessed this with tray and coffeepot in hand, and it appeared to affect him in the oddest way. Across the cups and saucers, he turned eyes full of pity towards the young midshipman, and said: "I help. I know way. I show you gunroom. Sir."

For a moment there was silence. It was the nearest to a sentence Sam or Will had ever heard him say, and possibly his longest utterance. They stared, waiting for Kaye's inevitable explosion. But Kaye was not the one to speak.

"How dare you!" said the midshipman. The words were hot, the voice was high, but still retained its chill. He glared at Black Bob cruelly, as at a piece of nothingness. "If you speak to me again without express permission, I will strike you, understood? Go to your tree, you monkey. Go."

Black Bob's dark eyes fell down, but that was everything he showed. He pushed the tray forward, and went with it towards a table. Not a crock or spoon that rattled, as he put it down. Rex Shilling bowed towards Post Captain Kaye.

"Sir," he said. "With your permission, I shall seek my quarters."

"I will send for you," said Kaye. "Proceed."

"Well, there's a jolly chap!" said Gunning, as the midshipman disappeared. "You told me, Kaye, we'd have a splendid company if I threw in my lot with you. Laughing and carousing both day and night, fine wine and better song! And add to all, this one most signal honour!" He turned his eyes to Will, mocking the captain openly. "He was going to make me master, with a warrant and a berth all of my own," he said in explanation. "Better than the little hutch I used to have as owner. Ain't he the merry Andrew, then?"

Slack Dickie kept his course through this.

"Each family has its liability," he said, good humouredly. "Groat is mine." He paused. "Or one of 'em, at any rate; I have an ugly sister, too! But I told you true, Jack Gunning. With this fine ship, done out with good King George's money, we'll reach Jamaica and drink rum by the barrico, served up by titty-naked girls, and roll in money! I'll find a cane estate, bankrupt or abandoned; I'll get it factored into health again, and when the war is over, all there'll be to do is ship the sugar back over here and pull in cash. You're a rich man now, Jack, don't bother to deny it. Good God, that shipper could be you!"

Even by the standards of Slack Dick this was unguarded stuff, thought Bentley. But he knew he was a man who needed allies, who lived in desperation of their lack. Now Kaye was eyeing him intensely.

"No need to look like that," he said. "It's not so great a secret, Mr Bentley. Or if it is, it is a family one, of sorts. Your Uncle Swift is in on this. He is a prime mover, not to blunt the point. I would deem it in your interest to add your weight to mine. Jack Gunning should come too."

"But I'm rich already," said Gunning, with a smile. "So you tell me, Captain Kaye, and you should know. I'm rich and live in London and I love the place. As do my wife and little children, sir."

"You have more mistresses than children," Kaye replied, not unpleasantly. "The day your wife finds out—what then? In the Carib Sea the drink is better, the whores are dark and passionate, and if you should weary of it, you have money to desert. I know, remember, how much you took off of their lordships. You could live among the palm fronds in the golden sand, a beauty on each arm, two others in your bed, and drink yourself insensible every day. Jack, the rum comes out of taps! Listen, man, listen to me! What about the *drink?*"

A haunted look crossed Gunning's face. It was as if he heard a siren calling in his head. Then he relaxed.

"You are persuasive, Captain Kaye," he said, "but you don't persuade me, not at all. In truth I have forewent the demon, and that is fact. I always told men I was ruler, not the ruled. As to your money schemes—well, my needs ain't many, that's the truth. You keep your cold Atlantic, and I'll go home by coach at sunset, like a lord!"

"But not tonight, though, surely? I hardly think that we'll be through by evening. The more the work, the more the guineas, no?"

"As you desire, Capting. I am not expected urgently. No hogshead is calling me, neither. Their bungs can stay bunged up, for all I care."

A half an hour later, Will and Samuel took orders and advice from Gunning, as he moved about the new-rigged ship. A big man, he went soft and feline, and his eyes picked out a dozen things in minutes. At first he stayed in his shore-bound togs, pale linens, long-skirt coat and all, but shortly he was chafing at the bit. He went to the cabin for a word with Kaye (who was largely conspicuous for his absence during the "seadog things"), and emerged in what East Indies men call *dungrees,* and a sloppy canvas smock. The *Biter*'s people, both those who knew him and the newer hands, responded with enthusiasm. He knew the workings of the ship like an angel guardian.

Not all the men were with him, though—which, strangely, appeared to trouble and surprise him. When he'd seen his former hands about the deck he'd hailed them like long-lost friends—and been ignored. Until the ship had moved out to the buoy, they'd not been allowed the freedom of fresh air for fear they'd skip across the

Thames like ducks and drakes, so it was hardly a surprise they shunned the man who'd signally betrayed them, but Gunning could not see it, any how. He had hired these men and worked with them, been drunk with them on many an occasion; and then one night they'd gone out on the rattle with him, as so many times before, and woken up with shackles on their feet. Gunning himself must have been quite monumental fluted because he did not appear to remember doing wrong. He greeted them today with warm and smiling face; and then the smile blanked out. Willie Morgan, built like a muscle-barrel, spat on the deck between Gunning's feet, which were shod in rich, soft leather. Boatswain Taylor saw it very plain and pretended he had not.

Taylor, as he made it clear to Sam and Will, also watched others of the crew with extra caution. The three of them, at the main chains when work was smoothly underway, briefly discussed the *Biter*'s people, and how they shaped, and the prospects that they would get across the ocean in one piece. Happy for the present that no one could run, they focused on the men they guessed were trouble-makers, mainly the three Scots. Each had been face-to-face with one of them, and to a greater or a less degree disconcerted. Each acknowledged that the three could be open, almost sunny, but had a kind of mayhem lurking in the eyes. Their blond curly hair, their thin little goatish beards, their lack of bulky muscle—well, inside these strange, unthreatening exteriors lived something dangerous.

"I cannot understand a cursed word they say," Taylor summed up, "but it sounds like they would like to kill me. Hugg and Tilley feel it, too. I think Tom Tilley might kill them first to get in his advantage!"

"And do you see the way they watch?" said Holt. "Except their eyes are always on the swivel; you cannot catch the buggers at it, nohow. And they watch Gunning, and his old crew; they weigh them all the time. Keep 'em hard at it, Jem. Work 'em half to death. And tell Tom I'm on his side! I'll buy him fresh meat and brandy while he's waiting for the gallows!"

Bentley said, "They watch Jack Ashdown, too. Have you seen the bruises on his face? I believe that's them, although Ashdown won't admit it. What know you about that, Bosun?"

Taylor was dismissive.

"A bloody Irish from the bog," he said. He laughed. "Christ, hear me! As was my father, and his brothers too! No, but he sticks to his heathen tongue, and for certain gives them hell in it. Oh, I don't know. If he is scared of them, he shows it bloody funnily. Maybe he likes to fight. Men do, from County Limerick."

"Is that where he hails from, Limerick?" asked Holt. And Taylor smiled.

"An Irish answer, sir: if you want him to—then so he does. In fact, I think he came from County Cork . . ."

At luncheon in the great cabin—a proper, shore-side lunch, with everyone washed and back in smarts—Kaye carried on his test of Gunning blatantly. Black Bob, in his deep velvet suit and white silk ruffles at his neck, produced and served up bottles in variety, which Dickie babbled over like a *nouveau riche*. Fine, they were, of torrid vintage, chosen and laid down for him by his father's cellar man at home. To start, a crispish white, slightly *pétillant* in the best French manner, that danced upon the tongue (he said) and cleared the mouth out for each new morsel of awaited food. He conjured up for some of them around the table, unwittingly, a vision of one-leg, one-eye Geoff, hopping among his cauldrons while spitting tobacco at the range, but no one laughed. The fish, indeed, was good, straight from the river outside that morning, shit-fed but none of the worse for that.

"Well, John," said Kaye to Gunning. "You must be sorely tempted, sure? Just one small glass ain't going to kill you, is it?"

But Gunning, who had been working like a slave all morning at the tasks he loved, was untempted and untemptable.

"Not what I'm used to, any case," he said. "Red Biddy was my vintage in the normal run. Washed down with coal-oil, if the notion took!"

"You should be coming with us, then," said Kaye. "Our new Mr Pusser looks like a man who wouldn't know the difference. Out in the wild Atlantic he'd tease your palate sure. What say you to it, Mr Surgeon? Is this fine *blonk* to your taste? Or is it medicinal?"

So far the scrawny surgeon, Grundy, had spoken no word, except to grunt a sort of greeting as he'd entered in. He turned his thin face up towards the captain, reached for his glass, and took a cautious sip. He pursed his lips.

"Aye, sir." His voice was harsh, a little squeaky. "It strikes pleasant enough. In the normal run, however, I eschew the demon drink. I have seen it . . . it can lead men into degradation. Can it not, sir?"

Kaye eyed him. In fact his eyes glowed with distaste.

"Good Christ," he said, point-blank. "Thou'rt not a nonconformist, art'a?"

A normal man, thought Will, might have collapsed into confusion under such attack. Grundy did not. The lip-purse was accentuated.

"I believe in our dear Lord, sir, as you and all men must. The wine is pleasant, that is all I know. Pleasant and therefore to be avoided, to excess. You must not think me rude, sir, if I take no more beyond this glass."

Gunning was in tucks of laughter.

"'Fore God, Kaye! You've got yourself a sawbones and a sexton there, rolled into one! Do you preach, sir? A preaching man is good on a long voyage! Give 'em clysters with the one hand, and suck their souls as well! There see, Dickie, that's your reason I ain't coming with you! He'd try conversion and I might confess! And then the Lord would strike me dead; he'd have to with my multitude of sins! Next he'll be blessing biscuits and calling 'em God's bod!"

"That is Romish, sir!" squeaked a voice. Not the surgeon's, though—it was Rex Shilling, midshipman. His cold grey eyes, for once, were hot with anger, his pale face reddening. "Mr Gunson, or whichever way they call you, this is a Christian ship, and an English one! My kinsman, I am certain—"

He was cut off by Kaye's sudden movement and his furious indignation. The captain stood upright in the cabin—and could, so high the refit men had raised the poop above his head—and slammed one large fist down onto the table. Bentley, Holt, and Grundy stiffened, keeping their counsel very close. Shilling gaped, and Gunning renewed delighted laughter.

"Midshipman!" bellowed Captain Kaye. "You do forget yourself!

Your kinsman, is it? Your bloody kinsman? I am your captain, sir. My name is Captain Kaye! Do not forget it, sir!"

"And I am Gunning," boomed John Gunning. "Not Gunson, Gunport, or Gunbreech-hole and wiping paper! Jack Gunning with a gentleman's commission, brand, spanking new! Romish, kiss my arse; it was straightforward blasphemy! Dick—I won't sail with you, will you with *him!* It is a mealmouth nun-fucker!"

Shilling, without permission, stood. Pale to begin with, he was paper-white. He was shaking, and his small mouth worked.

"So now you stand, do you?" roared Kaye. "Who gave you leave, you popinjay? You may sup alone, sir!"

"But he insulted me!" The voice was trembling, on the verge of pipe. "Sir. Captain. He—"

"Dismissed," said Kaye. Nobody moved. He waved a hand impatiently. And then he smiled, his anger, it would seem, evaporated. "Go on, Groat, go sup alone. Mayhap Bob will bring you something, if he ain't learned his lesson of being kind to you. Don't stand there, sir, just go."

Humiliation. You could smell it in the air, mixed with discomfort from some of the viewers of the scene. Will noted that Rex Shilling's eyes had tears in them, nearly overflowing. A little boy, he thought. Fourteen. As he walked out, Gunning laughed again, without restraint, and Captain Kaye joined in.

It was a lubricated do, this luncheon, although both Bentley and Sam Holt held back as far as possible. But each of them had more than they desired because crossing Slack Dickie in this mood was not good sense. Gunning did it, though, with humour and impunity, and a familiarity that argued he and Kaye had done much together in the months since they had sailed out on the Press. The harder Kaye spoke up for a certain wine, the firmer were Gunning's refusals— while Grundy was quite frankly forced. At last, and suddenly, he went white, clapped his napkin to his lips, and entreated, with his staring eyes, to be excused. More laughter rang out as he left, and Kaye later sought to know if he had vomited. Grundy had not.

Gunning, though, had passed a test. When all the food was gone, and he was clearly restless to be back in *dungree* clothes and working, Kaye put to him a proposition that left his officers exceedingly surprised. He had to go ashore, he said, and do a journey up to Hertfordshire with his two lieutenants. Jack Gunning, if he chose, could stay on board of *Biter,* in command, and carry on the readying for sea. Gunning, sober as a judge, near blew the window glass out with his laughter, which Will and Sam, though not amused at all, could understand.

"What?" he shouted. "And can I keep Midshipman Pissface with me to dole out Navy discipline and blows? By God, Capting, maybe you should lay off the beggar-brew yourself!"

Kaye said mildly: "Well, you are off it, John, and you have proved it so. Who knows, if I give you this chance of being in command you'll get the taste for that instead, and come across with us to Jamaica. I know you for a master seaman, friend, and now I know the soberton, as well. You know the ship, you know half the men, you have an exact idea of all that must be done. I shall return tomorrow, or the next day at the latest, and essential time is saved if you should oversee for me. What do you say?"

Gunning shook his head, not in refusal, though. He allowed it to be rather fun, and profitable as well (he hoped; Slack Dickie nodded). The two lieutenants, who were mighty dubious at thought of leaving ship themselves, not least because there was so much that they could learn from this big man, knew better than to carp. They wondered what the hell was going on, and they wondered how Taylor and his boatswain's mates would take to it. They wondered also, from their sharp experience, how long Gunning's dry spell would last. He was a man of droughts and tidal surges, and always had been. Mayhap, when they returned, the *Biter* would be gone, be sunk, or be a floating gay-house or bordello. They wondered also, and most vigorously, why they were off to Hertfordshire with Kaye. It was where his family seat was, certainly, but beyond that, they had no idea. It disturbed them.

EIGHT

The captain, although he still did not put their minds at rest, waxed almost lyrical on the road to Hertfordshire. He had sobered himself since luncheon time, washed down, dressed up, and had the little black boy iron every ruffle and smart panel he could find. He wore a fresh fine coat of Navy blue, a brand new wig, a pair of shoes that one could see one's face in. A boat's crew hoyed them up to London in the dandy skiff, where a coach from home had come to meet them, and Cox'n Sankey told off two beefy oarsmen to half-lift Kaye across the mud to keep all bright and clean. He did not bring Black Bob to do the normal looking after, and in the coach, in an excess of friendly openness, he told them why.

"This house we're going to," he said. "My father's house, my lord's. Well, there are servants there enough to pull my boots off, ain't there? Why bring the little nigger, eh? In any way, Sankey's up on the box, and he don't care too much for Bob; he might have tossed him off into the gutter. My Dad, God bless him, might have asked awkward questions ditto, doncha know?"

Bentley shared a glance with Holt. The coach blinds were down to keep them from the common gaze of London, so not much could be seen of the outer world. Kaye belched noisily, and they hoped he would speak more.

"Not awkward, not to be exact," continued Kaye, after some short while. "But he don't like blacks around the house; he thinks they bear the mark of Cain. Now Sankey, when a lad, well he was my . . . procurer, I suppose. You know? Will, your land's in the country, ain't it? Walt Sankey used to set the maids up for us lads. I've got two brothers, did I say? Both bigger, and both demons for the quim. Same for you was it? Or similar?"

In the shady warmth, both his juniors smiled secretly. My land's in the country is it, thought Will. Another kind of country, yes indeed . . .

"Not being rich, I was procured by a friendly milkmaid," Holt laughed. "Not even vice versa! Since then I've paid for it, of course!"

"Ah, the fair Annette," said Kaye. "Aye, I've shagged her too, at Marigold's. Lovely and skinny, old Annette, ain't she? Just like a little boy."

Sam's smile, in Bentley's eyes, was a shade less warm. But he nodded, quite judiciously.

"Can't say I've seen it that way, sir," he said. "But then . . . well, little boys ain't never been my bent." A pause; a moment. "Don't know what I'm missing, would you say?"

Kaye lifted his wig off and mopped his shaven skull. He sighed.

"They don't talk back," he said, "that's one advantage. Double with Black Bob; he don't talk anyway. But Sankey don't approve. He never did back home in Hertfordshire, when we was spunky little kids. Any maid, no problem, no charge, no argument. He gave me all his sisters, one, two, three. But when I got in a hayrick with his cousin Harry, his mouth was like a lemon slice. He never dared to say owt, though; he wasn't stupid even as a youngster. I'll make him pull my drawers off tonight—that'll show him! Bloody prig."

Subtle form of blackmail, Will thought. He grabbed a handle as the big coach lurched. The driver bellowed, briefly and obscene. Through a gap in the slatted blind, he saw green fields, and water.

"It's enough to make you seasick, this contraption," he said. "It's like a boat that don't go with the waves. How long is it? To your country . . . estate?"

"Oh God, not far," said Kaye. "Not above another hour or so I guess." He reached across and dragged the blind open. "A river there. Don't know it, though I ought to, I suppose. But it can't be too long. This coachman keeps a cracking pace. Charlie he's called; I think I've got that right. Go it, Charlie, I've got an aching arse!"

Sam, who like Will found the motion quite unpleasant, sought distraction. He asked a question he did not expect to get an answer to.

"Why are we going, sir? Good man though Jack Gunning is, ah . . . well . . ."

"Well nothing, Holt!" snapped Kaye, but with good humour. "I know what you really mean, and you are wrong, I tell you. In the time since your disaster I have got to know him, and I have not a little faith. We go to see my father in a way not unconnected, and I will wager all I have that Jack will see all well. Without him selling me the *Biter*—or to their lordships, in actual fact, thus saving me the dollars—this expedition could not have happened, and the pity is he thinks to not come with us. Well, as for that—nay, profit lies out there for taking, and mayhap his mind will still be changed. We are going to my father, Holt, to talk of profit. Wait, and you will see!"

The talk of profit, if in the air, was yet a long time coming. By the time they pulled up the enormous driveway to the house near Ware, the conversation was at an end on any subject. Neither Will nor Samuel, in private, could say they liked their commander much, and his topics outside the Navy and its ships were not ones they would have chatted over in the usual run. Opulent though his father's coach was, also, it still gave aching rear-ends to men more used to standing up than sitting. Their feelings, as they approached the monumental steps to the front doors, were mixed, with relief at journey's end uppermost. The reception part, however, made them nervous.

The duke was there, Kaye's father, with a kind of dowager who was his Lady Ma. A butler and four footmen, and a little girl of twelve or so, called Arabella, though that was hidden in some sort of title that neither Will nor Sam could fully catch. Behind the leaders, trying to be lost apparently, was a tall, skinny maiden that Will thought very ugly, with a big hooked nose and lanky ringlets. Called forward by her father, peremptorily, she looked down at Will's face with cold politeness, hardly any social warmth at all. Will, indifferent, was nonetheless surprised. She offered him her hand, also, unlike any maid he'd ever met before, and shook his with an extremely solid grip.

"My gracious lady sister, Felicity," said Kaye, with strange effusiveness. "She . . . she plays the clavichord extremely well." At which the long-nose demoiselle actually snorted, unladylike in the extreme, and her father roundly told her off. Bentley, whose experience of high society was small, had to school his mouth firmly to stop it gaping. 'Fore God, he thought, I wish I was at sea! I am at sea . . .

It was many hours of such discomfort before the purpose of them being there was finally vouchsafed, by which time William was aching, almost desperate to be gone. They endured tea and dainties with the duchess, a tour around the nearer splendours and the ornamental lakes, an introduction to all the many horses, one by one, by Lady Arabella, who loved them more than life, and ten times more than humans. Sam, who lied daringly and said he hated them, except with carrots as a roast, was furiously dismissed and went off, bizarrely and unchaperoned, with Lady Felicity amid gusts of noisy laughter. Will, under the iron thumb, watched them striding out like long-limbed cranes with some sort of envy, although Felicity could have been no man's companion out of choice. Chaperone, he thought. Hah! No necessity.

At last though, the four men found themselves alone, full of mutton and good wine, feet on the fender of a gigantic pile of crackling aromatic logs, supping port and brandy *ad libitum,* and smoking clays. The duke waxed lyrical about the current wars, in fact the whole succession fought in the West Indies in recent years, and the wonderful new tobacco tastes they had brought to "good old England."

"Even the Cuban snuff, I've took the taste for," he said, "although Lady Arabella and her mama hate me for it and say it ruins all me clothes. I sometimes think," he added, eyes on son Richard, "that we should forget the cane idea and go for Hispaniola. Sugar is for maids and lower orders when all's said, but tobacco is a solace fit for kings."

Sam, who found it much easier than Will did to fit in with mighty men (or any other sort, to tell the truth of it) scraped his shoes along the fender rail, and laughed vulgarly.

"Oh come now, sir! We fight the French already out there, and I'm told the *Guarda-Costa* attack our ships although we ain't at war with Spain. If they did join in again with Johnny Crapaud, it would be hot as Hades. According to the captain here, the planters on our islands shit themselves for breakfast every day, and they've got a squadron guarding them already!"

The duke was very like his son to look at—bulky, rather clumsy in his build—but his face was keener. He was very sharp.

"Aye, perhaps you're right, Lieutenant," he replied. "In any way, they grow tobacco with free labour, not slaves, so I believe. Perhaps the profits ain't so good, at that. *Guarda-Costa.* Your accent is correct. Do you speak Spanish? Richard here does not."

He turned a look on Kaye that Bentley recognised too well—the

disappointed-father look. Kaye blinked, discomfitted, and Bentley felt
for him. It occurred to him there might be hidden depths to Dickie's
disaffection with his family, which might be the reason he refused to
use his title in the Navy. He was an earl or marquess, Will had heard
it rumoured, but would only use his simple name, eschewing courtly
pomp. A great loss to him, possibly, this title he'd been born with:
Slack Dickie was quite short of natural advantages . . .

"A few words only, sir," said Sam. "More French. They taught me
at the Christ's Mathematical." He caught the look, half laughing. "Aye,
I am a jolly pauper, sir. I was orphaned at an early age; my family
went to Virginia where they died. Do I take it you are planning a plantation, sir? Jamaica?"

"Father . . ." Kaye began, looking anxious.

"Oh fiddle-faddle, Dick! Of course we have to tell them!" He
turned to Will. "Gad, sir, what must fathers do with sons? Lieutenant
Holt's a jolly pauper, and Richard is a miserable one. Oh yes, Dick,
pauper is the word, for let us not mince it! You might take money
to the Indies, but whose? But mine, sir. It is an act of trust alone
that I should risk it with you!"

Will and his gallant captain were both robbed of social speech by
this, although Sam still managed half a smile. The duke, aware belat-
edly that he had been too sore, perhaps, sought for a softener.

"Ha, family!" he said. "It is not all bad, I suppose. Swift is your
kinsman, Bentley, and but for him, I doubt this would have happened. He is a stout man, sir. He aims to rise, and he has all the
tools. He has a new ship building, I believe? Did you know that?"

Will blinked. His Uncle Daniel's fingers lodged in many pies. He
guessed this was a test.

"I did, sir," he replied, carefully. "She is down the Thames still, I
presume. I've visited. She won't be fitted yet, though, surely? I believe
the work was halted when he went away."

"She is not complete. Any case, she is too small; Dan Swift thinks
he under-ordered. But if he returns in time, he may yet come over
to see you, even so."

"What, quit the service?" Holt was sitting upright, apparently
amazed. "But there's a war on. How could he do that?"

The duke was shaking his head, amused. "Nay, nay, not quit. He could sell the new boat, could he not? Lease her to the Navy, even, like Gunning used to do the *Biter*." He nodded judiciously to Will and Sam. "My idea, that, by the by—their lordships buying *Biter*, with Gunning kept on as her sailing master. It seemed a good neat way. Now Dickie has a post, and Gunning is beholden to him. He controls the ship, as in the past, and anything that goes wrong with her, he puts it right, don't he? Or drowns!"

There was a silence for a good brief while. The logs cracked and sparkled. The flames chased shadows in the flue. They did not need to check Slack Dickie's face to know to keep his secret. Masters did not drown who never went to sea, did they? The duke harrumphed.

"In any way," he said, "your uncle is easing from the squadron at the Straits, Lieutenant Bentley, and going private once again. It is his preferred way. He sets out in his letters, and their lordships are agreeable so long he comes up trumps. He's took another galley off of Tangier, recently, a bloody fight, quite brutal. Hold hard, I have it hereabouts somewhere. A minute, friends, I beg of you, a minute."

He hauled himself upright and went across the room to a bureau in the corner, where he started bustling through papers. The three young officers looked at each other, loath to talk. William was wondering, with discomfort, how well, and why, his uncle knew this nobleman: indeed, appeared to be in constant contact. Kaye, equally uncomfortably, was wondering how he could persuade Jack Gunning to fulfil the obligation he was certain he had made to serve on *Biter* as her sailing master, warranted. Sam, strangely, thought of a large nose, aquiline, and the body of a cat, buried and imagined 'neath a full-skirt gown.

The duke returned with not one letter but a bundle in his meaty hand. He dropped into his leather chair and leafed through them, discarding the rejected ones onto a little table at his side. He then pulled out a pair of spectacles from his fob and perched them on his nose. He turned the lamp beside him on the table up to full.

"Here," he said. "I suppose you did not know, young Bentley, that your Uncle Swift keeps up a lively conversation with me on suchlike affairs? Nay, I'll wager you did not."

I could have guessed it, thought Will, masking the inner bleakness with a smile. I *should* have guessed it. How else should I be so tangled with Slack Dickie Kaye?

"No, sir, indeed," he said, politely. "My Uncle Daniel rarely writes to me, I must say."

"He may not write *to* you, but you will permit me to reveal that you are *mentioned* very frequent," Kaye's father told him heartily. "Swift has a portrait for the future, for the benefit of all, and you have a most important part to play in it."

For the benefit of *all*, thought Bentley. Good God, that I most sincerely doubt! And even Richard Kaye, though wary of a new humiliation, managed a laugh.

"Lord sakes," he said, "we are Navy men remember, Pater. Swift's plan of benefit is for us alone, me and your good self as one family, himself and Will another." He smirked, suddenly recovered, and a little smug. "He heard about my action on the Goodwins," he told them. "'*A seaman-act of greatest skill and daring,*' I think he quoted to their lordships, was it, father? And suggested that because of it, I was the man to do their Indies job. I and my cohorts, of course," he added. "He'd heard that you comported well, like proper fighting men, if perhaps unorthodox, and thinks the three of us exactly what is needed. Not so, sir?"

The duke flipped pages, amiably.

"He calls the planters babies, who need ships like dummy-tits," he said. "But babies who have cash, and *ergo,* have got pull. Hold, let me pick him up again. Ah yes, here 'tis: '*Last and worstly for these nambies, their slaves are now revolting. A positive explosion of escapes and rapes and robbery and looting.*' Which means, according to his men in London, Swift further writes, '*an explosion of these cowards coming back to England. The streets by the Exchange all jammed with planters and their whining wives, all bleating tales of how they have been driven from the island by atrocity, and had to leave their houses and plantations to hired factors, dishonest to a man. Frankly, my lord*'—that's Swift to me again—'*frankly, my lord, having seen but lately the bestialities that the Africs revel in, the planters do quite right to fear the safety of all Christians and to run.*

But for ourselves, I smell much money to be made. A small and gal-
lant ship to take on the worst revolters and make our lambs feel
wanted and protected—and the chance of pickings, surely.' He fin-
ishes, *'At the very least, sir, could not your gallant son acquire an*
estate? Abandoned, bankrupt, I am told the range is endless. I am
also told that, truly run, the returns on capital can be enormous.'"

The duke smiled at them, across his spectacles.

"In that, Captain Swift only tells the half of it," he said. "I have
done my own work and the figures are astonishing. Twelve per cent
per annum, fifteen, eighteen possibly. There are fortunes to be won,
estates just waiting to be snapped up and rescued from defunctitude.
To cap it all, he hopes to pull some strings to come and join the
squadron in the Carib, or better still make it another private voyage
if he can. There! Is not that fine?"

The oafish smile on Dickie's face grew broader, and he nodded
like a German children's toy. Will, though, felt his blood run cold.
They were naval officers, but the idea was a spree, a jaunt, to set
Slack Dickie and his father up in owning a plantation or some such
nonsense. Their life would be the *Biter,* Kaye, and Uncle Daniel too.
Great heavens, it would not be bearable!

"Bravo!" said the beaming son, though, his eyes alight with oppor-
tunism. "Pater, that is fine indeed! Between the three of us, between
the four—great heavens, we will make a fortune!"

"He mentions Gunning, incidentally," the duke said then, a name
that wiped the smile off Dickie's face. "I told of him in detail as the
Biter deal progressed, and Captain Swift was mightily impressed. A
man of business, who never worked, and *Biter* paid the rent for him
until he sold her to the Office, lock and stock and all! What a man,
Swift thinks, to set up in a bankrupt cane estate, and watch the gold
pour in. Prior to which, to boot, he'll get you to the Indies safe and
sound. To our venture, my friends, he's worth his weight in gold."

Sam laughed. He said, with one sardonic eye on Kaye, "I'll drink
to that, sir. It's a safe wager Gunning would as well, eh, Dick, were
he but here? To Gunning! Good old London Jack!"

The old man nodded, with enthusiasm.

"Aye. 'Tis pity, indeed, he could not join us, though Dickie says that he is rough, as diamonds go. He is on board, ain't he, 'working her up'—if that is what you sailors call it. One good man to do the work while we disport ourselves. Most excellent."

Slack Dickie Kaye joined in, of course, but Will could see he had a heavy, nervous heart. Good reason, too. They drank some more that night, but not too late because the duke was fighting with his gout as usual, and over breakfast—substantial, nay, enormous—the talk was all of social things, and property and horses, and feelers from milady duchess and her younger daughter about where their land was, and who their neighbours were, and if they liked formal balls. The father glowered, the son chafed, Bentley considered self-destruction, and Sam Holt stuffed his face with sausages and kidney, and seemed to hold a raucous dialogue with Lady Felicity, conducted with the eyes. Raucous, and strangely vulgar because they both were laughing, although in virtual silence, save a muffled snort or two. As they made farewells, standing formally beside the coach, Felicity dropped a curtsy, then laughed out loud. Her mother's face was like a field of ice.

On the journey, though, Will did wheedle a thing or two from Kaye, while Lieutenant Holt lay in a twitching doze. He used his own status as a second son to introduce the subject, then found several grounds for outraged complaint that he did not, in fact, feel. Kaye responded with admirable self-pity, ranging across the advantages that both his brothers had, the complete lack of duty or benefit his sisters vouchsafed upon the household, his father's failure to appreciate or acknowledge or accept the uniqueness of his contribution to the common good.

Money, and his lack of it, and his father's cruel insistences rankled most of all, Will learned. Dick (claimed Dick) had been the prime negotiant over the *Biter,* wielding his skill and expertise to win their lordships to his point of view in the goodness of the deal that he (again) had brokered all alone. He had saved the Office hundreds; he had found the men to do the job at prices almost impossibly favourable; he had bespoke certain improvements—vital, absolutely vital—that the Navy had then reneged upon the payments for. He knew a Navy clerk, he said ("Confidentially. This must never go no further, Mr Bentley."), a Navy clerk whose name he'd not divulge, who had overseen and aided beyond all price and expectation. And then . . . and then, he said, his father had refused to pay the sum he'd pledged ("on some trumped-up story, some hateful claim I had not kept him properly *au fait").* Which left him owing Cam—

He almost gave the name, then swallowed it, and Will, indifferent, said politely: "It is a dreadful tale, sir, but . . . well, was it a large sum?"

It was, quite manifestly, although Slack Dickie would say no more. But he ventured, ruefully, that both he and Bentley, by virtue of their birth in the wrong place upon the ladder, lived always just one step from ruin and the debtors' prison. And it was sore, he said, infernal sore.

"My Pa hates me," he said. "He looks on me like turds, or dross. But I shall show him. By God, I'll spend his money for him wisely in the Indies, if I can, but what I really mean to do is get my own. I have the ship, I have the men, I have you two for my officers. Both pirates, and one a second son! By Christ, Will Bentley, I have hopes of prizes, very high! My Pater shall be made to learn. My Pater shall be made to see my worth!"

Cruelly, perhaps (but he could not seem to stop himself), Bentley mentioned London Jack.

"Gunning," he said. "He seems determined that he will not come. Can you persuade him, do you think? To stay on board with us?"

A hunted look. Slack Dickie sighed. "I think I can," he said. "I hope I can. 'Fore God, though, I could wish he had not got so much from their lordships for the *Biter.* He is rolling in it, William. He cannot be bribed."

"Ah well," said Bentley. He felt for this big man, suddenly, this big, soft man. "Ah well. I expect that he will come. I'm sure that it will be all right, ain't you?"

But when they pulled smartly back to the *Biter* later that afternoon, the man who had command of her was a whey-faced youth of fourteen summers: Rex Shilling, nicknamed Groat. John Gunning, former owner, former master, seaman and navigator consummate, had gone. Poor Richard Kaye was truly in the lurch.

NINE

Deb's flight from Portsmouth, up the London Road to find protection at Sir A's and, perhaps, some news of William, had ended in disaster far beyond what she had later admitted to her friend at Dr Marigold's. Thin Annette had described her to Sam as "starving and in terror," and capable of little except tears. All true—and it had taken long for Deb to build her resolve of steel back up again.

Things had started excellently, after her night near Hilsea Lines, with a lift from outside the George Inn given by a fat and cosy waggoner who was old enough to be her father, and a lot more pleasant. They had jogged along quite comfortable, with little friendly chat, no curiosity beyond the strictly welcome, and the sharing of a bit of cheese and good small ale. Well beyond Hindhead he had pulled into a drover's yard—his journey being almost done—and set her up with his cousin Abraham, who was due to head much further north next morning. She was given food, a place to wash in, a place to sleep. And slept there unmolested.

Abraham, like his cousin Ben, was the epitome of waggoning. He knew everywhere and everyone along his chosen way, and had little interest in the world beyond. Ten minutes after he had whipped his team up to a gentle plod, in fact, and before the sun had truly risen in the sky, he appeared to go to sleep again, which made no difference at all to the oxen. He woke from time to time, smiled at Deborah (if she was herself not dozing), waved his whip at fellow carters (whom he seemed to know, each one), and nodded off once more. Deborah, warmed by the sun, watching the bright green southern countryside, enjoyed herself immeasurably. As they got nearer Langham Lodge, it seemed more likely by the minute that Will Bentley would be there, and all would turn out wonderfully.

The idyll ended very shortly after she had been dropped off. She would not name Sir A's house as her destination, and she foolishly told Abraham she was expected at a local inn. He therefore stopped his team outside the coaching gate, despite her protestations, and looked askance when she declined to have a glass with him to say farewell. He made no more of it, however, and as he turned the first bend in the road he twisted on his seat and waved his whip at her, which made her feel appallingly alone. Then a maiden she half-recognised came from the servant entrance and looked at her, and looked again, and squeaked out, "Deb!"

It fell to her quite simply to deny it, and she knew plainly that it would not work. She could not place the girl, but knew she knew her, and was terribly afraid. Quite rightly so, as it turned out. Even had the maid reported her presence in all innocence—she did not—there were too many people who knew of her and her disappearance from these parts for Deb to reach her destination without a challenge of some kind. They exchanged a lying word or two, Deb gave false reasons for her presence, and a false destination she had to hurry off to—now, what shame she could not stay and talk—and the maid returned in kind. Desperate to be gone, and with palpitating heart, Deb walked casually away until obscured from the public house, but was far beyond the time she might have hoped to run and catch up to Abraham.

Then she struck out across some fields and scrub that she had got to know while she had been a chattel owned by Marcus Dennett, the mountebank whom Will had killed by shooting in the neck. She was a mile or less from Langham Lodge, but the estate was gated and high-walled, and men on horses would reach the entrance long before she could, if set on at the inn to search for her. Within minutes she heard horses' hooves, which to her frightened ears sounded most purposeful, then later shouts and whooping. Shaking beneath a bitter thorn bush, licking blood from a deep scratch on her face, Deb prayed, if somewhat incoherently, that she would not hear dogs.

In a copse that night, spying on the armed men now clearly hunting her, Deb evaded them with cold determination by using a band of tinker men, or maybe deserters from the current wars, as an unwitting shield. They had a filthy, sleazy, tented camp, and were cooking stolen conies in a pot. There were no women there to smell her out, nor children she could see, so it was easy to blend herself unspotted into the darkest edges, while the searchers crashed about not far beyond. The tinker men did square up from time to time, with furious words and shouting on both sides, but there were neither blows nor shots. Next night though, Deborah knew—if she were still not found—a man called Jeremiah, the vilest man in all God's world, would head them with his vile companion Fiske, and dogs. This pair, employed by Chester Wimbarton, would not give up so easy.

Deb hid there through the day, untroubled by the drunken woodmen. Then as the dusk was coming down, she headed for Sir Arthur's land. She knew before she reached the boundary, though, that she would never get across it, even if she could find a vulnerable place. She saw Fiske on horseback, men with dogs, men with muskets, and was certain they would they kill her rather than let her get to that house, and safety. Wimbarton had laid good money out not long ago; he thought he owned her. He was afraid she might tell things to the law to cause him untold harm. Deb had no illusion: if he should catch her, she might live, and never see the light outside his world again. Otherwise, he'd want her dead and buried in the deepest hole. Her body was her only pledge for bargaining, but his steward, Jeremiah, if he won it, would cut her tongue or head off for his pleasure and give the remaining silence to his lord.

Deb pondered hard, but not for very long. She knew she could not get away. There was no way of clearing from the area; she would be sought and caught. She knew she needed men to hide or fight for her, but men she could outwit and get away from when their use was run. She needed men to save her from the hands of Jeremiah. At whatever cost.

They did save Deb that night, the wild men, and for several days thereafter. Jeremiah and Fiske attempted sorties because after her disappearance they assumed, quite rightly, that she must have joined the vagabonds for hiding. There was a chance she had got into Langham Lodge, but they could not believe it; there was a chance she had escaped along the road, but, if so, why had she risked her life to come? They attempted sorties, but tinker men pay little heed to outside interference; they are the masters of evasion—and the brutal tactics of Wimbarton's bully boys impressed them not at all.

If Deb was there, she was invisible and would remain so, Jeremiah knew. The woodmen were armed and dangerous, and were prepared for bloodshed if need be. When threats and bribes and vigilance had failed, he withdrew his men to merely guard Sir Arthur's boundary.

The cost for Deborah, as Annette later saw, had been immortal high. The men gave her protection, in their fashion, and she did repay them, in her way. Then she had to fight, and scheme, to get clear of the encampment and the residue of Jeremiah's search. She reached Marigold's in the end despite her grievous usages, and despite her fear that she might end up on the rope for her part in the death of Marcus Dennett. Marge Putnam was horrified to see her, but more because the "poor maid looked near-dead," she said, than because of her own fears of harbouring a criminal. She smiled, and welcomed, and sneaked her in and swore the other whores to secrecy.

Annette was the maid who knew her best, and she was most pragmatic. She did not probe at Deb too hard because life had taught her long ago that she would learn most by accepting. She comforted her friend, and washed her hair and face and body, and her feet, and dropped a tear on her at so much evidence of abuse. Deborah loved her for it; they knew that they were sisters in distress. Annette could guess a story and be welcome to it. Deb knew the truth, and it was not a truth to share.

The worst thing, in some awful way, was that she knew that she would have to try again, and she still had no idea what she would find, and what would happen to her, if she should get into the Surrey house. She was certain that Sir Arthur was a friend—remained so—and would give her refuge if she could make it to him, wherever Will might be. She was certain, but she did not know. That was the awful thing, the worst.

Inside of her, deep inside, Deborah could feel a change. There was a hardness growing in her brain and soul; there was a cutting edge. Although she longed for sight and touch of William, her love was different: it had teeth and muscle. She no longer believed inevitably that she would see him soon—or ever, necessarily. She no longer felt that it would kill her, either, although the pain was very raw.

In fact, in some ways, she became determined. To find him would remain her aim, and—she did believe—her destiny. But she was sure of one thing, clear and absolute: she would live.

TEN

"What! Gone! How mean you, gone, sir? How dare you, gone!"

Midshipman Shilling, small and pale, stood in the cabin facing Richard Kaye and trembled in the stark sunlight. At first it had seemed the bellowing would begin on deck, but even Kaye, at last, had read the faces of his company, had seen suppressed excitement in their eyes and snapped a lid on his public rage. He had shouted at Jem Taylor to "set the scum to work," and hustled Shilling toward the poop-break, flanked by Holt and Bentley. He had slammed the door behind them, then opened it to look onto the deck to check the men were scuttling to rope's end and cane. They were.

"Well, sir? Have you lost your speech? Well, sir, what mean you, he has gone?"

Will, who had seen too many small boys bullied by men in blue, could not help but admire Shilling's courage. He was as pale as death, exhausted, and had a definite, ragged cut above one eye, with bruising. But although he trembled, he returned his captain's gaze unflinching, and until the ranting stopped, seemed unprepared to give an answer.

"Dumb, is it?" shouted Kaye. "Or stupid? Do you not understand the English that I'm giving you? Is it too hard? You say a man has gone, you drop it in as if it's nothing, and then you won't—" He let out a growl, a kind of cry, pure frustration. "Good God, sir, how *mean* you, Gunning has decamped? What, with all his men, the former crew I bought off him? How many has he left, the bastard! Oh, the London River *dog!*"

Shilling said quietly: "I did not say decamped, sir, and he took no others of his former crew. He went, sir, to escape them. They chased him off."

It was well-timed. Slack Dickie goggled at him, uncertain he had heard it right, and Bentley took the opportunity.

"Who chased him off, Rex? What, his own shipmates? Or was it *Biter* men?"

"The Scots," said Sam, flatly. "That's where my wager goes. It was those three homunculi, for a king's ransom! Did not Taylor seek to aid you? Did you not have a gun?"

The midshipman eyed him coldly. "We have marines on board here, sir. It is not my place to shoot men for a discipline offence. In any way, it was not necessary. I had a good control."

Captain Kaye began to shout again.

"A good control! A good control, you blasted fool! Then where is my sailing master, my navigating man? If they chased him off, why did you not stop them, Groat? Why did you not shoot them? What mean you, that you had a good control?"

"The Scotchmen are a handful," muttered Holt, "but Jem and Hugg and Tilley—"

"It was not the Scotchmen, sir," said Shilling. "It was not like that at all, I beg your pardon. Gunning had been on the deck, up forward, setting up the martingale, I think, and his former people rushed him. They had been shaping bad all day. They planned to toss him overside, I guess, and they were beating him as well, exceeding badly. The first I knew back aft was shouts and roaring. Lieutenant Savary was down below, I think, but his men were by the mainmast, so I drove them with me to the bow."

"They had their muskets?" asked Holt. "That would have turned the trick, surely?"

"It was a melee," Shilling replied. "Fists and elbows everywhere. The soldiers seemed afraid to get too close, in my opinion, and they could have levelled arms in case of orders, but did not. Lieutenant Savary, I have to say it, must have heard the rumpus; unless he's deaf or drunk."

There is something unpleasant about this child, thought Bentley. There is intention to him. But Kaye ignored the slight on Savary.

"What happened then?" he said, impatiently. "Come on, sir, spit it out."

Again the measured pause. Midshipman Rex was not for hurrying.

"I ordered them to cease," he said. "I ordered the marines to go among them. I climbed into the chains so I could be better seen. I shouted for the boatswain and his mates."

"And?"

"Taylor was on the main topgallant yard, sir. He was working with a maul and did not hear at first. Then he came down. His mates ran up from otherwhere, but Gunning had been lifted to the side by now; they would have been too late to stop him going in the river. Except I saw the Scotchmen, sir. They were by the capstan. Two of them had picked up handspikes. They were ready."

"Ready?" said Kaye. "What, so you ordered them? Hah! It was the Scotchmen saved him, was it? Hah!"

There was a momentary silence. Overhead, abruptly, seagulls screamed. The midshipman shook his head.

"Saved, sir?" he said. "Well, I . . . it was a sort of riot, sir, it was a madhouse."

Holt said: "How did it . . . how did you finish it, Rex? Were you still stuck up in the shrouds?"

He had been polite, suggesting Shilling had been in full control. Shilling took umbrage anyway.

"My name is Shilling, sir. I am midshipman. Please do not use me so familiar. Yes, I was on high. I directed Mr Taylor and his men when they appeared. It was a very violent time. It lasted what seemed many minutes. The brothers knocked down about a half a dozen, knocked them down unconscious. Taylor and Hugg and Tilley chased the others off, and I skipped down to stop the Scotchmen killing them. Those handspikes, sir, if they catch you right . . ."

"Yes, yes," said Kaye, "and where was Gunning all this while? Not dead, not overboard quite clearly, so where in hell?"

"He was overside, sir. Not overboard exactly, he was not *in* the water, he was on it. In the ruck he must have slipped away, I did not see the going of him, sure. He ran down and got out on the boom, sir. Those damned soldiers, slack again, they are surely paid and fed to stop such things? He ran along the top and jumped down into a boat and cast her off. When I saw him he was half a cable's length away, going like a gun."

"What?" said Kaye. "One man alone? What boat was it; how many oars? He is not a giant, sir!"

Shilling nodded, faintly.

"He hailed a wherry, sir, and transhipped. Around here they know him, most of them. I put a boat out instantly, but too late; they were almost in among the Deptford tiers. And the Scotchmen, sir, were still for killing all the mutineers. I still had pressing work to do."

Kaye made a noise, half impatience, half disgust. Rex Shilling waited.

"I lost the man, sir," he said. "For which I crave your pardon. But we fetched the stolen boat back smartly. And we still have all the London River crew, mostly intact."

"Aye!" said the captain, suddenly hearty. "Aye, you've done well for that. Or at least, the Scotchmen have! Aye, it was a stroke of skill indeed to winkle them from Coppiner, the rogue! I will call them aft! They must have extra brandy! And they know Jamaica, also! Maybe we do not need—" He broke off. He laughed. "Hah, Bentley; Holt! How capital if they could navigate, what? Ha ha, how very capital!"

Their eyes exchanged one thought: their commander, their buffoon. But Shilling was looking anxious.

"Sir," he said. "Captain Kaye, I must say—"

"You must say what, Groat? Is there no end to your munificence? What else have you done for me, you hero? How would you like to be lieutenant of marines?"

"Sir," said Shilling, ignoring this crude jest, "you should not think those brothers are so . . . sir, they helped me for a . . . for a reason. I—"

Kaye barked, "Backsliding is it, Groat? Fearing their praise will outshine yours, is it? Look, sir, did they help or did they not? Without them what would have been the upshot of it all? Good God, I hate this in a man! Ingratitude!"

Maybe it was a family trait. Maybe Shilling had seen his relative blow hot and cold like this before. But to Bentley's eyes he took it very calm indeed. He squared his shoulders and his grey eyes did not falter.

"They border on the insubordinate," he said. "It took all my . . .

it was a battle, getting them to do my will. I fear sir . . . I fear there is much violence in their hearts."

Slack Dickie laughed at him. He raised his large head to the deckhead beams and let go a shout of it.

"Capital!" he said. "From heroes to villains in one prissy mouthful, eh? Next you'll say they set about you, I suppose? You have a bruise, Groat, a cut and bruise above your eye, all unexplained so far. What—did they attack you? Did the villains set about you? Pshaw! Spit it out, Groat, say what you must say!"

To Will's eyes, the mark above the eye appeared to stand out starker. Perhaps the young man had paled. His mouth tightened, visibly. A muscle in his cheek began to work.

"No, sir. Of course not, sir, I am their officer. To attack me would be mutiny, and mutiny means death. I must say, sir, your inference—"

"To hell with inference," said Kaye. "To hell with you and mutiny, Mr Shilling Groat. Mutiny means death, does it, and dead men haul no halyards, as the Navy proverb says. So to hell with talk of violence, ditto. Those Scotch brothers saved the day by your account, and they are just the men for me. If I were you, I'd thank my lucky stars that they were on my side." He stopped, and gazed at Shilling, levelly. "Ah, Shilling, Shilling, you have a lot to learn. Now get out of here, and leave me with my officers. The Scotchmen I will talk to later. You may go. No! Stop! I have a better plan! Black Bob! Where are you, bastard boy?"

Will Bentley and Sam Holt were astonished, but Rex Shilling turned as white as bone. He caught his breath as the small black boy appeared from behind a painted screen; he was appalled. Bad enough to be dressed down so savagely: but when a little savage hidden boy was listening . . . Bob, who had clearly heard it all, compounded it by smiling at the midshipman, in shy sympathy.

"Bob," snapped Kaye. "Go find the boatswain for me, or a mate. I want the Scotchmen here immediate. The three of them. Lamont."

"Lamont?" repeated Bob. His velvet eyes were wide but puzzled. Midshipman Shilling's eyes, on him, burned with hatred.

"Lamont!" said Kaye. "The Scotchmen, three beanpoles with the scraggy whiskers! Oh, to hell! Find Mr Taylor. Find the boatswain.

Look him out and tell him. The Scotchmen. Go. The Scotchmen called Lamont."

Black Bob nodded, and muttered "Taylor, bosun" once or twice. As he moved toward the door Kaye waved the midshipman to leave as well, and Bob pulled it open to hand him through. Shilling glared at him and hustled past, as if to touch him would mean contamination. Bob's face, turned back, was stricken. Then they were gone.

There was silence in the cabin for a moment, with Slack Dickie regarding them as if distracted. Then his face cleared. He was smiling.

"That bloody Groat's a bloody prig," he said, "but there's spirit in him, I must say. If we'd left it up to Savary, we'd have lost the crew I do believe. He's just a pretty face, that pretty boy; he needs a roaring out. Now men, what do you here? Have you no tasks to—ah, I remember."

The smile became a beam. It was as if he had a bomb to lob. He did.

"Tomorrow," he said. "I had a letter from their lordships. I did not tell you earlier in case you were distracted by't. Tomorrow, *ante meridiem,* you are required at the Offices. And after that, to celebrate, I give you liberty to go to Surrey to make farewells; I know you have a mind for it. Day following, unless the sky falls down, we're setting sail. One captain, post, two lieutenants, accredited, official. D'you remember Captain Oxforde? He heads up the testing board. Lord Wodderley, I understand, has taken an interest also. Well, what say? You've twenty hours, less, to learn again your tables and your stars! You will not shame me, will you? I confide you will be excellent, indeed."

Will's face was blank, but Holt's was humorous. Then Will remembered Deb, and his heart jumped. First the examination, then to Sir A's. Good God alive, just what to make of it?

Kaye was nodding vigorously.

"Aye, aye, well might you look concerned, boys. I hope you've done the work; I gave you time enough, for sure. In anyway, it is a load of flannel, is it not? Christ, when I faced the board my heart was so high in my mouth I could scarce articulate, and every other question left my mind a blank. I passed with colours flying, as they say. We all know more than we give credit for, leastwise to ourselves, that must be it. Take heart!"

We know more important people, that is more like, thought Sam. But he could not be bitter, could he, for through Swift, and Kaye, and Wodderley, he guessed he knew some, too, in terms of names and interest. He wondered though, uncomfortably, how the ship would get halfway round the world. How she would even reach the Downs without a pilot.

"Tomorrow, sir?" he heard Will say. "Is this not jest, sir, is this for serious? But I . . . but we . . ."

"But nothing, Bentley. But remember this: if you make a muff of it, you'll have to face your Uncle Daniel, will you not? He has confidence, and so do I. You have tonight to finish off your preps. I will give neither of you any other duties. I would even let you take the night ashore, except I know you'd fuck your strength away at Dr Marigold's. With Annette's legs locked around his waist, there is no certitude that Holt would even turn up at the Offices! So—what say you both? Am I wrong to place my trust in you? Just tell me I am right!"

They pulled their shoulders back, they put on keenest faces, they chorused, "Aye aye, sir." When Bob's face peeped around the door, back from his errand, they made their bows and left with resolution. Outside the cabin, they met the Lamont brothers. The three Scotsmen glanced sideways, sardonically, and touched their curly forelocks polite enough. But there was something odd about their faces, something smirking, and as they passed, Will heard a squeak from the little African, a squeak of pain or terror. He spun upon his heel, but saw nothing but the brothers' backs, lean and wiry, as they forged into the cabin.

Later that evening, as they watched the quiet northern shore of Kent in lovely starlight, Sam and Bentley became aware of the boatswain, in the shadows watching them. Will raised a hand and beckoned, and Jem Taylor padded barefoot across the deck to join them. Like

Shilling, it was noticed, he had a mark upon his face, but worse. A livid bruise, a jagged cut with blackened blood attached. Sam pointed at it.

"Go on," he said. "Explain."

"Those Scotchmen are the devil," Taylor said. "I can speak frankly, Mr Holt? They will put us all in danger, sir. And tonight they boast they've taken brandy with the owner."

The word introduced a tiny thrill in Bentley, but not a pleasant one. The owner was what men had called his Uncle Daniel, on the *Welfare*. But Swift's command had had a grip of steel.

"Do you doubt it, Jem?" asked Samuel. "Or is the question why?"

A small noise from the boatswain.

"I do not doubt it, no. That they have power over poltroons is—" He broke off suddenly. He coughed to hide embarrassment. "Not that I suggest, sirs—not that I do impugn . . . Ah Christ, sirs."

"We've heard naught wrong, Jem," Will told him, gruffly. "Better to be frank, please, downright blunt. It is not as if we have not . . . oh speak, man. Tell us your fears."

"They did take drink with him," put in Holt. He glanced about the empty deck to make sure no one overheard them. "Midshipman Shilling told a story how the brothers saved Jack Gunning from his former people, who would have slaughtered him. They saved the man and saved the day. Mr Kaye, I have to tell you, has the highest hopes of them. Of Shilling too, I guess, although he don't find that so pleasing as a prospect."

"The midshipman did try to warn him, though, in some way," said Will. "He blew hot and cold about them. First praise, then talk of violence in their hearts."

Taylor gave a quiet laugh.

"Violence in their hearts, was it?" he said. "Poor boy was lucky that he got away alive. I thought one moment we would have to rescue him, me and my mates. In all that bloody mayhem."

"What?" said Sam. "They hit him, did they? He has a bruise, but said . . . go on, finish it."

"I think the face-hit was an accident," the boatswain said. "But they . . . well, he tried to order them, to give commands. They insulted him most horribly. They laughed and mocked him. They held him for a toy."

"Humiliation," Will said softly. There was pity in his voice. He recalled Rex Shilling's pale and tortured face. "But these are common sailors; they are pressed. Where was this, Jem? Did many of the company observe it?"

"No, sir, I think not. It was in the 'tween decks. The Scots had beaten the rioters down there to shackle them, subdue them. There was still hot work on deck, but I had followed down to give the boy . . . the officer . . . a hand. I heard them rag him, call him seven kinds of . . . I heard the insults, sir. The threats."

There was something hidden in the words. Something Will was unsure of, but Sam grasped or guessed.

"Are they buggermen?" he said. "Come, Jem, tell true. Were the threats to make a toy of him? That sort of toy?"

"Aye, sir. Among other things. Not the sort of things that he could tell, poor boy. They set out, sirs, to bring his spirit down, to make him know that they were in command. It was an act of brutes, in sorts. Of brutish men who . . . who seemed to have command." He stopped, embarrassed. "I cannot say it right, that's the rub. It sounds stupid, mad. They are like . . . officers in some wise, sirs, like men of . . . certain skill. If they get to that midshipman on his own, sirs, far out at sea . . . unless he tells, sirs—how can he survive?"

A small breeze blew up, ruffling the water down from the northern shore. A smell of dockyard fires, rank and harsh, rolled over them, mixed with the acrid fumes of iron foundries. All three of them, caught in the throat, began to cough. Their panting afterwards was somehow companionable.

"What shit," said Holt. "Night and day they cast and forge. What filthy shit they pump into the air."

"We'll be at sea soon, sirs," said Jem. "Another half a dozen lighters came today. But he needs warning, sirs, Captain Kaye. He needs it telling and explaining, sirs, come what may. Those Scotchmen are the devil, sirs; they're as fatal as the grave. That midshipman is haughty, but he is just a little boy. Beg pardon, sirs, if I ha' overstepped the mark. I live in fear, sirs, honestly."

At a nod from Holt, Taylor slipped away. The two stood another half an hour, sometimes in sweet river air, sometimes coughing. To the north a newly fired furnace burst out gouts of orange flame, and even when they went below, the fumes dragged at their lungs and noses.

"Well, we must warn Kaye," said Will. "It is our bounden duty. Though God knows, he won't take kindly to it, will he?"

Sam laughed.

"He don't like Groat that much," he said. "Don't trust him much at all, I think. We'll keep an eye on him at sea, and make sure they can't get to him, and otherwise he need not have much to do with them, I guess. Kaye don't see him as a commander, does he? Far from it!"

Next day, though, Captain Kaye felt confident enough, apparently, to leave Midshipman Shilling in sole charge of the *Biter* and all her company, including the Scots.

It was a terrible mistake.

ELEVEN

Despite their nerves at their impending test, both Holt and Bentley had a certain blitheness on that pleasant morning at the prospects of what the later day might bring. Open-eyed and open-hearted, they walked into an ambush that neither, on his own, could easily have survived. They were not far from the waterfront, in a very measly area, as they approached the environs of Seething Lane, and at first it seemed the attack was of that not-unusual nature—to rob poor sailors of their hard-collected cash.

One turning more to get a sight of the Navy Offices, and they were picking through the mud and filth like well-bred dainty ladies, to protect their shoreside leather shoes. Each carried a small valise with stouter gear for riding down to Surrey with, which—from the footpad point of view—was surely bait enough. They had been discussing Langham Lodge, and the possibility that Deborah could be there, and wondering if an express might reach the house before them, to forewarn. Where to get one, though, with a trusty messenger and good strong horse—on top of which, it would cost a deal of cash, which neither had to spare.

"And capping *that*," said Sam, merrily, "what if we fail the test most miserably? Would you then be so keen to go and claim your pretty bride? Would she, indeed, be prepared to throw in her lot with such a failure? Could you afford a licence, what is more?"

Will, hit by a sense of longing and ridiculousness, was forced to laughter. For months he'd crushed all thoughts of Deb, all hopes. He had, indeed, more than half assumed that she was dead. But she was living. And she might be there.

"We'll just turn up," he said. "We'll ride in unannounced. She won't be there. She can't be; it would be too much on the lucky side. We'll keep our money in our pocket where it's needed most."

Now Sam laughed.

"We'll have to hire nags," he said. "They don't come free. But if we get our tickets from the buffers, we'll have silver in great store—so long they shell out something in advance! Any way, there'll be Mrs Houghton who will welcome us as heroes, even if we fail. We are her blue-eyed boys."

It was at that moment, as they crossed the entrance to a narrow alley, that the attackers flew at them. Three men in cloaks burst out, one with a naked blade and two with clubs. They were roaring like wild bears, and the bigger two made a set at Holt as if he had been targeted. A smaller man swiped sideways at Will, his cudgel catching him across the chest with force. Luckily, Will's feet both slipped in the mire, and he skidded before the weight of onslaught, followed by the ruffian, who lost his footing as well. Will, light and nimble, was able to twist, still on his feet, and jerk the other man across his leg, to sprawl headlong. Then he turned to help his friend.

But Sam, as pale as death, had also got a blade out, a long and wicked dirk that he must have had concealed. One assailant, face uncovered, was caught in Will's sight, open-mouthed as the steel ran across his cheek and opened it like a piece of uncooked belly-pork.

The other knife-man, already served, was gaping silently at his fist, which held a weapon still, but in a pulsing sea of crimson. Then Will's man jumped up to swing at him, took in the scene before him—and stopped his cudgel in mid-air, demoralised. Will kicked out sideways at his knees and dealt a twisting crack that made the villain shout and drop his weapon, turn and run.

"Follow!" yelled Will. And "Stay!" riposted Sam. Will, who had already made a half a dozen yards, pulled up reluctantly. Sam came up to him, and, panting, they watched the three men disappear. The dirk, Will noted, with a quiet admiration, had disappeared.

"Blood," he said. "A dangerous place, this London. 'Tis worse than Petersfield after summer fair. I like the blade, Sam. Without it, I would have ended dead. Fool robbers, though. We do not look like rich men, surely?"

Sam was wiping mud from off his leg. His clothing, not too sharp at best of times, was looking truly shabby.

"They were not robbers, though," he said. "Just the other kind, indeed. They were employed to seek me out, for *I've* robbed *them* is the way their masters see it. They were coming to collect."

Will blinked at him, his lack of understanding comical enough to set Sam laughing once again.

"I may not look rich," he said, "but what I've got ain't mine, and rarely has been. You owe money, Will, you must understand? I owe money also, and this was meant to be the reckoning. That's why I took up with the dirk. Man's best friend. Fuck dogs!"

They were almost at the Office entrance now. Slightly muddy, slightly dishevelled, hardly calm and collected, in any eyes. Will owed money, he was very short, but then . . .

"How much?" he asked.

"Hah! You'd have to ask my creditors for the exact sum, keeping tally ain't my finest skill. I must owe Marigold a round twenty, and he's not the biggest shark in my small pond. Our escapade, and dodging prison, and all that . . . well, you know the story. Suffice to say, when I see men in mind to slinking, I duck into the shadows. Sing ho for the examination; I need the extra pay. Except I owe their lordships plenty also, according to their clerks!"

"Do you gamble, Sam?" said Bentley.

"No, I live, you po-faced turd! I live, and take from lenders, and then they want it back! You have a father. You are lucky. I do not."

"You have an uncle. Well . . . Sir A is—"

"Sir A is generous to a fault, and through the years I must have cost him hundreds, must I not? I can no longer borrow from him, Will, I can no longer ask. Why? Because, my friend; because. Now come in here and stop this pissy blather. Do I look smart enough? To be a true lieutenant? Now wipe that worried look away, and wipe your boots, and smile. Here's to success, friend—success and deeper debt!"

"Oh lord," said Bentley, and it was half a prayer. "Oh lord, success. Oh lord!"

Strangely, though, from the moment they set foot into the Office lobby, both had a certain feeling that they would not fail. They were greeted by a clerk, who told them off indifferently to wait in a side room until summoned. It was a small and fowsty place, with an unlighted fire in the grate, but almost before they sat down, the clerk looked round the door and beckoned them to follow. Two flights of stairs, a polished door in oak, and after a knocking from the clerk, a gruff order they should enter.

The room was large, with a shining oval table and tall windows. They were closed, but light streamed in and kept them blinded for a moment. Will then saw five men around the top end of the table, backs to the light, and recognised Lord Wodderley, who half stood— the soul of courtesy—and made the slightest bow.

"Young men," he said. "No secret of the fact we've met before. How is your uncle, Mr Holt? Yours, Mr Bentley, is very well; he asked me most particularly to say so. He was impressed by both your actions in last year's nonsense on the *Biter*, as indeed was I. Another open secret, then: we are not here to fail you, or otherwise to do you down, but solely to assess if we concur with other men's opinions. I shall not even waste your time with introductions, as, being young, you will instantly forget our stuffy ranks and faces. A test, sirs—who is this?"

Smiling broadly, he waved a hand towards his right, where sat a thin and acid post captain. Even had not Kaye forewarned them yesterday, they would have known him. He had come on board of *Biter* once to investigate a death they had had part in, and had found Slack Dickie Kaye not guilty of a crime. His gaze was level, not unfriendly, and both Will and Sam felt a certain weight of shame.

"It is Captain Oxforde," said Sam, and Bentley nodded.

"Captain Kaye did tell us, sir," he said. "But we both remember him."

Oxforde said, "It was a difficult circumstance when we last met. Both of you, I thought, acquitted well. Now, my lord. With your permission?"

"Oh, if you must, Oxforde," said Wodderley, jovially. "But no trick questions, eh? One young man of these two has battled round the Horn under jury rig and the other's beat three hundred smugglers and Frogs. No doubt they know which sails to douse and in what order coming to an anchorage. They're seamen born and bred."

Will, blushing at its pointlessness, heard himself say, "We did not get right round, sir. The Horn. We were beaten back. And I was down below in—"

"Pshaw!" went Wodderley. "Fishing for compliments, is it? And when you sailed an open boat down Channel in a hurricane, I suppose you had a ten-man crew and navigator? Give up, boy! We haven't got all day!"

There were chuckles from the other officers around the table, and Oxforde gave a sort of shrug. He shook his head at Wodderley, amused, and carried on.

"All right, then," he said. "We'll take most of it as read; Lord Wodderley has the right of it, I'm sure. I am bound to ask you, gentlemen, on your words of honour, how you assess your skills at navigation, taking sun and star sights, converting tables, dead reckoning with log and timing glass. Mr Holt, you first. You went to Christ's Mathematical, so I believe?"

Sam's turn to blush. He wondered if it was a loaded question, to show him as an inferior, a child of charity. Oxforde's face, however, did not tell that at all. It was frank and grave, and clear of prejudice.

"Aye, sir," said Sam. "I came out top in everything, if I may make so bold to boast, sir. I am fairly confident of crossing open water,

Start Point to Finish Headland holds no fears." He stopped; they liked the joke. "And then I'll call a pilot, sir. I would not wish to ship on any boat in unknown waters with only me at con."

There was the briefest silence, then a boom of friendly laughter, even a lemon-slicey smile from Oxforde. God, thought Will, dare I be so very honest? I am on my honour, but . . . But Kaye passed this examination once, and Kaye spells danger on a village pond. What are they looking for? Oh, what?

"Your answer, sir?" said Oxforde. Will coughed. He glanced from face to face, five pairs of eyes, no . . . no, four pairs and a singleton, one of the officers, a meaty, swarthy man, had one eye and a socket, skin collapsed. Will coughed once more and bit the bullet.

"Around the coast, I have no fears at all," he said. "Sea marks I know well and remember headlands and other features with facility. I can interpret charts with confidence, from those made for your lordships and thus well-made, to scrawls on paper, so long they're pretty accurate. At picking my way through soundings, with lead and line . . . well, I've done it and enjoyed it, sirs. It is my . . . I do it . . . sirs, I *revel* in it."

He drew breath to tackle the confession side, glancing around the assembled faces before he leapt. He would be completely honest, that he knew. He could learn, would learn, but had a lot to learn—a mountain. But he did not get the chance to open mouth.

"Good," said Wodderley, "well, excellent, in fact! What say you, gentlemen, are not these two officers the perfect complement? Lieutenant Holt takes them across the ocean like an arrow from the bow—and just when he'll put her on the rocks, Lieutenant Bentley takes the helm and slides her into harbour like a lamb! Ineffable!"

"And Dickie Kaye," began the swarthy captain loudly, and with clear comic intent. "Slack Dickie Kaye—" Then stopped, as his fellows looked at him aghast. His good eye closed, then opened on a bark of merriment. "Locked mouth," he said, "locked mouth! I'm not the man to rock the boat, you know!"

And that was it, to both their blank astonishments. They were given small applause, their hands were shaken, and they were congratulated by every august person present in the room, including

Captain Oxforde, whom they thought should know much better. On shaking Will's hand, though, he did look hard into his eyes, as if he was going to make a grave pronouncement. But all he said was this: "A good ship needs a sailing master, Lieutenant, does it not? You are lucky in John Gunning, I believe?" Will, then, suffered a collapse in telling truth. "Lieutenant" he was called. The die was cast. Lieutenant Bentley, an officer of the King, a repository of signal honour and integrity. But he could not tell them that Gunning was gone. *Biter,* across the wide Atlantic, would be in his own tender hands, and Lieutenant Samuel Holt's.

And those of Captain Kaye, God spare the mark.

Captain Kaye, in fact, was at that very moment preparing to abandon his most precious ship—and into tender hands his Navy masters would have goggled at. He did it on a whim of sorts, but not a sudden one, entirely. He had drunk and spoke with the Scotch brothers the day before, and had hit upon a train of thought and action when he'd pondered on the conversation afterwards. The sight of Holt and Bentley heading up to London encouraged him in thought, and before the forenoon watch was through, his strategy was complete. He instructed Bob, got figged up in shoreside gear, installed a new wig on his head and had it powdered—then called in Midshipman Shilling. His manner was avuncular, and almost warm.

"Groat!" he said. "My second cousin's boy! I have a task for you, a trust."

He was almost sentimental, rather than just warm, and Midshipman Rex Shilling was suspicious.

"Aye, sir?" he responded, rather coolly. "Well indeed, sir, whatever you command."

"It is a simple thing, young Rex, although it might surprise you, I would hope. I have to go away to London Town, this morning, now, upon some pressing business. Gunning has quit us, thanks to you— and you must take his place!"

Groat's face displayed astonishment, not mere surprise. He did, in fact, seem not to believe. He feared betrayal of some sort, or ridicule.

"Yes," he said. Then, "Aye, sir?"

"It should not be for long," said Kaye. "I will be back this evening, I should imagine. Yes, certainly, I should be back tonight, unless . . . And there is naught to do, in terms, is there? We are safely on our buoy, the fellows cannot run no more, the worst are back in shackles, and although you will command, there are other men to back you, are there not?"

Rex Shilling was unsure of that, and showed it. Kaye laughed.

"Savary, between ourselves, is a milk pudding, despite he is an officer and you are not. An officer of soldiery. Pah. But I have kicked his bollocks black and blue about his laxness and his men's, and I'll wager they'll use their muskets next time they are needed. Then there's Taylor Boatswain and his merry band of bone-crushers, and backing them are . . ."

He stopped, as if suddenly a touch uncertain. A quick small smile, a lick of lips. He turned away to shuffle papers.

"I have decided that the Scotchmen should be—What?"

Shilling had let out a noise, and Kaye had sprung around. Shilling's face was stricken, which he struggled to disguise. Kaye's manner was no longer of an uncle. His eyes gleamed prominent. He stared.

"Nothing, sir."

"Good. Those Scotch are valuable. I will not hear it said . . ." He cleared his throat. "If you should need them, you may call upon them for any aid. It is understood. I have spoke with them."

Now Shilling licked his lips.

"Are they . . . ?" He selected his words. "Are the Scotchmen warranted, sir?"

"Not yet. One must not be too sudden. But rest assured . . ."

Shilling rested unassured, far, far from it, but he could not let it show, for Kaye was gazing at his face intensely. The captain let out a noise, relaxed.

"Well then," he said. "That is the way of it. You are midshipman, Taylor has sway upon the crew, and the Lamont brothers are trusted also, with a certain power of command, however minimal. You may trust them, Mr Shilling, and you will. And remember this—on board a ship there is only one true demon. He lives inside a bottle, and the bottle must be corked. Do you perceive me?"

Rex Shilling nodded. But a picture of confidence he was not.

"Good. So keep the devil in the bottle, and do not let him out. The spirits are all locked and barred, the wine and barrels also. Keep it so, and nothing can go wrong."

"Indeed, sir. It shall be so."

Kaye twinkled at him.

"If *you* should feel the need, of course . . . Black Bob remains on board and is privy to my own small store of bottles—ah no, you do not indulge, do you, except in the way of *politesse!* Most excellent behaviour in a young gentleman. Now—go and find out where my bloody gig might be, and bloody Cox'n Sankey. Is there no one save the Scots on board this ship that moves with any *fizz?*"

As the gig pulled sharply from the side ten minutes later, Midshipman Shilling and Jem Taylor—who had been most briefly briefed, along with Savary, about the new world order—caught each other's eyes. The look held for several seconds; then both looked away.

TWELVE

The mood of Lieutenants Bentley and Holt—true lieutenants, not the acting variety—was fragile as they urged their tired hacks along the last few hundred yards of curving driveway up to Langham Lodge. They had ridden very hard to get there at a reasonable time (for uninvited guests), and both had mixed feelings, anticipation churned with fear, as they reined down for a more sedate final approach. Bentley, who had hardly spoken for an hour, had been hollowed out as they got further down the Surrey Road, his mouth like parchment, his stomach filled with flitting butterflies. For months he'd crushed all thoughts of her, all hopes. For months he'd more than half assumed she might be dead. But Deborah was living. And she might be here.

It had been the year before that he had made the journey last,

and the memories it stirred this time were mainly tragic. He and
Sam had tried, and failed, to find and rescue the baronet's adopted
son, Charles Yorke, and in the process uncovered shameful secrets
that touched very deep both friends and families. Will's certitude of
what was right and patriotic, even normal in the way of commerce
during war, had suffered blows he was not certain he'd recovered
from, and the fact that he had grown closer to his father because of
it, instead of simply cutting off all ties, still gave him sleepless times.
His father had visited him in prison, and been (as Will imagined)
completely frank about his part in all that wicked trade, and yet had
made Will see that it was due not to villainy, or evil, but was an hundred times more twisted up in complex life than that. He had an
image yet of Mr Bentley—soon to win or buy a parliamentary place—
saying to him, on his seventh visit: "How else do you want it, William,
how else? Your father starving, your mother on the beg, your little
sisters on the gutter-edge at Point, selling the only thing young
women have to sell by birthright? Good God, young man—grow
wise! There are but two ways to get through this life for people such
as us: we rise, or fall. If rising is our plan, we have to use what
weapons we can find."

Suddenly, in front of them, there was commotion. Around the
house, although the doors stayed shut, a pair of people, then a knot,
came hurrying: a farrier, a groom, and girls, and striding through
the middle, Sir Arthur Fisher's steward, Tony. The frankness of his
face, alive with pleasure at the sight of them, was the restorer that
they needed. The maidens who knew them, also, and the men, were
full of greetings as they gathered round.

"Tony!" said Sam, one hand raised in salutation. "Well met, friend
Tony, well met indeed! How goes the battle?"

"Mr Sam! Oh, well indeed, sir! And Mr William an' all! Well met,
sir, and well come! Jack, Timothy! Take the masters' 'orses there.
Maids! Go fetch some ale, or stir the kettle up. Mr Bentley, at least, do
love a goodly brew o' tea! Mr Will, sir? Is that the truth or ain't it?"

"It is indeed, Tony. Well remembered. Good God, I'd swallow a
cup whole; and put a mass of sugar in it, do! Here, take this nag,
Tim. You might have to carry me, and all!"

The stretching over, though, and the servants' smiles, they walked with Tony to a side kitchen door to freshen while Sir Arthur was informed. Despite his jollity, Will had a deeper hollow in his pit. Tony had not mentioned her, nor had the maidens who had been her friends. He felt it was his role to keep it buttoned in. He could play the love-calf, but to what effect? If people knew he'd held a candle for her, if they remembered, they would surely think it over long ago. Perhaps, indeed, it was.

Mrs Houghton, fat and bluff and motherly, treated them like long lost boys. She admonished Sam for his absence, and chid him for the sparseness of his letters, but clearly understood as well as he did—better—the reasons for his reticence. Sir A, she said, having moved heaven and earth to save him from official anger after his leaving of the *Biter* in the lurch, thought it most natural that he'd shown the normal ingratitude of a wayward son—and had forgiven him. She warned them though, that he was older than he had been, and they might not think he was ageing very well. The last two years, she said with meaning, had took a dreadful toll.

Sir A, however, when they went into his room, tried his hardest to belie her gloomy forecast. The room, as ever, was aglow with light from the giant windows giving to the lawn and from the quite enormous fire blazing in the grate. He stood, he walked, embraced them, slapped their backs, and seemed less stiff than they did from their ride. He was thinner than Will remembered, certainly, and his hair was whiter and less thick. But he did not have the air of someone waiting for the grave.

"Will," he said, "how good it is to see you. You have suffered much and I have suffered for you, in a minor, selfish way. And now I hear the both of you have took up with the *Biter* once again, and that oaf, Kaye. Ah, young men! I don't recall that I was ever mad as that!"

"You are very well informed as ever, sir," said Sam. "Mrs Houghton told me off for not writing you enough, but I see you are up with us as always. Way ahead, perhaps? Maybe you can tell us when we sail!"

"I know not when," Sir Arthur laughed, "but I do know where. The West Indies, the sugar islands, among the naked coal-black maidens. To fight the French? Or to protect the pockets of the fat commercial men? They are a very fractious crew, the sugar growers, I have had dealings with some of them over years. Cutthroats for money, and bleaters when they feel a breath of war or competition."

Sam smiled.

"I guess they feel out on a limb, sir, be not too short on charity. Stuck out on a little piece of land in the middle of a foreign sea, with every bugger and his dog after a piece of 'em. Hollanders in one direction, Swedes in another, Don Spaniard north, south, and west, and Frenchmen everywhere."

"Aye," Sir Arthur said. "And the slaves, of course, who'd chop 'em up and eat 'em for a ha'penny. Well, it serves them right. They're jealous because the Frenchmen do it better: better planting, better crops, better purses. And their blacks are freemen mainly, as I understand it, so they don't spend their waking hours planning pillage, rape, and bloody mayhem. I wish them joy of it. I have no sympathy."

"They do it better, sir?" said Will, brought up by what he thought he'd heard. "Frenchmen do? How's that?"

The old man looked at him for some long moments. Then he went back to the fire and sat down. He looked a little tired, all at once.

"I had forgot how young you are," he said. "Just because we English think we rule the roost it don't mean that we do, on all occasions. It is possible, you know, that other nations get it right, or righter, some of the times. The French islands have better yields, less native trouble, more returns on capital, and in general run things better than we do. Why do you think we fight these people? It is a constant struggle, Will, for wealth and power, and supremacy."

"And the slaves?" asked Will. "Do you tell me, sir, the French do not use slaves? But how can they work plantations, then? The need for labour is enormous. They need thousands, millions."

"And the Frenchmen do use slaves, uncle," Sam put in. "I have seen French slave ships. Indeed, I've smelt them from downwind."

Sir A poured himself a small glass of something sweet. He took a sip and made a face.

"Aye, most unsavoury, I'm sure," he said. "They do use slaves and slavers, certainly, and they deal them, also—there is much money to be made in that. But their own slaves serve a term and then are free. Likewise the Spaniards'. The best tobacco from the Spanish islands, this lovely snuff we're getting now, it is all produced by free men on free land. And we English have to smuggle it, as always, because we have not the wit to see the other ways. You all know the trouble that smuggling can cause, my boys. Even within the closest families."

The three of them fell silent for a while and had their thoughts. It was not a subject they wished to air aloud, though. The time for that was past.

Will said, "How can it be, though, sir, that we need cost-free labour and they do not? The planters must know what can be afforded, surely? If we cannot afford to pay them, how can the French?"

"Who says we do not pay them, though? We pay them food, we pay them shelter, we pay them men and medicine to keep them on their feet and working. French workers also eat. No doubt they also live in shelters of some kind; they also suffer the illnesses of too much work. But pay them wages, and they buy all these needs themselves from their own pockets. The planters' outlay may not be dissimilar, but there is this difference to men. Slaves are not freemen, and freemen are not slaves. Give a man his food and call him captive, and he will hate you for it. Sell a man his food from out his pay—and he will not."

He took another sip, then waved a finger.

"Slaves do not come free, from God or charity likewise," he said. "Before our planters pay to keep them alive and working, they must pay shippers and merchants for bringing them from Africa. The Frenchmen do that, too—but charge the slaves for their freedom when it comes at last, thus clawing back the wages they have paid out. So, given careful management, their freemen cost them less than any slave. Plus, freemen work much harder, and live much longer, do they not? A Jamaica slave, a British slave to say, lives only seven years or so, as I understand it, or can only work that long at least, but still must be fed and watered, I suppose, in his retirement or dotage. It is the logic of the madhouse, not the counting house. The planters are the slaves—to lunacy! Samuel, be useful. Put on more logs; my poor old bones are sore."

While Sam fettled the fire, Will struggled with a question. Knowing, as he did now, some of Sir Arthur's business, and where his wealth came from, he found it difficult to frame. Some men thought slavery disgusting, he knew, from a moral point—a question he had never really pondered. But Sir Arthur's business in the East, his use of native labour, was that not . . . ? Will sighed. Perhaps he'd better not to ask.

"Talking of lunatics and lunacy," said Sam, his work with fire tongs and poker almost done, "that leads us straight to Dickie Kaye. He took us out to meet his father, Duke Whatseecalled. Big lovely house, sir, but not as fine as yours. He wants to get himself some blackmen and a sugar crop, bought and paid for by his son. What say you to that, for lunacy?"

Sir Arthur stared at him.

"What, as a side bet to fighting off the French?" he asked. "I wonder what the Admiralty lords would make of that idea? But the duke is not a fool, even if his son should be. He'll surely not give him a bag of gold to carry over there? It will be a fishing trip, won't it, what the French would call *reconnaissance*. Perhaps he wants to give the lad a good *divertissement*."

"Aye, may be," said Sam. "Although there is some talk of Daniel Swift, as well. He corresponds with Dickie's Pa. There is some talk, somehow, of him going to the Carib also."

The baronet stared at the fire. It was blazing well again.

"Well," he said. "That paints it differently, I guess. It's true that black and white is not so clear in all of this, in any way. We're talking use of money, capital; and any venture, at the nicest time, can pay off handsomely, pay quite enormous dividends. Alternatively, if you cross the danger line, it's poverty and ruin, or, at the least, gigantic loss. Your uncle is a firebrand, young Will. But is he a man of capital and commerce. There's the rub."

"He's good at slave driving," said Sam, with a bark of laughter. "Ain't he, Will?" He paused. "It's not a trade that I should like to be in, though. I think it is a foul, filthy thing."

Sir Arthur sighed.

"I know it not, the whole Atlantic trade," he said. "Men rail at slavery—not many, it is true—and men rail at the way we make our monies in the East, merchants like me. But what, when all is said and done, is the alternative? There is none. It only becomes unbearable when the terrible injustices and blows of rock-hard fortune fall on ourselves, or those we love. My three sons were lost, remember, and my dear wife. Not because they or I was evil, but because things happen thus. Had I not made my wealth in the far Indies, they would have died of a far more common disease, perhaps, called penury. Life has talons, boys, and bloody claws, and men are forced to do things that good upright souls regret, and wish there was no need for. That is it."

Will cleared his throat.

"But . . . but slaves, Sir A? You do not deal in slaves, or use them, I believe? But if you had to—"

The old man's eyes stopped him. Will coughed.

"I do not deal in slaves, it's true," he said. "I do not use them in the East directly, in any way at all. But I do ship cotton cloth from India, the bulk of which is sold to merchants in Bristol, London, Liverpool—who mix it with some English stuff and ship it on to Africa. It is a favourite there, a staple, and the Africans pay for it with other Africans, called slaves, to go out to the Carib, and the Main. So without my cotton cloth from India, the trade would be much curtailed, or crippled, would it not? Despise it if you like, good lad, but understand it, do. For us and people like us, it is simply life. People like us, Will. There are irons to be struck."

The light was fading from the sky outside. Long shadows grew across the close-scythed grass. Will Bentley felt a shade misunderstood.

"I do not despise it, sir," he said. "I do not have a very strong opinion, to be frank. But whatever Uncle Daniel Swift might think— I do not see myself as a plantation owner! God forbid!"

"Not even if it turns out the only way?" said Sam, half-serious. "It is the times, Will, and the times are out of joint. The world is in a helter-skelter now; things change so quick you have to dance a jig to just stand still. Look at England, back to my grandfather's time, no longer. Kings with their heads off, no stake complete without a burning Catholic, a Dutchman taking charge. New colonies, the fortunes of the West and East brought home, and all the wars with all the other raveners—French, Spanish, Dutch, or any combination of the six! What is your plan? To stay at home in Hampshire with your sheep?"

Sir A was nodding.

"What breed of sheep, though, that's a question, too," he said. "You know how farming's changed and changing, Will. Then there is manufacturing, and foul, filthy air, people pouring into towns and cities like wild animals, London the open cesspit of the world, the River Thames a sewer. Good God, they say men cut your throat up there to get a poke of sugar or a taste of tea. And what of coffee? My, not so long ago we used to sing 'How shall I name thee, Shameful Bean?' You will not credit that, I'll wager!"

They looked at him, perplexed.

"But why?" asked Sam. "What was wrong with coffee, for dear's sake?"

"The devil's brew," said Sir A. "It made whores of women and revolutionists of men. Unlike good old English ale, that merely made them drunk and stupid. And the women fart, I guess!" He sighed. "Fact is though, Will, that money is the force that drives the times. If you have no money in Jamaica, you are just a slave. With money, you can make a fortune using slaves. Spend your money on a ship, and fortune comes from *selling* them. So what is right, exactly? What is wrong?"

"That makes the money that they pay us worth double, Will," laughed Sam. "We don't have to think or worry on such questions; we're paid to fight, is all. This week the French are brutes, last week the Spaniards. Although come to think, if I'm allowed a preference, the Dons are ten times worse. Too much spicy sausage, and they conquered half the world!"

"They stole Jamaica from the Carib Indians," said Sir A. "That's as I understand the history. And we stole it from *them,* on the barest pretext, not so very long ago. And now we're friends against the French, except the Spanish treat our ships like pirates and seize and pillage them and burn the bottoms out, as we'll do theirs again, you have my pledge for that. So tell me what the moral is, I beg of you."

A silence fell, but not uncomfortable. Outside the birds had ceased their noises as the dark came gently seeping down. Our life is all coercion, thought Will Bentley, mine and Sam's. We have no cash or station, and unless we rise and then take prizes, that can scarcely change. Prizes with Dickie, though—some chance of that! However—only *because* of Dickie—they were now lieutenants, and their rising could begin. Morality, it seemed, did not come into it. Perhaps the best way out was marriage, after all. Perhaps Slack Dickie could find him a rich match!

The thought stabbed him cruelly, and he heard his voice say, as a simple shock, the name he thought he had completely in command.

"Deborah, Sir A," he uttered. "You have not told me; I have not asked. I must though, sir. Deborah Tomelty. Where is she, do you know, sir, please? I had hoped . . . indeed, I'd almost prayed she would be here."

No going back on that, at least: his boats were burnt. The old man glanced into the fire, then looked at him steadily, then dropped his eyes away. Will's stomach dropped also. He could not guess what he was going to hear, but his stomach dropped and clenched. He felt desolated.

"We thought she came here, sir," said Sam. "We know that she left London. We know she was in pretty desperate straits. We hoped that she had made it to your house, and . . . sanctuary."

Sir Arthur Fisher raised his eyes to Sam's then, but did not hold them long. He let a breath out slowly, and it was heavy with regret.

"She was here, Will," he said. "She did come here. She stayed a little while, then went away. I gave her money—although she said she had some of her own—and . . . and she went away. She . . . I think she hoped to find you."

"To find me? Where?"

"When was this, sir?" Sam asked. "Was it long ago? Will was in prison. Where would she go? Why?"

Sir A's features had taken on a greyish tinge. He was exhausted suddenly. Will had a strong impression he was going to lie, or had been lying.

"She spoke of Stockport, so I think," he said. "That northern town she ran away from. Her life had been quite harsh since your disaster on the Shoreham beach. I think she might have had to . . . keep bad company."

Will felt bright anger spring inside him, but he crushed it in his throat. Sir A was clearly stricken; he was clearly almost beat. It came to Will that they must leave, immediate. They had to go to London, ask at Marigold's, search. But what if she'd been forced back to Portsmouth, as Annette had said she had been once? What if she was a nymph, a Shitty Corner slattern? Why had Sir Arthur let her go?

"That magistrate?" he said, abruptly. "That Wimbarton who raped and held her once? She could not . . . ?" Sir Arthur shook his head. "No. Well, thank God for that, in any way. But sir—where is she? Why know you not where she might be?"

Sam had an edge of anger in his voice. "Did she *insist* on going? Was she so sure then that she would find him? I fear, sir . . ." His voice trailed off. The thought hung in the air. "Aye," he finished. "I fear."

Sir Arthur, slowly and with not much trace of dignity, stood. He faced them, and his face was misery. He reached out for a bell.

"I fear I have done wrong," he said. He jerked the bell-pull. "If I have done so, I did all for the best, believe me. She left here of her own free will; she left with some good sum in money; she seemed . . . bold and confident. Boys, you must forgive me. I must rest; I must lie down a while. Pray prepare yourselves for dinner, then afterwards we'll—"

The door opened without a knock, and Mrs Houghton came in. She read the case instantly, and tutted with concern, hurrying to Sir A and laying her hand upon his shoulder.

"Now, sir!" she said. "Oh, you look terrible! Now come along with me and take some rest. Boys! Why have you let him get like this? For shame, sirs, shame on you."

Sir Arthur shook his head, touching her hand.

"Nay, Mrs Houghton, the blame is all on me. We were talking of the pretty maid, and William—"

"Ho!" she said, impatiently. "Why Master Will, surely you do not still . . . ? Now look, sirs, can't you see the bad effect? Poor Sir A is in a pother about the lass. We knew not what should be done. She said herself she must move on. She had a plan, I think, to . . . she had a plan. Sir A was very, very kind to her."

"She needed help and kindness," said Sir A. "Nay, she deserved it. But I—"

"Tush for shame!" snapped Mrs Houghton. "Come, sir, you must to bed awhile. Sirs, forgive me, but dinner . . . I am not certain sure Sir Arthur should attend."

"Oh, Mrs Houghton!"

But Sam, quick thinking, already had it in control. With smiles and words he told the baronet that they must go to Deptford anyway; they were required on the *Biter,* no excuses for delay. In a day or two they would be sailing and—as full lieutenants—they had to do their duty. All four of them felt great relief.

THIRTEEN

On board ship, Captain Kaye had told Rex Shilling solemnly, there was only one true demon; it lived in a bottle, which must stay tightly corked. An easy proposition, Shilling had thought, given locks and keys and armaments, a few marines and good strong honest warrant men. Drunkenness, as Kaye's gig disappeared towards the distant city, seemed the least of his concerns, and he found Taylor's worry on the subject but mildly irritating, and distasteful. Savary tried tentatively to back the boatswain up, but Shilling was scathing, and the mild-faced boy was too ready to be scathed.

"What are you thinking, Mister Boatswain?" asked Rex Shilling. "That they can conjure liquor from thin air? I have the keys to everything, and they remain with me."

Savary coughed, politely. "Sir," he said. "Mr Shilling. My experience in tented camps, indeed in some fine barracks, has been that men can . . . well, they cajole, and they threaten . . . sometimes force."

The midshipman was contemptuous. "The army. Well. Mr Savary, if you should see an attempt—any attempt, be it never so small—on my person or on any drink supply, then you must order fatal shooting. And there's an end to it."

There was not an end, though. Nor, indeed, was there any such attempt, not visibly. As Taylor and his mates knew, men could spirit drink from any void, or none. Wines, or ales, or brandy—anything to make tars crazy.

"That bastard's mad," said Taylor, to the giants Hugg and Tilley. "As mad as Kaye for going off and leaving us. As mad as giving us the Scotchmen for our help. Eyes skinned, friends, and handspikes at the ready. First sign of drunkenness, break heads. It will be the only way."

"So far as I can see," said Tommy Hugg, "them haggis-shaggers are half-flanged already. They came out of Dickie's den last night reeking of distilleries, and I doubt they'd finished. They look the men to drink three days away and yet stand upright. I'll take the opportunity to kill the lot, if they cross me."

"We'll do a sweep below," said Tilley. "We know the places, don't us, boys? By God, it's not so long ago we used 'em all ourselves!"

"And I'll speak to the haggis-shaggers, as you dub 'em, Tommy," the boatswain said. "On our side, thanks to Dick, God spare the mark. By Holy Mary, such allies have I never had before!"

The watch they kept was steady, the watch they kept was firm. Under Taylor's instruction—which Shilling acknowledged as the only stratagem—the people were put to shipboard tasks that kept them jumping, which tore their muscles to the last. Spare yards were shifted, checked for rot, re-tarred; cables great and small were overhauled; bolts of flax and canvas broken out, opened out, refolded; everything that was heavy and unwieldable moved around, and jiggled, and restowed. Throughout the daylight hours there was no discernible movement to fray the normal discipline, although the men kept grumbling as they were ground into the work. The

Scotsmen, who were nominally part of the afterguard on this occasion, were conspicuous more by absence than by overlooking sweaty
toilers—but gave no trouble either, as Taylor reported it to Groat.

"However, sir," he said. "I have a fear that they are getting drink.
Not the Scotch alone, although I guess that they are behind it, but
all hands. I see that—"

Shilling interrupted him.

"If you think it is their fault, you must pull them up on it," he
said. "You are the boatswain. You have the measure of the ship and
people. If they are getting drink, then stop them."

Taylor, a mild man, hard to rouse, considered a sharp answer,
then abandoned it.

"Sir," he said. "The Scotchmen show no signs of liquor, and I
have seen nothing definite. I would say, though, that the generality
are looking . . . there is a slacking off; you know the signs, sir—"
He stopped. It occurred to him that this midshipman did not. But a
boatswain could not suggest that of an officer, nor yet a snotty boy.
"You know the aspect. It is growing fast apace. The people are the
worse for wear, sir. The bare end needs a whipping."

"Is that a metaphor?" said Shilling, icily. "Would you use irony
to me, sir? I would exhort you to recall your place. Insolence is a
vice I will not tolerate."

Jem Taylor, although not unwise, was by no means an educated
man. He had never heard such words before, leastways not used in
anger, and had no idea, even, if he should feel insulted. His low opinion of such bugs as Rex, however, was slipping ever lower. He almost
felt a satisfaction at the ruckus he was pretty sure would come.

"Aye aye," he said. "Beg pardon, sir, if I have caused offence."

Lieutenant Savary approached them at this point. He was excited.

"Sir!" he said. "Mr Shilling, an' it please you! A soldier has been
hit. One of my men, Simms. A broken bottle! It got him in the face!
They are milling by that armoured store, sir, underneath the poop!
I fear they wish to get the swords and guns!"

"Good God, the roundhouse!" Shilling's face was wild. "Has he
got his musket? Can he not shoot?"

Savary stared at him. "He was hit, sir! His face is bleeding. He was alone!"

Taylor said decisively: "They must not get in there, sir! The small arms and cutlasses." He bellowed, suddenly: "Hugg! Tilley! Scotchmen, to me! On the double! Roundhouse!"

"Aye aye!" said Tilley. Appeared from nowhere, he went roaring along the waist, six feet of handspike like a feather in his fist. "Hugg's going through the 'tween!"

"Prime your piece!" Shilling snapped at the soldier-officer. "If they touch that storeroom, we must kill them!"

The deck, although fairly thronged with sailors, was peaceful still. No whoops, no shouts, no rushes. Then out of a thick group of them Jack Ashdown pushed his way. He went straight to Taylor, but addressed his news to Shilling, out of deference.

"No use shouting for the Scotchmen, sir," he said, "they—"

"Who are you?" said Shilling, rudely.

"Why not, sailor?" Taylor asked. "Beg pardon, sir."

"They're in the cabin," Ashdown said. "They are not after weapons, they want—"

"Good God!" said Shilling. "The captain's cabin? What mean you, man? Why?"

"Black Bob," said Taylor, flatly. Half a statement, but a question too. Ashdown nodded.

"They plan to make an arse of him," he said. "Them first, and then a general arse. They had him cornered by the manger, but he shot away. They are in drink, sir. The company is in drink."

To the boatswain and the Irish seaman, this was merely information, day-to-day, and coolly given. But Shilling was in stays entirely, while poor Savary had turned pale, then—furiously—began to blush.

"An arse?" he faltered. "But . . ."

"Buggery," said Taylor, brutally. "May be you do not have it in the army." It was no time for jesting really, he thought, but what the hell? They went to sea with babies, and the babies had command.

"Good God," said Savary, but his voice was cut off by a shrill and piercing scream. It came from aft, and was too high to be a grown man, and was followed by terrific shouts and roars too low to be from boys. Suddenly the men packed in the well were also on the move, surging towards the poop-break, and a rising, throbbing noise came from their throats.

"Sir!" said Taylor, urgently. "We must act!"

Shilling, to give him due, was already galvanised.

"Shoot the leader!" he roared at Savary, and his high voice cut through the fug of liquor and excitement like a knife. He snatched the cutlass that he'd worn all day with ostentation and almost sprinted across the deck to reach the drunken men.

"But my man is hurt!" said Savary, forlornly, and Taylor shouted: "If he can see, sir, he can shoot." He raised his voice a notch. "Bloodshed, you bastards! I'll break your heads, the lot of you, and string you from the mainyard! Do you want to die, you goats!"

"Can I use a weapon, sir?" asked Ashdown, and Taylor tore a belaying pin from off the nearest rail for him.

"They'll try to kill you, man," he said, but Ashdown only smiled and went his way. Savary, stock-still and white as cream, was gasping with the effort to grip his courage. He snatched a long dirk out, had an army cutlass in his other hand, and rushed towards the poop.

At this instant, amid a general screaming uproar, the tiny form of the African burst from the captain's doorway and went across the broad deck like a hare. The drunken crewmen split apart in some confusion, although some did try to seize him as he ran. Then the Lamonts came out, one by one, their faces awful in their concentration.

"Stop!" shouted Savary. "Stop before I cut you down!"

It was cruelly comical the way that they ignored him, even when he waved a cutlass in the face of one. They hardly glanced, they hardly broke their step, they swept on across the crowded well-deck and the people cleared a path. As they clattered down a hatchway, Tilley, who had run along between decks to head them off, appeared from out of the dimness, handspike already swinging for a blow across the leader's face or chest—and was overwhelmed. The two bigger of the brothers took a flank apiece, then moved out sharply while pushing back his arms by the power of their onrush. And the youngest

Scotchman, like a coiled wire come unsprung, went between them into him, full in his face, full in his stomach, and Tilley went down backwards like a slaughtered ox.

They might have fallen on him then, and wrought some fearful damage, but Tom Tilley struck his head as he went down, and lay unconscious, like a dunnage sack. Other drunken sailors eyed the fallen giant, and maybe wondered at their chances, but the Lamonts, it seemed, were determined not to lose the small black tail that so enraptured them. Within a dozen paces they had gripped him, and his renewed screams split the darkness as shrilly as a rabbit's in a fox's teeth.

Taylor had gone aft with Savary in his wake, but Ashdown, belaying pin in hand, braved the drunken rioters between decks. It was darker by now, almost full night, and down below few glims had yet been lighted. But Ashdown, following the screams, soon came on the brothers and their prey, although he could not see the details of their infamy. He allowed himself no time to think, or fear the odds, but threw himself into the seething blackness, and lashed about him with the iron pin.

With other men he might have triumphed, but with the wild Lamonts, Ashdown—as he had fully been aware—had no chance. His intention was to clear a space for Bob to vanish in, and it appeared he was prepared to lose his life for it. His first blows landed hard, and the Scotchmen—bleeding—shrugged them off. Before he had withdrawn and struck three times they were on him. The belaying pin, his only hope, was in Wee Doddie's hand, was jammed into Jack Ashdown's stomach, reversed, and smashed across his arm. The blow had been directed at Ashdown's elbow, and would have crippled him forever, but Dod's palm, luckily, was full of his own blood, and the two-foot iron flew from his grip and disappeared after a glancing hit.

Then it was fists and feet, gouging fingers, tearing attacks on vital organs, butting foreheads, teeth, and knees. Ashdown, a man of no great stature, but formed of steel apparently, fought them like two tigers, fought and held them long after it was possible for a normal human being. His dedication, coupled with their hatred, swayed them from their first purpose also; they were consumed in their determination that they would finish him for good. Had Tom Tilley regained his consciousness half a minute later they surely would have killed the Irishman, but as the boatswain's mate came to and lumbered into sight, the Scots relinquished this secondary objective, and renewed the hunt for Bob. Ashdown, breathing blood, was left for other men to save (or finish off), and they had disappeared when Tilley came upon him. Tilley—even Tilley—was horrified by the wreck of man before him, and terrorized some of the drunkards in an instant to pick him up and take him to the surgeon's cockpit. He wanted desperately to track the brothers down, but knew the people would not save Jack Ashdown unless ordered to like children. In any way, he needed reinforcements. Black Bob was screaming, he could still hear him. Black Bob was screaming, so was still alive, and could be found. To judge by noises from on deck, from noises aft, the riot was getting worse.

Sam and Will Bentley, once Sir A and Mrs Houghton had left them on their own, tracked down the steward Tony, told him of the change of plan, and in fifteen minutes were dressed and mounted for the weary ride. Will, although his head was void of clear ideas, was desperate to be started. Sam was not so eager.

"My arse aches," he announced, from the saddle he had sat upon for only thirty seconds. "And we ha'n't even jogged a jot. Tony, this horsemanship's unnatural."

Tony's frank face, turned up at him, was troubled.

"Mr Sam," he said. "There is something that you have to know. And Mr Bentley."

"Deborah," said Will. His voice was flat. His heart was full of fear.

"She is safe, sir," said Tony, although his voice was grave. "I am confident. She went off from here some weeks ago, and she was, well, full of vim. The master, see, and Mistress Houghton—Well, maybe they got the wrong idea."

Will's horse began to stamp. It was a fresh one. Tony would send the others back to London in a train. They were inexpensive hacks, not quality like Sir A's.

"Go on," said Will. "What wrong idea?"

Tony heaved a breath. Divided loyalties.

"He'd heard intelligence," he said. "Well, rumour, maybe. Talk of shooting at that place I took Deb to, that gay house, Dr Marigold's. Talk of brawling. Talk of murder. Mistress Houghton, sir, was . . . full of horror, so to say."

"But I was part of that," said Will. "I did the shooting. If it was murder, Tony, then I'm the murderer, not poor Deb. What was the wrong idea? Was I not mentioned? Did I get away scot-free?"

The steward held his silence. One shoulder moved a fraction, almost a shrug. Sam said: "Don't treat Sir A too harsh, Will. Or Mrs Houghton. To them she must have seemed a liability. At best unsuitable, at worst a snare. A drag."

"Aye, that's it entire, sir," said Tony. "Might not be fair, but you're an officer, while she's . . . oh, sir, I liked her, sir, I like her, and, sir— I think she is all right! Sir Arthur thought she was a danger to you, that he had to rid you of somehow, even *any* how so long it was no harm, she must have nothing more to do with you, d'you see? He gave her money, sir, much money, and I, sir . . . well . . . I think she is all right."

The horse, impatient, moved about erratically, did dancing steps. Will tried to still it, but used the time to catch his thoughts. Then Tony blurted, "Sir, I should not lie to you. She went off with an officer, a high-up in the Customs House. He had fancied her before, sir. He had mentioned it. To me. And I . . . I . . . ."

"You played the pander, did you?" Holt said, harshly. "'Fore God, Tony! This man is in love!"

"Aye, sir," said Tony, bravely. "I hoped, indeed, that he would understand. You are sailing, sirs, for the Americas, as I have heard it, soon, and the maid, sirs, is then beyond all reach. She could have gone to London, sirs, and settled in the gutter. She could have become another Spithead Nymph. She'd spoke of it to the maidens, not just once. Ask Eliza. She had already almost trod that route before. This man had a carriage, sirs. And a wife."

Bentley had been about to speak. This stopped his mouth. The horse, snubbed on the bit, fiercely shook its head.

"Oh, good!" Sam's laugh was genuine. "So she'll live in comfort, will she, but not be put at risk of being took to wife herself and so lose her chance with William? Ho, Will, that's capital! Tony is looking for a very noble tip!"

Tony, not at all nonplussed, took Will's horse's bridle and nuzzled at its ear. His eyes sought Will's. He smiled.

"It seemed the safest way, sir," he said. "It is Sir Peter Maybold. A fat man whose main problem is his wife. He loves her, sir, and she despises him. He comes to see the master here, but is discreet. Sir A will never know of the involvement, or that the maid went off with him. And I, sir; well, I cannot keep an eye on her, exactly, but I will hear intelligence. Thus might be in position, sir, to catch her if she falls."

Not long after this they took their leave. They conferred often on the way, wondering where they should go to find out Deb, or what to do, but knew in both their hearts the thing was useless. They knew Sir Peter Maybold's name, as surveyor general of the riding officers, but knew not where he lived, or what to do if they had had that information. The more they rode, the more Holt felt that Tony's solution had been the best one to be hoped for. Except he dared not say so to his friend.

But Will could see it too, and worked at it, through the hours. By the time they put their horses into livery at the Bear's Paw, in Southwark, where Sir Arthur's men could swap them for the hacks, he felt that he had come to terms with it, could face the information squarely.

"She is not dead, nor is she like to be," he said to Sam, as they waited for a wherry that would take them to the *Biter*. "She will be safe; she will not starve."

"Aye," said Sam. He quoted from a sailors' song: "*And she will be safe, and be loyal and constant.* Well, not that exactly! Oh God, there goes my tact again. She will be constant, in her lights, Will. I'm sure she will be constant. In her way."

A wherry nosed into the jetty, and they settled in the sternsheets for the long pull back to Deptford. As they left the lights of London town, Will felt a grinding loss. Next day or the day after, they were due to drop down the murky Thames and set course for the far West Indies. Three months, six months, a year or more? Would Deb still be alive when he came back again? Or if, indeed. Or if.

The thought chilled him, but he knew the Indies and their reputation. More men died there out of illness than ever fell to war. He realised that Sam was singing. Quiet, absentminded, his voice surprising sweet.

> *And you must be safe, and be loyal and constant—*
> *For I shall return, in the spring as you know.*

The black, sleek water carried them along.

FOURTEEN

When Tilley reached the deck in search of help to save Black Bob, he found the fabric of the *Biter* truly on the rend. The blackness of the evening was near complete by now, with only flares from furnaces on shore flashing through the dark from time to time. The men, safe in obscurity, had let the drink course freely through their veins, and the excitement of the yells and whoops above, mingled with the smell of blood and fear from Ashdown's torture down below, had knocked them rapidly beyond control by normal discipline. As Tilley spoke of Bob to Boatswain Taylor, the first concerted move along the pitch-dark deck began. Its target was the ship's boats at the boom, and had it succeeded, *Biter* would have lost her people, certainly.

Tom Hugg saw it first, and yelled to Taylor, who bellowed what amounted to an order to the pale child-officer of marines.

"The boom! The boom, sir! Captain Kaye will kill you this time! Man the boom!"

Savary, whose courage had come back under duress—and the weight of a shiny cutlass in his hand, perhaps—scurried for the ship's side as if completely fearless. There were men in tumult clambering on the bulwarks, and he swung his army sword and caught one of them a smacking blow across his shirted back. The man, more shocked than frightened, swung round, then swore in anger as if to jump down on the officer and tear him limb from limb. But other men climbed over him to his place, using him as a ladder and a handhold. Then Groat appeared, also sword in hand, and shouted, "Soldiers! Soldiers! Shoot the first man that sets his foot on there!"

The marines, including Simms, who'd had a bottle in his face but was recovered, were mindful of the last disaster and the dressing down they'd got from Captain Kaye. All three had their muskets ready now, with long bayonets glittering in two of them, and they moved up smartly with the blank looks of men quite prepared to use them. The sailors, whose hatred of the redcoats sprang from the soldiers' perceived indifference to the brotherhood of degradation shared, remained defiant and noisy and obscene, but made no more moves to cross the rubicon and catch a hot lead ball. In a sudden mass, they jumped down to the well and lashed out at each other, not the soldiery. For some of them, at least, the mood had changed to liquor-fired joy and jollity, as in a good-time shoreside fight. Fists flew, and blood began to flow.

Not all the men were mollified by this free-for-all, though. Some, maybe drunker than the rest, maybe more disaffected by Navy life or the sight of the riverside at tantalising distance, retained their steel-bright fury. From down below the screams and shouts of hunters and prey were overlaid by the thundering and clamouring of the Gunning men and others held in irons, some fearful of what might be happening, others insanely jealous of the feast of havoc that they were prevented from enjoying. And others yet, blinded to all reason, were moving inexorably on the roundhouse and its enticing stock of weaponry. Rex Shilling and the soldier Simms spotted this danger, and they were within a breath of being just too late. A crowd had gathered with a long bar and a jemmy, and enough drunk, heaving bodies to obscure their intent—which was to get beneath the new poop deck and force entry into the armoured house, also newly built, that was approachable from every side. It had one door only, though, of course—and Shilling got there first, while Simms slashed furiously with his unsheathed bayonet to keep back the interlopers and to protect the young gentleman.

At the last instant, out of nowhere, Grundy the surgeon appeared, clutching his box of medicines like a favourite dolly, and begged entry, too, his white face streaked with tears. As if bemused, the seamen cleared a path for him while Shilling, not bemused, seized his skinny arm and jerked him in and slammed the roundhouse door and pulled a bolt across. Outside, the cheated seamen awoke in fury and made a concerted rush, kicking at the stout woodwork, beating at it with anything to hand. Shortly, the long iron clawbar and the jemmy came into play, and the dark compartment—no light lit yet— shook and vibrated to the determined onslaught.

Tilley and Taylor, alerted by the purposeful din, ran through the fighting men on deck with Tommy Hugg, while Savary and his two other soldiers made to cover them. As they arrived, though, Simms thrust out his musket from a defensive port, took swift aim, and without an uttered warning, pulled the trigger. Taylor saw the gush of smoke and flame envelope a pig-tailed head at point-blank range, and saw the man go down before it. The jemmy bar went one way, the crowbar was tossed another, and the howling, roaring mob, as the smoke and stink dispersed, fell almost silent. In the midst of them, the shot man clambered half upright, clutching his smoke-blacked face most comically. There was blood pouring from his scalp, his hair was parted, and his mouth was one large gape. Outside on the open deck, Hugg shouted triumphantly, "Now move, you bastards! Move! Oh Christ, I'm going to break some heads, boys! Move!"

Men milled about still, men rushed here and yon wild-eyed, but the desperate mood was broken. Lieutenant Savary seemed to puff with pride, delighted with Simms's brainpan-dividing shot, while Hugg and Tilley quickly gathered up some trusty men—new-trusty, now they saw which way the wind was blowing—and moved like tornadoes into the fray. Taylor, his mind more full of Black Bob now than easy triumphs, approached the soft-faced army man, circumspectly and polite.

"Sir," he said. "I need my mates here to go below and rescue the little nigger boy, if he still lives. Might I ask that you instruct your stalwarts to keep order here when we have dinned it in these beasts? It will be hot work down below, and we need safety up above, if it should please you, sir."

Savary, who might have taken offence, was startled at the thought of poor Black Bob.

"My God," he said. "The nigger boy. We must come too. We've muskets, bayonets, swords. And you have . . ."

Taylor laughed.

"Handspikes, belaying pins, a fid or so. It will be less easy than this mill-match here, but a sight more fun, I'll wager. We'll clap some in irons, maybe cripple one or two. Most are much too drunk to fight like real men now. And we have some real hard cases here, I promise you. Just make sure this lot stay subdued and do not run the round-house door again, or try to steal a boat from off the boom."

The officer stood still a minute, pondering. Taylor, from his knowledge of the breed, knew that he might well be overruled. He could swallow that, he would do if he had to. But the black boy's chance of life was very small.

And then Bob screamed. Through solid oak, and several decks, through bulkheads, God knew what. The thin scream wavered, sharper than a surgeon's knife. Bob, in the dark below, his long, desperate game of cat and mouse with the Scots brothers lost at last, had felt a hand lock on his ankle in a tight hole in the forepeak. And begin to pull.

Savary heard it, and turned pale.

"Go quick," he said. "Go quick."

Tony, although he did not spell it out, had moved a mountain to try and save Deb's life. It had fallen upon him to shift her out of Langham Lodge, and he had taken it upon himself to do it with humanity. He had worked for Sir Arthur since a child, and within the normal lights of master-servant would have said, if pressed, he loved—at least, revered—him. Sir A, over this maid, was in an awful, searing bind, and Mrs Houghton, for once, had hardened her heart, lost for alternative. Tony knew his task was to get rid, to remove a present danger. Tales of murder, prostitution, Shitty Corner ale-dives, accosting smugglers on lonely beaches, were all too close for comfort. Neither Bentley's father nor Sir A would escape with unscathed reputation, Tony knew, if push should turn to shove.

He had approached her when she'd been at the house a week, and he had made his inquiries and his preparations. Deborah was not a fool in any way—her intelligence was like a beacon in her eyes—and he knew within a minute that she'd been expecting something dire, drastic, from him. He had passed a message down from Mrs Houghton through the girls about this meeting, but so subtly that they had no suspicion what his true reasons were. They, romantic creatures, guessed that it was about her "lovely Navy boy," whom they said for certain loved her still, was well, and would be back some day, most likely soon. Deb, whose mind had grown out of all proportion to her age since gaily leaving home with Cecily, was convinced that she knew better, despite she sometimes screamed with inward pain for facing it. Sir A and Mrs Houghton, so kind to her the year before, had made it plain her presence was a trouble to them, but a trouble they could neither admit to nor explain. They did not know where Sam was, they said; they had no inkling about Will Bentley. True or false, the upshot was the same: she was a refugee, but Langham Lodge could not be her place of refuge.

Tony, once they had cleared the air, was visibly relieved at her grasp of the realities. She had come in hope, they both knew, and the hopes had failed. Sir A had moved her up to London one time previously to protect her, but it had ended in disaster, and she was now, to all intents, liable to tracking down as accessory to a killing. At Langham she was also in a current, constant danger from Sir Arthur's neighbor, Chester Wimbarton, and his predatory cohorts, who would hear, inevitably, of her presence there. Servant maids and men, even those who said they were her friends, were incorrigible gossips. "You must go, maid," said Tony gently. "You cannot stay. Sir Arthur is frail and ill now. Despite her sympathy, Mistress Houghton, I can promise you, will turn against you soon."

They were sitting in his quarters, which were small but neatly

furnished, very comfortable. Deb had a flash of longing for an apart-
ment such as this, an ordered life, a person she could depend upon.
To her amusement, if not her shame, she wondered for a moment if
she should offer something for the privilege to this stable, kindly
man. He was old but not decrepit, forty-fiftyish, and strong and spry
and healthy. She gave a little laugh. It trickled out, and when he
asked her why, she told him. Tony, unembarrassed, unexcited, only
smiled.

"I'm glad you have not lost your humour, maid," he said. "These
days I do but little in that line, and what I do is not worth sharing."
He stopped, and twinkled at her until his answer had sunk in. Then
both gave out a belly laugh—which ended, for Deb Tomelty, in a sigh.

"Ah, Mr Tony," she said, wistfully. "What can I do? It is the only
asset that I have, but truly you are too kind a man to waste your
time on that with me. I mean . . ."

She laughed again. Strangely, he knew just what she meant, even
if Deb was not so sure herself.

"You love your sailor boy," he said. "I know that, maid; I believe
that. If you have to use your person for a bargain, you must do better far than me. The pity of it is Sir A is not himself inclined. He is
a widower of the most truest kind. He mourns his wife."

He noticed her slight shiver, and he gave a tut. The face Deb
made was rueful in return.

"Too like my father," she said. "Well, older and more richer, but
you know the way I mean. If he offered, even, I would have to run.
For a man like that, I could bring only misery."

"You are in love," said Tony. Again Deb did not reply. She made
another face, though. It spoke of pain, but Tony, who had been pondering for days, assessed the time, sadly, as ripe as it would ever be.

"There is another way," he said. "At least, I think there is. It is a
sort of whoring; you might deem it so, but it would save your young
man from destruction, which is what Sir Arthur fears, and it would
not be like a death with Wimbarton or genteel filth as Dr Marigold
purveys. You love your sailor boy, but you will not destroy yourself,
I know. Will you consider anything within these lights?"

Her clear brown eyes were frank and calm.

"I am a lost girl, Mr Tony," she replied. "I have got to live, and what has love to do with that? My body is my own, whoever lies beside it. Even after Wimbarton I knew I was myself. Like a death, perhaps, but I was still alive."

The steward's face was sombre; he did not try to smile.

"I know a man who wants you, maid," he said, "and I would ask you to consider him. He is a rich man, quite a kindly man, who would not do you harm, I'm almost sure of it. It is a man who's noticed you before. Has made inquiries, in a discreet and quiet way. Do you allow it's worth considering?"

Deb, sitting on a leather-covered chair, looked young and lonely and forlorn. Which was, indeed, just how she felt. She wondered vaguely who this man might be, and her stomach hollowed slowly, by degrees. She did not know him. She did not want to, ever.

"I am lost," she said, almost inaudibly. "So what have I to do with it? And I have almost been a Spithead Nymph."

Tony, quite suddenly, was brisk.

"I know a man who wants," he said, "but even better, maid, I know a man who maybe won't be able. He'll try; I'd wager gold on that, but the chances he will get it up aren't worth a silver shilling! Nay, it is not a joke, I know, but there are good sides, even to pandering. When he first mooted it, he hinted that there might be money in the scheme as well, and I made a haughty face. But to be a harlot from necessity, as you must be, is honourable, and the cash could come to you! Five guineas as an introduction fee, reverse!"

His tries to make a jest of it were laudable, but only made Deb cry. She pulled the kerchief from between her breasts with unconscious grace, and dabbed her eyes and cheeks.

"He loves his wife," he said. "But is in desperate need of some affection. There are other safeguards, though, if you agree to let me move ahead. I am always here, and he knows it, and he knows Sir A has tried before to see you are protected. I do not think, girl, it will fall adrift."

She nodded. She tucked her kerchief back and covered up her breasts, again unconsciously.

"I do it for I have no other way," she said. She smiled, wet eyes glistening. "I do it for another, Mr Tony, although the chances are that he will never know. No, I will not say that; I'll be damned before I do! If I sleep beside a hundred men, I . . ." The thought was bleak. The kindly face in front of her might break her heart.

"I am prepared," she said.

It was two days hence from then, the final step, and Deborah was required to do little, except think and wait. After her interview with Tony, she was escorted back to the room she had been sharing with a girl, and told to collect her things together and to keep her movements very mum. The other maids guessed that something was up, but Deb was expert at dissembling, and they soon gave up the asks. She met with Mrs Houghton twice, alone in that dame's chambers, who spoke to her with kindness, very frank. It was a step up for the girl, she urged, and if she played her hand right she could be set up for life. A rich man's mistress was every young girl's dream, was her opinion. Deb held her peace.

The switch came in the evening, after Sir Peter Maybold and Sir A had had a supper *tête-à-tête*. Deb, forewarned, had dressed to travel clandestinely from the household maidens, and been hidden by Tony in his quarters. He had given her a pepper talk, some money in a purse, a small bundle of fine underlinen he had got from who knew where, and a glass travel-flask of brandy, just in case. At a certain time, arranged beforehand clearly with the Customs man, he escorted her outside into the gathered dusk and stood with her a good way down the drive to await the coach. Sir Peter's man was looking out for them, and pulled the rig to a standstill smartly behind a clump of trees. There was a dim light in the coach, and as Deb was propelled forward by Tony's gentle hand, it illuminated Maybold's face. Eager, concerned, congested, red. He was smiling, very nervously, and on his bulbous purple lips there was a dew. Deb breathed in and held her breath, and felt the chasm yawn within her.

"Ha," said Sir Peter Maybold, awkwardly. "By George, you are a pretty one indeed! You are beautiful."

She looked at him. She stared.

And you, thought Deborah Tomelty, are most exceeding fat.

FIFTEEN

As Holt and Bentley dropped down on the *Biter* in a wherry, there was an air about her that had both of them, on the sudden, keen and tense. There was no noise that they could hear unusual, there were no people visible, but something was wrong. It was a pitch black night right down the river, and the furnaces and kilns along the Deptford shore were belching flame and filth like hell a half a mile removed. Then they saw lanterns moving on the deck.

"There's lights!" said Will. "What o'clock is it? What's going on?"

The watermen glanced across their shoulders, indifferent. They were working; why should there not be lights? But Holt felt inside his pocket for his dirk.

"Know not," he said. "It's too late for—What's that? What are those cries?"

The boatmen, interested, rested their oars, till Bentley barked at them.

"Swing round! Put us head to head! Don't lie to the boom until we've—"

"Ahoy! Boat there! Is that you, Mr Bentley, sir?"

"Jem Taylor," Sam hissed. "Well it's not a mutiny, thank fortune! But where is Kaye? Hey, Jem!" he yelled. "Boatswain, ahoy!"

"'Long there," Bentley told the boatmen, feeling for some coin. He stood and gripped the pendant off the boom, as Sam, much taller, swung his body up. "There, catch, I haven't got all night!"

The money fell, the rowers scrambled, and Will and Sam balanced along the boom in a frantic hurry. At the gangway they met Taylor, with blood all down one cheek, and Savary, who was almost squeaking with excitement and had his sword in hand. By the forward hatch stood two of his soldiers, their muskets in a guard position. By them lay two men.

"Good God!" said Bentley. "Taylor, what is this? Where is the captain? Who are those bodies? Have you been attacked?"

"The captain's gone!" said Savary, his voice extremely high and light. "This afternoon. He had to go to London, urgent. He said he would be back betimes, but so far he isn't. I thought your boat—"

"Jem!" Holt cut in rudely. There was a sudden racket from up forward, and below. "Is she in command or are there factions? Christ, I do not have a gun! Who has the roundhouse?"

"Secure," said the boatswain. He wiped blood away so that he could grin unhindered. "Groat's in there, locked. Midshipman Shilling, sir, I beg your pardon."

"What mean you, locked?" demanded Will. "Is he a prisoner?"

The young marine lieutenant was wild to have his say. He stayed Jem Taylor with an upraised hand. "One of my men is with him! They were—They were forced to make a stand. My man fired, but the devils still came on. 'Twas done to save the armaments!"

"And is there fighting still?" demanded Sam. "What is that noise from forward, Jem? Where are your mates?"

The noise became more violent, roars and crashes, maybe blows. But no shots, no sounds of steel. And Taylor was still grinning.

"It's mainly drink now, sir," he said. "As usual. We've got them all in irons; we've broke a head or two. But no real trouble now. We got the Scotchmen all locked up. That was the start and end of it."

Bentley and Sam exchanged a look. The Scots. Inevitable. But how, or why, had Richard Kaye thought that he could go ashore?

"The Scotchmen," Will said. "So drink's their demon, is it? Who killed those men? The Scotchmen, I suppose?"

One of the corpses, in fact, at this point started moving. Even along the deck-length they could see that it was Josh Baines—ship's rat as he was known without affection. He hauled his torso upright, then collapsed. The soldiers looked aft enquiringly, to see if their lieutenant had an order for them.

"They're not dead, neither of them," said Taylor. "Alf Wilmott's worst. He picked a fight with the smallest Scotch, and—" He stopped, and the amused look faded rapidly. "There is one dead, sir," he said, stiffly. "I forgot. Well, maybe dead. Black Bob, sir. The little neger boy."

"But we don't know that," Savary said quickly. His light voice was a little sick. "Sirs," he went on, looking at their faces, "no one saw him going overboard, no one heard a scream or splash. My feeling is, my hope is that . . . well, I hope he's hid himself. He's very small and black."

That came out almost funny in its way, but no one was amused. Will remembered the cry of pain or anguish he'd heard from Bob last time he'd seen him with the Lamont brothers, and his concern grew.

"Was that the Scotch?" he said. "By God, they're going to end up hanged! But why was he not on shore with Captain Kaye? And who is in command, if he is gone to London? The midshipman? They're going to end up hanged, they must do!"

"The midshipman was given the command," said Savary. He was embarrassed, as if he thought he should have been, perhaps—an even more absurd appointment in the lieutenants' contemplation. "And also . . ."

He tailed off. Taylor spoke, after an interval for politeness.

"The Scotch were mentioned, too," he said. There was an odd note in his voice. "He told me I could trust them. Use them as warrant men. But it was them got liquor to the people, certain of it. By the time we were aware, it was too late. Explosion, sir."

"Good God alive," said Holt, soberly. "He wants to warrant them. Good God alive."

"How did it end, then?" Bentley said. "This explosion. Not by the Lamonts's hands, surely?"

Taylor did not laugh, although he sensed the irony. He mopped blood, calm and frank. "The soldiery," he said. "Mr Savary and his men. They held the boom and saved the boats. I must say they were sterling, sir. That I must."

The officer of marines—who blushed too readily, that was for sure—blushed once more. "Captain Kaye had made it crystal—" he started, and Taylor interrupted.

"They held their corner and when the madmen went to breach the roundhouse, one of them jumped in with Midshipman Shilling like a shot," he said. "And he'd already been cut in the face severely by a broken bottle. The surgeon got in, too, the dear knows why. He had his drug-chest in his arms. They barred the door."

"The dear indeed," said Sam. "And was he drunk?"

Savary said excitedly: "It was Robert Simms. The oldest of my men. He only loosed one shot off and it damn near split the leader's skull. The neatest groove you ever saw upon a head. The man was howling."

"Not killed, though?" asked Bentley.

"Not killed indeed! It was a splendid shot! I think the captain now may see us with new confidence as his protection force. You asked us how it ended, sir. I dare to say that Simms's shot was the single key. I dare to think that with some confidence."

Holt raised his eyebrows quizzically. "And your opinion, Taylor? Is that assessment right? And if it's ended, what of Black Bob, then?"

"It fell to pieces, I will say that," said Taylor. "A bit of blood's a goodly soberer. Sam Megson went to tears; it all came flooding on the very instant. You know Megson, sir? A corkhead, daft like all the breed. He was squalling like a newborn babe. We went in among them with spikes and clubs, and it was pretty easy, when all's said. A soldier held a gun on them while we went below to sort the worst ones out. And then the Scotch and poor Black Bob. We got some lamps and tracked him to the forepeak, sir. They'd been making play with him."

Bentley and Holt were silent for a while. The racket from below was dying down.

Taylor continued, "They'd catch him, and they'd use him, then they'd let him go again. It was a game of chase. When we got there he'd wormed into a space they could not enter—not for the first time neither, I don't guess. They were darting with their arms and bits of batten, they did not see us coming, they were . . . well, sirs, how to hide it? One of them had his britches round his feet. I could have drove my handspike up his hairy arse."

Savary, pride gone, looked sick as any dog at this. Sam tutted.

"Damn good job you di'nt, Jem," he said. "Might have lost a hand-spike otherwise." He laughed, without much pleasure, though. "What then? You rushed them, did you?"

The boatswain nodded. "Candy off a maid," he said. "Tom Tilley took the biggest 'un, Hugg seized the bugger with his britches down, I and two other lads grabbed Wee Dod. Wee! He damn near broke Dusty Miller's hand off. And they yelled blue murder into the

bargain. They were bloody banshees. Even when we'd got the shackles on they were yelling for the Pope."

"The Pope?" said Bentley. "Why the Pope?"

Taylor gave him a look.

"Expression, sir," he said. "Don't mean a thing. Angus was yelling
for the captain at one point, and I do mean that, though. He said
the captain would see us flogged. He might still be at it, if you want
to go and listen. Mind Dod, though. He can spit eleven fathom."

The scene along the deck by now was quiet. The two injured
sailors were sitting silently; the marines still held their guns, although
uneasy at the pointlessness involved. Light still flowed upwards from
the hatchway forward, but the noise was hidden by a gentle breeze
that played among the rigging and top hamper. Across the river, flare
and furnace blazed, but intermittently. It was an almost peaceful
scene.

"So what of Bob?" asked Sam. "Is he dead, or what? You did not
leave him jammed up in his hole, for sure."

"You thought he had gone overside, maybe," said Bentley. "You
thought he might be drowned."

"Aye," said Taylor. "Well so he might indeed, sir. We could not
get him out, no how, and when we'd finished with the mad Lamonts
we could not see him, neither. Hugg thought he'd seen him rushing
out from under, but if he did he must have gone right into the darkly
parts where some stragglers from the riot were assembled. We heard
a whoop or two, some screeches, but as this officer here—beg pardon,
sir, Loot'nt Savary—as he've said, no one heard a splash nor anything.
He may've . . . well, I don't know."

"He may've hid?" asked Bentley.

The boatswain nodded an affirmative. "He may've, sir. But we
looked and searched a bit, and we found nothing. We flushed a few
more drunken buggers out for locking up, but no Black Bob. I'm
sorry, sir, but I wouldn't be surprised . . ."

They stood there for a moment, thinking. Then Holt let out
breath.

"Right," he said. "Jem, check the fighting's over. Tell Tom and
Tommy not to kill no more, we're short of seamen anyway. Me and

Lieutenant Bentley will dig out Midshipman Rex and Sawbones and marine, while you, sir, should check out your two men and tell 'em to stand easy. Rat Baines and Wilmott won't offer no more grief, and when we've all drew breath we'll go and beard the Scotchmen in their den. With luck, we'll need to shoot the buggers then! I'll get some pistols from the roundhouse, just in case."

Rex Shilling, when they had persuaded him to open up the bolts, was still shaken and white around the gills. He had not wasted time, though, for the armoured house had been arrayed with loaded muskets and hand-pieces, with a brace of dirks and cutlasses for each man. The small space stank of sweat and farts though—the lieutenants guessed the soldier, naturally—and the surgeon, Mr Grundy, looked worse than useless if it came to fight because he was wall-eyed drunk. His open chest contained many bottles, which, although all small, were clearly potent. And this, thought Will, is the man who won't take wine. Perhaps the eructations were not so military, after all, in origin.

Shilling, though pale, was haughty still. No word of pleasure at his, and the ship's, delivery passed his lips, no word of thanks or even greeting. He said stiffly that the men had risen, in a state of drunkenness, but that by strategy and use of honest loyalists he had retained command. Will found this almost breathtaking, and Sam had a coughing fit. Later, he opined to his friend that Shilling would rise fast and far, far, far. He'd be an admiral, Sam wagered, by age seventeen! The midshipman also, on the instant, demanded that he be let to confront the Lamont brothers in their shackles and to teach them a lesson with a rattan cane. When Bentley vetoed this, then Sam for emphasis, Shilling took it badly, with a sulky muttering and a sour folding of his meagre mouth.

The Scotsmen, when they went to see them—without Shilling, who was told off to muster all the people not in chains and mark some discipline upon them—were neither worse nor better in their attitude and temper. They, too, were haughty, achieving this despite bruised eyes and smears of blood; they, too, were smouldering in their level gaze. Both Sam and Will asked questions, firstly civil then more and more impatient, but elicited not a single word. The brothers, not very large, not very strong, not brutish about the body in any way, gave off an aura of suppressed violence that was almost palpable. Smouldering maybe—but they sat easy in their chains and shackles.

"Well," said Samuel in disgust, at last. "We'll see how well your silence serves you when the captain has returned. I warn you, Scotchmen, there will be flogging done for this—and you will get the first and hardest."

Their faces showed neither smile nor sneer. The grey eyes continued calmly burning. It was weird, unsettling. Holt and Bentley, not at all at ease, got up without a mutual signal and went back to the cabin. Inside the sanctum there was a light on still, and they went to check for theft or damage. Will heard a noise, a scuffle and a moan, maybe, and they began a search. Under the captain's massive bed, naked and abused, they found Black Bob. He was bleeding from the body, and from mouth, and ears, and anus. Like the Scots, he could not be made to speak.

Later, after they had settled him on a pallet in the drunken surgeon's bay next to Jack Ashdown, they talked it through exhaustively, reaching no conclusions, then Bentley went to sleep and Sam took watch. Richard Kaye's first action, when he returned next morning, was to free the Scots from their captivity.

SIXTEEN

Sir Peter Maybold, though fat and quite unhappy, was a kindly man. When Sir Arthur Fisher's steward had approached with hints of Deb and her availability, he had blushed bright scarlet and denied any interest beyond the fatherly. Sir A had told him, he told Tony, that she was a runaway, whose life ahead seemed blighted by her circumstance. Tony, with his usual wisdom, had played on this, seeding ideas about a sponsorship, protection, the role of quiet benefactor. The Customs man—quite desperate, in fact, for kindness from a female—had let his needs and longings do the rest. By the time he had her in his carriage, looking frightened and alone, he felt himself a Titan and a friend.

Fear, in fact, was an emotion Deb did not feel. She arranged herself beside him in the carriage, where he patted the cushions with his hand, and tried hard indeed not to drown in mournfulness. Tony's farewell had wrenched her in its kindness, and the sight of Langham Lodge's gatehouse, unlighted but secure, gave her the sense that another chapter of her life was done, a chapter which was fairly safe and comfortable. Will Bentley would come back one day soon, she guessed—but would most likely not be told that she had been and gone. She was leaving for his sake, they would say; she accepted he was not for her nor ever could be. The trouble was—though in her head she quite believed it—her heart did not, at all. To them a noble sacrifice. To her, a twisting knife.

"My dear," said Peter Maybold. "I welcome you into my purlieu. I wish to tell you, from the earliest, that you have naught to fear from me. For the present, you need not even speak or smile unless you wish to. But if you do—then do, and more than welcome!"

Ah Christ, thought Deb, I do this for your sake, Will Bentley. I sleep with this lard giant for your sake, and will you thank me for it, or forgive? Ah Will, I wish I'd never met you, friend.

"Where will you, sir?" she said, faltering. "Where do you take me, please? I am not feared, but . . ."

He harrumphed. The coach rocked on its springs in sympathy. Or, more probably, thought Deb, they'd hit a rut.

"Ah," he said. "A forward-thinking maid, I see. Master Steward said you had a brain between your ears. Well, my dear, I take you to a village that I know. Heard you of Chiswick, ever? On the London River, out of London a good way?" He stopped, discomfited. "Hhm. Well, not there; I do not take you there."

She glanced at him, but made no comment. Chiswick then, she supposed, but she was not meant to know it. Who would I tell, she thought? And why . . . ?

"It is no moment that I know the name, sir," she said, quietly. "I meant, to a house, a stable, whatsoever? You are not married, I suppose?"

"No, no!" said Maybold. "No, indeed I—yes, I am." There was a pause. He stared at his knees, then turned to her and caught her eyes. "Maid," he said, "I have a wife, she is . . . she is very fair and young. I fear . . . I fear she does not understand me fully."

Deb had heard of this from whores at Dr Marigold's. Wimbarton, though, had never talked to her when she'd been his, and did not give a fig if he was understood or not. Fair and young, she pondered. She could see the woman's point. What was to understand? she wondered.

"I do not have a great experience, sir," she said. "Of men. But I am willing to talk, and listen. I can listen very well if so required of me. Will I have a proper room?"

He nodded. He was a little easier, she could tell. She would have a room, he said, in a small house on an estate owned by a friend of his. There would be another woman there, an older one. She was a housekeeper.

"I will visit," he said, wistfully. "When I can. It should be . . ." He became yet more wistful. "It should be not infrequent. If you wish it so."

They hit another patch of rocky road, and while the swaying banged them promiscuously together, it enabled both to hide in silence. Deb felt sorry for this fat old man and wondered what that meant. She sneaked sly glances at him, sideways, to see if she found him hideous. He was and was not, all at once: a pleasant smell, clean clothes, not smeared with food like some of his age, his wig not perched on sideways but snug, smart, unridiculous. His breath smelled sweet from lozenges (but that could change), and he had not tried to press upon her, in any wise or guise. Could it be bearable, she thought? Better than death, in any case.

The trip was several hours, and she dozed (by pretending to, at first), and so did he. She woke one time to find him snoring, noting the long glaucous dribble from his slack mouth onto his neck with fresh despair. By the time they came off of the road and up a side track from a chip-stone drive, she was tense, and nervy, and dying to relieve herself. She thought that if she had to sleep with him this night, then she might rather die. He awoke, and did not recognise her, and was overcome with panic. Deb patted him, and genuinely smiled.

The house was small, and by Deb's standards, rather wonderful. It was a cottage, near but not too near three others, built for a woodsman on the estate and now lived in by his widow, Mrs Collins, who helped out at the big house kitchens, so she said. She was a pleasant body, quiet and comfortable, who found Deb's accession no surprise, it seemed, although she later told her that she'd never heard of such a thing before. She lived on the bottom floor, "because my leg ent right," and the rest—a sitting room with bed and two small lobbies up above—were Deb's domain. With ostentation and embarrassment, Sir Peter pressed a purse of guineas into the old dame's hand, but did not do the same for her. So I can't run away, thought Deb. I wonder if he doesn't know Sir A provided for me?

She wished to see upstairs, but was not certain of the protocol. She was still near bursting, for she knew the rich had different attitudes to simple needs than she and her type did, so, in a rush, she said to Mrs Collins: "I'd better go outside, I need the privy quick, and then we'll go up, shall we, sir?" and he blushed brick red again, which she found quite endearing.

When she returned, though, he had thought it through, completely. He would not come up, he told her, because he wished that she might have some privacy, and in any case he had . . . business that he must do. Privacy was quite humorous, thought Deb, but did not say so, and when he'd left, at long last and awkwardly, the old widow, with unexpected candour, told her that the "business," surely, would be his wife.

"Didst know that, med? That this man's got one, like? She'm a wild one, half his age, scarce old enough to be your big sister, and she'll shag near anyone, save poor old 'im. Treat him badly, and he'll be no trouble, my advice to you. Leaf out of 'er book, like. Make good sense?"

In ways it did, she saw that, but it was not Deb's way. As it happened, she needed neither guile nor other forms of lying and dissembling to keep Sir Peter from forcing himself upon her. It was a week before he came to visit next, to find her drinking tea in the back kitchen with Mrs Collins, now her friend; and even then, upstairs in her sit-and-bedroom, he made no move to touch or use her person. There was a fire going, and they sat on opposite sides, decorously, and Sir Peter sighed a lot, but seemed otherwise content. Deb was embarrassed, and developed a head pain through trying to think up anything to say, then gradually relaxed. At the end of one hour and a half he got to his feet, apologised profusely when she sprang to hers, moved his head forward as if for a kiss, and then back again as if his neck was stiff and he'd been merely looking for an easement for the ache. Deb laughed, but did not kiss him, and he went away.

"Contented?" Mrs Collins said, when asked. "What, him? What's that to you, my med? If he do not be contented the remedy is his, for surely, ent it? Anyways, I think he'll be content with talking to a woman what answers back without a sneer, what I've 'eard. Just so long's you don't make 'im too 'appy, so he brags to 'er 'e's got you, you'll be fine is my advice."

It took him several visits, in fact, before the fat Customs man felt the urge to try the physical, and then he signalled it so far ahead with gifts of cut blooms and sweetmeats that must have come from a London craftsman shop, that Deborah was not only ready but could hardly keep a face. She was easy in the cottage now, and easy with her old companion, and even easy, in a certain way, with him. They normally retired "up aloft" (as he put it, gallantly) and sat and chatted little talk, and drank dishes of tea, or sometimes coffee, or sometimes merely sat. When he did speak seriously it was brief because his only subject was Laetitia (his wife, as Deb now knew), and as soon as he realised what he was saying, he would collapse in embarrassment. It was after one of these occasions that he pulled up to his feet—wheezing a little from the effort—and produced his presents from a bag.

"My dear," he said. "You must like candy, for you are so sweet. And these blooms—from Covent Garden, from the Netherlands— well, they are not so fair as you are, that's the truth!"

Truth or not, he blundered forward then to seize her, and Deb— who could have stepped aside and had him fall flat on his arse and called it accidental—Deb did not have the heart, and let him grab and squash her, and fold her in his arms. And thus he kissed her, and a boundary was crossed. That night, alone in bed, Deb cried. The bed was soft and white and warm, and hers. She wanted no one in it, ever, except William.

Mrs Collins, also, when she told her, was gloomy for her sake.

"Ah well, med, it 'ad to 'appen," she opined. "Leastways it means you'll not 'ave your eyes scratted out, don't it?" Deb looked blank, and she continued. Apparently, some of the household maids, who had young men on the estate, were beginning to get hot about her being there because she did no work, but swanned about just being beautiful. The feeling was that one day some young groom or footman was bound to fall and land slap on her belly, bottom up. The girls were gossiping, the venom on the flow.

"But once Sir Peter's done the deed with you, why, all's all right again, ennit? How will they know? I'll tell 'em, won't I, med? I am your friend, and looking out for you."

It worried Deb that her presence was such common currency, for she knew that Maybold's house was not too far away. He had urged upon her several times that she should keep silent about her "gentleman," but having naught to do with younger men and women in the day-to-day brought problems of its own, for she was seen to be standoffish and stuck up. Aloof, and she must suffer isolation; fraternise, and she became a whore.

There came an evening though, inevitably, when the die was cast. From the moment he stepped into the house from out his coach, Deb knew that the fat man's mind was up—and his dander! He carried flowers and a bottle of the finest, finest brandy (this he told her), and he was as clumsy as a first-time youth. Deb's smile of welcome, shot through with amusement at his shambling, faded away when she realised. She bit her lip, then had to smile once more, but hardly carried it. Sir Peter, in a rush, came up to kiss her. He dropped the flowers, hit her elbow with the bottle, swore like a trooper, then apologised.

"Madame," he said. "Mademoiselle. Deborah. Oh what an oaf I am, I've spoiled it. Take me upstairs, an't please you. I wish to propose a toast."

Well, it would not be marriage anyway, thought Deb, and that is one thing. But he's going to swive me; he is going to get it out. And I must smile, and make some noise of pleasure. Oh Christ, I wish I did not have to.

Upstairs in the bedroom, Maybold was nervous as a cat, and blushing like a bride. Deb, amazed at his gawkishness, was disinclined to help him, had trouble not to let her feelings show. He tried to clutch her with romance, but his arms were too short, his corporation too gigantic, her bones and figure too unyielding.

"My dear," he breathed. In fact, he almost panted. "My dear, tonight's the night that I must . . . that you must, we . . ."

With luck he'll spend before he gets it near me, thought Deb, with neither charity nor passion. Oh I do not want to do this, how I hate to be a whore. Now he's plucking at my kerchief and my tits will soon be out. Oh I hate it all. I *hate* it!

"My lord," she said, pushing him politely back from her. "My lord, you must get ready; you have your britches on. Would you like to use the little room to make your preparation? We ladies, Sir Peter, must prepare. Excuse me for a moment, do."

She swept away from him, and then—having nowhere to go—turned back and harried him towards the other door. He went reluctantly, but with an eager look, and Deb stood for a moment, suffering. Her preparations would be minimal—lie down, pull up her skirts, she had it off by heart—but she had to steel herself, she had to smile. When he returned two minutes later she was still on her feet, still suffering. But Sir Peter, red as brick, was ready as a man could be.

"Sir Peter," said Deb, aware the sight was funny in despite of all, but desperate not to laugh, or cry. "Sir Peter, you are very bold. But come."

He was in a brocade tunic, but naked from the waist. His belly was enormous, round like an orange, and his legs were patched with purple, quite peculiar. His lips were drawn back from his teeth in an agony of self-control, and beneath his lower dome the prick poked out and throbbed, most painfully. At any second he must spend. It was inevitable.

He did, with a gasp and cry of pathos mixed with joy, and as he did so, the bedroom door burst open with a crash, to reveal a woman with long hair in ringlets, and a pointed and triumphant face. Behind her were two serving men, with pistols in their hands. Deb, still fully clothed thank God, just stood and stared. It was Laetitia Maybold. They had been betrayed.

Dick Kaye, when he came back on board, was like a whirlwind. He could be noisy in a fury, and today he was damn near apoplectic. The ship was quiet when he came along, with no one smart enough to notice him and muster a saluting party, which set him off wrong-footed for a start. On deck, though, when he met Rex Shilling and asked some pointed questions, the thing began to fizz. Will was down below with Black Bob and Ashdown when it erupted, and he cut and ran. Holt was still sleeping, but that did not last for long. Kaye's voice, vibrant with fury, was like a cross-cut saw.

Will hit the deck in time to see Shilling quailing, his face flecked with spittle from the tirade. He heard Kaye bellow of the Scotsmen, demanding who had locked them up and why, ordering their release, *immediate!* When he saw Bentley his voice went even higher, approaching screaming pitch. Around the deck the seamen—many of them marked with cuts and bruises—averted their eyes, tried to become invisible.

"Bentley! Lieutenant Bentley! What means this boy, what means this raving *boy,* sir?"

Shilling's pale face seemed to go paler, but he held his ground and pulled his shoulders back.

"It was a mutiny," he said. "Captain, I beg of you, please listen. It was—"

Kaye stamped his foot and raised his fist and screeched. Bentley approached with caution.

"It was a dereliction, sir!" Kaye shouted. "A dereliction of your duty, sir! Good God alive, I put you in command, you ninny! The Scotchmen were to help and they're in irons! Christ, I will have your entrails, boy. I'll have your bloody *entrails.*"

"Sir," said Will, and "Captain Kaye," said Holt, appearing at the hatch.

"You boobies!" bellowed Captain Kaye. "I leave my ship for half a day and—oh, you bloody, bloody *boobies!*"

All four were standing still now, in the morning sun. It was a strange sight, four men in some degree of uniform, stunned or bawled to silence. The Thames smell was sweet today, with the breeze wafting the London filth up to the Essex shore. Kaye blows hot and cold, thought Will, he has no bottom, no authority. Even a man as young as Shilling could not fear him for very long.

He said, carefully: "I think, sir . . . in the cabin? These people have big ears." Enjoy a show, he added, to himself alone. Mr Punchinello, make 'em laugh . . .

"Where's Bob," demanded Kaye, aggressively. "I need some coffee. Bob! Come out and serve your master, skulking scum!"

"The cabin, sir," repeated Will. "We can talk of it in there. Mr Shilling, perhaps you'd be so good? Geoff Raper will have put the coffee on, I have no doubt. He will have heard of Captain Kaye's arrival."

For an instant he feared the midshipman might get up on his high horse at being used as cabin boy, but even this one saw the sense, after a hesitation. He strode towards the galley, as purposeful as if the captain had been a normal man, and any sailor who dared to look at him soon dropped his eyes. Kaye gazed after him with bemused disdain.

"My second cousin's son," he said. "How did she ever get such shit? What has he done? Why are the Scotchmen held? Call Bosun—where is he skulking? I want them out immediately! Now."

"It can't be done instanter," Holt improvised. "We'll need to get the blacksmith to heat up the forge and knock the shackles off. I'll go find Taylor to set him up. Will can fetch you to the cabin and explain. The mess."

Despite the clearing that had been done, Kaye's cabin still bore marks of the struggle for the roundhouse, and there were bits of broken furniture, although he showed little interest in them. Will guessed he had been drinking, which he did with zeal on runs ashore. He had a whiteness round the eyes, a looseness of his grip on things.

"Groat said you were on shore, the pair of you," Kaye said. It was half a statement, half a question, accusatory. "He said you had not returned, and then the men got drink in them. Lax, lax! I warned him ere I went to keep them from the liquor, then half the company go in a riot. Why did he arrest the Scots? It is insubordination! It is dereliction!"

Will said, carefully: "There seems not any doubt, sir, if you will pardon me. The Lamonts . . . were them that started it."

Kaye's bulbous eyes fixed on him. They were angry, not a hint of acceptance in them.

"Fiddle-faddle," he said. "Who told you this? You were not even here! Rex Shilling has a grudge for them because I put them in a half-command. They are good men, Bentley, have not a doubt of it; they are exceptional. How many others of the crew are chained? Why think you these brothers were the ringleaders?"

Will licked his lips. It would place many men in most tight positions if he told Kaye what he knew and he chose not to believe it. He had seen Kaye's way with facts in times gone by. He was a man with little grasp of right and wrong. He wondered if he should bring Black Bob into the picture. How would that work on Dickie's addled mind?

"Six or seven are in irons, sir," he said. "And those others from the time they tried to murder Gunning. This band, this new lot, so we're told, went mad in some wise, sir. Mad for the drink. And for . . . they chased your little servant, sir. Black Bob. We thought they'd killed him."

Shockingly, Slack Dickie Kaye let out a laugh.

"He'd take a lot of killing, that bastard would!" he said. "What was their plan, to use him for their sport? He's got a great advantage in the night, he goes invisible; I know. Sometimes I think he disappears. He is a spirit!"

Will viewed this with distaste from many aspects, not least the way it had put the captain in a better humour. Bentley had spoken with Bob—had tried to—and the boy's eyes had shown as pools of terror; he'd been out of speaking, far beyond. He had lain still and trembled when approached.

"It is more serious," Bentley said. He kept his voice indifferent, but his words were quite concise. "He was hunted like an animal and used quite barbarously. He is badly injured, sir. The Scotchmen—"

"Oh, to hell with him," said Kaye. "He is a boy, a thing, a toy, an ornament, no more. The Lamont brothers are most useful men, and if they need some sport, what of it? Black boys are two a penny where we go. I spoke with them yesterday, Mr Bentley; we spoke at some good length. They know Jamaica—they were prime movers in society until detractors brought them down. They could help us make a fortune."

Bentley's face must have betrayed his blank astonishment, for Kaye began to bluster.

"Now, sir, your memory's at fault!" he said. "We spoke with my father, did we not? We talked of pickings, an estate. These men can set us on. They are well versed in fields of planter commerce!"

Will was almost speechless. Ashdown had known the men in Port Royal, Ashdown who had near lost his life in saving Bob. He had told Will earlier that they had been run out for bestiality on a servant girl. They had hunted her, and raped and murdered her, just as they would have done the boy, and had escaped the gallows by a half an inch, on account alone the servant girl was black. He had begged Will to warn the captain, to tell him if he shipped these men he would be mad. Black Bob would die, he said, and many other men as well.

"But sir," said Bentley. "I have been told that . . . I have it on authority . . ."

He stopped, and they held each other's eyes. Will knew he was on shaky ground, on very shaky ground. But Kaye was challenging.

"Authority? On what authority? What have you heard about these Scotch?"

"There is a seaman, sir. One Ashdown. He—"

The captain cut him off. He expelled breath hard; he made a sound of great derision.

"Pshaw, Ashdown! I have heard of Ashdown! The Lamont men are on to Ashdown, sir! It is a niggler of the most petty kind, a carper. He it was who was thrown off the island, not the Scotchmen. He is determined that he'll do them trouble, and you've fell for it. He is a Romish, is he not? A Jacobite. He would rather join the Frogs or Spaniards than fight for King and country. He is for a Romish God. And he has a thing for black men, Bentley, a truly strange thing as the Lamonts tell it. He has incited slaves to rise against their masters. He was damn near hanged for it."

That Ashdown was a Catholic, Will had no doubt. He was Irish, after all. But he had not mentioned faith, nor any of the other things he stood accused of in Kaye's eyes. And Black Bob had been attacked, for certain.

"The brothers, sir," he started mildly, "are drinkers."

"And so am I! And so are you, be not so mealymouthed! They are good honest men of commerce who were ruined by a lack of capital; it is the same old story." His eyes narrowed. "The eldest one, whose name is Angus, was a factor, too. They know estates. Lack of capital, that was their problem, and rival factions in the planting trade. They are Scotch, and therefore work too hard in some men's eyes. There is prejudice in Jamaica against the Scotch. I will have them free, Mr Bentley. It is disgraceful. I must go on shore again today, and I will have them at liberty. Where is Mr Holt?"

"Go on shore, sir?"

"Aye, on shore! Unfinished business, that's why I went to London yesterday, ain't it—or did you think I'd gone and left my ship for pleasure? In command of fools and poltroons, despite one of them is my family's blood! We sail, sir, we sail tomorrow, if I have my way. And we are short a sailmaker, and a soldier, and a man to keep the ship while I get sleep, if I should be so foolish as to dare. Even a man of God, good Christ—and if sailors ever needed one, it must be this benighted crew! There are things to do ashore, sir, and only I can do them. I ask you to guard the *Biter* safe, is all, to keep her clear of bloody drunken mayhem in the way of yesterday, is that too much to hope for? I doubt it on a proper ship, with proper men to help me, but on this—but on this, sir, I sincerely . . . well, I fear!"

You fear, thought Will, with cold contempt, but you will go; and if the thing flares up, you'll shuck the blame, as always.

"I would ask you only, sir," he said, "not to release them ere you go. For the sake of discipline, if nothing else. Men perceive the Scotch have chosen Midshipman Shilling as a target, and men take sides. There will even be some wagers. There will be provocations, deliberate attempts. I ask you, sir, if you must go away, to keep them locked below."

"I am going," Kaye said, harshly, "and the men will be released. If there is trouble, you and Holt must look to it. If there is mayhem, it will be your fault. You are my chosen officers, Mr Bentley, and it is best you learn to fill those offices. Go fetch Holt to me; he is taking too much time. I'll have those shackles off without delay."

There was something in his manner, though, that Bentley found suspicious—a sudden lightness in his face, a quirk of humour. Indeed, when he had told his friend the news, and the two of them faced Kaye once more, they found the case had changed: but for the better or for worse they could not tell. When the captain set out later, he took Coxswain Sankey and his usual boat's crew, but minus three. Their places at the oars were taken by the Lamont brothers, and Kaye told his two lieutenants he would return that night, at whatever length of time this final task should take.

"We sail tomorrow," he said, loud enough for men around to hear, and for the news to race around the ship like wildfire. "We sail tomorrow when our complement is full."

Sam and Will did not try to still the buzz and babble as the gig was pulled away upriver. They noted that the Lamonts—men of commerce, factors, gentlemen, whatever they might be—were definitely seamen also, who could pull an expert oar. They hoped and prayed that they would run the moment their bare feet should touch the shore, the way that seamen do, pressed ones especially. At the very least, they told themselves, it would prove to Richard Kaye that he was mad.

But Will was on the quarterdeck when the gig returned, and three of the oars were still manned by the silent, straw-haired brothers.

There were other forms in the boat, two bound and gagged, and on the bottomboards, bulky and folded awkwardly, was a very large man, his head completely buried in a sack. He was unconscious, unconscious drunk it would appear, and he reeked of shit and liquor. Tom Tilley and Tom Hugg, when roused out (it being three hours of the morning), had to rig a tackle, so heavy and unwieldy was he, but they were laughing when they laid him on the deck. Will knew the man as well, despite the covered head, and Kaye's look of triumph made his stomach chill.

Poor Jack Gunning, in a golden coat with vomit trimmings. Master before, and owner, now merely master, and in the drink again. Kaye said to Bentley, brusquely, before going to his bed: "Those Scotchmen, Bentley, are the men for me, the men indeed.

"We are sailing on the morning tide."

SEVENTEEN

Laetitia Maybold, much as her husband feared her, was a woman with a sense of humour, it appeared. When she saw the state the poor, fat man was in, she laughed. It was, true, not a pleasant laugh— harsh and brief and like a corncrake's cry—and her lips, rather than smiling, were locked into a sneer. He stood there, crouched to hide his shame, and his florid face went white, then glared and glowed brick red. The brocade tunic was too short to cover him, and his flabby legs were pallid in the tallow glow.

"Sir Peter," said his wife, "you are a buffoon, sir, and an adulterer. This is your latest whore, I see. She is too good for you."

The two armed footmen, torn between duty and pleasure at the spectacle, turned eyes to Deb. On one face was clear regret that she was fully clothed. A juicy harlot with her clothes still on was unlooked for disappointment.

"No!" said Sir Peter, in a strangled voice. "Not latest, this is the only—this woman is the first! It is misunderstanding, dearest! It is . . ."

Deb almost laughed herself at this. He stood there, like a padded pudding, with a dripping withered thing between his legs, a pathetically meagre puddle on the floor in front of him, and claimed misunderstanding. It would not have took Judge Jeffreys to hang him, certainly, she thought. Laetitia did not laugh again, however.

"You. Whore," she said, "what say you to this? Will you tell me you don't know this man, you have never seen his face . . . and parts . . . before? Go on, tell me that. I will believe you, that is a pledge. Go on, harlot. Say it."

"My dearest—"

"Shut mouth, you!"

"My dear Laetitia—"

Laetitia Maybold stalked across the floor (with careful feet), and slapped her husband on the face, a ringing, stinging blow. He raised his hands, remembered, dropped them down in front of him. Laetitia was smiling: a smile of satisfied derision.

"Oh go and get your clothes on, you fat fool," she said. "You are a steer, a gelding, half a man. And you, you trollop. Have you a cloak? A nightgown? While my husband hides the flabby German sausage thing, you may gather your essentials. You will not be coming back here. Have you boots?"

Deb looked to Sir Peter—without much hope—but he was on the move, a rapid shuffling towards the smaller room. She turned to face the gentlewoman, and her eyes were calm. Her heart, however, was hammering like horses' hooves.

"But I am going nowhere, madam," she said. She was aware, on sudden, of her accent, and she was ashamed. Laetitia's voice was like cut glass. She glanced at the two footmen, who were stolid now again. Maybe their accents were country also, Deb thought inconsequentially although a different part of country from her own. The lady's gaze was level on her face.

"Oh, but you are," she said. "You are a whore without a home. Do you plan to sleep beneath the stars tonight?"

Where is Mrs Collins, thought Deb. And then she knew. Mistress Collins would have more sense than putting in appearances.

"I live here," she said, her stomach hollow as the words. "The rent is paid."

"By my husband. Yes indeed. And he has stopped. Do you have another source of income?"

Her sarcasm was withering. But Deborah fought to retain her temper and her dignity.

"I have done nothing with your husband, Mistress Maybold," she said. "That is the simple truth. You have no cause of jealousy."

The woman paled, and Deb realised she had made a signal error.

"You slut," she said. "I'll slice your eyelids off. How dare you use that word! *Jealous?* Of *you?* You think I want the fat and useless eunuch? Of course I do not! You think that you might have him? You are a filthy little whore, a slut, a tart, a cesshole of disease! In case he's ever touched your parts, he shall no more come near me. Not ever. *That* is my jealousy, harlot! You are nothing, and he is less!"

Her fury had brought Maybold back, and for a short while he was inclined to remonstrate, or maybe plead. His wife, though, was beside herself; she was incensed, a performance new to Deb but which he recognised too well. The servants too, apparently, for they took it very calmly, seemed almost in a small *ennui* while Mistress M played out her rant. The upshot, though, was that Deborah must come with them, to be locked up in their house or stable until such time as Maybold would dispose of her. Her panic at this word did not last long, as she noted that the footmen treated it with indifference. When she dared to ask why she could not just be let go free, Laetitia was contemptuous.

"Why, you ask. Why should I answer, I reply. But I will, as you are too stupid to understand. This house, this whole estate, is owned by one who knows us. My husband is his friend, he tells me. His people know the story, they know your face, they will have mocked these most ridiculous cavortings. And you think I'll leave you hereabouts, do you, to keep the merriment alive? To let them gaze upon your painted cheeks, and marvel? To let you seduce the common menfolk and make mock of me and mine? Seduce his lordship, even? Oh that would be most prime, I do believe. You stay, and swive, and end up as the mistress here! You're mad, you slut! We leave here instantly! You will not return!"

Deb considered shedding her own tears, breaking down and screaming. Indeed, she felt she was quite near it. But something in this young woman—not many years her senior, if further gone in hardness—something in her face and manner made her fearful. There was something taut and brittle, dangerous. Deb felt keenly that if anyone were mad, it were not she, but more likely Mistress Maybold. And she thought she'd better play along, be emollient, and wait and see.

Sir Peter, though, had moved into a different mode. Fully dressed and still pathetic, he now was pleading, with tears standing in his eyes. He stood in front of Laetitia—not close enough for easy striking—and was imploring her belief in him. It was love he felt, he told her, and it was love for her alone. This crazed liaison (Deb, presumably) was a way of getting women's intercourse, meaning conversation, nothing else, without imposing on his dear wife, who found him overbearing, he would concede. He was begging her, he said (indeed he was; he was almost on his knees), to believe this was a mad mistake, a venture into territory he had never trod before, and never would again if she, Laetitia, could just this once forgive him. Then he looked at Deb Tomelty, full in the face, and swore he had never touched her parts, not even kissed her lips, and had not realised she would be a fount of all manner of disease and filthiness. Then he *was* on his knees, fully on them, and forcing sobs out from between his hands. His wife, Deb noted, looked as revolted as she felt herself.

Revolted by her husband, but not moved to pity for the girl, it soon appeared. With a signal to the gunmen she swept out and down the stairs, followed by Sir Peter, who neither looked at Deb nor made a sound. Deb made a sound, a sort of strangled cry, put out a hand, then dropped it to her side and closed her mind and heart. She was pushed and hustled, although not ungently, down to the front, where a carriage was already moving off along the drive. At head a muffled driver, at tail a muffled guard, and its windows tightly curtained. For her and her gentlemen escorters, there was a pony-trap. One drove, one sat opposite Deborah, facing forward, his pistol on his knee. She, facing back, caught sight of Mrs Collins at the cottage door as they whisked away. Neither woman waved or made acknowledgement of the betrayal.

Laetitia, as well as being bold and resolute, was a dissembler, it soon appeared. Deb had thought she was to be taken to the Maybold dwelling to await her fate, but quite soon she realised this was not so, for they were heading in the wrong direction. They hugged the river, true, but the village character of the settlements they passed gave way gradually to an area more populous and filthy. Sweet smells of field and animal manure were overlaid with acrid fumes of smoke and furnaces, and they passed a group of brick kilns whose lowering gases, for five whole minutes, almost choked them. Then clumps of masts, black against the sky along the river banks, became more thick and frequent, which meant that they were on their way to London. They were on their way to London's land of docks.

Her guard, who seemed a pleasant man enough, although he did not put up his gun and had said that if she tried to jump he'd shoot her, was not forthcoming for some little while about their destination, or her fate. At last, though, with a hungry look that Deb was tuned by all her recent past to recognise, he made a gambit. Subtle at first, but—when she pretended she did not get his drift—rapidly more crude. She was going, he implied, to face an awful fate, but there might just be a way to make it easier. What sort of fate, Deb wondered, could be worse then rutting with this pock-marked oaf and his companion in some grubby ale-house bedroom or a ditch, then being used, no doubt, as concubine or earning whore? Finally, she asked that very question, couched in a different way.

"Where are you taking me?" she said. "That lady said I was going to Sir Peter's house. She thought I would be an embarrassment, is all. What do you say will come to me of harm?"

Her captor scratched his temple with his pistol-barrel. He had a smile on that was more a smirk.

"Laetitia is a liar," he said. "She would accept my offer, though, if I was rich. I ain't, but I'm richer than you, my maid. I keeps my bargains, too, not like her. Try it with me. I can give pleasure, in

spite my pocky phiz. You can come and live with me. There ain't
no missus in the way. She died last Michaelmas. Not of the pox,
neither."

"I'm almost tempted," replied Deb, with polite sarcasm. "And
what of your companion, on the box? Is he part of the bedding offer,
or is he to remain my carriage driver, now you've made me up to be
a lady?"

He made a gesture with the pistol, obscene and graphic.

"He has no taste for maids," he said. "That's why the master keeps
him, for looking after madam. He makes a fortune that way, with the
bribes he gets by sneaking suitors in, and master's none the wiser,
fat old fool. So you'd just have me. What say you?"

The trap was in the dockland outskirts well and truly now. They
were dim and dirty, and looked deadly dangerous. Deb wondered if
these "guards" would throw her off to face her fate if she refused the
offer, but guessed Laetitia would be expecting proof the mission was
accomplished, whatever it should be. This man would use her first,
then do his mistress's bidding afterwards, most like.

"Tell me the alternative," she said. "What has the mistress got in
mind for me? Are we going to a ship?"

He looked slightly shaken, then he laughed, and she knew. Her
mind was filled with memories of Marcus Dennett, the man who'd
brought her down from North to South, the man who had ruined
Cecily, the man Will Bentley had shot through the neck. He had
made his money in many ways, all unsavoury. When possible, he had
sold young maidens into servitude in the Thirteen Colonies. He had
spirited them away.

"You're too sharp for me," said Pock-face, with another laugh.
"You'll have a knife under that skirt, I reckon, and if I tried to force
the issue you'd cut my yard off, wouldn't you? Aye, that's it, med,
you're going as a five-year passenger to Americkee, two birds with
one stone for the mistress, see—she gets rid of you for good an' all
and gets paid into the bargain. She's an ever-open 'ole where money's
in the question. Well—most things, come to that!"

Quite calmly, Deb thought things over. She had talked about this
business with Marcus Dennett, her first procurer, and she knew she

could, with luck, come out well from it. She'd be indentured to a farmer or plantation man, and then she'd have her freedom—again, with luck. Some women were abused, raped, murdered, died of disease or destitution—but others fell upon their feet. There was a shortage of white servants in the colonies, and a shortage of white wives and mothers ditto. Planters needed to rear up sons and heirs just like anyone, and the slaves and native redmen were mere savages, it was held, not breeding stock to found an English dynasty.

"You couldn't take me off even if I said yes, you silly devil, could you?" Deb said merrily. "You've got to take back money to Mistress Maybold, money or proof. Which part of America? What do they grow there? How long's it take?"

The guard was charmed by her good humour, which Deb hoped would stand her in good stead when he sorted the transaction. She did have a knife, the one from Margery, but to use it would probably bring about her death, she knew. Tony, she remembered, had predicted Will would end up in "the Americas," which was a thought, but not one to be taken serious, however much it gave her instant longing. According to Dennett there were a thousand miles of coast, and England was a pocket handkerchief compared with the smallest part of it. She was unlikely to bump into anyone she knew . . .

"What part?" he answered. "That I do not know. What grows there? Money, they used to say, when men believed in faeries and suchlike. How long? Depends on speed and luck. West Indies would be best because there's a war on and the packets are fast sailors and carry arms, so gossip has it. On the other hand, though, the Carib is alive with French and Spaniards and other foreign rogues, so you might end up a morsel on a plate of frog's legs or a bit o' Spanish baggage, take your pick. The captain that has bought you ain't a bad man, though; we've dealt with him before. I'll have a few words with him, med. Thou art a spunky lass."

She was staring at him. He noticed and guffawed.

"Oh no, not dealt with him for things like this!" he said. "You are the first one, honestly, even the mistress don't make a habit out of it! But she does a bit of smuggling, which would cause Sir Peter grief, as he's the top nob among all riding officers, ain't he? This

Captain Harding brings her items in, and takes Sir Peter's money off of her, a comfortable arrangement. So I could not have had you, lass, and got away with it; you speak quite true. By Christ though, thou art worth a try, believe me! I wish you luck. I mean it. I wish you God's own luck."

The ship slipped from her berth next morning, pulled out by dockyard boats to take the early tide downriver. It was a pleasant passage west across the ocean, and a quick one. Deb, as the only "passenger" —Captain Harding's business was done, in the normal way, for much higher yields—was largely left alone, but sadly took aloofness one step too far. Her indifference to the mate's advances, a young Cornish man called Godfrey, whose aspect she found rather threatening, angered him deeply, although he kept the anger hidden. He it was, when they reached Kingston, who found a buyer for her and sealed her indentures.

He chose a man called Sutton, who had constant trouble with his slaves and servants, and who had two brutal sons. Deb, who could not read, thought she had signed her life away for five years when she left England, and that, God knew, was more than long enough. Godfrey had other plans. Captain Harding, when he heard of the transaction, raised his eyebrows, but remained indifferent. The price agreed was good, to him—what else mattered?

EIGHTEEN

Biter's trip down London River, and then along the Channel to the Atlantic, was a revelation to Will Bentley, and a holiday. The last time he had sailed this water was in a screaming northerly in an open boat, with his friend Sam Holt unconscious in the bottom and his French saviour, Céline, heading, as he now supposed, to her death. When he had fought the stretch before that, in a full-rigged man o' war, it had been a ten or twelve day plug against wild westerlies, and running seas at lower topsail height. This time the sail was easy,

fast, and beautiful, with the weather like an aromatic balm. Even the
pressed and shackled men—now released—snuffed the warm air with
appreciation, and forgot their maids and children left alone on shore.
Mad Captain Kaye—Slack Dickie living up to it—eased the situation
in a wondrous way by apparently forgetting all the troubles they had
faced while moored. Men who had expected flogging, could at first
not quite believe, then got used to it. Slack he might be, this pop-
eyed popinjay—but what a walking wonder of the world!

This time, indeed, by some weird chemistry, Captain Kaye got all
things right. Bentley and Holt, with trepidation, assumed he would
force Gunning to con them down the Thames, and Gunning would
put them on a bank from fury, spite, or even craftiness. Gunning was
a three-day drunk, in general, and his level of incompetence could
only be guessed, not gauged, if one did not know when the drinking
had begun. If he put her on a mudbank hard enough and purposely,
the voyage might be over before beginning, and he could go back on
shore and try to have Slack Dick arrested for kidnapping him. Too
drunk to work this out, though, he might still hit another ship and
kill them all, himself included.

In fact, Kaye had engaged a pilot priorly, straightway to the Nore,
and Gunning's fate was a washing-down with buckets, and being
shackled in the hold with men he had betrayed. At first they raged
at him, but he raged back, in fury and an agony of deprivation, desperate as he was to have a drink. And shortly they forgave him, it
would seem, or saw the joy in his predicament, ending as he had
done like them, and with as little justice and a bigger, harder thirst.
Then, when they had been released but he was chained still, Kaye
pulled an even smarter stroke by giving Jack a bottle, then two or
three, *ad libitum,* until the thirst was gone, and he was prepared to
lie quietly unconscious for a day or so, and then forswear hard liquor
for evermore—again. When Gunning next appeared on the quarterdeck at the con, he was pale, and clean, and workmanlike, and they
were half way to the ocean, two days without a sight of land.

The strangest thing of all was that, having been kidnapped and
cheated, robbed of his family, friends, and home, he did not find it
terrible. With the weather staying clear and good, and getting warmer

as they ran down their southing before the long push west, he became expansive, happy, and abstemious. On that front, he was not so big a risk as the so-called surgeon, Grundy, whose inability to hold a knife and fork at dinnertime gave little confidence should he ever need to come at one with a scalpel in his shaking hand. Grundy still swore, black was white, he did not drink, and indeed no one had ever caught him at it. His chest was always locked, and he was never seen around the spirit-store replenishing his "medicines," so bribery and buying silence was the only answer feasible. There were always men on any ship who could get liquor as by magic, and mostly they were not the ones who drank. Not many sailors went ashore with money in their purses at the end of any voyage. Some did. Some were very rich. And all thanks to their lordships at the Admiralty.

Holt and William, contemplating Taylor dousing three drunken men with water-buckets one afternoon, three drunken men dragged from below almost unconscious, wondered why the Navy did it; although, of course, they knew.

"Eight pints a day," said Sam, disgustedly. "A bloody gallon down each neck, while still we've water in the tanks, sweet, fresh, and clean. Then a nip of brandy as would kill an ass or my old Auntie Mabel, even. Christ, when we reach Jamaica and the rum, they'll all be dead or pickled in advance. How do we ever fight the French?"

"Maybe they're worse," said Will. "They grow the grapes and make the wine and brandy. Strange if their sailors don't get as much of it as ours. Though, come to think of it, our smuggler friends were sober to a man, almost. Small-boat hands, however: if half your crew's unconscious, who's to save your life?"

Gunning, big and bland in shirtsleeves and bare feet, had come up with them upon the quarterdeck to watch the boatswain's operation. He was relaxed and comfortable, no concession made at all to the fact that he was the *Biter*'s sailing master, as everyone supposed. He shook his head and sighed.

"The devil drink," he said, lugubriously. "I'll tell you why the Navy do it, sirs—to keep men who can't run from jumping overboard. Christ, what a life for those boys there. See Willie Morgan— the curly one, built like an ape? He's just got wed, and his doxy's fair enough to tear your heart out wishing for a grip of her. And Charlie, next beside him: his old lady just had twins, two month ago. Any wonder they hits the bottle? Life saver."

Sam, who had quite taken to the Londoner in the past few days, eyed him with amusement. "Two things to say there, Jack, if I can be so bold? Firstly, did you not love the bottle before you were pressed into the Navy, so what's your excuse? And second, weren't it you that pressed those men, who thought they were immune?"

Bentley was amazed by Sam's outrageous gambit, more so by the response of Gunning. He gave a whoop, and then a chuckle, then said merrily: "Aye, fuck 'em, so it was! To keep 'em on their toes! They'll be back upriver someday, and if Willie's missus hasn't any childer— or only the one he's put in her already—then it's proved she's worth the marrying, ain't it? And likewise, if she's gallus, he'll have living witnesses, sucking at their mother's milk, and save the time of hearing lies and stories. He should thank me for my benefaction."

"And the bottle?" Sam pressed.

"And anyway," continued Gunning blithely, "I ain't joined the Navy, who told you that? Have I signed articles, or took a bounty, or dressed up in shitty cast-offs from out of Pusser's chest, like stink I have! What's been done to me was done against the law, and Mr Kaye will pay for it one day. He thinks that he can be my friend, he thinks I'll keep him company, poor lonely captain bastard, and he can kiss my sweaty bollocks. I can navigate and run this ship, but I'm a passenger. It's going to cost him dear."

The breeze was blowing gently from a clear and lovely sky, and the *Biter,* hardly heeling, was running at a cracking speed, with stunsails drawing. Around them men worked quietly, and Kaye was nowhere to be seen. Will, despite the conversation, could feel his heart expand. All problems, at the moment, were well below the threatening.

"Not for an argument, Mr Gunning," he said, "but me and Mr Holt here can do those things now, I would venture. You yourself have checked my sights and seen my reckonings, and I get better every day. Sam can do positioning as well as any man, and between us and Taylor and his mates, the vessel runs on grease. We've got your hands ditto, Morgan and Charlie Bond and what's the tall one called, Mike Symonds, is it? They may be drunkards, but then what matters that, in our King's Navy? They can hand and reef and steer, as so can many of our people, and your men know the *Biter* like their mothers' faces. Not say you're not needed, but might say we'd get by."

Gunning spread his hands in apparent agreement, nodding.

"Oh surely, Mr Bentley, surely. And you know the Carib, do you? You've sailed in hurricanes? You know when the season starts and when it ends? You know when the reefs in clear blue sea below you are at safe depth, although a hundred fathoms shows no less sharper than two meagre feet? Do you know how well your anchor holds on volcano ash? What time of night the wind blows onshore like clockwork, and on which island? Of course you do, sir! You're an officer!"

"We're very young, Jack," Sam put in, as if he meant it, gravely. "Try to make allowances, won't you?" He twinkled. "But you have sailed the Caribbean, have you? Does the owner know? Whoops! You were the owner, weren't you? Will be again by sound of it! Or want to be!"

Gunning laughed. "Not I. I dropped out of *Biter* before her bottom could; she's served her turn for me. But in the Carib there's more to learn than what you glean by years of merchanting, believe me. There's Monsieur le Toadfrog with his long lean guns to fight, there's Señor Spanish with his garlic and his thumbscrews, there's savages who eat folk up for breakfast, and for all I know there's pirates, still. Thank God for men of such experience as you, Lieutenant Bentley, I should say. Without you I'd be shaking in my shoes."

Will was not inclined to take umbrage at the tease, for Gunning had a point at end of all. In any way the man was very interesting, as Sam had told him several times. He was starting to discern his friend as right.

"Well, we have guns an' all," he mildly said. "And the dons are on our side, unless there's been another treaty I've not heard about. We've fought before, we'll fight again, I guess."

The big man curled his lip so obvious that both Will and Sam turned, inquiry on his face, and waited. Gunning, as if he'd been caught out as schoolmaster, sighed. He leaned across the rail, and hawked, and spat. No Navy man indeed; no officer would do that, and no seaman dare on pain of lash. He cleared his throat.

"If we meet a canny Frenchman, I'll take my chances overside, among the sharks," he said. "How long we been at sea? Ten days, twelve or more? When did you last hear a carriage gun? Where's your gunner, armourer? On deck, examining his pieces? Down below filling cartridges? The shit he is! How long to run a big one out, do you reckon? Clear it, charge it, load it, haul it out, and set the bastard off? If Dickie is the owner now, he don't take care of his possession, does he? Even the Spaniards, half drunk, could outgun us for speed—and probably for straightness, also. These things don't aim themselves."

"But you have sailed with him—" Will began.

"Aye, and found him slack. What care to me, Slack Dickie's slackness? I ran a tub for him, for profit, on the Press. What chance of battles with the French in them times? If we saw one we could run, and I could sail her, no fear on that score, eh? That Navy clerk I know, remember? Ed Campbell, you met him with his doxy on *Biter* once, Sal Marlor's friend. He said the Navy's hot on gunnery; they see it as the coming thing. Some captains—and Dick would not believe this—can loose off shots as regular as tides, once in five minutes, less; I can't remember. How long on *Biter*, do you reckon? Five hours? Days?"

Will cast his mind back to his other life, his other ship, the *Welfare*, his Uncle Daniel, martinet. Good God, this man was right: they'd passed the days with gun drill, cutlass drill, fist fighting, single-sticks. The big guns had been in and out a dozen times a day, loaded, set, unloaded, cleaned, run out again, sometimes fired if the captain cared to use some powder for the sake of keeping men on their toes. If the people were not up and down the masts—setting, furling, bracing, sheeting, slushing—they were up and down from magazine to gun-decks, arsehole to breakfast time, sweating till they dropped. And when the wind was calm, they got the boats out and towed until their muscles screamed for mercy and backs cracked.

Holt's experience was not so wide by far, but he could clearly picture it. He had spoken to other men, and been mocked because he sailed on a Press tender and thus fought English tars, not with the enemy. He knew the *Biter's* Navy hands were lazy, overfed, and soft—too lazy, overfed, and soft even to run, which other shipboard slaves did as a bounden duty, a kind of nod to great traditions of the service. He had known of something wrong, but had not realised before that they might have had the remedy to hand.

"By God, Jack," he announced, "I think you have the right of it! By God, Will, this could help to pass the time! Let's call upon the man instanter; let's get some action going!"

"Instanter?" responded Gunning, with a smile. "If you mean the captain, you mean tomorrow, don't you, Mister? Urgent means tomorrow on this ship, tomorrow or the next day. And tomorrow never comes, they say."

Good jest, and one Sam Holt appreciated, but Sam Holt meant today. There was another matter he was determined would not get away from him, however; he wanted one thing more.

"Jack," he said. "Oh, not 'Mister,' by the way, call me 'Lieutenant,' for sake of Navy form, and 'Sam' in private, if you wish—but Jack, you slid away from my important question: what of the bottle? You came on board unconscious, you drank in irons like a fish for two days, you call the liquor 'devil,' or 'the demon,' and—"

"And then I swore," said Jack. "All that's behind me, that I can promise you. I had been took, remember? Kidnapped, forced, plucked from my hearth and home—well, from an ale-house, anyway. It was a little need I had, for comfort and replenishment, and me and drinking now are sundered, that partnership is dead. See that cloud there, Mister Lieutenant?" He pointed, to the far horizon. "I could be misreading but I'd say that is bringing dirty weather. Strong winds, big seas. I welcome it. 'Twill wash the stink of piss away."

"You change the subject."

"No, I don't. I have naught to hide from you, I promise you. I'm teaching you, is all. This calm blue sea, this vault of tender firmament—it's going to blow like buggery. If not today, tomorrow. I'll put money on it. I'll bet a quart of brandy."

He's incorrigible, thought Will, with keen amusement. He drinks himself insensible, and pretends that he don't like the stuff, then makes a wager and a joke of it. Holt was in tucks.

Gunning said: "Why should I lie though, gentlemen? I drink the way I whore; sometimes it's necessary. You know that, Mr Holt, don't you? They say that you're in love with one. That's the hardest, is it not? The tearing off, the ripping out of some maid's bed and heart. Do not you sometimes feel the pull of drunkenness?"

Sam smiled, easily. "But men don't miss whores, surely, if it's true that mine's a whore. You've been pulled off from a lawful wife and home. Children too, for aught I know."

Will watched, fascinated, and held his peace. This sort of talk was out of his experience. These two men sparring made him think of wary dogs, stalking round each other, shaping up to see which was the stronger or more dangerous. Not for the first time, he realised his early life was of a different class from that of many men he knew and worked with.

"Aye, childer too," said Gunning, "but that's just complications. I'll tell you frank, Lieutenant, I'm glad to be away from land at last. No word to Kaye now, I depend on you for that, but what drove this man to drink was not the loss of one, but the grabbing claws of many. Wives ain't the worst of it, at least they only want to gossip or to moan. But you've seen Sal; Christ, she was locked on like a bulldog-bitch, all talk of love, and little houses in a leafy spot, and children of her own—*our* own!"

Sam gave a hoot of genuine amusement.

"But don't she know you have a wife? Now that *is* foolish in you, John!"

"Damn me to hell she knows! She sees no right in it, is all! As if there was some way I could get out of it! As if I wanted to! Then there's the others, too: Becky and Flit and Jane and Janet and the rest of them she do not know, I hope, but she'll find out. Just 'tween the three of us, it is a favour Dickie's done me, although I'll make the bastard pay for it! And in the islands, I believe, the maids are black, and don't speak English, and so don't answer back. My friends, that sounds like paradise to me."

"So it's not the lack that drives you to the bottle, then, but superfluity! By George, you'll not go thirsty, whichever way! And your pledge to drink no more is straight a lie, I guess?"

The big man spat across the rail once more, with levity.

"God's truth," he said. "I swear to you Lieutenant, I will never touch another drop."

Whatever the lieutenants thought of Gunning's good intentions, Sam in particular was fired by his plan to smarten up the people, and sought the captain's ear on it in good short order. Kaye, languid at first, soon changed as it sank in. The trouble was, as Holt told Bentley later, he seemed to get the process arse about. Within a half a day—before he would allow a gun drill—he ordered floggings. He had, he claimed, been well aware the people were all idling, and had decided that a bomb be put amongst them. All Holt could offer, he averred, was advice as to which of all the scum most needed the whip. Groat, he added with amusement, had made it clear he thought the Lamonts were prime candidates, which only showed that Groat was mad. Who were Holt's nominations?

Holt, as he told William, was in a quandary. Scarce one on board did not agree with Shilling, however much or little they cared about the boy himself. The Scotsmen, almost blatantly, made mock and thwarted him, while if confronted with the captain near, they were as meek and mild as muted sheep. Muteness, indeed, was their most telling tool against the midshipman. When he ordered them to any task, they would not respond, and the more his passion rose, the tighter went their lips. He stopped short of striking them—which he would have done, and did, the bulk of men—because there was something in their silence so deeply menacing.

Groat's only triumph, and only he alone thought of it as such, was in the matter of their being warranted as boatswain's mates. He had boldly brought the matter up at the captain's table one early night when Kaye, relaxed and softened by the weather and their easy progress south towards their goal, had hosted a minor feast for all his gentleman (save Grundy, who was lying down below dead drunk and claiming a recurrence of the ague) in the cabin. It had been at

first a sticky do, with the tragic, clumsy form of Black Bob—since
the river incident a kind of listless ghost—casting a long shadow on
easy conversation. But as the wine flowed, then the brandy, the talk
got easier, with opinions passed about many of the men and cir-
cumstances on board the ship. Kaye raised the brothers first for
devilment, it would appear, for he held mention till a point where
Bob was standing at his side with a large hot bowl in hand. The boy
jumped visibly at the name Lamont, and slopped some juice, and the
captain laughed at him, and winked at Arthur Savary, who blushed.

"They are galvanic, see?" said Captain Kaye. "Their very name
makes even monkeys jump. Beg pardon, boys, to all you three, but
I wish they could be officers indeed! Except that they agree they cannot navigate!"

Bentley and Holt, politely, let it ride, for they thought Dickie said
this for mere effect. But Rex Shilling, quite drunk and slightly flushed,
began to sputter quietly. He did not dare to speak it out, but his
views were plain, and Kaye found it amusing in extreme.

"I'm going to build them up," he said. "Jem Taylor is a useless
article, and his mates are worse. I see the Lamonts taking over from
all three, Angus as boatswain, the younger ones as mates. What say
you, Rex?"

Groat swallowed.

"Well, sir. If I might make so bold? I think it . . . I think it dangerous," he said. "It is not to me, sir, do not think that. But . . . but
other men . . . the brothers are . . . they anger people, sir. I fear if
they gave orders, there would be . . ."

He tailed off. He was blushing worse than Savary, whose face
burned in sympathy. A most odd army man, Bentley thought.

"Well?" Kaye enquired silkily, after a pause. "There would be
what? Speak out, Rex. We're all friends here, y'know."

"There would be bloody mutiny," said Sam. He laughed. "Mr
Shilling is right," he added. "'Part from any other thing, Jem and
his lads would fight it tooth and claw. They—"

"In any way, it's wrong," cried Shilling, interrupting. "They don't
deserve it, sir. They are disobedient. I mean—no, that is wrong, they
disregard . . . there is insolence in them."

Kaye's amusement was clear to see.

"Disobedient," he said. "Well well."

His humour was still high, so Holt traded on it.

"I tell you, Captain, a damn good plan might be to have a milling for the prize," he said. "Jem and Hugg and Tilley facing the Lamonts across a chalk-line on the deck. They could slug it out to kingdom come, and the best men win it all. It would come to that, in any way; Mr Shilling is right on that score. If you make the Scotchmen up to boatswain and mates, the boatswain and his mates will make a war of it. To death, I should not wonder."

"A milling match," said Kaye. "Hmmm, interesting. It would be a bloody afternoon."

Will said: "And Taylor and his boys would win it, sir. Jem's small but hard as adamant; Toms Hugg and Tilley are just veritable bears. If you wish to give the brothers fair reward, this would be one way of doing it!"

"Fair reward!" said Shilling, sounding furious. Then bit it off, although he damn near choked himself to do it. Ah, Will noted gloomily—he learns at last. But Kaye was musing now.

"They would win, would they?" he muttered, almost to himself. "Aye, a bloody afternoon, indeed. Well, I will think of all this, gentlemen," he continued more publicly, "and thank you for your views and information. Thank you, Mr Groat. Illuminating."

In the days that followed this, Rex Shilling convinced himself, apparently, that his ideas—"illuminating"—had put the captain right about the brothers. Somehow, it appeared to give him confidence, particularly face to face with them, who bristled enmity when he approached still, and failed to give voice of any kind to anything he might demand of them or say, although they did his orders, with bad grace. Below decks, Will heard it rumoured, the mid took care to keep well clear of them, singly or in group, in case they cared for confrontation, and he should lose. But in company, he would boast— and even to the Scotchmen's faces—that he had kept them down, and put the captain straight on their deficiencies. Their eyes now filled with hatred for him just at sight.

He tried to have them flogged, when Dickie decided flogging was the way to "smarten ship," but luckily for him, perhaps, the captain seemed to think that he was jesting. What had they done that was so wrong? he asked, and something in his eye quelled Shilling's answer in his throat. Both Holt and Bentley mildly averred that they had no one in mind whose transgressions needed whipping out of them because they largely thought it true. Apart from a little drunkenness, a little swearing, a little incautious sodomy, the people had been very well behaved; their only fault was sloppiness and slack—which Sam and Will had hoped to school them off with working up the guns.

However, once he'd had the good idea, the captain went whole hog with it. His first candidates were the deserter he had brought on board the night before they'd sailed from London (on the grounds he'd cost good money, but turned out too unstable to replace the soldier stabbed in Deptford, who had later died), the three ex-Gunning crewmen whose drunkenness had set the whole thing off, and Josh Baines. Poor Baines, the ginger rat, had done nothing worse than usual (which was very little), but Kaye did not like him, as nor did anyone, which made him very popular as a choice. Bentley pointed out stiffly to his captain that one man was merely half-demented, one was guilty of not even that, and the other three could not receive three dozen lashes as proposed because that was illegal by the articles. Kaye curled his lip, contemptuous, but avoided argument with this young, but stubborn, officer. All five, he said, would get a dozen straight. Clear decks and set them on—and call all hands.

Slack Dickie Kaye was infamous among the officers of the Navy that knew his name, and famous, possibly, among the other, lesser, ranks. By reputation he had never flogged a man, and it was widely held to be through idleness, or lack of understanding of the art. Discipline on the *Biter,* when a small-manned tender of the pressing service, had been bought with sheer indulgence, and the presence of Jack Gunning and his paid crew to do the seaman-work. Her Navy men—almost alone in the service in a war—had been given leave on shore, and what's more had chosen to return each time because their life was such a fizz. In and out of London River, good food from one-leg Raper, tarts and taverns always close to hand except when in the Downs or the Approaches (sometimes as much as five whole days at sea—disgusting!), and so much space below, they could forget their hammocks and sleep on the decking if they so desired, to share their beds with rats and cockroaches, and sometimes lovely ladies from the docks and dives. Now she was crowded, like other ships of war, and Geoff Raper's good fresh food was giving way to shit, provided not by the local Thames-side markets but from out of Purser Black's dank barrels, purchased God knows where and God knew when (but had forgotten). And Dickie's first reaction to increasing disaffection—was the cat.

In an odd way, that first time, it was almost festive. Savary's soldiers mustered in their finery, looking fitter than soldiers did normally. Sunshine, food, and lack of marching had been a rest-cure for them, and their officer was startling in his cleanliness and healthy glow. He looked so much like a pretty maiden that Will idly wondered if some of the sailors' songs he'd heard had come to pass, and Arthur Savary was indeed a lovelorn maid who'd come following her poor pressed man to sea. Somehow he doubted it, however, for Savary showed little interest in any man on board, and in fact used to shave, in the sunshine, in the waist, with a big cut-throat razor that made the sailors who lusted for his slender tail go weak in case he nicked his peachy skin. Any case, when Will had gone to the quarter gallery one time to defecate, he'd been at squat already, and Will had glimpsed his yard.

Tom Hugg had seen the gratings lashed in place—two side by side, for Kaye had decided on a show—and the company had mustered for the spectacle with good grace enough. They were well out by now, not far from the Azores, where they might stop with luck to pick provisions up, and the weather was killingly hot. Pitch was bubbling on the decks, and the smell of sweat from many bodies, sweat and dirty clothes, could catch the throat when wafted on a zephyr. Zephyrs, too, were all they hoped to get, for ventilation. As if by showman's clacker, or a signal from the Lord on high about the flogging (Approval? Disapproval?) the wind had dropped to nothing when the gratings were made ready, and the *Biter*, so used to ploughing through the mellow creamers, was now racketting and crashing idly in a leaden, lumpy swell. No headway of any sort, but she was rolling like a bitch, main yardarms threatening to make a splash from time to time. It was most uncomfortable, and Midshipman Shilling, first time in a proper sea in all his landlocked life, was showing it.

The five transgressors, hands tied in front of them, were brought up together and positioned by the rail. Kaye stood at the poop-break in his smart dark coat and wig, with Sam and Bentley flanking him, and Shilling a short way off. Savary stood down below them, next his three gallant soldiers, whose muskets-butts, Will noticed, were glazed with sweat. If one slipped out of hand and hit the deck and fired . . . he bit his lip, remembering another time and place, still vivid, still an unexpected pain. He looked at Taylor, and remembered the giant boatswain Allgood, and his vicious mates.

Taylor was not vicious, though, and nor, despite their size and rough demeanour, were Tilley and Hugg. Their faces were completely blank as they listened to the captain's litany of the sailors' dreadful crimes, which at times was shouted to overcome the crashing of the gear above. Taylor was glancing constantly aloft, fearing that the hamper might break free and come raining down, smashing heads. Jack Gunning, ditto. He had scorned to come and see his former shipmates whipped, but could not stay below in the event. The torture of the sails and yards and rigging was a torture to him also; he could not hide it from his face.

Kaye's hoped-for soldier was the first triced up, alongside him Edward Higgins, pressed from *Biter*'s early crew. Higgins, stripped to the waist, stood stoical, not bothered by a punishment considered well-earned by such a drinking session, considered almost a nothing to a man as hard as he. He laid his cheek against the grating, closing his eyes as if drifting off to sleep. His back, broad and hairy, was criss-crossed with old scars. So he had been a Navy man before his river days—or in some common jail.

His peroration finished, Kaye gave the nod to Taylor, who passed the order on to his two mates. They stood like bulls, cats hanging from their hands, knees bending as they rode the dreadful roll. Bentley, on the poop, could see the faces of the people, and not a few of them showed some distress. Not at the brutish punishment they had to watch, but at the motion of the sea. Of the newly pressed, there would be several who had been dragged from dry land life, however hard they'd screamed about it, and some of them would be throwing vomit before long. Will would have liked to shut his eyes on the whole distasteful thing, but he knew men better than his captain did. He had to forge a fighting, sailing crew from this gang of motley. Showing weakness, at any time, was not the way.

Although he hated this game he knew it, and from the first blow of the pair of cats, he knew that Taylor and his men were pulling back. He saw the bare backs jerk, and he saw the dull red streaks on the white skin. Not yet broken, though, nor even like to be at this gentle rate. The half-wit face of the nonsoldier broke into a slack-lipped grimace, denoting pain and anguish, true. But Higgins, whatever his intention to dissemble, revealed a half a smile before he turned his head to cover it.

"Good," said Captain Kaye, and "good God" thought Bentley and half the *Biter*'s crew.

"Not hard enough," said Bentley, as if by accident. Not loud, but loud enough for Taylor to hear, as well as Richard Kaye. The captain looked at him, his hazel eyes half angry, but seeking knowledge, too.

"I beg your pardon, sir?" the captain said. "Did you have commentary to bestow?"

"Beg pardon, sir," his junior replied. "I merely thought the rolling spoiled the warrants' strokes. Those cuts would not have lifted a milk pudding skin. They were not serious, Mr Taylor? Surely?"

Dick Kaye regarded him with different eyes, too stupid to understand his full intent. Taylor knew, though, as did Tilley and Tom Hugg. He acknowledged with an apologetic nod, and gritted to his mates to lay it on, or else they'd feel the lash themselves. The next stroke made the captain jump, the half-wit scream and howl, and Edward Higgins smile a shade more bitterly. Still no skin broke, though, and Taylor's inquiry to Will, their talking glance, had them in full agreement: it was convincing, but way this side of beastishness. Most importantly, Kaye remained in ignorance of their

collusion: he and the people knew this flogging, however unde-
served, was earnest. Transgressors would be hurt, and go hang guilt
or innocence.

The pain felt by the idiot was fearful, though, heartrending, and
quite clearly affected Kaye. After seven strokes the blubbering was
constant, an embarrassment, a shame, when luckily he passed out of
consciousness, collapsed. He had shit himself, what's more, a liquid
horror running from his trousers to the deck, and Kaye, pretending
fury, ordered him cut down and given to the surgeon, who stood
swaying by the port-side shrouds. Grundy was staggering, two sailors
told off to drag the soldier slipped in the shit and fell, and several of
the greenhorn seamen threw up their beef and biscuit. Sam and
Bentley, cold-eyed, efficient, brought order back in half a minute, and
the last three men were flogged, Ed Higgins having been released
like his companion after only seven strokes, for which luck, he showed
no gratitude at all. This time the whippings were perfunctory, with
no one much interested any more, so the infliction of great pain a
pointless exercise. Josh Baines was therefore fortunate—although
later in the 'tween decks he received a black eye somehow. He must
have fallen badly, it was said . . .

The main reason for the quick end to flogging was the weather,
however, which went rapidly from bad calm to ten times worse, with
wind. Gunning's prediction, which had been discounted in Will's
mind, was merely some hours late, but the wind and seas that shot
the men into the rigging and washed the filth and vomit from the
decks was on them before the gratings could be unlashed and stowed.
Of a sudden, the sickness that had already started flashed through
the ship like wildfire, with thirty men or more retching and heaving
up. One of them, who fought till after dark to save his self-respect,
was Shilling. But he had come down off the poop-break looking
green as grass, men had noticed, and some had dared to laugh behind
their hands. Sent below to make sure ports and hawses, and any
other leaky points, were firmly plugged and lashed and bunged, he
ran a gauntlet of more open cruelty in the heaving dimness, and, out
of sight of his fellow officers in a roaring squall, was also quickly
out of mind.

Full dark came early with the lowered cloud and heavy, rain-filled wind, and the general lack of vim and keenness of the people made the work very hard and dangerous, both below decks and aloft. It was not till after midnight that the officers foregathered in Kaye's cabin, with Gunning himself, and two of his better, stronger men at helm. The *Biter* was snugged down to reefed foretopsail and latino mizzen, with a rag or two at head. She was on the wind and punching, with the scuppers running constantly with breaking sea.

"Where's Groat?" said Captain Kaye, who had been sick himself, sick as a dog, and now was settling digestion with half pints of brandy swallowed neat. "Has no one called him? Bob! Bugger-boy! Go out and call the midshipman! Go fetch him, bugger-boy!"

Bob, eyes cast down, slunk out for fifteen minutes, returning wetter than a half-drowned pup. But he could not find Midshipman Groat, he muttered, and stuck to it however hard Kaye struck his face. Later Sam went out with a lanthorn, then Sam and Will joined with Savary and the two of his men not too sick to stand or hold a musket. They searched the fetid 'tween decks, poking and pushing everywhere, amid the groaning timbers and the groaning men. Taylor and his two mates then joined, and others of the seamen they could trust. In two hours the ship was quartered, and they had drawn a blank. Rex Shilling had gone overside, and he was never seen again.

NINETEEN

Next morning, when the news was general, it had a strange effect upon the ship. No one had liked Shilling, but there was an all-pervading sense of shame at his demise. No announcement was made, naturally, but everybody knew, and everybody thought they knew the culprits. Many men went overside in storms, including officers, but this was different. Rex Shilling was disliked, Rex Shilling had insulted and antagonised damn nearly all the people. Rex Shilling was at daggers drawn with the three Scotchmen, and they had murdered him.

Slack Dickie Kaye, alone, did not believe this. It was brought up first at breakfast time by Sam, at his most cutting, and Kaye jumped on it. At first he was lyrical, talking of injustice, proof, and high-flown concepts then—when Sam responded with a shocked obscenity—notched up to violent anger. His florid face grew flushed, his eyes protruded, and he shouted Lieutenant Holt down as a calumniator of the innocent.

"How dare you, sir?" he roared. "How know you that? Good God, sir, in a court of law you would not dare!"

This was so extraordinary that Holt would have laughed, except his mouth was gaping.

"In court of law?" he sputtered. "But . . . but . . ."

"It is defamation!" the captain said. "Last night there was a gale, the night was filthy! Shilling was sick, and puking, and he's never been to sea! You have the knife in for those brothers, Mr Holt, and I will not allow it! What makes you say such things? He lost his feet. He slipped. He lost his footing."

"Pray God he did not lose his cherry," Sam said, deliberately. "Please God he was not fucked before he fell. Sir, those men are animals."

"Where is your proof? What is your proof of that? God, Mr Holt, if I should tell them what you say!"

This caused silence in the cabin. Bentley and Savary both kept eyes downcast. Gunning, who had been awake all night, gave a sudden and gigantic yawn. Then Holt attacked, though quietly.

"You will not tell," he said. "As we will not tell your cousin how your nephew died. Some things must be unsaid." He stood, and wiped his mouth. "And now I leave, with your permission, sir, before this nonsense gets out of hand."

Kaye looked set for renewed fury, but Gunning also stood, large and exhausted, head bent under the deckhead.

"I'm for my bed," he said. "I don't care how the mealmouth died; he's dead that's all. The way your people acted, the wonder is we're any of us living. When we make it to Azores, I'm minded to walk off of here. You'll need the Scotchmen then; they're seamen. Mayhap the only ones."

Not asking for the captain's by-your-leave, he shouldered out and Holt went after him. Will and Savary stayed for a while, while Slack Dickie chuntered at them. As they left, he clouted Black Bob in a fit of pique as he cleared the table.

Outside, the day was fine and mild and beautiful, the sea calm and friendly, swept by a splendid breeze. The line of bronze that had marked the far horizon before the storm was gone, the few clouds left were high and tiny. Hard to believe that such a short time before they had been under press. Hard to believe that somewhere beneath these waves lay poor Rex Shilling. Will wondered about the vile things Holt had said. Poor Rex.

Sam, not content to merely wonder, had gone angrily about the task of finding out. He could move about the ship, above, below, even in the heads if he so desired, where most officers would neither care, nor dare, to venture normally. But although he clearly read a mood of muted regretfulness, or guilt at least, he could not crack the wall of silence. The only man he found prepared to open his mouth was the impressed soldier-boy who had been flogged, and he was almost lunatic by now. He gibbered at the officer, not happily, and clutched at him from off his pallet in the sick berth. Sam suggested to Mr Grundy that he should be tied, if only for his own safety, but Grundy, reeking of old brandy and despair, ignored the point. In fact, some days later the man went overside, like Shilling, but in full view of all hands, and screaming as he ran. He was as little missed, or less.

Most of the men Holt approached merely played confusion, pretending they had no thought of what he might be looking for. Some older men expressed frank sorrow, and one murmured that the boy had been so very young, but no one had a fact, or even view, to offer. Men came and went on board a ship, not just in the King's Navy. If you could do, you would bury them, and if not . . . well, hard life, easy parting. As Sam approached the Lamont brothers he saw them share a smile, then watched it fade from all three faces as he looked at them. To hell, he thought, and went to waste his time elsewhere.

That night, though, as he and Will stood silently beside the main shrouds, hoping to attract some sly informant, they became aware that such a one had drifted up. The night was pretty clear, but moonless and exceeding black. The nearest watch member was twenty feet from them, but could have been two hundred for all the chance of recognition a seeker might have had. They had guessed it would be Ashdown, if anyone should dare to come, and so it was. He stood there for some seconds, peering round and up aloft to see if anyone was aware of him. Then he relaxed.

"Good evening, sirs," he said. His voice was deep and low and pleasant, with a powerful tone of Ireland in it. They heard a wet sound, as he licked his lips.

"You need say nothing," Holt said, quietly. "We guessed it was the Scotchmen, is that so? Were they seen? Would any tell on them? Did they kill him first?"

"Say nothing?" said the Irishman, amused. "How would I do that, with all the questions you are asking? I did not see it, though, and nor did no one else, I'll wager. It was a shambles down there when the weather struck, there were men and bodies all around the place. I saw the midshipman, and he was being sick just like the rest of 'em, but he was being got at, too. Then I was up aloft, like all the able men, with Taylor and Tom Tilley on my arse."

The lieutenants digested this. The Scotchmen, likewise being able, would have been working aloft, most like. They must have done the killing in a lull, or taken opportunity by the horns as it presented. At least not a long-drawn thing then, Will thought. Were there no guards below, he wondered, no marines? Then dismissed it.

"If any saw it, and should tell, what would the Scotchmen do?" he asked. "They would kill again, I guess, or threaten it?"

Ashdown nodded.

"They've killed before, out in Jamaica," he said. "As I've told previous. An' she'd been a planter's daughter, or a white servant even, they would be dead for it, but she was black, unlucky thing. However, it was such a fearful crime they were run out for it, and those who knew them said it was not uncommon for them, they'd done murder before, and rape on other maids, and men. No one on this ship will speak up against them, you may depend on that, sirs. Aye, sure they would kill again. They seem to get some pleasure from that sort of thing."

"But what will happen if and when they get back there?" asked Sam. "Are they still wanted men? At least, are there none there to avenge the maid?"

"Or will they run?" Will added. "We'll put in at the Azores, I guess, to get fresh fruit and water and some wine. Most pursers don't give up that opportunity, and I'm sure the captain's game."

Ashdown shook his head, his grey eyes thoughtful.

"I think they will get back in safety, and I do not think they'll run," he said. "No one avenges black dead, do they, less it is their own weird gods? Or maybe the Maroons—some bands of them are pretty vengeful on the whites. No, they'll go back; I think they want to. If they die there, as well die there as anywhere, and there's rich pickings to be had if you are pitiless. I don't think they argued too hard against being sent straight back by Coppiner."

He made a quiet noise into his hand, expressing amusement, maybe. "It's me that needs to get off this vessel, sirs, before we sees Port Royal. But I think I'll get off in me shirt and breeches, to feed the fish like little Mr Shilling is, more like. The Lamonts fear me, if they fear any man, because I know their crimes and I might tell when we get safe on shore. If I go like the little snotty boy, don't let them tell you I liked swimming!"

The bell rang on the quarterdeck, at the con, and men began to change the watch. Ashdown drifted invisibly away, silent as a wraith, and the two lieutenants moved aft to join ship's life. So now they knew, they thought, how Groat had died, and knew for sure they could do naught about it. They both felt warmth and admiration for the quiet Irish man, and hoped that he would run at the Azores. With that in mind, indeed, they both dropped hints to Captain Kaye next morning, then at dinner, too. Some men were showing signs of scurvy, they suggested, the store of wine was looking awful low, some fresh meat, newly killed, would grace the captain's table very well.

But for all the purser, Black, sulked and cajoled to back them up, Kaye was adamant. The wind was fine, the speed was good, the prospects excellent. Whatever they should think—or anyone—the ship was cracking on.

■ ■ ■

To say one thing for Richard Kaye, his taste for flogging men was excellent, in sailors' terms. After the first flush, when all hands feared he would make it a daily exercise, might get the lust for screams and blood like many captains seemed to do, he scarce mentioned it again. The deed was done, a storm had come, and his second cousin's son was disappeared. If he brooded on it, he surely gave no sign. And when Will mentioned the subject, tentatively, he was indifferent. Although he did reveal his hand regarding the Azores.

"It is a messy, useless business to flog a man," he said, "and I am not convinced it has much value. That bastard shitting on the deck upset me, I must say. The blood was bad enough, but at least it does not stink. There'll be stinks aplenty in Jamaica, I should think. Why add to them?"

They were ranged upon the quarterdeck, enjoying the windward breeze, as captains and the favoured few can do. The sky was clear, horizon clearer, and the flying fish were flying to Geoff Raper's pan. Holt, who liked to dig, put in a word.

"Dan Swift would not agree with that, sir, surely? Will's uncle thinks the whip's the soul of it, don't he, Will?" Swift was Kaye's great hero, he believed, and wondered how he would respond to it. But the captain just drank wine and scratched himself.

"But Captain Swift's not here," he said. "And we ain't had a mutiny, have we? I think some men already have the taste for running, and a flogging might just make up their mind. They'll not get a chance at the azure islands, though, whatever that fat purser wants. Have you ever seen a purser that ain't fat? Is there such a breed of men?"

They laughed, and the bottle went round again, no servant pouring. Gunning, lounging in his shirt ten feet away was offered, but he declined. He drank only water these days, even at meals.

"No landing then," sighed Sam, regretfully. "Ah well. I need a whore, sir, is the long and short of it. Well, long and long, if I might boast! The Azores whores—what colour are they? Are they very fair?"

Kaye, who almost surely did not know, squawked with amusement.

"They're Portugee and fat, with moley faces and long black whiskers! Not much your style at all! If you like maids with skinny arses you'll have to wait until you reach Annette again, at Dr Marigold's. Or court my sister! She's scrawny and she's got cash as well! It will cost my father dear to get her off his hands, depend on it. Her nose would put an elephant to shame!"

"I think your sister very fine," said Sam Holt, calmly. "Her conversation is excellent, and her looks far more than adequate, at the least. And if I may make so bold, sir, what you have said is not meet in talking of a lady. Slander is slander, even in the Western sea."

Gunning, watching the log-line leading from the taffrail, lost his languidity at this, hoping for a fight, perhaps. Slack Dickie found it only charming, though.

"It is not a lady: Felicity is a *sister,*" he said. "You clearly have none, Sam, but Will will understand. I note your interest, though, sir. My father shall be informed by early post!" He barked. "If they have such thing as post out in the islands. The blacks can't read and write, for certain. I wonder if the planters can?"

The subject died, but Will was interested. Later he tackled Sam, but got a dusty answer. It had been said, he was informed, as a way of rebuking Kaye for his awful rudeness and lack of rectitude towards a female family member. Something in Sam's manner was unconvincing, though, and Bentley wondered on. The thought of "fineness" and Felicity, however, he found difficult to grapple with. Ungallant though Dick's attitude, he felt it had some merit, in despite though sad. But if not pretty, Felicity was rich, for certain. Could Sam, with all his debt, be thinking . . . And Will felt a minor twinge of shame.

Kaye, with flogging rejected as a way to smarten up his people, remained convinced his officers were right about their general lack of fitness as a force, whether the fight were contra man or elements. He raised the gun drill plan, and told them to get to it, rapidly. He still thought kicks and beating were the way, so told them to lay on the blows and threaten slackers, but Will and Sam ignored him in great part. Martinets were born not made, they knew, and whatever else his faults Slack Dickie was no martinet. He would kill you from incompetence, or lack of care, but not from vicious discipline. So they began to forge the crew the way they knew and thought was best. To this end, Henderson, the gunner, was called to confer with them, plus Taylor and Sweetface Savary, as the marine commander now was widely known. He was not a gunner, but could train them on the small arms, it was hoped. In fact, one of his soldiers, Rob Simms, was not just a marksman with the long musket (as he had proved with Shilling in the roundhouse once), but could strip the beasts like clockwork, and fettle them, and teach men how to load and aim at speed. For a soldier, Sam conceded, he was a very useful man.

The *Biter*, since her buying for the Navy, had been built up quite sturdy as a way to carry guns, although the raising of her poop and hamper gave her a tendency to tenderness that Gunning quite disliked. When they hit their first real blow, he said, "the bitch would just turn turtle with her frillies in the air," and he suggested, as a starting point to getting spry and seamanlike, the men should rearrange the guns, with more on the lowest deck and lighter ones above. Although the greatest weight of ball they carried after refit was still not above seven pound, the shifting of the guns themselves and carriages was a massive task, and served to get the men's blood pumping and sweat bursting from their skin. Taylor and Hugg and Tilley organised the seamanship—the tackles, lifts, and stoppers to sway chunks of wood and metal up and down between the decks—while Gunning and his former men prepared positions and worked out the ballast points. Then Sam and Will divided the watches into teams, six of them all told, and began it as a competition, playing off for speed, and strength and skill. The Scots, despite their clear desires, were spread around the ship, and had to fight each other for the beer and brandy prizes.

Two days of this, and all the men were leaner and much faster than before. There were broken heads and fingers, cuts and bruises, but far fewer gripes and moans. After the lifting and the hauling came training on the pieces, with Henderson a happy man at last. He had worked on many ships, but none as dull as this, he told Jem Taylor, but given time and shot and powder to expend, he'd get their firing up to a half-respectable rate. Kaye, at Sam's suggestion, put his nose into the magazine, and felt the powder and made approving noises, and exhorted men who had never packed a pudding-cloth to stuff cartridges that would give the Froggies hell. When they had piles enough, the word went round to let some off, for fun.

The crews at first were frankly hopeless, and one man, sadly, lost his hand by not clearing from a muzzle fast enough. This was spectacular, as were his screams when Grundy plunged his stump into hot pitch (he having felt no pain at all before, he said), but it gave a useful lesson, quickly learned. Others included not touching red-hot barrels or the blades of scouring worms, keeping bare feet clear of trucks (five toes lost, among three men), and not breathing in too fast when a muzzle poured out smoke, the black and massy swirling hiding red hot sparks of wad and blazing powder. Soon men stripped down to drawers, no ends or strings or tapes to catch and jerk, and wore bandannas wet across their faces, hiding mouth and nose. The decks around the carriages ran black with filth and sweat and water and thick soot. The people were in seventh heaven.

Even Slack Dickie took a lesson from it, although he complained bitterly each dinner time about the filth and stink of burnt explosive, and the taste it left on all their food, however fresh or deeply seasoned. He could not resist temptation, either, to single out men for favour and high compliment, most of all the three Lamonts. Even when one of them discharged a musket too high, and nearly killed Jack Ashdown, who was working on the foretopsail yard, Kaye managed to berate both Scot and Irishman for the "careless accident" with a flippant smile. The Scots were good at the small armament, no question, but then again there were other men their equal, probably. But their special skill was cutlass, and a knife held in the free hand, and a smile of pure fury, just controlled. Few men would take them on a second time, even with stewards standing by with singlesticks and podger bars. They were prepared to murder, not a doubt. For which the captain smiled on them—and gave them rum.

Within ten days or so, the *Biter* was a different ship in terms of fighting, and even in sailing, too. As the killing skills were honed, Will Bentley and Sam Holt worked on the other arts, the arts of seamanship, with Gunning as their mentor and their aid. He had a way with him that they grew fonder of as time went by, a way of showing, teaching, informing, without a hint of side or tendency to mock or crow at inability. His ranging eyes took in the smallest sign of wear or weakness in the gear, and he had a knack of treating seamen as his equals, which he claimed they were, while directing them, ordering them, to smarten up their ways. In all, he wanted seamen, he told Bentley seriously one afternoon. He wanted men who'd look at a spar, or piece of cordage, even a hitch, and see from yards away that there was something wrong, or a problem that might grow. He was adept at complimenting, also, making sailors glow by praising them for tasks completed, or, even better, instigated from their own initiative. He told William, quite seriously, that he had the making of a great seaman, and in small-boat work, and trimming sails and balancing, was already there. Will, dubious, checked if he had said similar to Sam—the old way, praise everyone equally, but keep them unaware—but Gunning had not. Indeed, while giving Sam advice, he had told him, also, that Bentley was a natural, a rising master of the sea.

Jack Gunning's secret, he said laughingly, when the two lieutenants questioned him one sunny afternoon beneath the friendly shadow of the course, was that he was low. Had been, was now, and always would be, and it had been his lodestar and his guide. People like Kaye, he said, whose father was a duke, could never come to anything because they were too high. They could not talk to anyone, could not think like normal men, could quite possibly not wipe their arses without help. Will had the same disease, but luckily much lower down the scale, and Holt was poor, despite he was an officer, so might survive, with luck.

"But you're not poor, Jack!" Sam said, and Will told him, "Sam's got protection! Sir A is stinking rich!"

"Which gives Sam nightmares," said Gunning, easily. "And I made my cash by lowness, did not I? I can sail a ship, and navigate, and make men jump to my command without a whit of trouble or the whip. And I ain't an officer in the Navy, nor ever will be, neither. Slack Dickie kidnapped me, and he regrets it. In time the feeling will be ten times worse."

Will glanced aft to where Slack Dickie stood, alone and upright on the windward of the quarterdeck, shaded by a small awning of white canvas. Even at that distance his isolation was sadly striking, and Will knew why it seemed so. Dick Kaye made overtures to his inferiors, which were getting more plaintive by the day. Within the lights of splendid isolation—any captain's lot—he tried to intermix, to enter into dialogue, to be easy with them, expecting something similar in return. Most signally, as Gunning was hardly an inferior, having no position in the Admiralty hierarchy, he hoped for conversation, intercourse, with him. And Gunning shunned it. Politely, without coldness, he made it obvious that Kaye was not forgiven, nor ever would be. In the cold eyes of his sailing master, his erstwhile comfortable companion, Kaye was no one any more; he might as well not be breathing the same air. Since Black Bob was become a thing of wood, a kind of zombie of cold ebony, Dick Kaye was loneliness itself.

"Well, Jack," said Holt, following Will's gaze, "I think you've chose the right way to plough the ocean tracks. With your skills, you would have been made post by age of twenty is my guess, then no one would talk to you, neither. But given you're the only man I've ever met who's glad to get to sea for once to get away from women, this ship ain't *so* bad, surely? You could be captain here quite comfortable, do not you reckon?"

Gunning grinned. "Oh, easy said, Sam, easy said. But how do you get post by mainly staying home with maids like Sal Marlor, and Flit and Becky? It's sea-time their lordships go by, is it not? And this ship's got a captain, any case—he's the problem! If it was just you two as my officers, we could have a goodly time, admitted. But if I joined the Navy, I would not be me, would I? And when you're post captains, both of you, you'll most probably be evil bastards, too. God knows, from what I hear, it's in Will's blood." He paused, and saw Will's face. He laughed, to indicate, perhaps, that he was jesting. "I'm low," he said. "And I was born low. It's in the blood, maybe, that we gets problems. Like Dick was born an idiot. It will out."

There was no doubt that as Gunning grew more popular with men and officers, Kaye was more and more put out by it. In these calm latitudes, as they plugged fast and gentle out towards the West, Kaye went for social intercourse, but grew more clearly galled by Gunning's

easiness. At table, where the gentlemen, including Sweetface and the
surgeon, were called each night to eat and drink and talk, the resent-
ment was sometimes almost open. Kaye drank heavily, Gunning not
at all; the Navy men showed deference to rank, Gunning did not; the
captain's opinions and pronouncements were heard out respectfully,
but Gunning laughed at them. And he told home-truths that Kaye
did not want to hear, at all. On health, for instance.

"There is scurvy," Gunning said. "I'm surprised, Mr Grundy, that
you have not noticed it."

Grundy, who was drinking water and was as drunk as a fiddler's
bitch, gave a startled jump and blinked, his eyes trying to focus in
Gunning's general direction.

"Beg pardon, sir?" he said. "Scurvy, did you say? Nonsense, sir.
Are you a medico?"

Christ, thought Will, he don't recognise Gunning, after all these
weeks and months.

Slack Dickie's face went taut. "Scurvy, Mr Grundy? Could this be
possible? They've had good meat enough, and bread and beer."

Grundy turned his face to Kaye, eyes swimming. He dabbed his
lips, trying to collect himself. "Scurvy?" he repeated. "Not a bit of it.
What . . . what *symptoms,* do you claim, sir?" He thought this was a
test of expertise, extremely shrewd. But Gunning roared delightedly.

"Just the usual ones! Just sitting down and falling down and lying
down, and bleeding gums and ulcer-mouth and teeth you can pull
out between your thumb and finger! They've got scurvy, man! Have
you ever been to sea? Come and smell some of my sailors' breath!
That will flare your nostrils back, I tell you! They need some fruit
and cabbage, and damn quick!"

Captain Kaye put on a stern expression.

"Mr Gunning, sir," he said. "This is offensive. You may be master here, but you do not have jurisdiction across another's field. I
take it, Mr Grundy, scurvy is not a problem on my ship?"

"Perhaps no men have come to see the surgeon, sir?" suggested
Holt, diplomatically. "For surely, if scurvy had been seen, he would
have recognised . . . ?"

Grundy was nodding.

"The main symptom is a tendency to shirk," he snapped. "It is the shirker's joy and *vade mecum*. Tell them to come to me if they've disorders or complaints, sir. I will fetch them to their toes. Short shrift, sir. That is the cure. Short shrift and ha'pence."

It looked as if Gunning might argue, but in a half a moment he moved his shoulder in a shrug.

"There's one can hardly walk," he said, laconically. "I'll shoo him down to you, shall I? I'll send him in the morning, so expect him in a week. Better, I'll tell Jem Taylor and his lads to start him down with rope and rattan, shall I? That's a lesson would be worth the watching!"

Will, who did not understand this remark, was not alone apparently, but Sam, once the meal was over, explained. Men with scurvy, he said, men with scurvy bad, got very weak and lost their grip on life. Will did not need reminding how Sam knew: his father, mother, and his little brothers had died of it in sailing to Virginia. And Sam, in the early light next morning, took a careful look among the people and confirmed Jack Gunning's diagnosis. There were several men with several signs, he said. The cure? (In reply to Will's inquiry.) Fresh provender, and land. All Grundy could achieve, should he lay hands on them, would be to hasten their release—to the grim reaper!

But luckily for all of them, especially the sick, Grundy's administrations, it appeared, would soon be redundant. According to Gunning's calculations, and his figures were matched pretty well by those of Will and Sam, they were on a latitude just south of a Jamaica landfall, and their longitude (a far less certain figuring) looked fair to being well within the Caribbean Sea, despite they had not seen any of the outer islands, the weather having been quite murky for the last few days. They had seen piles of clouds towering into the milky firmament, however, which probably denoted land beneath them, and they had caught whiffs of vegetation, sweet and musky, fresh and warm. Throughout the *Biter* there was certitude: their Atlantic crossing was almost at an end.

Bentley and his friend, keeping watch one night—together for pleasure, though one of them should have been asleep—discussed the coming landfall and what they were like to find there. The warmth and blackness of the sky, few stars through the heavy muzz, was overawing in its way, and both of them were philosophical. Will in particular felt dwarfed and vaguely saddened, despite the balmy pleasantness. He felt that he had left his land for good, and all his people.

"Christ, Sam," he said. "It's all so bloody vast it is a giant, giant world. We've been at sea for weeks and weeks; we're doing about eight knots or so. It feels as though we're running on forever."

Holt yawned. He filled his lungs, then let it out luxuriantly. "But there'll be women there," he said. "And good dry land, fresh fruit and meat and coffee, they pluck it off the bushes, did you know? There'll be fresh water, Will. That's what I miss most. I'm going to have a good, long, lovely soak. And then I'm going to find a woman. Oh God, yes!"

Will's mind turned to Deb Tomelty then, and a painful emptiness spread out, as if inside his chest. He felt a vast, dark longing in him, but felt that he was stupid, weak. How could he love her still, who had had no idea what love might really be; how could sensation remain so sharp? Months, many months, since last he'd seen her, he had thought she'd died. And if he loved her, would she still cleave to him? Most probably—ridiculous.

"I think of Deborah," he said to Sam. "I wish I did not, but I do." To make it sound less hopeless, less a question of such crushing loss, he added: "I suppose you think of Thin Annette, as well?"

"Felicity," said Sam. It slipped out unbidden, and he found it quite astonishing himself. "How strange, Will, that I should think of Dickie's skinny sister! Felicity's the Latin word for happiness, an' all, unless I've got it wrong. How very strange!"

They stood in silence for a while. The dawn was breaking astern of them. The pink flush threw lustre on the seas ahead, tingeing the black with blue. The world was very large, and they were quite alone.

In fact, they weren't alone, while at that moment the world, in terms of metaphor, was small indeed. Some miles ahead of them, on a crossing course, was a Spaniard, freighted with plate silver from the isthmus and boxes of gold coin, escorted by two *Guarda-Costa* ships, severely armed, that had latched onto her when she had been separated by the wicked weather, out of season, from the force assigned to sail with her to Spain. She was badly damaged, her escorts less so, and they were looking to reach southern Cuba and regroup with a Navy force, or put in, if need be, for repairs.

And not much further, in this small world, Deb lay in her meagre bed and thought—among, however, many other things—of Will.

TWENTY

The sun, sending its feelers to the west, revealed to Bentley and his friend a black mountain stark ahead of them, with flickering veins of white-hot fire inside it. As the sun rose, the mountain range changed shape and constitution to become a bank of cloud, made jet and silver by the play of violent lightning. It spread to north and south across their whole horizon, and climbed to heights they scarce believed. Their wind was blowing towards it, warm and almost gentle, and the sea they rode on was still smooth and undulating. Neither had seen its like before.

Gunning had, though, and he approached them silent from behind to startle them. He had a spyglass in his hand, and he was thoughtful.

"I thought the seas were lumpish in the night," he said. "It's our sea meeting his and tumbling, dost understand? Give him an hour, and ours will be running back again, towards the east. We'll maybe see some vomiting again."

The two stared for a while.

"Is it a hurricane?" asked Will. Gunning hissed breath through nostrils.

"Should not be, although it's possible. Your Carib is a weirdly place for weather, sweet and lovely except for hurricanes in season, but often with a cracker up its sleeve. It's the volcanoes, maybe. When they blow, they blow everything to buggery. Weather changes, it goes all to cock and sideways." He gave another snort. "Port Royal disappeared one fine day, you know. Not so many bloody years ago. Fell into the sea, under a wave, half the population gone, white, black, and redman, all the ships and all the brothels, all the churches, too. You'd think God might mind his own a little, wouldn't you, but he don't. When all is said and paid for, he doesn't give a shining shit."

Will, despite himself a little shocked by such unbridled blasphemy, said quickly: "I didn't know that. About volcanoes, I mean. I knew Port Royal went, of course. Two thousand killed, or more."

Gunning seemed oddly contemptuous.

"What caused the fun, then, if it weren't volcanoes? Don't you think you *ought* to know these things? You're officers, ain't you, with little bits of paper?"

Sam studied Gunning's face with interest. It seemed to him there might be something going on behind it—and wondered if it could be drink. How long since Jack had last broke out? Some weeks, some weeks . . .

"I always heard it was a judgment on such a wicked place," he said. "It was bursting at the seams with whores and pirates, so the good God put his thumb down on the lot. Maybe the priests and vicars that got hammered in their churches had their fingers in the penny pile? Or in the nuns and choirboys, even."

Gunning, though, was no longer listening. He had his spyglass to his eye and he was studying. Sam's eyes followed, as did Bentley's.

"What is it, Jack?" said Will. "I thought I saw a dash of white. Is it a sail?"

The sun was blazing ever further westward, accelerating. As the sea turned from black to royal to a greenish azure, white flashes appeared above the rolling waves, rhythmic, tantalising.

"It is a ship," John Gunning said. "Spanish by her cut, but something strange. She only has one . . . she's a clumsy galleon, but she's only got one mast. I think—"

"Another one!" said Will, whose eyes were very keen. "There is another sail, Jack! To north of her! It's . . . no, I've lost her. I—No! There she is!"

Sam, frustrated, tried to get a borrow of the telescope, but Gunning would not give. Their faces close, Holt got a whiff of liquor from the master's breath. Oy oy, he thought. Oy oy . . .

In a minute more, Gunning picked up another vessel, somewhat

astern of the other two, and decided that the biggest one had lost a
mast, or perhaps some upper yards. *Biter* was flying down the wind
towards them, though, and he observed, with quiet amusement, that
perhaps it was past time they told their lord and master.

"If she is a Spaniard," he said, "those others must be escorts,
must they not? Which argues she is a merchantman, worth guarding. There will be treasure to be took, maybe."

"Spanish?" said Sam. "We are not at war with Spain, Jack, are we?"

"You never know," said Gunning. "Nor don't you never know with
Dickie, do you? He owes money left and right, ain't no one told you
that yet? Remember my friend Campbell, young Ellen's beau? Who
do you think greased the selling of the *Biter* with the Office? Do you
think it cost Slack Dickie nothing? He owes Eddie about—"

He was cut off by a bellow from aloft. It was the lookout, up on
the main royal yard. A sail, he roared, then another, then the third.
As Kaye clambered onto deck, Will shouted, "On the bow? We have
them! Peel your eyes for any more!"

Kaye, whose face was flushed from sleep, was pointed in the right
direction, then clapped Gunning's spyglass to his eye. Will went to
weather, to the shrouds, and scuttled up two dozen feet or so. As the
light strengthened he could see the ships quite clearly. A crippled
merchantman and two smaller fighters, not lofty, but distinctive, in
the Spanish manner. It was an amazing picture, for beyond them,
a massive backdrop, the sky was black as pitch, with lightning flickering like blazing silver threads. They were close-hauled though,
and *Biter* was running easy, so all shared a wind of one direction.
Impossible to say at this stage which way the storm was making,
though, or how fast.

"That's weather damage," said Gunning, who had retrieved his
glass. "She's not been attacked. The pinks are battered, ditto. One's
got a main sail split, the other's got a jury yard. Easy pickings,
Capting, easy pickings! She'll be loaded up with jewels and silver for
the King, depend upon it. We've got the wind gage, our gunnery's the
very acme, and we need a fight to blow the farts away!"

Then, all pretence forgotten, he hauled a small flask from out an
inner pocket, and sucked liquor from it. Smiling, he offered it to

Kaye, then Sam, who refused it, too. 'Fore God, thought Sam, this could shape up a good one. They had not had breakfast yet . . .

"Mr Gunning," said the captain, stiffly. "Those ships are Spanish, as I think. We have no quarrel with them that I know. And I would thank you not to drink upon my quarterdeck."

The closing speed between the vessels was swift, and it seemed most of the people were of Gunning's mind about the protocol. The rumour spread like lightning that the big one was a treasure ship—no evidence at all except that Spaniards in the Carib "always carried treasure from the mines"—and also that she was sinking, and it would be an act of mercy to board and save her men and loot. The gunner presented himself, as if awaiting orders, and Sweetface's soldiers turned out unbidden in sweat and scarlet, standing stiff and formal and expectant in the waist. But orders came there none, save directions to the helm to ease her up to pass the trio safe to leeward, offering no hint of pugnacity at all. Knots of crewmen stood round in clear attitude of disaffection, glaring at the poop and muttering.

A voice from high above boomed down, "She's running guns out, sir! The frigate to our larboard, if that's what the Dons do call 'em. I can see men on the quarterdeck, and at the prow. She's got bow chasers, sir. They're loading them."

It was the boatswain, Taylor, leading instinctively as usual. He was high up by the main truck, clinging like a monkey. Gunning, also, was in the ratlines. It was hard to tell if he had his spyglass or his bottle in his hand.

"Coastguard," he shouted. "*Guarda-Costa*. They think all English ships are smugglers, and he'll try and board. Luff up, on the wheel there! Luff up and let him see we'll rake him if he dares."

Both Will and Sam felt general excitement, and both understood the captain's reticence full well. Foreign ships, but not the enemy. To attack would be an act of piracy, which could cause a war. They felt for him, and felt the grinding pressure from the people.

"We are a Navy ship," snapped Captain Kaye. "He will not try to board us! Hold your course!"

It was Big Angus, of the Scots, who had the helm at present, and his face and stance reflected a rare affinity with the feelings of the crew—of anger and accusation at Kaye's peaceable intentions. If up to them, they would have steered across the Spanish squadron's hawse—but Dickie would prevent it, the poltroon.

But Kaye, for once, was not for turning. He indicated to Lamont to ease the spokes, as per his earlier instruction, and raised a spy-glass to his eye, a glass he'd shouted for from Black Bob. The small, sad boy stared at the ships as if excited for a moment, then, shoulders slumping to their normal stance, turned and slunk below.

"She's flying signals," Taylor shouted. And then: "A squall, a squall! It's going to get us with its tail! Up helm and let fly all!"

As the Spanish ship broke out its signal flags, it was overtaken, then enveloped, in a murky, ragged, cloud. The black mass ahead had spread a wide, deep tentacle in an instant, surrounded still by blue sky and hot sunshine. The merchantman, if such she was, and her two snapping escorts, were swallowed completely as in a rolling plume of smoke, with grey spume and vapour flying from its edges. In the instant she became invisible, the leading gunship fired a shot, and then the *Biter* was buried in a steaming, stinging rain that was as hot as coffee from a stove. There was a thunderclap of gear, a roaring and a hurrying of men, and Slack Dickie's smartest neckcloth was plucked from off his throat and lost. Within half a minute the *Biter* was pressed down almost on her beam ends with her people, newly smart and seamanlike, swarming everywhere to most excellent purpose. The racketing of cord and canvas was like a firecracker show, but she lost no major sail and no spar of any kind. Big Angus, with the help of Ayling and Tom Tilley, wrestled with the wheel, and kept the *Biter* under command, shooting forward ever faster athwart the fetch. Gunning and Will, at a weather shroud together, watched the display with satisfaction. Gunning, indeed, raised his bottle in salute, before he emptied it and tossed it overside.

The squall was clear of them in twenty minutes, leaving the *Biter* with her decks awash in a rolling, angry cross-swell. The sun burst out, the dirty clouds shot off downwind, and within the shortest time the drying deck was lost in mist, with rainbows. Gunning bellowed to loose the brailed and clewed-up sails, tend sheets and braces, and sweat up on slackened halyards. They had a good breeze now, warm and kindly, despite it was ahead of them for fetching the Jamaica coast, and to Will the storm looked blown-out, finished. The Spaniards, moreover, seemed quite lost.

Gunning, apparently, did not agree on either count.

"Mr Kaye, sir," he shouted, exuberantly. "They fired on us, sir. I told you so! The cripple's on her own out there! I say we board her while we've got the chance!"

This caused a flurry, as neither Kaye nor any others had spotted the galleon, but Gunning, on seamanship, was rarely wrong. He climbed on to the rail, pointing ahead and half a point to leeward, and the captain lumbered after him. The sea was darker than before the squall, a writhing mass of foam-streaked rollers. Almost out of sight, on the horizon and dipping, was the single mast, with rags flying from her topmost yard.

"Higgins!" Gunning shouted to one of his former seamen from Press tender days. "You've got the peepers, man. Get up aloft and see if you can spot the others! Mr Taylor, did the stunsails all survive? Get 'em stretched again and lively, we'll run the bastard down before the storm comes up our arseholes like ten ton of bricks! Mr Black, you fat disgrace! Get me a bottle of your finest, and put it on my slate! And if the seal is broken this time, I'll tear your bollocks off!"

Black, the pasty purser, who had been fighting with Geoff Raper about a sack of flour spoiled in the squall, smiled sickly, as if he found Gunning amusing, but dared not answer back. He disappeared, and came back seconds later with the goods. Gunning broke the wax off, plucked the cork out with his teeth, and spat it overside. No need for corks when Gunning was a-drinking, said his smile. No need for corks at all.

The captain's quandary was tearing him, it was written on his face. But he struggled with his own desires.

"We will not fight them, Mr Gunning, and there's an end," he said. "We are here to aid Jamaica against the French marauders, not take on three armed Spaniards."

A knot of seamen grouped around the con made a sudden noise. An unknown voice (certainly it had no Scottish accent) uttered words that sounded like "They shot at us! They *shot!*" Big Angus Lamont stared across at the captain, and his eyes spoke volumes; they glittered with contempt. Another sailor's voice said plaintively, from out the ruck, "It's fucking treasure, mates! It's fucking *gold!*"

But it was Gunning, half drunk but crammed with subtlety and guile, who played the clinching card.

"God bless your soul, sir," he said silkily. "I don't mean fight *all* of them. You say three, sir, but I see only one. It blew like seven bells, sir, and it will again, I promise you; we're in the tropics and I *know*. They're scattered, and the cripple's left behind. They went downwind, and we went athwart it. They'll have to claw up to it, and up to us, if they can do it and if they dare to. In the meantime, Mr Kaye, sir—we've got a sitting duck."

There was a cheer, started by the Scotsmen, and taken up by many throats, and as if to settle it, Silas Ayling roared down from the eagle's nest that the "big 'un" was the only ship in sight.

"She's lumbering!" he shouted. "She's like a bleeding sow! Not one full sail upon her left untorn! We can run her down in half an instant, sir!"

"A quarter!" roared Ed Higgins, upping the bet from his slightly lower perch below the fore-truck. "Let me take her, Jack Gunning, and you can trim the sails! We'll show these Navy lily-boys how it's done!"

Jack's former crew roared their backing for this idea, and Kaye's originals, whose loyalty to Slack Dickie was suddenly beyond question under this absurd attack, whooped their own defiance. Men came streaming off the yards to deck without instruction and took up stations to handle tacks, sheets, and braces. Ed Higgins slid down a hundred feet like lightning and then dashed aft to take the wheel (which Angus made clear he'd have to fight him for), while the gunner, Henderson, called his mates and favoured crews to open ports, clear decks, and get the powder up, instanter. All this without an order or a word from Kaye or any officer. Bentley, indeed, was struck with amazement and amusement the way the ship was galvanised. She and her people had a mind and spirit all their own to fight and take the treasure ship, and her lord and captain was simply a part of it, not the brain. Will was fascinated to see what Kaye would do. Spain, for God's sake, was not a *bona fide* enemy.

Slack Dickie—on whim or goldlust, who would ever know?—threw in his lot with the rolling tide. Remarkably, he played his game with shrewdness and élan.

"A sitting duck!" he roared. "Aye, a fat duck for the taking, too! They fired on us, on a warship of His Majesty. Our duty is to teach the Dons their folly! Mr Gunning, you are our sailing master, give chase with all dispatch, I beg of you."

They cheered him to the echo this time, both factions giving voice as one, and lieutenants Holt and Bentley went to work to weld them as a single team, to solder up the splits. Taylor and his mates were called and given their instructions, Sweetface Savary spoke earnestly with Kaye upon the quarterdeck, and Mr Henderson spoke to his keenest crews as man-to-man, while cajoling the rest. In a half an hour, *Biter* was scurrying down the breeze under everything she had to spread, with all guns charged and ready to run out, her upper ports already open. The sky was largely blue by now, enormous, with only high white clouds racing overhead. Captain Kaye, indeed, thought to open up the lower ports, to bring the guns to bear the instant they were layable, but Gunning shook his head, and took a long pull at his bottle.

"You look to sink her, do you, sir?" he said, insolently. "Ah well, she's yours to play with, when all's said." He jerked his head towards the sky to windward. "D'you not see that? Another squall is coming, by and by. Perhaps the whole damn storm is blowing up again. So open them and bravo, that's the style. And hope."

Gunning, to those who knew him, was clearly drunk. His face was rosy, his lips were curving wetly in a dangerous smile. His curly hair was somehow wilder than the normal run, his bright eyes brighter, his good humour tinged with sharp aggression. He held a bottle by its neck, open and defiantly, and swigged at ever shorter intervals. His whole attitude was scornful; each time he lit upon a face of Navy officer, his eyes gleamed certain insolence. How long, Will wondered, before he was incapable? It was dependent on the time he started; the process was inexorable. If this was day one, great trouble seemed to lie ahead.

Holt said mildly: "Is that a jest, Mr Gunning? The sky is like a sunny day at Beachy Head. Do you really mean the dirty weather is still stalking us?"

Before Gunning could make up his mind to give a friendly answer or spit blood, a man dropped from the lower ratlines of the weather main shrouds and lay crumpled on the deck. All three Navy officers, plus Gunning, were on the quarterdeck, all four of them were astonished. Then Tilley, standing nearby to the man, moved up to him and pushed him with his foot.

"Tilley!" snapped Bentley. "What do you there? Is that man drunk, or ill?"

Grundy, strangely, who had been in the mainmast shade, moved to the seaman, unsteady but determined. He crouched over him and pulled his face up to the light. Bentley noticed blood around the nose.

"What ails him?" he called, approaching.

"He is shirking, sir," said Grundy. "Shirking for a guinea."

Tilley made an expression at the surgeon's head. He said to Will: "It's Abel Phillips, sir. He has the scurvy."

"Shit on scurvy!" cried the surgeon. "He is lying down!"

"He dropped off the ratlines," Tilley told Bentley. "He can hardly stand. He does naught but drink. Won't eat."

"Is he hurt? Did he fall far?"

Grundy shouted: "I can smell the brandy!"

This begged an answer, for so could Will and Tilley—off of him. Then Gunning took a hand, then Kaye.

"Of course he is not drunk," sneered Gunning. "He's not a King's man, is he? He is one of my boys, and they can hold their liquor. He has been ruined by the food on here. I would not feed a pig on it. He's dying, Capting, and it's you and Pusser Black have done for him."

Kaye, prodded beyond endurance, perhaps, by such unremitting

disrespect, bellowed: "The man is drunk! The man is an arrant idler!
Send him to the royal yard immediately! He is our lookout for three
watches straight!"

Gunning said cheerfully: "How will he get there, Capting, if he
cannot climb?"

"And you are impudent!" cried Captain Kaye. He moved across
the deck, as if to strike or kick the fallen man, then thought better
of it. "Tilley! Start him, man! Get him on his feet! Whip him up the
rigging, instantly!"

"And when he falls out, bury him," said Gunning. "Christ help
us, I need another drink. Black! You pasty bastard! Black, where are
you, fat-arse thief?"

Grundy was pulling ineffectually at Phillips, and Tilley, with a
shrug, put in a kick or two, without much heart in it. The man, blood
trickling from his nose to lips, pale and blotchy, with a fat tongue in
his mouth, was hauled and helped till he was upright, when Tilley
called a man across with water, and gave him to drink, and poured
the residue, quite gently, over his face. When Kaye had wandered,
falsely casual, off the deck and Grundy had been wooed and shooed
away by Bentley, Phillips was guided down into the 'tween decks,
where his friends might aid him if they could. He would have to go
aloft, though. Will and Sam, for all their disapproval, could see there
was no way out of that.

The time it took to run down on their prey was short, but even
in that interval they could tell Gunning's prediction on the weather
would be right. Out of the blue sky astern of them, high white fronds
of clouds came speeding overhead, thickening and twisting like a villain's fingers reaching for their neck. Below the fingers was a bar of
iron-black, its top hard and definite as a ruler made of ebony. As the
first movements on the surface caught up and overtook them, the
easy rolling swell got shorter and more lumpish. The *Biter*, stretched
to capacity by her canvas, began to plunge and labour. Overall began
a hum of vibrating cordage, which rose rapidly in pitch.

"When Gunning's drunk he'll overstrain her," Sam said, laconically. "What do we do? Give orders to reduce, or call the captain, or
keep mum until the sticks go overside?"

It was tempting to watch stubborn men go pigheaded to disaster, but not an option when the cards were down. Bentley shouted: "Mr Taylor, boatswain's mates! Why do you wait to get it off of her? Baines there! Call up the captain, lively now! Jump!"

Gunning's big face took on a twist, but he was not a fool, for all his wildness when in liquor.

"I've got you up to spitting range of her," he muttered, as he stumped towards the hatch. "If it's gunnery and stuff like that, I'm going to take my drink below and let you get along with it. I cannot bear to watch Slack Dickie's seamanship."

They were indeed quite close, and the speed was almost critical. As Kaye came onto deck, Tilley led Abel Phillips out from down below and took him to the main shrouds, to weather. Other men were gathering, waiting the order to reduce the canvas, and which specific sails. Phillips could have an easy climb if he went now, with mates to help him on the way.

Sam, on a nod from Kaye, was passing orders to the boatswain, calls were shrilling, and soon the yards and rigging swarmed with men. Will, at a sign, joined his captain at the weather, and they studied the great Spaniard. She was lumbering and her decks were chaos. There were soldiers, but not a lot of them, and sailors, cows and sheep and pigs. Up aloft, on unsecured yards, were rags and fronds of canvas, swinging blocks, and five sails, baggy at the leeches, not bowsed up block-to-block. Even Kaye was unimpressed.

Bentley said: "Where are her people, sir? Good heavens, there are more porkers than masthead hands. There should be hundreds. What is going on?"

"They'll be skulking," said Kaye, crisply. "You know the Spanish cowards. They'll be hiding down below."

As if in answer, there came a flash beneath the Spanish taffrail, then a dull bang as smoke went pouring off to leeward. A lucky shot or natural brilliance, but the heavy ball passed close indeed, growling and droning as it tore a passage through the air.

"Aye, sir," said Will, dryly. "Cowards indeed. Shall we return it? We're close enough. Perhaps he wanted to vouchsafe us with a ranging shot?"

Kaye had good grace enough to grin and raised his hand to the gunner, who was waiting eager as a dog.

"When you're ready," said the captain. "Stop her, dismast her, anything you like. But if you sink her, Mr Henderson—I will murder you!"

Gunning, too drunk to miss the fun, burst onto deck at this point and went to give instruction at the wheel. He gazed aloft, assessing the sails Sam had chosen to bring down or douse or furl, and found no problem worthy of the comment. The wind was freshening by the second, but *Biter* was snug enough. Her decks, though, were still dancing and heaving in the rising sea, and gunnery would be a lottery. Compared with her, the galleon was like a stone-built fortress on dry land. At a cable's length, or a little more, she took advantage of it. Along her starboard side there was a clutch of flashes, blown smoke, flat bangs, and on *Biter*'s larboard, tense men clenched their teeth involuntarily. This time the gunnery was not so lucky, though. Will heard no screeching buzz, noted nil damage to men or fabric of the ship, and saw but one single plume of water—that might have been a ball hitting a wave, or might have merely been a breaking crest. On the *Biter*'s deck a cheer went up.

"Come on!" Kaye shouted to the gunner. "He'll think we have no heart for it! Fire, God damn you!"

Some of the gunners took Kaye's spleen as an order, overriding Henderson's lack of one by nature of the thing. Others, Will guessed, chose to pretend to think so, to show the captain what a fool he was. Whatever was the truth of it, seven guns fired in a quick succession, and seven balls sank without trace about a hundred feet off *Biter*'s side, at an angle to plunge them to the depths. As she rolled to starboard and the deck rose level, the remaining cannon fired to better effect with at least three balls striking home. One struck a gun; they saw a barrel pitch into the air and then crash down. After that the Spanish ship loosed off a half a dozen more, which missed, and then there was silence. Gunning, off his own bat, shouted he was taking her about, which made good sense in view they were still making too much way, and would shoot past in half a minute. Also, they would be bow-on when the Dons let fly again and would be hard indeed to hit.

The manoeuvre went like clockwork in every department. Tacks and sheets were raised, braces stamped out at terrific speed, and her head went through almost without hiatus. At the same time, Henderson and his gunners, as smart as were the seamen at their tasks, prepared the guns for a second broadside, then reloaded the larboard pieces as the ship plunged round. Henderson had pulled men off the main gun deck because the sea was gone atrocious by this time, and the lower ports would probably stay closed unless they had a lull. The Caribbean might be warm, but on present form it could kill as easy as the Western Ocean. In any way, the Spanish ship seemed disinclined to fight.

As *Biter* filled upon the other tack, her starboard guns came round to bear in smart succession, and as they ranged they spoke. There were four strikes this time, and a ten-foot stretch of bulwark was beat down. Through it, most bizarrely, a line of screaming hogs came running, to plunge and thrash and disappear beneath the driven foam. Madly, a soldier with a long musket stood in the gap and aimed and fired—Will saw the flash and smoke—then threw his musket to the deck in anger.

"I'll wear her, sir," roared Gunning, in a delirium of excitement. He swung his bottle in an arc while shouting at the helmsman, "Up, up, up, damn you! We'll get the other broadside in!"

The wind was rising like a thing gone mad, but as the brig spun off it, Taylor and his new-trained seamen played her and her complex of thrashing sails and cordage as a master plays an orchestra. She turned in a pirouette, yards were swung and braced, tacks, sheets, and bowlines hardened home, and more sails doused and quieted. Henderson was ready as his new side came to bear, and five more balls slammed home into the Spaniard, from closer this time, in through gun-ports, across decks, spreading blood and consternation. But none below the waterline, thought Will. Good man, Mr H, good man. She will live to yield her treasure up.

Their fire-rate, compared with what the bigger ship could do, was clearly devastating. They could see men sweating at the Spanish pieces, and they could almost feel their shock at the weight of iron this lightweight Britisher could hurl at them. Men were seen abandoning the guns and running to the larboard, out of sight, although the soldiers kept up a ragged fire, way out of range. Then, as *Biter* loosed off yet another cannonade, two big guns, low down near the waterline, belched smoke and iron from the foreigner, and both balls struck giant hammer-blows, causing the *Biter* to stumble like a racing bull struck down. Sam Holt and Bentley, side by side at that instant, almost lost their footing, and took each other's arms.

"Christ," said Sam. "No more of those please, Pedro. You're meant to run away!"

But the Spaniards, for whatever reason, had shot their last of heavy metal. There was a general scattering on the decks, and suddenly a cry came down from *Biter*'s watch position on the main topmast cap. It was Phillips, whose voice, though thin and shaky, could still convey excitement.

"They're running, sir!" he yelped. "They're going in a cutter, overside! They're abandoning the ship!"

This caused new chaos on the deck, with seamen scurrying and whooping randomly. Hugg and Tilley laid about them with a purpose, while Taylor despatched some "better men" to be the *Biter*'s eyes. The captain, desperate to see, jumped on the rail once more, clutching at a hammock net to stop him going overboard, and attracted an instant hail of Spanish musketry.

"They still need working on, our lads," Holt said dryly to Will Bentley. "Not one of them can keep at post, and the captain leads the silliness, as usual. Look—they're cocking up their main yard for a crane. For want of better, I suppose. *Faute de mieux.*"

"Lay off!" yelled Gunning to the seamen at the wheel. "We'll be in stays, you bastards! We want to reach her, not go arsewards all to hell!"

"Mr Henderson!" roared Captain Kaye. "The bow chasers! Lay into her with those, man! I want the bastards stopped!"

On board their target, work was going on apace. The main yard cocked, the main course clewed and thundering, they saw the bulwarks of the cutter rise into view. They had a heavy tackle on it, which argued lack of manpower, and as yet no one had boarded, but were guiding it overside with ropes and podgers. Then the big ship rolled, and they lost their view of her deck. They heard halloos, though, and guessed their meaning, quickly confirmed when she rolled back the other way. The cutter had been launched from off the bulwarks, and men had swarmed on board of her. Short stubby mainmast was going up already, and grew a big tan sail in moments. Then a little mizzen, this sail white. They were full and pulling, sheeted home.

"Hah!" yelled Kaye. "The bastards! They've took the treasure for a guinea! Mr Holt! Mr Bentley! Mr Gunning! We must after them! We must launch boats!"

"Dickie's bedlam," Sam said quietly. "How much treasure have they got in that? Has he seen the weather yet? Has he even looked at the horizon?"

On the Spaniard, something else was happening. Men were running at the bulwarks, climbing up, waving their arms and shouting. Some were trying to attract their own cutter, others were screaming at the English ship. Yet more were at the smaller boats on deck, apparently to ready them to launch. As Will puzzled, a half a dozen of the men dived overboard on the far side. Then the big ship rolled and men jumped off towards the *Biter,* from this side. The seas by now were boiling. He saw arms and heads for moments, then most went from view. From afar he thought that he heard screaming.

"Christ, Will," said Sam, "what are they *doing?*" There was a flash, a whoosh of grey-blue smoke and sparks, a thud that rolled across the intervening sea. Sam was answered.

"They're scuttling," said Will, and his voice was low with shock. "Good God, Sam. Look at all those men on board. Good God, we've got to save them!"

Kaye was beside them then, and almost beside himself with fury. He was screeching out abuse and spraying spittle. "Save them, the bastards? Save them? We've got to save the ship; we've got to get on board and put the fires out! Gunning! Lay on to her! Henderson, rake the decks! Shoot the bastards if they try to board us. Shoot them in the water!"

"Boarding party!" shouted Sam. "Taylor, gather up some men! Hugg! Tilley! Choose your people! Get small arms from the gunner's mates! Mr Savary! Where are you, man! Where is Mr Savary!"

Savary appeared, in full uniform and smart, followed by his three men, in full fig. The effect was spoiled rather when one of their hats blew off in a gust from round the mast to go flying overside, but they looked like soldiers, no argument. Most of the opposition, though, on the Spaniard, had sadly disappeared.

Captain Kaye was roaring. "I want to ram her, Gunning! At least to lay along her, double quick. Can we grapple? I want to get my men on board and strip her of her cargo! Get up to her, man, get up to her!"

Gunning, drunk as a lord, was laughing with delight. He was waving his drinking arm about, endangering his helmsmen's lives with the black bottle, essaying little dancing steps as the quarterdeck went skew.

"She's on fire, man!" he shouted. "When the magazines go she'll blow up like a bomb! And us alongside of her? Christ, we're in a squall! It's getting tasty! Aye, I'll lay along her if you want to lose your shrouds, and then your masts, and then the lot when all her powder blows! If it's suicide you're after, Capting, then we're your men, eh boys?"

Smoke was pouring from the Spaniard's hatchway—or perhaps a hole torn in the deck—but there was a marked lack of flames and fire so far. Bentley, assessing it as a sailing problem, considered Gunning right on every count. The Spanish ship was rolling fit to die, sliding beam-on to the seas with no one, presumably, at the helm. If *Biter* went along her, she would be crushed and smashed up by the roll, and she'd lose her masts inevitably. As to boarding her by boats—well, madly dangerous, as the sea went madder by the minute, but do-able if needs must. What for, though? They could not take off treasure in the open boats, and soon she would blow up.

"We need the boats to save the men, sir!" he shouted at Slack

Dickie's face. "There's a dozen of them in the sea, sir! Twenty! I'll launch the yawl! Mr Gunning, heave her to!"

"Fuck the men!" screeched Dickie. "The sharks can save 'em! Fuck heaving-to! Gunning, do your duty! Ram if you have to! I want that treasure off!"

Big John laughed harder, but he gave no orders that would heave her to or close up to the galleon. He was hauled hard on to the wind, spilling it from almost every sail, almost every leech ashake. The *Biter* punched and juddered, hurling spray across her deck from bow to stern, and men stood about, uneasy. They could not hear it, but they knew some row was going on. They were waiting for a resolution.

Angus, though, would wait no longer—and would do the captain's bidding. Shockingly, the Scotchman ran onto the quarterdeck as if invited, and bellowed something in Kaye's ear that Bentley did not catch. Kaye, startled, said something back, and looked aft to where the brothers, and a knot of other men, stood round the lightest cockleshell, which was the captain's dandy skiff. As Angus arrived, they lifted it and swung it neatly onto the bulwark cap, then flung it bodily onto a rising wave. They had prepared it, unnoticed among the clutter on the deck, and jumped on and off the rail like monkeys, getting into her. The lifting sea slid back, the oars were out, and on the instant the skiff was dancing on the crests, as light and buoyant as an empty brandy bottle. In her were the three Scotch brothers, a man called Dusty Miller, who had once fought with them and later had palled up, and little muscle-barrel Morgan, who hated everybody because he'd been torn off from his wife, and loved to fight and bully, which made him a natural in their company. They did not bother with a mast and sail, the wind was now so hectic, but they lifted her across the seas like whalemen on the chase.

"They will board her for me!" Kaye said to William, triumphantly. "They will take her as a prize and douse the fire. We will hold station till this squall blows out!"

"We must save the Spaniards!" said Will, and Holt, joining them, added his weight. Two boats were ready, he told the captain, and their crews would stand the danger. Kaye looked aloft, ignoring him.

"Where away the Spanish cutter? Ho! Man aloft there! Where away the bumboat?"

The thin cry drifted down, "Dead to l'ward, sir! And making heavy weather of it! I think she's filling!"

Then there were shouts and cries from forward, as *Biter*'s second boat was launched. As it hit the sea it was turned turtle by the back-wash from a wave, and five men went roaring overside. Bentley shot off to help his men, as ropes were thrown for them to grab, and oars and handspikes were used to keep the yawl from smashing into *Biter*'s side. Holt, his own boat safe on deck with Tilley looking on, was scanning the water near the Spaniard to see if he could spot swimming survivors. While Kaye had mind on other things: like profit.

"It's going out!" he said. "God, Holt, I think the fire has gone out! There's too much water going down!"

Certainly the flames and smoke had died. There was a wisp or two, but diminishing, not on the increase as it should have been. Seas were breaking across the galleon as she rolled, with white water visible when she presented her deck to vision from the *Biter*. They could see the sea in lumps, going pouring down the hatchway. If the bomb had been put underneath it, then it was in the swim indeed. And the dandy skiff was fast approaching. They were close enough to see the oarsmen pause, reach overside, and haul at something. One Spanish seamen, then another, was dragged in. In the *Biter*'s waist, a few men cheered. Sailors were sailors, anywhere. You saved them if you could.

"I hope the Scotch are armed," Kaye gritted. "If those bastards try to fight." He grunted. "Nay," he added. "Not against Big Angus they won't fight. The Lamont boys will kill them all."

"Save them just to kill them," Sam said lightly. But he thought, grimly: please God not, that's all.

Gunning came rolling up to Kaye, still in a high good humour, his curls plastered to his dome, mouth slack and red.

"Well, Capting! Shall we chase his little cutter, eh? You've got a good crew on board the prize, almost, and I can't get much nearer if you want to stay afloat. Or shall we send young Willie, when he's fished his yawl out of the drench? He's a good hand in a lickle scudder, he could catch him—if he's got a week!"

Dick Kaye was in a turmoil. He did not want the cutter to escape, for he was sure she had the best part of the loot on board, the gems and stones and sacks of doubloons, too. But if he chased her in the *Biter,* the galleon would be lost in probability—and she was likely packed with solid silver, in the Spanish way. If they left her, they might refind her, or might not. The weather was exceeding dirty, and night must sometime fall. Will, the yawl recovered at no greater cost than a seaman's rupture and a few lost teeth or so, was hurrying towards them.

"Mr Bentley, can you catch her, sir?" demanded Captain Kaye. "It is a long chase but a necessary. Or"—turning to Jack Gunning—"would it be quicker if we on board here clapped on sail and chased? What time is left? How much will she carry in this gale?"

Will said, "The cutter is two times faster than my yawl, sir. My yawl could carry but a wisp in this. I'd never catch her."

"Ha ha," cried Gunning. "A quandary, Capting! A quandary! What's it to be from Providence today? All debts paid off, or lose the lot! How much canvas will she carry? How much are you prepared to risk!"

Kaye's face, indeed, Will found remarkable. It was contorted with a wild desire, or a need. His earlier reticence at the illegality of fighting with this ship seemed swept away by mad determination. And Gunning was mocking him. Openly, and with a drunken joy.

"Oh, it's such a lot to gain or lose!" he said. "Capting, what will our friend Eddie say? It is a quandary!"

Then Taylor, exploding from the hatch ten feet away, shouted, "Sir! We're making water, sir! Those shots we took have started her! The ship is flooding."

And Gunning roared, as if in full command: "Oh, man the pumps, you bastards! What a lovely tub! Oh, what a lovely, lousy arsehole of a tub! Man the handles! *Pump!!*"

TWENTY-ONE

As Deb's ship had sailed into the harbour of Jamaica on a pleasant, aromatic breeze, her heart had lifted with a sensation not unlike cautious joy. Kingston town was sprawling, ramshackle as seaports are, but the whiteness of the houses and the blazing greenness of the land behind was tonic after near three months at sea. Despite herself, she searched along the wharves and moles and outer buoys for Navy ships, and somehow felt she would not be surprised to see Will Bentley waiting for her, absurd though that might be. There were none, naturally, and he was not. The Squadron was at sea as usual, ranging far to windward in case the French fleet ever came. But it had been a fantasy, is all, so Deb was not cast down.

That started when they came up to the main dock wall, which already held two merchantmen. So far her view of the West Indies had been pleasantness indeed—warmth and weather such as she had never known, and scented, spicy air, even out of sight of land. But as they passed the two unloading ships towards their packet berth nearer the middle of the town—passed very slowly, under sweeps with sails clewed up—her eyes and nostrils were assailed with choking suddenness. It was shit she smelled, tons of it, mounds of it, rivers of it pumping across the decks from out the bilges down the sides, as the ship that had been offloaded of its cargo began the end of voyage clean-out. And on the other ship she saw bodies—but still alive and standing on their feet—black men and women and some children, most naked but some in caked and putrid rags. Some faces, though alive, looked dead, some were contorted, some shed tears. Round necks and wrists and ankles they wore chains.

"Slave ships," said Captain Harding, at her side. "Thank your lucky stars, eh, maid? Thank your lucky stars."

The slave wharves led on to the marketplace, a mud arena of pens and auctioneers' small pulpits, which was fairly crowded at this time, with wagons, traps, and gigs manoeuvring like a market day at home. It shocked her that she thought of Stockport then because it was not beasts on sale today, but human beings, and she had a harsher pang, of shame and pity, that they had been brought to this. They were not animals, whatever some might say, and even at a distance, even despite the filth and reek, she saw bodies fine and muscular, men and women of amazing tallness among the normal run, and eyes that seemed to snap with pride and fire.

Deb, however hard she found it, with whatever trepidation she anticipated the next few hours or days, did not foresee the things that happened next to her. She felt pity for these people, certainly, but an expectation, knowledge absolute, that such things, such degradations, were naught to do with her. She was to be a servant, a five-year servant, with indentures, a place in house, and benefits in cash, a little land perhaps, when that time should be served. But once the ship was moored up alongside and the captain—without farewell—had left to see his agents or his offices, she found herself sweating in the marketplace, in the care of the first mate, the skinny man from Redruth with a glinting eye. Deb knew that he had been slighted by her indifference, but had no idea he would hold that to her disadvantage as a way of getting back. But now he smiled a certain smile, and Deborah was uneasy.

"Mr Godfrey," she said, politely. "What happens now? I do hope I don't have to find a situation for myself?"

He found this delicious. She was like a chicken to the slaughter. And he would make some guineas from her, also. Better than swiving, even—however lovely she might be.

"Nay, surely not," he said. "You need me to make a transaction for you, med, and I am almost famous for it. See over there? Where those gentlemen are standing, upwind of the nigger pens? That's where the lucky white folks go to be sold."

His smile grew nastier as Deb digested this. But she could accept it as an ugly fact; she had known that Mistress Maybold was not doing it for charity. In fact, Laetitia had paid Captain Harding ten pounds "to take the harlot off my hands" in England, and Harding, a business brain, had sold her on to his first mate for thirty, which was the normal rate, but made the deal for Harding rather wondrous—forty pound profit, except for food and drink and bedding on

the voyage, which was infinitesimal. Now young Godfrey—also on
the up and up—was confident of getting thirty-five with little argument, plus the piquancy of vengeance, and could hardly wait. Across
the square he had seen the vilest planter on the island and had
known Miss Snooty's fate was sealed. From a proper, upright owner
he might have pushed the price to thirty-seven, maybe forty, with a
maid as fair and young and strong as Deborah, but Alf Sutton was
mean, and hungry, and had two hungry sons. At thirty-five he would
swallow her like a shark. He would take her even if he did not need
a female servant.

In fact, Alf Sutton always needed servants, and wanted females
even more. When Alf had come from Yorkshire many years before he
had had a wife, called Anne, a baby daughter, and no sons. He had
brought out money raised by like-minded yeomen and some rising
artisans in his parish on the edge of Halifax, made glassy-eyed by
tales of golden grass and sugar cane that grew to six-foot piles of
cash. Sutton had a mind and chin like granite, and had torn farm-
land out of Pennine uplands as few other men had had the strength
to do. Papers were signed, which said that when he made his fortune, profits would accrue back in his homeland. He lied, and the
men who'd given him the money lost it all. It was put round that
Alf had died, as had his wife, in sad reality, two months after arriv-
ing in Jamaica, but even those who did not believe it knew that they
had no redress. Go out there and be killed, by Alf, or fever, or the
savages? They were Yorkshiremen. They learned and knuckled down.

Being bluff, and strong, and unafraid of any man, Alf Sutton had
done very well in Jamaican society of that time. There were already
well-established towns, but years of piracy and buccaneering had left
it a dangerous and unlawful place. The Navy and the military, brought
out originally to fight the Dutch and French and Spaniards for the
easy wealth the western islands represented when the natives had
been killed or shifted, finally brought some sort of order, first by sea
then on land—a sort of order ripe for exploiting by ruthless, uncaring men. Sutton had obtained his first plantation by helping black
slaves to slaughter its rightful owners, leaving it as derelict, then won
position in white society by slaughtering those blacks.

In remarkably short order he had gained another wife, who had died in childbirth, and then a third. She had been forced into marriage by her family, borne Alf his second son, then had run away. Jamaica was a wild and trackless place, and thousands of black slaves had run over the years, to become Maroons high in the mountains where white men did not go. White women either, it was assumed, but Ivy Sutton's body was not found, nor was she ever seen again. He did not care. He had had her, taken money off her father, and had got a son. Slave women could be forced, but he did not speak their language, and they were often sullen and ungrateful. White servants could be bought for three or five or seven years, but ran away. One, pregnant by him or either of his sons, once hanged herself.

When Sutton saw Deb Tomelty with Godfrey, he knew his God was in his heaven after all. He had dealt with Captain Harding and his mate before—usually for contraband—and he knew they understood him well. Godfrey he admired as a rat, and guessed the whole sad picture (correctly) as they walked across. The other planters— low like Sutton, not gentlemen-colonials at all—could see by Alf's hard eyes that he would have this girl, so did not even pause to dream if they could try. All saw her bold eyes quail as she took in the picture, which amused them mightily. A maid of brain and spirit! Now there'd be some sparks!

Deb said, low, to Godfrey before they had arrived: "I do not like what I can see here, Mister. If I have a choice in this, I would go somewhere else."

Sutton was in his sixties, and squat and brown, and not unlike a toad. As she approached, his mouth came open, displaying broken teeth and coated tongue, which slipped out to lick his upper lip in deep appreciation.

"You do not, of course," said Godfrey. "Why, you foolish thing!"

Beside her, to the right, Deb could see crowds of filthy blacks being herded into pens containing open horsetroughs by men with whips and clubs. Other men, black men, held buckets and long canes, which whistled as they flew to cut black backs. There was whooping as the wash-down started. It occurred to her the slaves would need to look their best to fetch a price, even in this savage land. It sickened her, for many subtle reasons. She looked at the toad who'd be her master and felt sicker yet.

"Mr Godfrey!" he said. "Well met, sir. Sir, tha must read minds indeed. That is just the very thing for me, just what I wanted. How much?"

Deborah could not believe her ears. And then again, she could. His accent was country Yorkshire, which made her jump with recognition, and his attitude took her back to the Pennines, ditto.

"Tha mebbe fain fer't bah me, but tha winna get thee knob in me, owd mon," she said. "Keep tha dirty leerin' to thasen."

The planters all around them goggled, then laughter burst from many throats. Alf Sutton did not laugh, he scowled. He stumped forward up to Deb as if he would hit her, and Deb, eyes flashing, stood her ground. Inside though, her guts had turned to water. She knew this kind of man, Christ, how she knew them. If he got her into his household, she was done.

"Tha cheeky mare," he said. "When we get home there'll be a whipping, lass. Mr Godfrey. Two pound off for that. I'll gi' thee thirty, not a penny more."

Godfrey said easily: "It's thirty-five, sir, depend on that. They say that them as spits do shag the best. She'll be a marvel once you've tamed 'er."

"Tek it or leave it, lad," said Sutton. He drove his stick into the dirt. "Thirty pound and not a farden over. Shake or go, 'tis all the same to me. Thirty-five, for a three-year servant! Bollocks, lad."

Godfrey was smiling, as were all the neighbours. Job done, they knew. No one had mentioned three years: Sutton's escape route.

"Well, let's say seven then," said Godfrey. "Shall we, sir? Thirty-five for seven year. Ar God, you drives a pretty bargain, don't 'ee?"

Deb's head was buzzing. The heat, the flies, the screams and reek that wafted in the throbbing sun towards her, made her think her brain would burst.

"Seven years?" she gasped. "But I'm not up for seven! I am a five-year one. I signed in . . . I signed in . . ."

"Indentures," Godfrey finished for her. "Indeed you did, med, proper job. I've got 'em in my pocket. Want to read 'em, do 'ee? Oh,

I forgot, you cannot read, can you?" He flourished papers. He pointed with a stubby finger. "Seven years, see that? It goes across, then slashes down, and that says seven, don't it? It's a proper job, is that. 'Tis legal."

Alf Sutton said: "With a tongue on thee like that, lass, tha'll not last seven, 'appen. I'll brek thee neck for lip. I winna shag thee, lass; I've got better pigs than thee to do it wi'. But I've got two sturdy sons who will, eh lads? Right bastards Seth and Little Ammon, innot they? They'll fuck owt."

His bold companions nodded in amused agreement, tinged possibly with civilised regret. Deb knew she'd lost the argument, the fight, the war, and possibly her life. Beyond the harbour she could see the rising hills, clad in verdant, violent green, and shimmering as the sun struck down on them from the cloudless, enormous heavens.

"Tha may stretch eyes till they do go blind, lass," said Sutton, with contempt. "Tha'll get no joy up theer. We've got bloodhounds on this island, two legged ones and four. When our niggers run, our other niggers run them down for us. When our women run, we lets the blackhounds keep 'em."

In desperation, Deb turned to the ship's mate.

"Mr Godfrey. Sir." Her voice was almost breaking till she mastered it. "This cannot be, sir; this is akin to rape. I have connections, sir. There is a Navy officer. He is in these islands. I give you warning, sir. It is across the law."

Alf's eyes, and those of his planter friends, might have changed at this, but Godfrey, through his master Captain Harding, had been clearly briefed. The young mate threw back his head and laughed.

"Spithead Nymph!" he said. "Mr Sutton, she knows Navy officers aplenty, and the Jolly Jacks an' all. She's a Portsmouth harlot, sir, a prostitute of Point, a Broad Street bitch! Med," he added, "you should thank providence that you're a servant now. For you'll get bed and board and payment, if you shags or no!"

"Payment!" said Sutton, his sense of humour cut. "Who says payment? Not even whores—"

"It is a nothing, sir," interrupted Godfrey. "It's in the contract, merely, and the contract shall be yours on payment as agreed. In any way, the harlot cannot read, can her? If it said she had to service horses she'd be bounden, don't you see? Do you want the horses serviced, sir?"

Humour was back again.

"Mules and geldings is all I use," said Sutton. "Mules do more work, and stallions are too much fratch; they fright the niggers. Too many stallions on our spread, any case. Me and Seth and Little Ammon do the serving, don't tha know!"

The men, it seemed, had time to talk forever, but Deb was wilting. She felt—she hoped—that she might fade away. The noise from the slave lots grew ever louder as more were poured in, and washed, and parcelled up for sale. She did not want to watch, but some scenes were so extravagant they could not be ignored. She saw strong men whipped and beaten to their knees, weak men cuffed and kicked, women stripped of their last rags of clothing, then stripped of their children, some stripped of babes in arms. But when the auctioneer clambered into his pulpit, it was time to go, apparently. Sutton had got his bargain for the day. As he told his fellows leeringly, it was time to test it out.

Alf rode a big black mule, but to her amazement Deb was to walk. What's more, he tied a rope around her waist, which he jerked at every now and then as if to remind her who was boss and who the servant/slave. Deb had a small parcel with her, containing clothes that she had fashioned on the voyage, a piece of mirror, a brush she'd had off one of the sailors who'd hoped to get a kiss. This she had to carry. She also picked up a piece of stick betimes because the dogs that lurched around the roads and tracks were lean and wild, and most unfriendly. They came up boldly she struck them boldly off again. And the heat was killing.

The plantation was some miles away from town, and her interest in the surroundings was quickly worn from her. Lush it was for certain, and green and aromatic, but its very difference from the fields of home made for desperate loneliness. The roads were hard and flinty also, and her feet were soft from too much time on shipboard, and began to cut. As she lagged she dragged, and Sutton, with malicious pleasure, jerked. Once she fell to her knees, and when the mule stopped (human compassion, in a beast?) the human drove his heels into its sides and swore it onwards. The mule, as mules do, ignored instruction and turned its head to stare at Deborah with its dark brown, gleaming eyes—which frightened her and moved her. Her only friend, an animal? However hard Sutton kicked and swore, the mule stood watching her. Then, when she was upright, it turned its head front and plodded on.

There were other mules with white men on them and traps with white girls and women in various sorts of finery, who stared at her in fascination. One man on a horse stopped to talk to Sutton, and Deb realised he was a minister of some sort, a reverend, with black tricorn and drab coat of fustian—despite the heat—and high black gaiters above his boots. He raised an eyebrow at her and wondered, indirectly, why she was on a halter. Sutton twisted his little mouth into regret and said she was a fallen woman, fresh from England, which he had bought to save her from herself. The minister was mollified.

"Do you go to church, whore?" he said. "You may come to church with Mr Sutton's people, if he will be so kind. We have all sorts at the back; you will fit in."

"Will I be welcome?" Deb gritted, with hatred in her voice, and the minister ignored her, tutted, tipped his hat to Sutton, and moved off. Sutton chuckled.

"Th'art red hot, art thou," he said. "You wait till you meets my Seth and Little Ammon."

There were black people on the roads as well as whites, but they were in profusion, not in dribs. That some were working slaves she could perceive, as many were in chains and shackles, driven by thin black men who carried whips and switches of stripped wood. But some blacks seemed to be of different class and wore shirts and britches, although of mainly rag. They were in smaller groups, some on their own, and women were among them, with wicker baskets on their heads. All were barefoot, however, and all but the men with whips looked downwards as they passed, their eyes well hidden, their faces blank. Deb, exhausted, could make nothing out of it; it was just a passing scene.

It was similar when they reached the man's plantation, which was marked off from the road by a pair of untrimmed wooden gateposts driven into verges, with neither gates between them nor a fence or hedge on either side. The land was light and sandy, not far from the shore in fact, and almost beach itself, held intact by clumps of grasses and stretching gently upwards to a stand of palmy trees. Deb had seen growing cane by now—there was almost nothing else along the way once the outer town had been passed by—so saw that Sutton's plantings appeared to start in earnest to the right side of the trees. By looking harder she discerned a house within the clump, white from a distance, with a reddish roof. As they got closer she saw that it was in desuetude, surrounded by outhouses, sheds, and barns in all kinds of decay. On their route they had passed the mouth of one broad driveway leading to a grassy crest, and Deb had looked up along it at the opportune and seen a gigantic mansion, apparently of white marble or similar, with pillars and columns in the grandest style. Alf Sutton was not a successful planter, then—nor yet a gentleman. What a surprise . . .

There were servants there to greet them—at least to notice their arrival—and their faces held the expression she had seen before. All were clothed, the women with their bosoms covered, and the tallest had a long whip in his hand. This man was black as polished ebony, his thin cheeks marked with patterned scars, his eyes as cold as ice. When Sutton called him over, he came slowly, almost regally, and stood there with his shoulders back, his lips in curled contempt.

"This is the mistress," Sutton said to him. "She is a whore, and if you or any of your nigger bastards lay a hand on her, I'll cut your bollocks off with my own hands and broken glass." To Deborah he said: "This is my Number One. His name is Fido."

Deborah, sweating, blinked. She must have misheard, surely? The heat was killing her.

"But Fido is a dog's name," she said, weakly.

"And Fido is a dog," replied his master. "Ain't thee, Fido? A great big black bullmastiff."

Deb stared into the haughty face, and the dark eyes held her own, unreadable, unchanging. Sutton went on, "They've all got nigger names as well, tha knows. But not pronounceable by Christians, as fur as ah can tell."

The black man was head and shoulders taller than the white, and half his age, built like a marble god. He had a whip; the road was only half a mile away. Why did he stay there, calm, indifferent? Why not cut—then run?

"Fetch the women," Sutton ordered him. "Tell Mabel, Mary, Mavis that the new mistress is here." He threw a smile at Deborah. "We calls 'em all by names that starts the same," he said. "It meks it easier, sithee? Mabel's top bitch. Keep her well beat and she'll look out for thee. She's got a child of mine, so she has hopes. The silly bitch. Nowt's what she'll get. Nowt and the gutter."

Within an hour, Deb had "settled in." Sutton had left her in the care of Mabel, a woman in her twenties, and when Deb spoke to her in English she replied immediately, but in a form of language so debased that it was to all intents incomprehensible. There was English there, undoubtedly, but whole words and phrases were misused and mispronounced. Deb, on leaving Cheshire and the North, had been amazed by the diversity of Englishes she'd heard, but even London's bitter nasal twang was clearer far than this. And Mabel was not friendly, she was very far from that. Only when Deborah, alone, burst into sudden tears did the temperature move up a little. Mabel returned to the scruffy bedroom where she'd left her and uttered something in a kindly voice—and smiled. Deb's tears became a flood, and when she sank onto a chair, Mabel moved to stand beside her. She did not touch, but did not move away, for several minutes. Then she gave Deb a piece of cloth from out her apron pocket to wipe her face.

Later, Deb toured the house and saw some other servants, and met the cook, a fat and solid Irishwoman of maybe forty years. Bridie clearly thought herself the mistress, and made it plain she would not be displaced by some young flighty piece, and stayed suspicious for a good long while. She did, however, brighten up when Deb discussed her prospects of survival, and asked if she could run, and where to run to. Bridie laughed and said, most like, it wouldn't come to that. When Deb insisted she was serious, the laugh got deeper.

"Listen, girl, you're in Jamaica now. Alf and his *spailpíns* go through *cailíns* like you like fire goes through thatch. But most well-brought up ladies are gone before then, unless they're very strong. Have you not heard about the ague? In ten days, two weeks or so, you will fall ill, and God love you, then you'll die. I'm sorry for you, *mo chroí,* but there's an end to it. And if you live you'll be a cripple, and Sutton and his sons will kill you with the childbirth anyway."

Earnestly though she stated this, the woman's very fervour gave Deb heart that she'd survive, that in some way it was a sort of testing joke. Bridie's manner modified, in fact, when she saw Deb was not about to have the vapours, and—at last—she got the kettle off the hob and made a mash of tea. She had been at Sutton's place for years, she said, and had seen women come and go, some on their own legs, some in coffins. It was a failing farm—she called it "farm" with an Irish intonation of contempt—which made it feel much like the world she had been thrown out of by the English. "I feel like I'm at home," she laughed. "God love you, Deborah, this place is as cruel and hungry as the west of Connemara, so it is. You have not come to paradise, *mo chroí;* you've come to hell on earth." Sutton's place (it had no name that Bridie knew of) had, the Lord alone could guess, what number of slaves (she did not know numbers, either), but she knew it lived on debt.

"They are all old, you see," she said. "That's why it's failing. That bastard Fido, for to speak. He's over thirty, mebbe, and lives so long because he does no work. He is a driver; he whips his fellow blackmen for reward. He has been here for longer than I have, even, and I first saw him with a whip in hand, so he has never worked. Do nothing and live long, that is his secret."

"But he's not old!" said Deb. The dog name had made her wince again, but Bridie did not notice. "You say he's thirtyish! That is not so very old in England!"

"Oh, thirty is a grand old age out here. Not many slavemen make it that far." Bridie took a mouthful of tea and savoured it. "It depends on the age they start at," she went on. "The planters don't like children off the boats because they do not have the strength; they cannot pull their weight. But let's say most slaves come here in their twenties, some more, some less—you know the picture. Well, they'll not see thirty, most of 'em. Seven year is roughly what it takes to wear a man out, bit longer for the *cailíns,* if I may call them that." She laughed. "*Cailíns!* Some of them, would you believe, have never worn a garment in their lives when they first get here! They've rings in their noses and their earholes you could hang the washin' on! Their titties swing quite shamelessly. *Cailíns* indeed!"

Bridie had grown quite merry over this, but Deb could feel her spirits quailing. Without ever meeting these poor people, she could feel an ache for them. She missed her Cheshire land, sometimes she missed it very bad, and she had left by her own choice, however much she might regret it now. As to shame and bosoms, she'd been forced to show hers off, to sell herself.

"I don't know what a culleen is," was all she said, and quietly. "I'm truly sorry. And do they die then? When they're worn out?"

"Indeed they do," said Bridie, crisply. "They die, and Master has to buy some more, and Master doesn't have the money—not many of the rich men do, despite appearances—and so he lives in debt. He swives them because he wants to breed more up, he says—although it is because he is a dirty ram in truth—but that don't work with the *cailíns,* neither. *Cailín* is a girl," she added. "It is the Irish. A *cailín* is a girl, is all, whatever creed or colour she might be, poor thing. Master rapes them, and Seth rapes them, and Little Ammon does his best, the eejit. And the slaves grow old and die at twenty-five or thirty, and the Master's debt gets bigger by the year." She stopped, and grinned hugely into Deborah's face, displaying strong white teeth. "And it serves him bloody right," she said. "I can't wait till he starves, the wicked *spailpín.*"

They sat there in the silence of the tropics for a while, a silence that was in fact the clamouring of insects and the screech of birds. Then Deb said: "Why does it not work then? If he and his two sons use the slave maidens as their broods, and the slaves as well, I guess, live with each other in the normal way? Even Christian maids get with children, and these are savages, surely? In any way, he told me one of the women had a child by him. It was Mabel, as I think, who I have met, although she did not say a word herself on such a subject."

"Aye, Mabel is his latest fancy," Bridie said, "and Mabel has a little baby boy. But will it live, though? Few of the women have children of the lasting kind, although some fall pregnant, as you say. Mabel came to term, the baby was alive, and that is not so usual, believe you me. Stillbirth is the African way, out here. They are experts at the art."

As Deb digested this, Bridie sat quiet for a while. Then she sighed.

"Most do not even get with child," she said. "Leastways, that is how it seems to us white folk. They have spells and hoodoo as they call it, and they know herbs and poisons in great profusion. Some babes are born and smothered on the spot. It is quite deliberate. If you had been torn from hearth and home and made to breed with men like Sutton, or Fido even, would you want to give up your babies to be worked to death and murdered? You would not. Best be ugly like me, and suck old bones to make your breath stink vile, and leave the duty to the younger hens. I pity you, *mo chroí*. It's not a case of drawing lots with Sutton and his boys; they'll all have you. And then Fido can feast upon the leavings, can he not? And spit you out for his noble brothers."

"Fido," Deb said, after a pause. "How can men call others 'Fido?' And has he many brothers? Are they called dogs' names also? Alf Sutton is a monster of depravity."

"He has no brothers, it is just a word, and they're not noble either, don't let your heart be leading you astray," said Bridie. "If Master is a monster truly—and I don't say that he ain't—then he is no worse than the most of them, so to say. One man, Sir Simon Walton, named his best team after his hounds back home in England. Nudger and Whitehawk, Ranter, Flier, Flash. Is it worse or better than giving the females English names that they don't recognise? I don't know, but you will get used to it, for sure. And when a slave's wore out, their name can come in useful down the line, can't it? It's easier than thinking up a new." She smiled at Deb's expression. "It is not a pretty life," she said. "Much better would have served you, if you'd stayed at home . . ."

Later that evening Deborah, who had had as good a wash as she could manage in a basin without even a sliver of soap, was called down to have her dinner and meet the family. She had assumed the dinner was with the family men, but Bridie called her into the kitchen, where there were places set for the two of them, and three or four more settings for the household women. Deb had met Mabel, who moved her lips at her, and was introduced to Maude and Mollie, who seemed uninterested in her presence, and ate sullenly and quickly, ignoring her. The three black women, when they talked together, did so in the tongue that Deb had heard before, and which struck her, already, as more and more like English. Then Bridie joined in, as fluently as them, and threw a smile at Deborah at one point when they laughed, as if she ought to understand what they were saying. Deb, trying hard, began to pick words out and then discern a pattern. It was a private English, maybe, a tongue all of their own. When the blacks had gone—they ate quickly and with little fuss—Bridie called it *Kreyole* and said that Deb would pick it up.

"It ain't a private language, though," she said. "It's what we speak here on this island. A lot of white folk can't—planters and their ladies, and the rich—but don't put trust in that, for many do. And some like the master and his friends pretend they cannot, but they know the gist and fall upon you like a ton of bricks if you should be talking out of order. There's slaves have died by thinking they were safe in Kreyole talk."

Deb wondered why the slaves did not use African, but Bridie laughed at that, as well. Because Africa was not a country, but a place, she said. Africa was many, many countries, and the people from each part spoke their own languages and could not understand each other half a jot.

"Do you speak Irish?" she said. "Do you speak Welsh, and you from just beyond the border? You do not, so. Why then should Mabel, who's a Coromantee, say, know the talk of Mildred, who might be Ebo, or a Paw-paw, or Mandingo? By sea they could be months apart, from what the traders tell us. And by land in Africa—impossible!"

And then the bell went, and there came a shout, and Deb walked through a broken door to meet her fate. The master sat at the head of the table, shortish, bullish, with his toad-face flushed, while two young men were flanked along the sides and facing. They were rough-dressed, like their father was, and more like hands than farmers in

Deb's eyes. One was big and quite well-looking, with tight-curled hair and wide, firm mouth, while his brother was a different kettle altogether. His eyes were dull and staring, his features in some subtle way displaced, and the smile upon his lips a combination of vacancy and lust. As she walked in, he stood up behind the table, rattling the platters, cups, and cutlery almost to the floor, and licked his lips.

"Sit you down, Ammon," said the toad, affectionately. "You'll have to wait your turn. Miss Tom-tittery, that there's my second son. His name is Ammon, and he's looking for a wife. What say you?"

"Tom-tittery?" said Ammon, with astonishment on his features. "Is that her name, feyther? My golly, that's a pretty one! Am I to change it for thee, lass?"

He sat down heavily and stared some more, while Miss Tomelty felt as hollow as a drum.

"She answers to the name of Deb," said Sutton. "I expect she'll allow thee call her that, Ammon. She is a Cheshire lass. Good breeding stock."

"I heerd she were an 'ore," said the other one. He smiled at Deb, an open, friendly smile. "I'm Seth, don't mind me 'alf-bro," he went on, "'e's simple, like. I don't know which 'alf of me 'e's got, but it wa' not me brain, no'ow." He paused, a short, timed pause. "'E's got the Sutton podger, though. 'E's donkey-rigged. Mebbe his ma were black, eh, Pa?"

"Get off wi' you!" said Alf, as if annoyed. "I don't have m' nigger sons at dinner table, do ah?" He gave a bellow of amusement. "Need a bloody big table, when all's been counted—there's enough of 'em to fill a bloody cattle pen!"

Ammon was blinking, eyes puzzled. "'Tent right though, that, is it?" he said. "'Bout nigger podgers being bigger." He turned his face to Deb, with care of explanation. "Ah checks, tha see," he said. "Theer's only two got bigger ones ner me, and ah fucks theer women to show as who is boss." He turned the eyes to father next, then brother. "Ah swived that Bonzo's yester'een again," he told them, full of pride. "He tried to stop me, Bonzo did, but I had me pistol in me hand in case, and I smacked his face with it. Then Fido got two lads on 'im and give 'im a fine kicking for his cheek." The eyes went back to Deborah, the smile was kindly, broad and frank. "Ah'm very good," he told her. "You can try me, an' you like. Would you like to see m' podger now?"

There were roars of laughter and derision from around the table, which made him blush although he could not see, in truth, what he had said so wrong. Deb felt her stomach dropping down and feared that she might faint, or vomit on the hard earth floor. Not faint. The thought revived her. If she fainted among these animals they would strip and use her, one by one. She had fallen among wolves. Or maybe all the English planters were like this. She took the dishes out, as her excuse for leaving, and Bridie told her not to return, but to go outside and vanish for a while—but being careful in what company she fell—in the deep black night.

Next morning, and in ensuing days, Deb (with Bridie's connivance) spent much time hiding in the open largeness of the plantation, and doing her duties in the house—which were minimal and ill-defined, and largely pointless—and avoiding contact with the men. It was a busy time in the planting year, and all three of them were scarcely in the house, and scarcely sober when they were. Interested in lechery, certainly, but exceeding easy to avoid or give the slip. Deb smiled at their advances when she had to, and apologised as she skipped off to do some chore she'd dreamed up, and nodded seriously when they told her "just thee wait!" Little Ammon, who was six feet tall of bursting flesh and muscle, did seize her once, but as he tried to get his penis out, she bit his hand and streaked away—and by the time she had emerged to lay the supper out, he had forgotten all about it.

After ten days, as predicted, she came down with an ague, but it was not a major one, and she survived. Had any of the Suttons wished to join her in her bed, Deb would most likely not have cared, or noticed, but sweat, coughed blood and vomit are effective prophylactics, and she remained unvisited. Bridie ignored her, too, but Mabel took it on herself to save Deb's life. In the days of her recovery they started to communicate, she teaching the Cheshire maid Kreyole, and Deb asked her why she'd cared for her so selflessly. As far as she could understand the answers, it was because Mabel hated

Alf, and Alf did not care if Deborah lived or died. Alf was the father of her son Wasambu, she said—but called him Spot. Sadly, Deb could not pronouce Mabel's given name.

Throughout the weakness of her recovery, Deb haunted the plantation, watching. She saw the poor black people being gathered up outside their shacks, then walking to and working in the fields, cutting and transporting stacks of cane to pick-up points for carting to the factory. The poor black people were driven on by other blacks, she noted, who carried whips they used with casual liberality. None of them—drivers or the driven—acknowledged her, and Deborah felt invisible in some wise. Even the few children would not meet her eyes, and when she turned round suddenly to catch them peeping, were in fact indifferent, as though she were not there. Of white men she saw none, save for a glimpse of Sutton, on his big black mule, on the skyline every now and then. Little Ammon, great big hulking Little Ammon, had disappeared from open air, as had Seth. Above, the sky was always blue, and calm, and clear—and Deb was desolate as the grave.

The factory, when she at last drew near it, was another hellish vision in her eyes. It was a huge building, with open ends, and inside a maelstrom of furnaces and vats and mighty boilers. There was machinery, groaning and racketting as it slowly turned by man and mule-power, and chutes down which she saw chopped cane fed constantly towards great rollers, which cracked and screamed and screeched under duress. She had little idea what might be going on, but over all there was a pall of sweet steam, hot and heavy, which she realised soon was leaving an awful stickiness on her skin and hair and clothes, a stickiness so all-pervading she found it most unpleasant. But although she ran away the first time, she felt it as compulsive, and returned quite often as her strength came back to her, careful to sit on the windward hillside, clear of the blowing vapour, lost in the rhythmic, violent noise. Thus it was, one day, she did not hear the scream as Little Ammon died within the boiling-hall. She saw the running, though, watched the commotion as people poured from out the factory, ran about like headless chickens, wailed and hid themselves, then burst out and ran and wailed again. She saw the lines of mules on the turning wheel falter then stop, heard the screeching of the rollers fade and die. She saw dozens of black men and women running in every direction, saw overseers and drivers lay about them with their whips in violent paroxysms. She saw Seth burst out of one end of the factory blowing a whistle, loud and long, then saw him hold a pistol in the air and fire it. Shortly afterwards, she saw Alf Sutton, at a gallop, driving his black mule across the yard and straight into the factory, and heard shouts and blows and many other screams.

Little Ammon, Bridie told her later, had fallen into a vat of boiling sugar cane, and it served the bugger right. She had it on authority that he had slipped by simple accident, like the clumsy oaf he was, while prancing about demented in the way he always had, dicing with death and taunting all the niggers for their cowardice as they refused to follow in his path. The master, though, and Seth had called it murder on the spot and had taken Bonzo into the lock-up to wait his execution. Ammon had raped his wife the day before, as he so often did, and Bonzo, it was held, had dared to take revenge.

"You know his wife," said Bridie. "We've had her in the kitchen, friend of Mabel. Her name is Moira, and she's six months gone." She laughed, a little bitterly. "Whichever one the father was," she said, "the babe will be an orphan, won't it? If it should live so very long . . ."

TWENTY-TWO

It took the Biter one full night to lose the Spaniard, and cost her three more days in seeking her again. Throughout this time the pumps were manned, without any break at all for the first few hours, until the carpenter and his crew had found the leaks and worked on them with caulking, matting, and gallons of hot pitch to staunch the major flow. Mr Carpenter, however, had a long face from that moment forward and would complain to anyone about the vessel's hull. So much so, indeed, that Will, at last, was told to fetch him to the cabin, where the captain had a quiet word with him to tell him to desist. Not that quiet—it was heard throughout the aft part of the ship. The captain, it would seem, was locked on one thing only now—his need to have the plunder. Mr Carpenter, it would seem, was therefore bound to keep his mouth tight shut.

When the Scots had got on board the galleon to leeward—and they had picked up a drowning man or so to add to the first two—Kaye could see through his spyglass that she was being snugged down "almost comfortable." While all his *Biter* men were running round him "in a devil's funk," he said contemptuously. He was pleased indeed he had "a good prize crew" on board the captured vessel. In fact, he swelled ridiculously, with a small smile fixed on his face, which Sam was sure was to do with money. While he dreamed of silver ingots, though, Holt and Bentley, along with Gunning and his bottle, worked hard to save the ship. Ideas of pursuing the cutter or following the Scots on board the galleon were abandoned when they'd clattered down below to see the water gushing in. Will raced aft to tell Dick Kaye they were in straits, Big John ambled happily to issue orders to set and trim her canvas to take off all the strain he could, while Sam worked with Taylor and his better men to stop the ship from sinking. The weather, just to do its part, blew squall on squall on squall until the Carib could have been Charybdis.

To start with, Slack Dickie was insistent they must stay close to the cripple, ease in by slow degrees till they could put a line on board and take her under tow. Gunning laughed out loud.

"Tow the bitch!" he cried. "Tow her where, with what, and how? The only line we've got that's man enough would be the cable, and if that should break and we should need to anchor, what do we then? In any way, think of the strain when we come to the snub! If it didn't pull our arse right off, the bottom would drop out, I'm telling you! We're taking water, man; we have been hit!"

He was in high good humour all the while, although his words struck Will as ominous. He did agree with Gunning, though, that a tow was not in question. For a start-off, even if they could come up with their "prize," how would they get a line on her?

"There's not the weight on board to haul a tow-rope in, sir," he told Kaye. "We could maybe get up close and pass a messenger, although if we got near enough to throw it we'd be much too near to get away without a hit, I'd guess. But there's no muscle for the rest, is there? The bight of cable will be down in the sea, and wet, and sinking. You'd need ten men on her capstan in a blow like this."

"And what's the point?" said Gunning. "We could only tow down-wind. She's twice the size of us. Even with only one mast she'll slide to l'ward faster nor we can, and we can't carry much until we've patched the bottom up. Bloody Hades, I ain't so sure we'll even catch her at this rate!"

The light was fading from the sky, and the Spanish ship looked suddenly quite far away from them. She was still rolling, but no longer to her beam-ends, as the Scots had squared her off from out the troughs. In fact, she had her stern to them, and it struck Will, by a quirk, that she was on the run. It struck him urgently.

"Sir!" he said. "The night is falling soon! If she goes on at that rate, we might miss sight of her. Had we not best up helm?"

"Aye, that's what I'm saying, is it not?" said Kaye, all snap and temper. "We need to get a line on board. Not to tow, maybe, but at least to keep her tabbed." Gunning hooted, and Slack Dickie glared at him. "What is it, Mister? Have you some words to say? Will you stop mumming like a fool and get her sailing? Taylor! Call the hands there! We're going off the wind and setting canvas! Gunning—do your duty!"

Jack Gunning smirked, while assessing what to set aloft and how to trim it before he gave his orders. "Gets dark like thunder in these parts, Capting," he said. "Drops like a stone, the night do. One minute broad daylight, next minute—whoof. A monkey's armpit! I'd signal while we're still in sight of 'em, if I were thee. Signal 'em to carry lights." He stopped. The smirk grew deeper. "Can they read signals, though?" he asked. He was sneering. "Them Scotch brothers? I wouldn't bet my pay on it, would you?"

"Gunning, you are a fool," said Captain Kaye. "If they put lights on, who do you think might find them? Where do you think those *Guarda-Costa* ships might be? In any way, the signals are agreed already, thank you very much, between myself and my prize crew.

They will show lights at intervals, responding to our own, whenever we should show them. Mr. Holt, I shall leave that up to you, sir."

Lieutenant Holt acknowledged smart enough, as was his duty, but Gunning, chuckling, took another pull at his brandy bottle and wandered off to rouse his men to trim the canvas. Will wondered, but did not dare to ask, just when the captain had done his detailed planning with the Scots, and why the hell he placed his trust in them.

Kaye was expansive, though, and needed no outside prompting. "I told them I would try to get a line on, Will," he said, "but Big Angus was quite sanguine either way. The signalling will go well enough, long as we stay in close. Double up the lookouts, will you, sir? All eyes skinned and peeled, a flogging for the man who loses her! No, I mean it," he said earnestly, seeing Bentley's face. "Now is the time for blood and fire, lad, not slackness. Double up the lookouts and give that as my warning. There!"

At present the lookout at the highest point was Abel Phillips, who everyone save the captain and his surgeon, Grundy, thought was ill of scurvy. When Will, relieved, suggested he should now come down, though, Slack Dickie's new resolve was hardened even further. Phillips was a malingerer, he averred, and his punishment should not be curtailed in any way. The weather might be windy, but it was warm, and slackers should be shown the folly of their ways. Thus Phillips stayed up high aloft, and made Will Bentley think of earlier such punishments he had seen, and their awful consequence. He did, however, send others on to lower points, to back the main man up. When darkness fell he shouted as a test, and all of them, Phillips included, responded.

But in the night, although the weather eased considerably, they lost the Spanish prize completely. As dusk fell she was visible, going straight downwind as easy as you like, and when it went pitch black not many minutes afterwards, in the Caribbean way, she disappeared as well, as though she was a lantern newly doused. Bentley and Sam were on the quarterdeck alongside Captain Kaye, and neither wished to be the one to say first that his sight of her had gone. In fact, Slack Dickie taunted them.

"Well," he said, after some few minutes. "Which of you can point her out to me, for a golden guinea? What? Can you not see her, then? But was it not your duty to report?"

Will, decisively, stepped away from the captain so as not to offend his ears with bellowing.

"Aloft!" he shouted. "Lookout, there! Where away the Spaniard?"

It was abnormal long before Phillips replied. His voice was thin and reedy, not sounding right at all.

"I can see him, sir," the hoarse shout came at last. "Direct to lee. But very faint, sir. Very hard to pick."

"Make a signal, Mr Holt," Kaye ordered crisply. "One white lantern to the foretopgallant yardarm, with a red one underneath. Lively now. I instructed Tilley earlier. He awaits you on the foredeck."

Holt and Bentley exchanged glances. Dickie was up to his tricky tricks again. But Holt shouted for the boatswain's mate, and Tilley responded. Ten seconds later the lanterns climbed into the sky— to be replied to almost instantly by a red one in the night ahead, with a white one underneath. How far away, Will wondered. A mile? A little more? Too far for comfort, anyway. Slack Dickie, though, was cock-a-hoop.

"You see?" he said. "The perfect system, is it not? Easy, constant contact between the Scotch and us, no chance at all that other ships might see. Now down our lanterns come, and Big Angus's will follow. At every turning of the glass, we do it once again. And in the morning, now the weather's easing, we'll come up to her and take the silver off. Then ho for Port Royal, and our hero's welcome in Jamaica! Capital!"

Gunning staggered onto the quarterdeck at this point, dropped his bottle, and stood and yelled profanities as the shattered glass and brandy spread around his feet. Captain Kaye, incandescent with a sudden fury, ordered him to leave the deck and go below, or better still to do his duty and bring them closer to the galleon. Gunning laughed, sat heavily, then rocked back and forwards in apparent mirth, calling for more brandy from Black Bob, who was nowhere to be seen. Kaye, almost screeching, called for Arthur Savary and his marines, and when they came running, in various stages of undress, ordered them to arrest the drunken master and carry him below to lock in irons.

Before they could touch him, Gunning was swaying on his feet, his leer become a bitter scowl.

"Capting, you are a fool," he said. "Those Scotchmen are accursed villains and all on board here know it except you. I will below, and gladly, and if you catch up with those bastards, I will stand you a puncheon of fine spirit when we reach Port Royal. They are gone, sir. You have lost 'em. How long will it be before you see it?"

"Savary!" roared Kaye. "Do your duty, sir! Do it! Why, never have I heard such insolence! If this man was a Navy officer, he would hang, I promise you!"

"Oh stop your bluster and shake out reefs and get more sail set," said Gunning. "I know why you are desperate, man, even if no other bugger else should do. Christ, I need another bottle. Bob! Where are you, boy? Black Bob!"

As Savary approached him, very gingerly, with his soldiers less sure than he was, if that were possible, Big Jack blundered at and through them, scattering them like pins, and stomped to the companionway and down. The marines and officer, aware of how ridiculous their aspect, clattered after him, more to remove themselves from sight than for a sensible intention. Dick Kaye, in a paroxysm, roared to officers and men to shake out everything, to get her lifting, to notice that the wind was now a gentle breeze (which it most certainly was not), to get her under way, and handsome! He shouted forward to Holt for another signal to be made, and he shouted aloft for Phillips to report a sight of them. Phillips did respond, after an aching pause, but said there was no sign at all; the sea to leeward was invisible, a field of blackest black. Will shouted at the other lookout men, to cover Phillips's back, and all reported similar.

Then Holt's signals went up, and after some delay—and to general astonishment—the reply came, distant and very dim. Slack Dickie almost danced in triumph at his rightness and made the signal yet again, in fifteen minutes time—to not a flicker. He demanded cleaner glasses, then, and bigger wicks, then caused burning bundles to be hoisted up, and all to no avail. Sail was piled on sail, until a royal blew out of its boltropes and *Biter* took a roll that looked at one stage as if it would roll her over, and after one more hour, a gunpowder flare was blown out of a bow chaser that lighted up the sea all round them and near choked all men on board with smoke and burning sulphur. In the black that followed this Chinese display, men saw many flashes in their eyes, but none of any substance from ahead. When dawn came the sea was black and empty, then dark blue, then turquoise, streaked with white. Still empty, though, a heaving, pale blue void. And up aloft, it was discovered, Abel Phillips was asleep.

The search went on three days, and the argument over Phillips's fate repercussed far longer, both among the people and the officers. For Captain Kaye chose to blame the prize ship's loss not on the Scotchmen, or indeed the filthy weather and the onset of the night, but on his chosen lookout's dereliction. Phillips's crime was discovered when the captain called for him before full daylight and got no reply. It was still blowing very hard, and any man aloft can fail to hear, but it was not above a minute before the "awful slackness" was established beyond doubt. In fact, Phillips was so hard asleep that he could not be made to move even when prodded hard by little Ratty Baines, who elected to spring aloft to do the captain's finding-out for him. Rat Baines, when offered, was not the man to miss an opportunity, and smacked the lookout's face from left to right and back again, then twisted his ears to try and wake him up. But Phillips was like stodgy pudding, and in the end Holt sent Tommy Hugg aloft to see, and ultimately to lift him down across his hulking shoulders. On the quarterdeck, when deposited, Phillips dropped in a heap, was poked about some more, and finally rallied himself and stood. His face was marked most clearly where the slaps had hit. Blue bruises in the shape of Rat Baines's fingers.

Captain Kaye—obscurely aware that his conduct in this act was under observation—of course called Mr Grundy up to give a fair assessment. The surgeon prodded Phillips cruelly and with clear contempt, and pronounced him a malingerer. Phillips stood blinking, indifferent, perhaps not even hearing what was said. His face was pale, his eyes were glazed, and the spreading bruises rather horrible. There was also, from his mouth and nose, a small amount of vivid blood.

"Well," said Captain Kaye, examination over. "You have been asleep aloft, in dereliction of your duty, man. You are lucky that you did not fall. And while you slept, the ship that you were watching for has disappeared. Made signals as arranged, no doubt, to no acknowledgement from us, who did not see them. Now that is serious. Now that, sir, to our enterprise, is damn near fatal. It is an enemy, a prize, stuffed to the gunwales with Spanish plate. And you have lost it. You will be flogged."

William was close while this went on, and an almost overwhelming heaviness fell upon him. His breath quickened, for he knew that there was nothing he could do. Abel Phillips, barely on his feet, his eyes unfocused on the captain's face, made no reply, indeed no sound beyond a little sigh. It came to Bentley that this punishment was not for Phillips, in reality, but for Jack Gunning, to blame his drunken mocking of the loss of easy riches, and Jack Gunning neither knew, nor cared. Misuse power where you can, thought Bentley gloomily: a first rule for the weak.

"Well, sir?" said Slack Dickie to Phillips, harshly. "What say you to that?"

"Captain Kaye," said Bentley. His voice was low and clear. "I think this man is ill, sir. He shows clear symptoms of the scurvy. You cannot—"

He stopped himself. Kaye's eye was on him. It was almost wild.

"Ill, sir? That is not what Mr Surgeon says."

Grundy was beside them on the quarterdeck. His face was pasty. There was a tremor in his hands and lips. Another twenty minutes without a drink, Will knew, and he would be in a worse state than poor Phillips. He felt disgust for this man, though, not pity.

"Perhaps, sir," he said, "perhaps Mr Grundy's experience—"

"Malingerer!" snapped Grundy. "A clear-cut case! I have been at sea for years, sir, and I never saw a clearer case! How dare you, sir!"

Kaye's tension eased. How pleasant, to have his dilemma solved so neat. "It is what their lordships pay him for," he told Bentley, mildly. "What man who keeps a dog barks for himself? A fool." Suddenly he spotted the boatswain emerging from the forward hatch. "Mr Taylor! Clap this man in irons, if you please. When the weather eases, I will have him flogged. Unless," he said to Phillips, "you care to rise aloft once more, and peel your eyes, and find our fortune? No? I thought as not."

Phillips, in fact, had not understood, or made response at all. Taylor arrived, looked at the captain with blank eyes, and detailed two men to escort the transgressor down below. Grundy was dismissed and almost staggered as he made for the companionway. On a moody whim, Kaye went aloft himself to use his telescope, and stayed up there half an hour. But the Caribbean Sea, white-flecked but moderating by the minute, showed no other ship or boat at all. And as the weather eased, they set more sail and plunged on ever faster. It was their only hope.

Kaye was not an unfair man, as he argued it to his officers in the cabin, and he held off with the punishment for as long as possible. The *Biter* swept the seas downwind, then, when they assessed they must have caught or passed their crippled quarry willy-nilly, took a board to the west of their trajectory, then worked back to the east. The mastheads were manned from dawn till darkness, and—triumph of hope over common sense—men were put to lookout through the night. Kaye had arranged his signals with the Lamont brothers, and nothing would persuade him that they had let him down. After near three days, when the sea was calm and turquoise, he did give in somewhat it seemed, but could not bring himself to call the searching off. He re-named it as a wreckage watch, and insisted the Spaniard must have gone down in the storms. No one argued with him, naturally, and to an extent, some of the lower people enjoyed his private pain, which as the time wore on grew almost touchable. Even the loss of a galleon stuffed with silver was not worth crying over from the common point of view. Their share of prize money was a paltry one to start with, and very prone in most of their experience to strange evaporation, not unlike a plum-duff fart on Sunday. They only hoped the Scotchmen choked themselves to death on too much greed.

So course was set at last for Port Royal, at their current rate a further two days or more, and Bosun Taylor was ordered to set up the grating so Phillips could be punished for his costly sin of failing to pick up the Scotchmen's signal. Jack Gunning, by this time, was as sober as a judge once more—indeed he swore that he would never touch another drop—and told the captain roundly that the lookout man was innocent of any crime. It was, unfortunately, red rag to a bull, and any doubts that Kaye may have harboured were washed away in ire. But in the face of Will and Sam's unspoken opposition, he allowed that six would serve the purpose, although it was insanely generous of him and hardly worth the laying on.

Six lashes, though, served the purpose very well, as Holt for one had feared they would. In fact, Phillips started bleeding after two, from nose and mouth, and all around the eyes, and on the third stroke his head dropped sideways on his neck, and he vomited a scarlet haemorrhage, and died. In his back, it was noted as they cut him down, the cat had dug deep grooves, the skin unbroken, like blue-black valleys across a white and blotchy plain. Next evening, near becalmed not far offshore a bare few miles before the Palisadoes, they heard appalling screams drifting from what Gunning assessed must be a cane plantation just beyond the beach. They smelled a smell that some of them identified as flesh, on fire. The heat of the night, when they at last dropped anchor just inside the harbour mouth, was almost overwhelming.

TWENTY-THREE

The punishment they chose for Bonzo was a savage one, but not abnormal, so Deborah was told. She could not believe that, though, and nor, it seemed to her, could many of the slaves. There was mutiny in the air, strange ululating noises that induced a great unease in her. Fido and the other drivers switched attitude themselves, became rank oppressive and aggressive, laying about them with whip and cane at any provocation, or at none. Within two hours of the rumour going round of Bonzo's dreadful fate, two more cane-cutting men had had their long knives torn off them and been beaten to the ground then penned up and bound alongside him. That night the drumming started, which made even Bridie nervous in the house. Mabel, Maude, and Mildred were like frightened birds and avoided conversation with the white women. Bridie told Deb that drums were banned, the use of them could lead to execution, then laughed.

"If it blows up this time, though *mo chroí*," she said, "the executions will be arsy-versey, won't they? The white ones will be first, that's you and me and Master and his Seth, except that they've got guns, of course. The Africs speak through drums, that's why they're not allowed, and for all I know they could be beating up an army while we talk." She called out: "Mabel! Kwaamyaeer, mayad, waas cahlinya!" Mabel, reluctantly, did come across, but her response to Bridie's stream of subsequent Kreyole was minimal. Dismissing her, the housekeeper told Deb that they were of a different camp now; it was whites and blacks as separates, not household women all as one. Moira, she added soberly, had miscarried that afternoon. Not by accident.

In the morning, on the day of punishment, there were three more men in irons, and a site prepared for the "starring" of all six of them. One was a little boy, no more than twelve years old or so, who had been caught up a tree by Fido's bloodhounds (human variety) with a makeshift drum. Both wrists had been already broken—sharp lesson for a drummer boy—but he was still to be destroyed, on Master's order. In case the thought of revolt still clung in some "simple minds," Deb learned, Sutton's drivers were being "beefed up" with some whites. Although he did not use white labour because of the expense, neighbours could be relied on in a situation to do their best to help—not from altruism, Bridie explained, but for self-interest. If Sutton's slaves ran riot and the hacking whim became a passion, it could spread like wildfire. Sutton's plantation was small, but on two sides of it were richer holdings, owned by richer men. Nearest, indeed, was Sir Nathaniel Siddleham, who had three sons and two lovely daughters, and therefore much to guard from harm. The sons, Jeremy, Jonathan, and Joseph, enjoyed a lark—the bloodier the better—so would certainly be there.

Deb found Bridie's attitude to the troubles, and the way she talked of them, quite difficult to hold down. The words *lark* and *bloodier* struck her as unusual, used in such conjunction, and the easing of her mood now she knew that there would be men with guns in plenty to keep the blacks in check was also hollowing. The whole thing, in fact, became festive in some way as the day drove on, with many slaves given time off from working to clear a site for punishment, and set it up. Deb herself was put to preparing special food and drink for the white guests and their white guard men, all of whom arrived with guns and clubs in prominent display. Sutton and his son over-saw the work, while the three Siddleham brothers stood about conversing with each other, ignoring them in most part, drinking wine. They also flirted hard with Deborah, whom they professed to find more wonderful as the wine went down, and on whom their advances became more pressing. They ranged in age from seventeen to twenty-five or so, were dressed like London gentlemen, and (as she saw it) considered themselves God's gift. She had met rich men before, although not this rich, perhaps, but never ones who so clearly had no work to do.

"Oh, Deb, Deborah!" said the middle one, whose name she thought might have been Jonathan, but did not care to know. "Why do you stay here in this awful hole? Come fly with me. We have a house two miles away or so. It is a palace compared with Sutton's filthy hovel! Why came you here? You cannot let him or his monsters touch you! Come with us, and be our sisters' serving maid!"

"Monster," corrected the youngest, with a laugh. "One of the monsters boiled himself alive, or got boiled anyway. You're lucky there, Deb," he added. "Imagine Little Ammon 'twixt your lovely thighs! He's not sweet and clean and gentle like I could be if that is what you wanted! Come take a walk, my love. My pistol is not the sole thing I keep cocked!"

Seth Sutton, who had heard this quip, ordered her roughly

to fetch jugs of beer outside and rum because the entertainment was to start. Deb called to Mollie for some help, and to Mabel. She was shocked by their frightened, tear-filled eyes.

The clearing, or arena, had become a crowded place. All field-work must have ceased, all field hands, men and women, brought down to see the fun, or learn a lesson through their witness. Deb took her position on the white side, nearest the house, waiting on the whim of all the men. They formed a phalanx of armament, Alf Sutton in the middle with a burning torch in hand, Seth with another. The Siddleham brothers and their men ranged outside the Suttons, eyes wary, longer guns and pistols ready. While the bringing in and tying down of the six sacrificial victims was the task allotted to the blacks.

Fido, in a coloured shirt, directed operations, and he revelled in it. The prisoners were brought in as a group, and those who still had clothes were stripped stark naked. All were silent, as if all protest had been beaten out of them, except the little boy with broken wrists, who squealed from time to time when the fractures were manhandled. Fido and his fellows slashed out with their whips or canes at every moment, and blood ran down dirty skin almost from the first. Then the prisoners were pushed and directed to their squares of death, and forced down to their knees or buttocks, then kicked out till they lay down flat, their faces to the sky. Then, their arms and legs were pulled out till they lay like starfish, and their wrists and ankles chained to wooden stakes. Around their waists another chain was snaked, and shackled onto metal bolts driven into the dirt.

Now it was the women's turn. Fido barked orders that were not Kreyole, but even Deb could almost understand. Beyond the house-yard, by a small wood shelter containing fuel, stood Mabel and the other house-women that she knew. Not all—Moira, despite orders to the contrary, had stayed away, had in fact disappeared, maybe had run. But the others, eyes down and sullen, gathered the makings of a fire, armful after armful, and brought and dropped them by the staked-out men. As they returned for more, Fido's cohorts began to kick the sticks and brushwood into piles around the feet and hands of all the "starfish," while from the crowded onlookers began a mournful chant, low and rhythmical, that rose and fell so subtly that Deb was not sure she heard it in reality. As the first flames licked off the Suttons' burning torches into the piles of kindling, the low moaning became a kind of vocal *whoosh,* long-lived and musical. To be drowned out by tearing, shrieking screams.

"That's how tha'll die!" yelled Alfred Sutton, moving from Bonzo to another writhing slave. "Tha killed my son and I'll kill thee, tha bastard! By finger and by toe, by ankle and by wrist, and when the time grows right I'll roast tha bollocks off an 'all. The lot of you! The whole damn lot! Tha' art murderous! Th' art coal-black murdering scum! He wa' my little son!"

Seth, in paroxysms of hate and rage, flew from man to man, igniting corners. The Siddlehams, which Deb found sickening, gave whoops and discharged their fowl-pieces into the air. Their men picked brands out of the growing fires and fettled up the parts that failed to flame so well. While Fido and his fellow slaves, faces impassive, cut alternately at the roasting men, and at the women if they did not bring wood enough to keep the torture burning bright. Over all, the chanting boomed from God alone knew how many throats and was drowned out by the rasping, hacking screaming of the men who had transgressed. The men, and drummer boy.

Of a sudden, overcome, Deb found that she was screaming, running at Seth Sutton with her hands outstretched in claws, as if to tear his eyes out. Seth, at that moment, was driving in a forked stick below Bonzo's knee, to hold the limb down now the ankle bone had burnt through and escaped the red-hot chain. Startled, he jerked upright and the two prongs tore free from out the earth and struck Deb's forehead. She fell, shouting, onto Bonzo, whose screaming mouth blew full into her face. Her hair caught light, flaring across her eyes, and her hand plunged into the fire around his wrist, which she felt, a slimy, melting stick that seemed to crack and splinter as her weight came on to it. Then Jeremy Siddleham dragged her off the fires by her hair, and kicked her from the blazing, stinking bodies into the front ranks of the audience. She was burning as they grabbed at her, her clothes on fire, hair crackling as it flamed and singed. And as she dropped, Deb saw Moira rush into the yard, rush frantic at the roasting prisoners, into the reeking smoke.

■ ■ ■

The death of Abel Phillips, which had caused some little stir on board of *Biter*, made fewer waves on shore next morning, although it did lead to some comment and to general conversation on crime and punishment with the leading planters. As the man had died so close to land, Captain Kaye had been constrained from the quick and easy way of burial overside, not least because he feared how Jamaica gentlefolk would take it if presented with a rotting man wrapped up in canvas bobbing off the Palisadoes when he rose up in a day or three. So their first task, he told his officers as they were rowed ashore new-shaved and in their smartest fig, would be to arrange a burial in the Navy cemetery, if Kingston ran to such a thing. There was a party waiting for them at the jetty, two Navy men and two civilians, and after handshakes and greetings had been exchanged, they were escorted to an out-department of government where the Admiralty was also housed. The Navy men were a captain on the sick and hurt (he had one arm and half a leg) called Shearing, and an old lieutenant, Jackson, who clearly suffered from the principal naval disease, got from a bottle or a bung. Two arrant failures, Will guessed immediately, left behind to keep the portwork ticking while the Squadron lived at sea out in the offing.

The Assembly men hardly inspired more confidence at first glance, though one of them, Mr Andrew Mather, turned out very sharp and honest, in his way. He was only the assistant acting governor, he said—and laughed outright at Kaye's fallen face. But he explained the governor was back in England at the present time, a device by which the richer gentlemen kept their hold on sanity (and their wives), and the deputy was ill of a recurring ague. He enquired gravely how long they'd been in Caribbean waters and wondered if that dread disease had seized them or their company as yet? No? Then I'm afraid you have that pleasure still to come, he said. Bad air. Bad air brought in, as some men said, by the filthy negro slaves from out of Africa.

The Assembly offices were well appointed, and by the time they were ensconced with cups of local coffee, the ice was broken. Several planters had come in for introductions, and it was explained that all the men of wealth and business took part in governing the island, raised necessary militias and so on, and sat as magistrates. Some of the planters were anxious to know what *Biter* was to do for them, how soon she could go out and show herself to warn off French warships (or "pirates," as they preferred to call them), and "fire a cannon or two into the Maroons to show them that their easy life was over." One planter, Ephraim Dodds, was particularly insistent, and it took Mr Mather a little time to damp him down.

"Ephraim," he smiled, at last. "We know you have good points to make, and useful ideas how the Navy men can best be used, but do not roll too far and fast, I beg you. Captain Kaye and his officers have been at sea for very many weeks. They have things they want to do, their own concerns and problems to resolve. There are letters for them from the Squadron, I have no doubt, perhaps even from the Admiralty in London. Captain Shearing? I trust that I don't speak out of turn?"

Shearing nodded equably, though Captain Kaye was steaming, Will could tell, by the idea he and his vessel existed "to be used" by wretched landsmen.

"There are matters to be pursued with urgency indeed," said Shearing. "Of course, Captain Kaye, there are instructions for your work outside main Squadron duties, but on a lighter note we have mail from England. Lieutenant Jackson there has brought a parcel in. Some of it is rather ancient—it seems the Office sent it, with the usual clerking madness, before you even left the Thames—but there is quite a tidy little bundle, even some few scribblings for the people, though God knows who will read it to them, eh? There's an enormous stack for one young gentleman, what was the name again, Lieutenant? Farthing, is it? Guinea? Shilling? Midshipman. I do not see him here, I think? Unless he's come up from gunroom to wardroom very fast!"

This gave Holt and Bentley quite a lurch, for both of them had lost Rex Shilling from their minds. So young, so troublesome, so easily forgot. It was quite chilling, that he had got letters in profusion. They had forgot Rex Shilling; but he was loved by someone, still.

"Oh, Groat," said Kaye. "Nay, he's not gone to the wardroom, sir. He's dead, poor lad, lost overboard. Must I take all his letters? Or can you send 'em back? That would save me time and trouble, would it not? There are some for me, I trust?" He stopped, aware a silence had come down. "Oh," he added. "It's sad about poor Rex; indeed, he was my nephew, that's the worst of it. His mother is my second cousin. But these things happen, do they not? We had a man who died just yesterday, and we must bury him. In fact, I need to find a place in a cemetery round here, one with Navy bodies in for preference. Is there someone that can help?"

To ease Kaye's discomfiture, some of the company rallied round him. Lieutenant Jackson, blinking with bloodshot eyes, asked how the man had met his end, and Kaye, with his usual tact and diplomacy, said baldly that "the villain had been flogged and could not take it." This caused a stir of interest, and the tale came out in dribs, a shade embellished to underplay Phillips's state of illness and overplay his supposed transgressions. Mr Ephraim Dodds, who did not seem to like the Navy much, snorted at the punishment, which he thought too kindly and perfunctory, but a man called Peter Hodge pointed out its "satisfactory end." Simple flogging, he said portentously, was all well and good within its limits—that is, if it worked. But on the island, he agreed with Ephraim, "there is a need for harsher acts."

Considering how Phillips had bled to death like a leaky bladder, Holt observed sardonically: "Death is quite harsh enough for shipboard men, I think, sir. Why is it not for your men here?"

"Our men here?" said Dodds, unpleasantly. "We do not talk of our men, sir; we talk of savages. The reason we need harsher acts is because we deal with harsher types of being. To call them men is blasphemy; they bear the mark of Cain, the stain of sin, the shadow of that ancient savage act. We roast them, sir. We roasted some last night. At least, the last ones died today, not till the early hours. It is extraordinary how long these monkeys cling to life."

Holt's sardonic smile had frozen on his lips. His scarred face, still pale despite days in the Caribbean, was white around the mouth.

"You roasted them?" he said. His voice was faint. "Good God, sir, as we came to land we smelled . . . we heard . . . good God, sir, and you call *them* savage? What, roasted men to death?"

Dodds was furious. "Not men, sir, no! You do not listen to me! These were monkeys, slaves, savages from Africa! Good God, sir, you are from England, and it is all too manifest! Know nothing, interfere with all! It is England's way and motto, and it is why we left you, sir, and there you have the truth!"

Captain Shearing coughed uncomfortably into his handkerchief. He appealed to the less fiery island men. "But it was well-deserved, as I believe," he said. "I had heard these . . . ah . . . slaves had murdered somebody. Most brutishly. I heard . . . a vat of boiling cane juice, was it not?"

Peter Hodge nodded vigorously. "One of Alfred Sutton's boys," he said. "The one called Little Ammon. Man was a simpleton, but that makes it no better in a white man's book. These savages crept up behind and tossed him in, no rhyme nor reason, not a provocation of the smallest kind. You should have heard *his* screams, sir," he added, straight at Sam. "If it's soft for howling you are. That would have wrung the heartstrings of an iron man. They burned a dozen of them, and they should have burned the lot. You do not understand, is all."

From a corner of the room a quiet man now spoke. He had been listening to everything but making no comment. His dress was rich, he was pale-haired and well-made. His voice was low, but listened to intently.

"Six men," he said. "Five men and a boy, in fact, that they caught drumming up a tree. One man as a murderer, and the others just in case the rest should get ideas. My sons were there." He nodded politely to Kaye and his lieutenants, but did not stand to bow. "I am Sutton's next door neighbour, for my sins," he said. "Siddleham. Sir Nathaniel. My sons went along to see the fun, and help out if the blacks went out of hand, or mad."

"They did, a bag of gold on it," said Ephraim, acidly. "Your sons are handy shots, Sir Nat. Did they get to bag a few?"

Siddleham shook his head. "The madness, mostly, was from the womenfolk," he said. "A couple threw themselves upon the pyres, so to speak, most strangely that new white maid Sutton's got. She ran out screaming and hurled herself on the murderer, the man the house called Bonzo, I believe. Odd she should have took a shine to a nigger quite so quick, and odd he should have murdered Ammon Sutton on her behalf, but that's the way of it. She is a Portsmouth whore, they told my lads, what seamen call a Spithead Nymph. Truth to tell, my boys were hoping for a crack at her; she was a juicy, lovely piece. All right for the slavemen still, I guess. They like 'em broiled."

"A Spithead whore," said Hodge, pompously. "And poor Alf Sutton paid good gold for her. You cannot get the servants these days. The maids of quality are all gone to glory."

Sam and Bentley, muscles rigid as moulded bronze, stared at each other among the crowd of men. It was not impossible, both knew, and both were racked with a conviction it was so. Will heard his own voice, as if from a great hollow place, a long, long way away.

"Is she all right?" he said. "I beg your pardon, Sir . . . Nathaniel. And do you . . . do your sons have a name for her? I . . ."

The distinguished man looked hard at him, still seated. He eyed him, up and down.

"I do not have a name for *you*, sir," he said coldly, there having been no formal introduction. "No matter, though, her name is Deb, or so my sons would have it. And what are you called, sir?"

"Bentley," Will murmured. He could scarcely speak. "Lieutenant Bentley, by your leave, sir. I . . ."

Slack Dickie gave a hoot of sheer delight. As men had said, she was a most determined maid! He bellowed out a "Hah!"

"Well glory be!" he said. "Excuse me, sir, but this is capital! Young Will here had a whore called Deb in London! I am Captain Kaye, sir, I do beg your pardon that I am so bold, but if this is his Deb, she is a lovely piece indeed, a thing of spunk and fire! Ho, Will! How truly, truly capital! Out here but one day, and you'll get a piece of arse, no waiting!"

Most of the planting men found it amusing—especially Will Bentley's obvious perturbation—but Ephraim Dodds remained unmollified.

"That is the measure of the Royal Navy, then," he said, distinct and bitterly. "We have Frenchmen would destroy and pillage us, we have black Maroons in colonies prepared to come down screaming off the hills and murder us, we have slaves who spread disease and idleness like a filthy plague. And all our proud protectors crave is swiving."

"And all their masters crave is dunning us for higher tax," said Peter Hodge. "You have no time for fornication, sirs. You have not earned it. Captain Shearing. I trust to hear you disabuse them, sir!"

There was a harumph of general agreement from round the room, and Shearing, leaning easily against a pillar on his one good leg, was expansively relaxed.

"I am sure that that is understood, gentlemen. These are sailors' dreams and stories, by which we pass away the boredom of the deep. I have business to talk of with the captain here, and his gallant officers, as soon as this get-to-meet-you session's done. As you know, the Spanish sent a schooner in, a day or so ago, with reports there is a pirate on the loose and requests that we should have the Navy keep an eye. Perhaps, Captain Kaye, we could head up the agenda with that item?"

The planters, reminded of the Spanish visitor, became newly animated, and there were calls and mutterings of "spies" and "perfidy." But Mather calmed them down, while Shearing and Lieutenant Jackson gathered in the Navy officers and guided them into a corridor. Not many yards away lay the Royal Navy suite, which was empty, wide, and spacious, with open windows that let in sweet breeze and sun. A black man in livery was set to bring in drinks, while Captain Shearing took his favourite seat—it had a rail and grabbing knobs—and waved them to sit down.

When they were settled, with long draughts of juice that all found soothing—save for Lieutenant Jackson, apparently, who went out twitching after two mouthfuls and did not return—Captain Shearing allowed his smile to fade, replacing it with a definite solemnity. Will and Sam, whose minds had dwelt on Deb, and how and when they could seek her, realised quickly that there was much more to be said than had been ventured while the planters had been there. There was a bundle of letters on Shearing's desk, some sea-stained, some quite old, but it was not to these that he referred at present.

"Gentlemen," he said, "I mentioned a Spaniard, and an act of piracy just now. It was a *Guarda-Costa* message boat; I said a schooner but it was a handy pink in fact, fast and light and urgent. The captain told me a heavy ship of theirs, a freight ship called the *Santa* something or the other, had been set upon in an act of seaborne theft that reminded the authorities—so he insisted—of the so-called bad old days. The ship, as he described her, the attacker or marauder, was a brig. And built on British lines."

He left it there, and let it hang in the sweet air. Will saw Kaye swallow and tried yet harder to tear his own thoughts away from Deb. He knew Kaye felt easy on the Spanish galleon (save for his sense of awful loss) because the ship was sunk and could tell no tales. But Will had no ease; *his* sense of loss was raw as new-cut flesh. Had Deb been injured, badly burned? What meant the man by saying "broiled?" But he'd said "whore," also, and "Spithead Nymph," and said that she was with a slave, the mistress of a neger desperado. But surely he had heard it all wrong, anyway? Deb was . . . she had loved him, and he her. Deb was . . . he would have to go to her, this day.

As he dragged his mind back, he heard Kaye talking. His voice was confident, but with a note of query in it. He was asking how the Spanish knew the brig was British. And how, indeed, they knew of the attack.

Shearing remained relaxed and pleasant.

"They do not know that she was British, Captain," he responded. "Just built on British lines. In England, men think the Spanish are not seamen, but I promise you, they're sadly wrong. If they say British-built, then British-built she was, for a King's ransom. Which, incidentally, is what I guess the Spaniards have lost, though they'll deny it to the very last."

There was a long pause. Will noticed not much birdsong, but a low, insistent, tropic buzz from through the windows. Kaye was swallowing again. He was not so much at ease, perhaps.

"They know the *Santa* was beset because they found survivors off of her," Shearing continued in a while. "They'd escaped and ran ahead of a little storm in a cutter, and barely managed keeping her afloat. The story was that *Santa* had been damaged in the earlier bad weather, and was limping back towards Hispaniola when she was attacked. Although she was a lowly freight ship, merely, two *Guarda-Costa* ships had been escorting her. They'd found her by luck, apparently, and fallen in with her until a new squall split them up." He stopped. Significantly. "Captain Kaye," he said, "that is where I find the story . . . thin. I do not believe it. Two escorts for a freighter? And finding her a cripple, finding her by accident?" He stopped again. "How think you, Captain? I must say, I get the whiff of . . . plate."

Kaye was staring through the window, where palm fronds gently blew. Perhaps, thought Will, his mind had drifted off. Perhaps he'd not been listening enough. For a man in such a fix, he looked untroubled past belief. But then he slowly smiled.

"She was a treasure ship," he said, "as you have rightly guessed it, sir. Ditto, the brig was me, but we approached to aid her, nothing else. She was short a mast or so, but when we closed I assessed she could have got to port without our help, and we indeed, sir, and of course—were not for touching her. We'd not have *dreamt* of it." The smile broadened. "And then—they opened up on us. Yes, Captain, they fired first I promise you; the aggression was not ours. Indeed, they fired twice, on two occasions, before we loaded a ball. Ain't that right, Lieutenant Bentley? Mr Holt?"

They nodded, and Shearing took it in. He assessed the two young men for honesty, a good, cool time. He sipped his long drink, thoughtfully.

"But that is strange," he said. "We are not at war with Spain, are we? They are our allies, so to speak. And when they fired on you, Captain, you fought back? You did not hesitate?"

"As was my duty," Kaye responded stiffly, "which is very plain. If any man shoots at a King's ship, we must retaliate. Is there another rule? They opened up on us; we gave back shot for shot. We won the day."

Captain Shearing sighed. "Ah well," he said. "I suppose they'll never know for sure, is one good thing. It was not a major shipment, as I guess; the *flotas* are not timely any more. She was a solo vessel so I doubt her treasure load was great. A solo vessel, with a little escort out into the open ocean, but she never made it there. I take it you took nothing off before she sank? You saw the cutter go, I guess? With the survivors?"

A longer pause.

"She did not sink," said Kaye. And added quickly: "Then." He cleared his throat. "I put a prize crew on, but another squall blew up that turned into an all-out blaster, and we never saw a sight of her again. Perhaps she sank in that one; to tell truth we do not know. It was very violent, and before they left her, the cutter men had planted bombs to blow her bottom out, although the fires all burned out without explosion, it would seem. She was a plate ship, Captain Shearing. I am certain of it. She was a prize it was worth dying for, if need be. We searched for her for three clear days."

Shearing half rose, as if he would have liked to pace about. Then dropped back, frustration on his face, his chopped-off leg thrust out. But his gaze was level, still. He had impressive self-control. "So she's out there floating is she, for all we know? With your prize English crew on board and a hold that may be worth ten fortunes? Alternative: they are all dead. Well, tell me one thing, sir. You were not flying British colours, were you, when you did this job? Please God."

Kaye's throat was troublesome once more. "In heat of moment, sir, I own that colours may have been overlooked," he said, as if regretfully. "The whole thing was very sudden, and the squall came on so quick. Remember, the shots they threw were offered without warning."

Shearing, although satisfied with that, was absorbed in thought. "So," he said, "that's one thing, then. I thought that Pedro's pirate must be you, and you admit it. But Pedro only *thinks* he knows, so far, and could hardly dare to say so here in Kingston Harbour, eh? You've broken every law and protocol between the nations ever written, Captain, all to steal some plate that probably ain't even there. And if the Dons can pin it on us, we'll be at war with them, as well as Johnnie Frog. What is your state of readiness for sea? Don't goggle, man—how quickly can you get your killick up and go? And I will not hear your horseshit, man. The truth!"

For a cripple, Shearing had extraordinary authority. Kaye goggled further, but not for very long. There was scurvy, he admitted (Hah! thought Sam Holt, *hah!*) but already fruit bumboats had flocked around the *Biter,* and the very sick could go on shore if need be; they were not many. There was bread and salted beef in plenty, he imagined (leastways the purser had not tried to up the price!), and the water should hold out a day or several, assuming they were not too long at sea. But why, he queried, oddly. Why should they go, for what?

Will knew, and his heart was growing colder by the second. They would go to sea, and Deb was lost on land.

"To find the *Santa,* Captain," Shearing said, "before she's lit on by the Dons. If she is still afloat, and she has Englishmen on board whatever their pretence—we are undone. The Spanish presence in the Carib is enormous. They have ships in droves and ports unlimited. To stop them joining with the French is our constant juggle in these parts, and you have risked it. Well, capital."

Dick Kaye was unabashed. It occurred to Sam he did not believe the ship could be afloat. His precious Scotchmen would have saved it, otherwise. He had given up the treasure—and his crewmen—for a total loss. But also any danger to his reputation.

"Well, sir," said Kaye complacently, "if I find the *Santa*—"

"*When,*" said Shearing. "It was an act of war, man, so it is *when.* And if she has got trove on board . . ."

"So when, then, sir," riposted Dickie, lightly. "And if she is a plate ship, sir, what do you propose I do? Sink her?"

He said it with a laugh, but Shearing was not laughing.

"Yes, sink her," he replied. "Get her underneath the waves as soon as ever possible, without too much smoke, if feasible, that might act as signal to any Pedros who might see it. Axe her bottom out, pour shot below the waterline, do anything you may, but get her scuttled and then go. If you are spotted in the act, God help us all. How many of your men speak Spanish? Aye, as I thought. If the Spanish find her first, and take your prize crew off, we will deny it all, whatever they might say to us, however strong their certitude. We'll say they are deserters, pirates, any bloody thing, but naught to do with George's Navy, understood? George's men are Pedro's friends, and if they hand them back, you hang them from the yardarm there and then, no trial or any other fiddle-faddle, to show them we speak true; or I will hang them in the harbour here if that's where the Dons should drop 'em, whatever they might have babbled under the thumb-screws. Woodes Rogers cleared these seas of pirates, so it's said, and we uphold that blessed state. Now Captain—go."

For a moment, Bentley used the thought of hanging Scotchmen from the yardarm to tear his mind from Deb, but he could see the fatal flaw in all this jolly talk too clearly. On board the *Santa* were not just the Lamonts and their fellow desperadoes Morgan and Miller, but an unknown number of Spaniard survivors. *They* could speak Spanish, doubtless—but were not likely to tell Shearing's version, were they? They had been captured by the English Navy, and that was that. And if *Biter* got them first, then what? They could not be clapped in a Jamaica jail, surely? They could not be prisoners of war when Spain and England were at peace. Yet still Slack Dickie Kaye was smiling.

"And the silver, sir?" he said, silkily. "The treasure trove, the bullion, the jewels? As I will have took the ship illegally, I confide you wish me to sink that all as well? A pity, though, that I've achieved so little good. And all with best intentions, I do swear."

Sam, who'd held his peace with fortitude for very many minutes, stifled a laugh so badly that it went off like a giant's fart. Shearing, to give him credit, joined in the ensuing fun.

"You are incorrigible, Captain Kaye, and so are your officers," he said. "Of course the silver must be lost—in a Seville sow's back fundament! But when you're shifting it from ship to ship, for God's sake keep a weather eye open for the Dons. To lose the lot would be far better than be caught with it, and I mean that absolutely. If you have to—sink it, let it drown, for if you don't, you will sink us, the whole damn boiling. The French fleet could be in the offing any day. We can't afford to meet him with one hand tied up behind Don Pedro's back."

In two hours time, after a fury of activity that was a sort of miracle, the *Biter* was towed out beyond the Twelve Apostles, all canvas set and hanging, until she picked up the beginnings of the Under-taker's Breeze to blow offshore with. Twelve men had been sent on land to rid them of the scurvy, and the decks were stacked in any way with fruit, and water casks, and puncheons of good fresh local rum. No men had run, Lieutenant Sweetface Savary reported with a quiet pride, although Black Bob had tried to jump off of the captain's quarter gallery to swim ashore or drown himself, no one knew which. Kaye found him tied up in the cabin beside the bed and gave him a good kicking. He had lost his store of riches, his chance of getting out of debt, and now he was on a wild goose chase. He gave poor little Bob a damned good paste. By late afternoon, in a steady Carib wind, they watched the island disappearing in a grey-blue haze of heat. John Gunning, stone cold sober, stood beside the helmsman at the con. Will Bentley stood beside him, and his heart was cold as stone.

TWENTY-FOUR

Deborah, after the star-fishing of Bonzo and his five companions, was thrown out of Alf Sutton's house, and given to the blacks. She was, indeed, of them already, for they had saved her life while the white men had stood by and watched her burn. The slaves she had been thrown among by the oldest Siddleham began to beat the flames out instantly, although the smell of burning hair filled Deb's nostrils as her heart was filled with terror. The pain was general and excruciating, from legs and arms and body and her face, but her eyes were open and she saw Moira throw herself on top of Bonzo. The black woman was dragged off, as Deb had been, but given far more blows and cut across the face by Fido and his men. Her body crashed into Deborah's, and the two of them lay screaming in the crowd.

The starring went on for some more hours, but after this Deb was not part of it. She lay with Moira in a smoking heap, fading in and out of consciousness, it seemed. The blacks all round her, men and women, continued with their ululating chants, and every now and then, apparently, others of them would rush on to the square to scream and shout, and be thrashed down like animals. The smoke, of wood and flesh, stayed low onto the earth in the throbbing air, and the screaming of dying people rose and fell. At last the darkness came, and the slaves were told to go away, then whipped and cajoled when they failed to move. Deb's pain was dull, unless she made a sudden movement, and she and Moira, somehow, soothed each other, cheek-to-cheek. Towards the end, the Siddleham boys came to look at her, but she was too damaged to be used for sex, and they went off. Later, Deb saw Bridie, and called out to her, but Bridie walked on by.

Both she and Moira had had places in the house, but neither of them was allowed inside again. Deb could walk, and Moira could be carried, so they went to the settlement of huts not far from the boiling factory where Bonzo had used to work most of the time. About twenty shared the hut they used, men and women, and two little children who had somehow survived beyond their births. Both were fully black, and both had mothers who were very young and hopeful, or so Mabel tried to explain to Deb as the days went by. But they were weak and sickly because they got no sufficient nourishment, so were surely bound to die in shortish time. Mabel's own son—Alf Sutton's son, who had no expectations—lived near the house and got good scraps to live on, so might grow. Deb found she wished to know what Mabel thought of this, but had neither heart nor Kreyole words to ask.

From the moment they got her to the hut, it was clear the slaves would treat her as their own. Both she and Moira were stripped of every stitch and gently laid down on beds of fresh-plucked leaves, and Deb, in her pain and misery, did not give a hoot for that. But later, when Fido came a visiting, she risked mortal agony to roll onto her side and curl up like a baby. She knew why he was there, and his attitude made it even clearer, and he spoke—not in Kreyole— words that she could tell the meaning of despite that she knew none of them. He brought some others of his men as well, and there was general nudging. Crumbs off the rich man's table, Deb thought bitterly. Not good enough for white men now, was she—but still a very juicy dish. When she had posed at Dr Marigold's her face was covered, and she could not see reactions of her prurient observers, which had made it seem less vile. But one of them, she recalled distressfully, had been William. Her Will.

The herbs and potions, salves and unguents, eased her body, and strangely, eased her mind. Some of the things they bade her swallow induced sensations as of swirling and euphoria, and—had her face permitted it—she might, at times, have smiled. When Bridie came, in deadly secrecy, at night and wrapped up like a corpse, the housekeeper was glad, but not surprised. She hinted darkly at other soothing things than rum and brandy in the world of man, and told the maiden she would heal, what's more. Deb did, with great rapidity, although much of her lustrous hair was gone, and she had scabs and blisters on her face, her neck, her arms. She asked Bridie if this was why she had been banished from the house, but Bridie guessed it different.

"They see you as a slaveman's whore," she told Deb simply. "The Suttons will not play seconds to a black in first instance, and nextly, if you got with child, they would not know till birth if it was white or mixaroon. Why waste their time, when there are other wenches to be swived? Had you left Bonzo alone they might have married you, or had you as a whore of privilege, but you've made your bed, insulted them, and so are damned. When you are better though, *cailín deas,* you'll become a toy for Fido and his men. I have heard the Suttons talk of it. Seth in particular thinks it a gallant jest. I come to give you warning, Deb. I would caution you to cut your throat. Or run."

Deb lay there, wrapped in the rich and aromatic darkness of the hut, and contemplated. Become a toy for Fido and his men, or throw herself alone into the wilderness. No money, no real clothes, no knowledge of the land and how to live on it, no language except the language of the masters. She was learning Kreyole fast—she spoke with Moira almost constantly, and with the other women—but it would serve her ill in any crisis. It was a tool without a proper edge so far.

"I was no friend of Bonzo, no special friend," she said. "I ran out then because I could not bear it any more, to see him and his fellows suffering so cruel. I do not know what I hoped to do, just end something, anything, perhaps my life. Bridie, believe me, I lost my sanity. He was the nearest one, that's all, and I knew Moira. She had lost his child that day, aborted it. I think the Suttons are the devil, Bridie. How can I run away?"

"Slaves do, all the time, or leastways not infrequent," Bridie said. "Then they are hunted down by bloodhounds and brought back. As you can guess it, most of them are killed for giving masters trouble, or crippled sometimes, feet cropped with axes, fingers torn off, ears removed, eyelids slit, that sort of thing. Then others, that are very useful, young strong men and some strong women, are spared and put to work again, usually spavined in some way to stop another flight. It is a constant worry for the planters to know what to do for best. To lose slaves costs great money, for they have to be replaced, but to catch them and forgive them is not possible, and to catch them and to kill them costs even more. Sometimes, around the dinner table, my heart bleeds for them at what I hear."

Said with great solemnity, but Deb took it for a bitter jest. Bridie, she knew, was as much a slave as if she had been bought, as much as Deb had been before she'd joined hearts with the negers. Deb also knew the bloodhounds were not dogs but men, that slaves would hunt down slaves and kill them or return them to their masters. She lay there in the darkness, and she wondered how she could stand it for another seven years. Three months ago, she thought, I had a house to call my own, and a poor, fat, naked man to care for me. Could one miss that sort of thing? Absurd, absurd, absurd.

But things got worse as she got better, for Fido and his boys were anxious for their just deserts. Moira—whose name was really Kaia, it turned out—was to be the pudding at the feast, and the young men decided on some jollity to work up their appetites. Her brother in the hut (and Deb could not fully understand if he were her brother in the English sense or not) protested at the violence that was planned on her, and some other of the young men stood up on Deb's behalf, as well. An argument outside turned to violence as the women listened, and quickly there were blows and screams and lashing of hide whips. One of Fido's dogs shed blood, and Kaia's brother's face was smashed in with a stone. That night, outside the huts and then around the whole plantation, there was the sound of drumming.

■ ■ ■

In the brief hours before the *Biter* passed the Twelve Apostles and picked up a useful wind, Will Bentley tore out his heart for Deborah, which was the grand total of everything that he could do on her behalf. The pain of sitting in the sternsheets while jolly oarsmen rowed him from the shore was worst because she was within three miles or so, she might be dead or dying, and he could not even turn around and gaze, however pointlessly, behind. He had contained the ache of fear and longing in the Navy offices, knowing in himself that he would go and find her soon—then Captain Shearing had sent them on their way. On board the *Biter* the situation had been lax but jovial, with the people waiting almost calmly for some liberty ashore. It turned to ugly in a way that he could fully understand when the news sank in that they were putting back to sea. He was an officer, and it was his role to force them—and himself.

John Gunning was the key in saving it because—sober himself—he persuaded Captain Kaye to break out rum puncheons from the fresh supplies and pass the spirit round the people willy-nilly. So long as the men were capable of pulling rope and hanging on a yard, he said, the ship at this stage had no other use for them, but if they started to revolt she'd never get to sea. Savary's marines were stood down instantly from their guarding duties and made to flank a table in the waist that Purser Black set up. This fat man, a smile of calculation on his face, tallied out the small puncheons as they emptied, and counted profits in his head. The lines of sailors, surly to begin with, drank raw spirit till they coughed, then smiled, then laughed, then pranced off to their working stations. Jack Gunning, Will was told by Sam, would be an admiral in weeks if he should ever join the Navy.

Even when the brig had towed out and was in a useful breeze, however, and half the men were half drunk and the others worse, it was still felt that the reason for their sailing was a nonsense and a crying shame. They had scoured the seas for three days when they had lost the Spaniard, so what chance of finding her should they have now? It was generally determined, given her condition when last viewed in daylight, that she'd have done the long dive, with the silver, Scots, and onion-eaters all on board. The silver was regretted, but the other losses could be viewed with equanimity, and even pleasure in some hearts.

Gunning, though, with his knowledge of these seas, put it round that wind and currents would have moved her to a certain place, in probability, and he knew where it was. All moonshine, doubtless, but worth the gamble to give the men incentive. In fact, with tall masts, good lookouts, and the excellent clarity of the weather after the recent storms, he told the two lieutenants, there was a more than even chance that she was findable, if still afloat. With almost no hands and her extensive damage, the galleon could not have moved far, and the Scots, if they had navigating skills, would be heading for the south coast of the island, to get her beached—and lootable?—on some friendly strand.

"Tell Dickie Kaye to find out his best-sighted men, and bribe them with rum unlimited if they raise the ship," he said. "A ticket to a whorehouse would go down, as well. And remind him Don Spaniardo will be hunting ditto, so have a word with Gunner Henderson. Let's see if these bastards can still shift them cannons while their brains are all muzzed out. The demon drink, eh? It should not be allowed on ships, is my opinion!"

As well as doubting that the ship still swam, Slack Dickie Kaye had other problems on his mind than gunnery, although he agreed the men should practise hard as soon as they were sober. The problem of the Spaniards on board the *Santa* gave him most pause, as he explained to Bentley and Holt around the dinner table. If they had helped the Scots, for having saved their lives, they might be almost friends and allies by this process, and bribable to keep their mouths shut or to join the English Navy. Or maybe they had revolted against the Lamonts and taken back their ship, which would be even better, for then the *Biter* could wage war on them, which they would not survive. Both lieutenants looked politely dubious at this, which Kaye accepted ruefully. There was no evidence that Spaniards were completely mad by nature, so the Scotchmen would be safe. He sighed.

"At any rate, they will have done their best for us," he said. "Even you two must allow that they were sterling fighting men. If anyone could bring this off successfully for us, the Lamonts were the top. But they'll be dead, no doubt of it at all. Ah well, let's open up the letters that we've had from home."

It was a pleasant evening in the cabin, with the windows open wide and the scented air filling the space and complementing the rich wine that Kaye provided. In the Navy way, as they had guessed, some of the letters had been following the *Biter* for an age, but they were nonetheless welcome for that fact. Will had a sweet one from his sister Lal, with a little note from Martha added on (in French, the show-off—she was barely ten!), and another, strange one from his Uncle Daniel Swift. This said he knew William had made contact with *"Fat Dickie's father,"* and that he approved it mightily. He was in almost constant contact with *"my lord,"* and had Will thought of a match between himself and the elder daughter? He had heard she was ill-fared, but her fortune was in no doubt at all, and Will might get as much as twenty thousand *"for his pains in prodding her."*

He added, *"Females are susceptible to flattery in my experience, and especially flattery through the mail. A man may tell no end of dastardy and be not brought to book, by passage of good old Father Time."* What was more, he wrote, *"One can make love to an ugly harridan in script and imagine her as fair as Nellie Gwyn to Charlie in the song. And on the marriage night, just close your eyes and think of bags of gold."*

This missive was so unexpected and so very lower-deck, that Bentley was completely knocked off guard. He gasped as he read the more scabrous portions, and when he'd finished became aware that Kaye and Holt were gazing at him with bated breath.

"Well!" said Will, as flustered as a maiden. "My Uncle Swift would have me married off! And to your sister, Captain Kaye! Good God, he is exceeding bold!"

Slack Dickie cackled like a giant crow, but Holt, who had a letter of his own, responded almost sourly. Before he had a chance to speak, Kaye expressed his firm belief that Will could do much better in the bedroom stakes, despite the fact his "pretty love had turned out black man's whore!" He did concede, though, that "Felicity is very pretty in the purse department," and pointed out that as his brother,

Will would be duty bound to pay his gaming debts for him! His own letters, both from Swift and from his father, were more on business matters, continued hopes of sinking money in some land and slaves, perhaps, continued hopes that Swift could somehow wangle it so he could bring a vessel to the Indies "privately." It was not until some hours later, when Holt and Bentley shared a section of the rail to look out at the velvet night, that Sam revealed, with slight embarrassment, that his own, unexpected letter had been from what he called, half-bitterly, "Will's betrothed."

It took Will some moments to comprehend. Then he could not see why ever she had written, which made Sam laugh.

"I told you, Will!" he said. "Be not so oafish, man! To you it might be just a hatchet face; to me, I promise you, it is a sort of female beauty!"

"But to write to you! That's . . ."

"That's unexpected. Unlooked for. But exceeding welcome, let me tell you! We did a little walk together, to get away from that horsey brat the sister, and we got along like fun. But I never thought that she would write to me—and on the instant, it appears. No other woman ever did."

"The only other woman that I know that *speaks* to you can't write, can she? But poor Annette. Hell, Sam, what will the whippet say if you should wed Felicity?"

"I can't though, can I?" said Sam. "For she'll be a match for you, and bring you wealth and whippersnappers. Good God, I hope they do not have your height!"

"Or her nose!" said Will. "Don't write her that I said that, Sam! I put you on your honour, such as 'tis! By Jingo, though—to think my friend's in love."

That was another jest, but Sam did not deny it, and sighed rather.

"That seems too strong a word; I've only met her once," he said. "But honestly . . . well . . . I thought her rather fine, as I have said. Is your uncle serious, do you think? About your prospects as Slack Dickie's legal brother? And would that make you some sort of earl, like Dickie's meant to be, and if so, would you use it? Christ, I hope I do not have to call you something stupid! Lord Billy Bentley, companion of the garter and the placket. Shit! In any case, I'm not the friend struck down by love, am I? That's you."

He knew he'd stepped too cruel with that one, and fell silent, staring at the water. Since the meeting on the island, he knew that Will had thought of Deb obsessively. Back in Jamaica they would go ashore, however great the obstacles, and seek until they found her.

"I'm sorry, Will," he said. "That was—"

But a cry came drifting downwards then, an unusual cry from a lookout. Pitched low, to travel but not travel far, to warn but not be overheard. Indeed, the night was very still and calm, with just sufficient breeze to light the ship along.

"Sirs," the voice hissed down once more. "A sail, to larboard. I catch the moonlight in her upper canvas."

"Where away?" Sam called back, soft but urgently. "We cannot see her from down here."

There was a short time before the man replied, and in it both lieutenants jumped on to the rail and stretched their eyes. By looking up they could see where he was staring. He was a good man, and good-sighted, named Locking.

"Fine on the larboard quarter," came the call. "Almost dead astern. It is a brig, I reckon. I'm getting flashes off two sails. Topgallants, as I guess."

"Ah," Will breathed. "Two masts, then. She ain't our *Santa,* damn it."

"Let's aloft," said Sam. "I still can't see a thing, can you?"

They climbed rapidly until they reached the main-top. Sam still saw nothing, but Will caught a flash, then another, which must have been pale canvas. It was several miles away. He stared up to Locking, who had shinned the last feet of bare pole, good man.

"Can you see which way she's heading? What is it, merchant or ship o' war? Hang on, I'll come up with you."

By the time he got there, disappointment. Locking, glancing down beyond his feet at Bentley's upturned face, shook his head regretfully.

"I've lost him, sir. The angle of the moon, I guess. Smallish ship, sir, with them low sticks the Spanish favour, I would wager." He smiled. "Well, I wouldn't put my mother's life on it. I'd say coast-guard, though. One of them we saw before, mebbe."

Will stared until his eyes began to play him tricks, but saw nothing more he could hold on to. He must assume, therefore, he told himself, that Locking would be right in that: it was the *Guarda*. We have seen them, he thought—have they seen us? He tried to guess it, from the way the moonlight threw.

"Will he see us from there, Locking? The moon's behind us, but it's high."

Locking said instantly, "Not a chance of it, sir. The light's on him and coming back at us. He could only see us if he was upwind, like we to him. Upwind, upmoon, you know what I mean. I say we are invisible."

"On your mother's life?" smiled Bentley.

"She died ten year ago, sir. So I will risk her, aye. For what it might be worth . . ."

Bentley slid down quickly to the main-top, and talked it over with his friend. It was some hours until dawn, and they thought it pointless to bring down the upper sails, for both agreed Locking was right about their visibility. In any way, the sky was clouding up appreciably, which meant God was on their side (as Sam allowed, with cheerful blasphemy).

"My guess is," Will said, "she's heading squarish across our stern, but away from us, thank heaven. When the sun comes up there'll be no hint or sign of us, but if we shed sail, she'd be that much closer, wouldn't she? We're making five knots, maybe, so by breakfast time we'll be twenty mile away or more, well in the clear. Let's keep Slack Dickie in the dark till then, or he'll have fits. Bad enough that the Spanish are so assiduous. I doubt it's just a passerby."

When they told Kaye at breakfast time that they may have seen a sail in dead of night, but were by no means certain it was not a chimera, he was indeed agitated. The chance of finding the *Santa* afloat he still rated very low, whatever Gunning thought, but it shook him that the *Guarda-Costa* might be active in the search. Worst case of all, he said, would be if *Biter* found the galleon, full of Spanish plate, and while they were in "the act of piracy" half the Spanish fleet heaved up.

There was a worse case even than that, however, and in six hours or thereabouts it started to unfold. To Kaye's astonishment, then disbelief, then joy, they raised the *Santa,* ran her down despite the failing wind and murky weather, and boarded her. They found the Scotchmen, sober, bold, and sanguine, and they found Morgan and Dusty Miller too, alive and well. They did not find the Spaniards, however, but they quickly found out why. There had been a fight, the Lamonts said. The Dons had tried to seize the vessel back again, and the *Biter* men had won the bitter day. There was treasure still on board, a mass of it—and the Spaniards were dead.

Will and Sam, between themselves, found it difficult to believe. Hard to believe, and not a small amount distasteful. But Kaye believed it, and his euphoria was a sight to see. The witnesses to the *Biter*'s act of piracy were now no more, killed honourably and through their own base treachery, and he was rich enough—once he had stripped and sunk the galleon—to blow his troubles all away.

"By Christ," said Holt, blaspheming but less cheerfully, "I hope Slack Dick believes in God, that's all. If this is true, it would convert the Devil."

Not many hours afterwards, back on board the *Biter* and dead drunk, Willie Morgan told a different story. The Spaniards, when they had finished helping save the treasure-laden *Santa* from the storm, had been deemed superfluous. Two had had their throats cut while asleep, a third was axed to death while struggling, and the others had been thrown overside to drown or feed the sharks. Even the men who shared the general feeling, that booty was welcome from whatever source, were silenced to the soul by it. To save seamen from drowning, then to murder them in the vilest of cold blood . . . it was unconscionable.

Will Bentley and Sam Holt also received the information. It fell to them to bear the knowledge, and convey it to Slack Dickie. That he was only safe—from anything—until the Scotch should turn their blades and minds on him.

TWENTY-FIVE

Cut your throat or run, Bridie had counselled, and Deb soon found the choice was made for her. Half of the night was filled with drumming, and the latter hours with attacks by the planters' loyal slaves. They came into the compound by the factory in silence in the early hours, but the men of the huts had moved to guard outside, and they were ready for them. The Fido-men had axes, whips, and staves; the defenders—who like all the slaves stole cane-knives whenever and wherever they could find them unaccounted for—had unburied their three-foot slashers, wrapped rags around the ends for handles, and whetted rusty edges razor-sharp.

In the blackness, the fight was swift and bloody, but the planters' men were at the disadvantage. The first attack was over in five minutes, and when the bloodhounds reappeared with Seth, who had guns and a lantern, their rout was even faster. A top slave driver, Patch, was speared between the shoulders to fall screaming, and as his companions turned to face the attack, a volley of thrown spikes brought three more down. Seth discharged two muskets quite at random, striking a young woman in a hut, then was forced to run with his own drivers. His father, Alf, who had already furiously berated him for his tactics, revealed that he had sent for the Siddlehams. With preparation time, it would take them about an hour and a half to get there.

It seemed to Deb that everyone must run, but the slaves whose homes these were thought differently, and it broke her heart. Kaia, among those who would not go—indeed was too much in pain to travel upwards of a mile or so before collapsing—tried to explain it in the language that they had in common only imperfectly as yet. Here, she said, they were a group who knew each other and were equals in their misery. The work was killing them by degrees, but they knew at least that all were doomed together. They could scratch out a little happiness by sharing life, and food, and speech, if only a Kreyole that mocked their individual languages. Off the plantation, who knew what they might find?

Deb, whose life had almost been defined by running, could not really understand this sentiment. Here, to her, was a place as evil as Wimbarton's, say, and a great deal more likely to be fatal. The white men who owned their lives were mad, and the Africans who acted as their drivers and their armament were blind to any struggle for survival but their own. Bonzo had been killed for doing nothing (Deb was sure), and the others would be killed for finding it unbearable. Alf Sutton and his one remaining son could not afford to lose more of their labour, but were prepared to kill them all, or see them die. She, who had run from a peaceful place beside a peaceful river because she had been young and stupid and dissatisfied, could not believe these people would not run to get out of this holocaust. As she looked at Kaia, hoping to convey all this, she cried, instead. And Kaia shared her tears.

After the third assault, though, some did run, and with this group Deb threw in her lot. It came not too long before dawn, and it was led by Sutton on his great black mule, by Seth on a white gelding, and by the Siddleham males, father Sir Nathaniel and all three sons. As they swept towards the factory compound the drumming in the thickets reached crescendoes, then swooped and fluttered before the onslaught like game birds beaten out of cover, and disappeared. The white planters led the charge, with the Siddlehams's white overseers like two iron flanks, and a roaring mass of black men, all on foot. They crashed through huts and shelters, laying waste to every normal trap of living and of life. Bones were broken, children trodden under foot and hoof, beds, and cooking pots and stools churned into pieces. Sir Nathaniel, as a salute to origins perhaps, blew on a hunting horn he'd brought from England and gave his sons a constant "View halloo!"

The blackness and the chaos was complete, and Deborah, after the first rush, was carried on a wave of black humanity. Mabel was in the mass, with her small, screaming son; and Kaia's brother, whom Deb had thought would die, was in the van, long knife in hand, his ruined face wrapped in a bandage and green leaves; two other young men that she knew, whose names she could not catch in their own language and she dared not call as Flight and True; Mollie from the kitchen (whose name was Goanitta); and a girl called Mildred, who was tall, and strong, and warned off young white men with her icy eyes. All around her in the fetid darkness of the bush, Deb sensed other people fleeing, heard grunts, and shouts, and screams. Behind all was the roaring of the white men and their hounds, the thumping of their horse and mule hooves. Barking too, and baying, as not all the hounds were human, and every now and then a gunshot.

It was chaos mostly, though, to Deb, who was a small part only of a body that she did not understand and in no wise could control. She appeared to run for endless ages, across terrain that went from loam, to sand, to bog, to thicket, and finally to blur. Her throat began to burn, her lungs to give her tearing, jerking pain, her heart and blood to hammer in her ears and brain. At one point she thought she heard an English shout—"The whore, the whore, there goes the Spithead whore!"—but maybe she was overwhelmed, or bedlam. She crossed roads with the fleeing slaves, she crossed a river with Mabel's son clasped to her and Mabel lost, she saw other slaves, as the escapees approached, go running off to hide in case of guilt by implication. The terrain was advantageous to them in the most part, and hindered men on horses with long guns and swords, even hindered Sutton's giant mule. The slaves knew where they were going, also, while the followers did not.

The hunt ended, for Deborah, on a great disaster. They came to a small river, not wide but deep and rocky, with steep sides, and their pursuers were not far behind them. To Deb's relief, Mabel had reappeared to take her child back, and was fleet enough to help the white maid down the unstable slopes and through the churning water. As they clambered up the opposing steepness, a bay hunter burst from the jungle they had come from and thundered breakneck towards the edge. It was ridden by a pale-haired man with a cutlass and a hunting horn, who realised too late he must either stop or fly. Mabel and Deb both gasped and cowered as he took off, Mabel's son howling as rocks and clumps cast by the hooves rained down. But the horse, eyes wide and nostrils flaring, knew it could not make the distance and threw its head back, screaming, just before it hit the other bank. It landed on its chest on the rocky angle and burst its heart presumably, and Sir Nathaniel was projected ungainly forward, hitting rocks and trees, his body twisting like a doll. Deb and Mabel, despite themselves, had to stop and see if they could help—but quickly doubted that they could. He was spread out like a starfish, staring at the sky, and he was grievously hurt.

As they stood and watched in silence, with the small boy moaning quietly, the man opened his eyes, focusing them momentarily on Deb.

"Ah," he breathed. "The English whore. Please help me."

Deborah, in a foreign land, stood facing Englishness and all the learning of her life so far. This man was rich, and old, and powerful and—like her—was far away from home. Theirs were the only two white faces in the gully, now crowded round the edges once again. Their eyes locked and spoke to each other across the great divide. She saw that he was dying, or crippled beyond restitution, or drowning in despair. His lips moved, he tried to open his mouth, form words, but for the present, no more came.

But Deb could hear him speaking to her, the drumming silence filled with words. A jumble, she imagined: he might be threatening, cajoling, offering a bribe. "If you save me," the silent man told her, "all will be forgiven. You need not go with these black savage wretches; you need not die. You are white. You are beautiful. You will be saved, forgiven, made much of. You will come home."

His eyes were bright with agony. Deb thought, with a rush of pity, that his back was broken. All around her, slaves were pleading that she should come on. Mabel took her by the wrist, her eyes bright with different pain from the old English gentleman's.

"Deb," she said. "Deb-bee come. Deb come. Deb-bee."

And Sir Nathaniel could speak again. So quietly, with so much agony, that she had to stoop to catch the words.

"Please help," he said. "Don't go. I beg of you—please help me."

The story of the murder of the Spaniards spread like lightning round the *Biter,* but the officers—Slack Dickie most of all—were not privy to it for some good long while. Slack Dickie got his facts from the Lamont brothers, whom he invited to his cabin when the ships were lashed securely side by side. Before the lashing was complete the captain had gone aboard her formally, and had them show him round the treasure room, which—in his newly awoken greed for riches— he found a trifle disappointing, for a start. As he had feared, the men who had escaped by cutter had loaded up the very richest stuff, had stowed it in up to the gunwales, it would seem. Sad that their boat had been so well-found and excellently handled; if she and they had sunk, none of this current difficulty would have arose.

But the Scotchmen showed him to the holds as well, and there he saw great stacks and chests of silver and worked plate and metal, which made his heart damn near implode upon itself with relief and wonder. She was not a bullion ship as such, but the quantity of precious stuff still made his eyes bulge with something like the dizziness of joy. He could not start to guess a value for it, but there was enough to please the King and all their lordships, enough to give him and his officers prize money to make their mouths water, enough even to make the people cheer his name instead of sneering as they generally did. Enough also, he considered privily, to secrete some bits away, to hide a little hoard. Christ, it looked like wealth beyond the common dream.

In the great cabin the Scotchmen took a drink—served them by a Black Bob who was more creeping shadow than a boy by now— and glowed quietly in Kaye's approbation. They told him of the sharp work when the Dons had set on them, and commended barrel-chested Morgan, and Miller, for their part in it. They said they'd set a course to northward from the point where they had lost the *Biter,* assuming that the captain would guess it was their safest way and sail to intercept them. They shook their heads about the lack of sightings after that, quite ruefully. But these things happened, did they not? At sea you never knew, not ever.

It was an hour after this that Bentley and Lieutenant Holt heard the other story. They had assessed the damage to the *Santa* as too great to try and jury rig her with any hope of evading capture if it came to chase, and had assessed the quantity of treasure that could be shifted from her hold to the *Biter*'s. Hatch covers on the prize had been stripped with great brutality, in fact the decks had been axed and dismantled where possible for ease of getting tackles down

below to lift the heavy stuff. The 'tween-decks in the *Biter* had been
cleared as if for action to make cargo space, although Henderson,
the gunner, had argued with great passion, and success, when his
captain had proposed that some guns should lose their recoil-space
to cram the silver in, and thus be useless in a fire-fight. Spare gear
and lumber in the hold was earmarked to go overboard if necessary,
although most bulky items—food, mainly—had been consumed in
the months at sea. Speed of shifting rather than space available was
the likely problem, everyone agreed. The Dons were in the offing
somewhere—even the trucks were manned with lookouts now—and,
inevitably, the weather was clearly on the slide. No great wind as yet,
but a greasy swell was rising, which made the vessels grind together
most uncomfortable. If it worsened much more, damage would ensue.

Ashdown approached them as they re-emerged on deck, and both
knew from his face that the Irishman had need of telling something.
He looked to check the coast was clear, then dared touch Bentley on
the wrist—sign surely of his great extremity?—and slipped sideways
behind a boat. Sam, quick as ever, took a position to shield Ashdown
from the general view, and they asked him what the matter was. Ashdown, calm and frank, said quietly: "They killed the Spaniards. They
slaughtered them."

As he had heard it, it was a simple tale that rang completely true.
Morgan and Miller, sober while in the Scotchmen's thrall, had smuggled brandy from the *Santa* back on board, made free with it, and
then begun to brag among their fellows. First of much small treasure that the five of them had hidden, which they intended they
would make away with, then of the Spanish deaths, not in honourable combat but through the Lamonts' treachery. When pressed
for details, Ashdown said, they had spoken freely of the murders, but
said almost nothing of the secret spoils. They had laughed, but made
it clear they could not tell, on pain of instant death.

"Myself, I fear discretion came too late to save them, sirs," he
added, with a sort of smile. "Loose tongues have signed their death
warrants, I would say. Indeed, I fear for all our lives if those Scotchmen should live, the miserable bastards."

Work still had to be done, so Sam left Bentley to confront Kaye with the revelation, while he went off with Ashdown to direct men to gather gear to keep the treasure-transfer moving. Bentley found Kaye at his cabin table, on his own, not even a glass of wine left from his victory celebration with the Scots. He was sitting with a page of paper in front of him, playing with a pen as if to write things down. His face was dreamy. He was calculating endless wealth. Why else, thought Bentley, was he not on deck, as a captain ought to be at times like this?

His irritation with this charming madman (as Sam had called him while they drank one night) robbed the careful phrases from his lips. Instead of circumspection he said baldly, "Sir, we must arrest the Scotchmen. They are murderers." He thought he should go on, but could not. He had left himself with little else to say.

Kaye looked him up and down, with nothing on his face but curiosity. He looked as if he thought Will mad. "The Scotchmen, sir," he said, in measured tones, "have saved your life and mine, and brought us riches to the bargain. The Scotchmen, sir, are worth your weight in gold. What is this nonsense now? What mean you by this idiocy?"

"Sir," said Bentley, "they have killed the Spaniards that they saved from drowning. Five of them. It was cold-blooded villainy, and they should hang for it. I have it on best information."

"What information, Mr Bentley? Tittle-tattle, I'll be bound. Jealousy and tittle-tattle from the meanest of the crew. The Lamonts told me how the Spanish died, sir, and I believe them, utterly. They rose against our prize-men as they were bounden by their country's oath no doubt—and they were beaten. Fairly, Mr Bentley, very fairly; the odds were even, five 'gainst five." He paused. "You know the Lamonts, sir, and Morgan is the strongest man I've ever seen. Do you think, fairly, that the Dons would stay alive in mixing with those men? They were bound to die soon as they rose, sir, and contra talk is filthy slander. It is unworthy, and must cease. Do you hear me?"

Will felt a touch of sweat break out beneath his arms. The sky outside the large windows was metallic, coppery. The breeze had come erratic, the swell was rolling in. He licked his lips once more, harder. His mouth was drying in the growing heat. How could he warn Kaye of the danger that he faced from these cold and desperate men? How would he make him see?

"Sir," he said, "I think I must arrest them. I have been told—"

He was cut off by a roar of pure rage from Kaye, whose hand shot out, knocking his pen and inkhorn to the deck. Oddly, there was a sudden wail from behind the bed curtain, a wail of fright from little Bob. Then Kaye was on his feet.

"Mr Bentley, sir, if you do not cease this folly, it is you will end in irons, not the Lamonts! They have done great service, sir, and you know it! I will not hear another word against them, not one word!"

Silence, at sea, is relative. All the ports and windows to Kaye's cabin were open, all the doors to quarter galleries and the stern. Undoubtedly his shouting was audible on deck, and when it stopped, a different sort of silence drifted in from there. Noises of blocks and gear, and two hulls grinding as they rubbed, but not a human voice, a void. Until, thin and shocking, came a lookout's cry: "A sail! A sail!"

For a moment the silence in the cabin changed. Kaye and Bentley stared into each other's faces, mesmerised. Then they bounded for the door, Slack Dickie grabbing up a sword and spyglass as he ran. When they emerged, the decks and rigging of both ships were alive with men.

"Where away?" Gunning was bellowing. "Damn you, where away?"

Bentley sprang into the lower rigging and raced towards the main top like a squirrel. He had no glass but his eyes were good, and his luck was in. As he steadied himself to stare in the direction every man was indicating, he caught a flash of white that would be canvas, for a pound. He shouted down to Kaye, "I see him, sir, I see him! He's coming square this way!"

"What ship?" Kaye shouted back. "Is it the Dons? How far away? What ship is it?"

No answer to that, but they had to fear the worst. From his vantage point, Will assessed the possibilities as bad. *Biter*'s hatches were open, her yards were cock-billed for the lifting tackles, her decks were strewn with sacks and boxes. As the swell had grown, so the warps and hawsers holding the two hulls together had grown in thickness and complexity, with bolts of gash rope and canvas torn from off the Spanish ship lashed and jammed between them as fenders. Even if they got axes to bear and cut everything in sight intantly, they could not be under way in less than God alone knew how long.

"Gunning!" Kaye was shouting. "For Christ's sake, man, I need some sense in this! How long before she gets here? How far is she? What time falls darkness hereabout?"

Below him, Will saw Lieutenant Holt organising the dropping and stowage of the treasure crates still in the air or on the decks, while sending boatswain's mates off to unrig the lashings and get the vessel clear to sail. He assessed the readiness of yards all round him, and shouted hands to get the ribands off and free up clew and buntlines. Then he shot down to the deck as fast as he could slide, and skipped across the bulwarks to the galleon.

"How much still below?" he shouted at Jem Taylor. "We'll have to leave it, Jem; we'll have to go like lightning. Haul the men out. Don't let them stay there gawping. We've got to go!"

"Aye aye," said Taylor, and roared down the open hatchway "Stand clear below! I'm going to let this drop! Come out, come out, we're getting under way!"

As men began to scurry, the boatswain signalled to a group tailing a tackle, and they let the falls run out. The crate of loot emerging from the hold shot back down with a screech of blocks, and hit bottom with a muffled crash. One man emerging seconds afterwards had what looked like a candlestick in hand, which Taylor snatched from him and tossed back down the hatch.

"Get overside!" he shouted. "Get back on the *Biter*. Watch your backs and heads! Look out there, Thompson! That fall's parting! Watch your back!"

Men were running here and there like animals in a forest fire, but patterns were emerging fast. As the *Santa* was cast free from *Biter*, each man on the brig raced for his station, while Gunning took control of making sail, and con. But as the two ships drew apart, as the last sailor leapt from one rail to the other, three men, then four, then five, burst out of the *Santa*'s aft companionway and headed for the far side of the deck. They had bags with them, long canvas sea bags, and bundles tied up in cloth, like marauding gipsies from the plains of Germany. The bags were heavy, but the men were quick, and helped each other. When they reached the rail, two dropped over out of sight, while the others let the bags and bundles down. As the last gear went, a light mast-pole head appeared above the capping, with a single sheave and halyard. It waved about until it found its seating, then settled, shipped. Angus Lamont stood on the *Santa*'s bulwarks, laughing as he waved towards the *Biter,* and his friends clambered down into the dandy skiff and hoisted a sail. Sweetface Savary, quicker than the seamen, grabbed a long musket and discharged it across the wide deck at the parting Scot, but Lamont only laughed the louder—fond farewell.

Slack Dickie stood gaping, thunderstruck. Bentley, gaping also, had a thought: *Perhaps he will believe us now, about his precious Lamont brothers! Perhaps he will believe us now.* He saw Jack Ashdown, standing by a pin-rail. Good God, the man was almost smiling . . .

And at that moment, a sudden cry went up from the mainmast head.

"A sail! A sail! Two points to west'rd of the other one! A sail!"

"God damn it!" shouted Sam Holt, springing into the lower rigging. "It will be another *Guarda!* God damn it all to hell, it *has* to be!"

TWENTY-SIX

If Dickie had a thought about the Scotsmen, he had neither time nor grace to share it with his officers. The skiff, indeed, had become visible beyond the *Santa*'s bulwarks, and she was going well. But Kaye's mind, in money matters, was as sharp as razors and had moved on from mere betrayal and his own false judgement. He had on board the *Biter* about half the treasure from the galleon, which meant a further fortune left abandoned (beyond the unknown part the Lamonts and their friends had taken in the boat) which he now planned to sink beneath the waves. Neither Will nor Holt could see their way to arguing with this, although they guessed it as vindictive. The

Spanish may not have seen them yet, said Kaye—unlikely but quite possible—and if they could sink the ship, then slide away, there would be no evidence at all "to hang them with."

Will blinked at this choice of words, but accepted there was sense in it, maybe. Gunning cursed the "capting" for making his decision only after they had cast adrift—a charge of powder in the *Santa*'s bottom would have been the quickest way—but he allowed at this range they could hole her pretty quick and fatally. The only problem being that the noise and smoke of cannonade must certainly alert the Spaniards, if they were not as deaf as posts! But Kaye's mind had switched on to devious, and he saw another big advantage to be had.

"Mr Gunner!" he shouted to the waist. "I want incendiaries; I want flaming bombs! I want to send her like a torch into the sky; I want her burning bright. But Mr Gunner, first: can you sink that jolly boat for me?"

From the quarterdeck the dandy skiff was an enticing target, about two cable's lengths away. In this wind, light and fluky, she was the ideal boat, and all on board knew there was no point in chasing her. The sea was rolling quite wildly, driven by some wind across the far horizon maybe, and she was laden heavy with her booty, but going very well. As Gunning said, she was a sea-boat, and the Scotchmen, whatever else, were seamen born. Holt added that there was heavy ballast, too, to be chucked overboard if need arose. When queried with a look of disbelief, he laughed.

"I don't mean the treasure, John," he said. "I mean their two companions with big mouths. I would not bet a groat on those men's chances with the Lamont brothers. Would you?"

But Mr Henderson, a sober man, told Kaye it would be a waste of time and shot to try and blast the cockleshell. He said that he could set the Spanish ship on fire, though, or sink her, or do both. Looking westward to the horizon, he expressed his feeling that there would be darkness before long, so surely a burning ship would act as beacon, would she not? Slack Dickie said "precisely," and gave the orders to proceed.

"Set her ablaze, sir, if you please. I want her burning like a bright volcano, attracting every ship for miles around like moths. But put some holes in too—not many, judge it right, so that she'll float a good long while. Afloat and blazing suits me very well. That is my purpose. Get to it. Mr Bentley, will you get aloft, sir, and assess those *Guarda* men, if that is what they are? Have they seen us yet, what sail they're carrying, some idea of speed? Mr Gunning, when we have set that tub afire, I want this ship to run off like the wind. I want everything she'll carry set and drawing, I want her to fly."

Gunning, impolite as ever, gave a loud guffaw, suggesting they should throw the treasure over if they wanted to go quick, then set off to confer with Taylor and his mates. Kaye, quite pleased by this response, commanded Holt: "You, sir. Make certain there is nothing English in our look. See if the sailmaker can mock up some Donnish cut in any of the upper sails. I wish to get away unscathed, but if they come close enough to see us in daylight, I don't want them to have an inkling of who or what we are. If we have to fight, so be it. But unless they beat and board us, there must not be any clue. And they won't do that, will they? Now you see what all that gunnery I insisted on was for."

The cheek of Captain Kaye was marvellous, but Holt, like Gunning had been, was more amused than anything by it. While he sought out ideas and skills to change the *Biter*'s looks, Henderson got to work with his best crews, and the blacksmith lit and bellowsed-up a brazier of bright coals. Across the water both Spanish ships (there was no doubt once they were in proper sight) piled on everything, to move down sluggishly on them in the failing, fitful breeze. The light was failing also, going from day to dark without the slow degrees enjoyed by Englishmen at home, but before too long Henderson reported he was ready to set the sky alight. Gunning took over at the con, a good helmsman was picked, and all hands took stations at their sheets and braces to lay the hull—and thus the guns—round sweet and handsome on their lumpen target, rolling in the swell. Working with the roll, at point-blank range, the gunner poured pound after pound of iron into the *Santa,* below the waterline, then dropped in seven red-hot balls about amidships, three feet above it. Not too much shot, not too much smoke, not too much to indicate they were a ship of war to the distant viewers, but within ten minutes of the cannonade's cessation, flames licked out of the cripple's holds, climbed mast and rigging, and ignited the furled sails. When night fell, the *Santa* was like a giant bonfire, placed between the coast-guard ships and the English brig. The moon rose, but it was bleached out, overwhelmed, by the blazing beacon. Despite themselves, both Holt and Bentley gave their captain best.

They sailed throughout the night, and as they sailed they piled on every stitch of canvas that they had on board. Gunning and Bentley conferred contentedly, as though it was a race on peacetime terms at home. They spread studding sails on every yard, low and aloft, rigged bonnets on the courses, and a spritsail underneath the sprit, then studding sails on that. The *Biter,* full of stolen silver, weed-infested from her cross-Atlantic plug, rolling in the lumpish, nasty sea, was hardly flying, but then, she hardly ever had in all her long and varied life. Worse, she was making water fairly quickly, which the unhappy seaway did not help. The firing of the guns, Gunning assessed, was what had done most damage, as it had the last time they had fought. Will wondered if he should have asked—as Sam Holt would have—how Big Jack squared the price he got for *Biter* from the Admiralty with her condition, but dismissed it as a waste of breath. Jack Gunning saw Kaye's behaviour in pressing him as per-fidy. It would never be forgot, and it answered everything.

The blazing mark that was the *Santa* flared strongly for a fine long time, then faded, then snuffed out suddenly. There had been no flash or gout of flame, so they guessed she had gone under before the powder magazines were touched by fire, and Kaye fretted to the gunner that the Dons had been able to get on board and damp the powder down and carry off the remaining riches. Henderson dared to doubt this, and indeed the flare had been so great for such a time that even the Spaniards were not deemed mad enough to have tried. Unless they'd slaves on board, said Sam, to do the work for them. To which Slack Dickie responded with such seriousness, that Sam despaired of his sardonic wit.

All on board had thought and hoped, though, that the blazing treasure ship ploy to keep the Spanish occupied would have worked completely. As the night had worn on the lookouts had sensed several times that there might still be pursuit, but the weather, the hot beacon, and the failing moon had made any proper sighting impossible, and the eye-tricks epidemic. As the sky lightened in the east, then raced to daylight in the tropic way, the spectral visions jumped rudely into life. One of the *Guarda-Costa* ships, taller and more graceful than the Spanish norm, was not so many miles behind them, and she was sailing like a beauty. Kaye, Gunning, and the two lieutenants stood to watch her from the poop, almost aghast at her sea-kindness.

"She's not got half the canvas up we have," said Will. "She's going through it like a knife through butter."

"Shit from out a goose," said Gunning, bitterly. "Them Deptford men that rerigged us have done a proper bollocks-job."

Sour grapes, and Sam and Bentley smiled, but Kaye was getting agitated.

"We'll have to fight," he said. "Shit, Gunning, do you think he'll catch us? Is there nothing you can do to make this tub go faster, man?"

"I could throw some bodies overboard," retorted Gunning. "There's a couple of men or so I've got my eye on. The one who lit the sea up with a beacon for a start, mebbe."

Will, studying the movement of the Spaniard, and the water in between, was not so sure that they would ever close. He felt the wind was getting fresher as the sun climbed up, and he thought that if it came to blow much harder their pursuer would lose his advantage. *Biter* was canvassed like a pyramid, but not labouring from it, and—had they had spar-space that would take it—could have carried more. Tub maybe, but a good old Newcastle coal tub, built like a parish church.

"We could whistle for a gale," he said. "That would show Don Pedro who can gallop."

"Or, with the solid way we sit," said Sam, "and Gunner Henderson to lay 'em on so sweet—we could pick her sails and masts off, nice as nice. That other one won't catch us, any case. I'll take any wager on that score."

As the long day dragged on, hotter ever hotter by the minute, the wind did pick up appreciably, and the rate they were run down diminished. But they were still run down, inexorably, and a confrontation, unless the nightfall saved them, was inevitable. They were not flying colours, and they had tried to hide her English cut of rig, but Kaye had it on his mind, and mentioned it too frequently.

"If it comes to fighting," Bentley said to Holt at one point, "I think he'll do it to the death, the very bitter end. He'll want to sink her and leave without a witness, swimming or picked up, who might report on us. Jesu, how far will ruthlessness take him, dost think? Or is it fear, not ruthlessness?"

"Not neither," laughed Sam, "surely? He's won a fortune, Will, ain't you worked that out yet? He's stolen treasure from the Spanish, and he's had the blessing from on high—the Admiralty. He'll get a good proportion of it by the rules, and maybe even extra, as reward. And don't you think some of it won't walk, in any way, into his capacious pockets? When we get back on shore with this, my friend—Slack Dickie's rich. Not to tear the arse out—this may have saved his life."

Sam did not say it further, but his smile led Bentley on. Not just Dickie rich, but in the nature of it, his company as well, and most of all his officers. If Dick was saved, then so was Sam, too. Will began to see the reasons for the captain's growing agitation, and, quite suddenly, to wonder if he himself might benefit, and by how much. His debts were not enormous like his friend's, but to ease himself of them, he knew, would ease his family ten times more. In many ways, the debacle of his last few months had cost his father dear, his mother, and his sisters ditto. Then there was Deborah, in servitude to God knows who in this awful, violent colony, a servitude that he could buy her out of, should he win such cash. He forced his mind away from that dream, and lighted on his Uncle Daniel. With money of his own, he could be forever free of that succubus.

How many of the people had made the same connection he could not guess, but Gunning, whose position in regard to prizes was ambiguous indeed, had clearly worked some implications of advantage out—unless his motive, as so oft before, was pure devilment. A half an hour after this, in fact, he went below in secret, to emerge again all sunny smiles. Glancing at the captain, he marched to the signal hoist belayed at the rail, fiddled with his hands in front of his large body, then hoisted bunting, still in ties, and jerked it out into a flag when the bundle reached the lateen-end of the driving sail; a flag that made men goggle, slap their sides, then yell with laughter. Crude and quickly made, but definitely a skull and crossbones. The *Biter*, of King George's Navy, was flying the black flag.

It may have been the weather, though, that saved them in the end, for as the sea got lumpier, the Spaniard made by far the worst of it, although she closed up on them still. When she was close enough Dick Kaye, in consultation with his enemy and ally Gunning, decided on a stroke. Henderson was called into the huddle, Bentley and Holt were told what the captain and the master wanted, and a number of gun crews were mustered to be ready. By now it was too late to open lower ports for fear what they might ship on board—to add to what was coming through the seams already—and long, light-ish guns were chosen to be charged and laid. Henderson selected chain shot, and some in canisters, and some grape. He did not want to kill this time, or sink because the officers and he agreed that crip-pling was needed, quick and from a distance, so they could get away intact. The shots would all go high, intended for the masts, and sails, and rigging, and they were going to round up and rake her by sur-prise, up helm, and scoot. The people, when they got the picture, became excited. Their dreams of money loomed anew. Money, and lots of celebration rum.

Gunning, as ever, was a poet of the ship manoeuvre. On a signal, the *Biter* was brought round sharply hard upon the wind, yards braced, tacks, sheets, and bowlines snapped in like bowstrings in a miracle of energy and speed. Presented with her broadside, the Spaniard could either keep her course and fly down square on it and hope her narrow target caused a miss, or swing one way or the other to get some guns to bear. It was even hoped, on *Biter*, they were not close enough as yet to have readied up their pieces. The Spaniards, after faltering one way and then the other till the captain made up his mind for good, came straight on at them—a disconcerting move, as she was going like a wagon down a hill, a juggernaut. Mr Henderson, in sole command of this part of the strategy, made some adjustments, went from gun to gun, then fired two together on one upward roll, and three more in quick succession as that side rose again. Mr Henderson, let none dispute it, was a master gunner.

The destruction was extraordinary. At first, as the rolls of smoke blew clear, the Spaniard showed no sign of major hurt, although the keener eyes could see her sails were shredded. Then her fore top-gallant mast went sideways overside, like some tall pine tree falling in a forest. Then her topsail dropped horizontally, a great white rush of canvas, which landed on the foreyard, hovered, then broke that from its chains to crash onto the forward deck, while behind the fore-mast the main topsail yard fractured at the truss and flopped downward like a seagull's broken wings. Then, as she dropped broad-side on, the Spaniards, good men, fired three or four of their upper guns, and one ball was heard to buzz and roar across the poop deck, hitting nobody and nothing. The *Biter*'s cheering was interspersed with sail orders, as Gunning upped his helm, braced yards round handsomely, and hauled in tacks and sheets.

The stern they showed so clearly to the Spaniard still flew the skull and crossbones, with humour and defiance. It had gone two hours later, to be replaced by Dickie's favoured ensign—a bare pole—when Taylor knocked, then burst into the cabin where the upper echelon sat and listened as the captain, in a mood of wild exuber-ance, regaled them with fine promises. Of rum unlimited, of furlough on the land, of women—and of money, money, money! One look at Taylor's face sobered all of them. It was immediate.

"Sir," he said. His voice was almost hoarse. "Sir, we are sinking. The bottom's dropping out."

Christ, thought William Bentley. Gunning's revenge . . .

TWENTY-SEVEN

Sir Nathaniel Siddleham's back was broken, but the tenacity with which he held on to life, and Deborah, was extraordinary. His eyes, now dull, now bright, kept up a constant communication, they flashed and signalled at her, imploring for her help. There were other men around her for a while, exhorting her to come, in Kreyole or their native tongues, and there were women, pleading with increasing desperate pathos. Mavis tried to drag her, tried to break her from the old man's vision, tried with cry and gesture to make her realise. But Sir Nathaniel—without a touch—held on. Needing her for help, offering solace for her body and her soul.

Deborah, finally alone with him in the river gully, knew that there were other men not far behind them, white men and black, Christians and their willing slaves. She knew that if they caught her, if she remained here till the followers came up, it would be the end, even if they did not kill her out of hand. She might, indeed, be lauded as a heroine; she might be hailed a saviour, or end up as a member of the white community, respected in the way that Bridie was, safe, with authority and some influence and position. But—she would not end up free.

She did not mean from slavery, she did not even mean from retribution, of some minor kind, for her running in the first place. She would not be free, if they caught up with her, to be herself, do as herself, a simple human being. All her life she had been forced. She saw it now with clarity, as she stood panting in the gully with this poor, broken old man. Forced to be a daughter, to be a hatter-girl, to be a liar, a thief, a whore, a runaway. She had been a sideshow, a kept female by a rapist, a rich man's comforter and toy and—close as a toucher—a Spithead Nymph. The only time she had not been forced, since childhood, was when she'd known Will Bentley.

And then she almost spat. She laughed, and almost snarled. Oh bollocks, she had been forced, been forced by love, as well! To follow, to seek, to pine, to hope. She could not blame him for that love. It had hit her. She had not looked for it, as nor had *he*, for certain. But it had made her weak once more, a thing of someone else's whim and want, a shadow and a follower, without her own clean will.

Deb looked at this broken lordship laid in front of her, and she thought: No more! She would turn away and leave him to his destiny. She would be hard on him and easy on herself. Her *self*. She would run into the mountains with Mavis and the men and other desperate slaves, and she would make a life with them. She would make a life, and try to live, and if she failed, she'd die. She would die unbidden, unadmonished, unadvised. She would die a mistress, not a maid. The mistress of her fate.

Sir Nathaniel was staring up at her, his eyes melting in the growing light. He was imploring her. His eyes were screaming to be helped, one human being crying for humanity. Suddenly, as if pulled by a wire, Deb bent over him and kissed him gently on the lips. She tasted blood and tears.

Goodbye Lord, she breathed (but did not voice the words aloud), goodbye. I hope someone will help you—but not I. Poor Lord, it can't be I.

She heard the hunters crashing through the undergrowth. She heard black women call, beseeching her to come.

She went.

They had whistled for a wind when they'd been fleeing, but as the day wore on and night came down, men on *Biter* began to pray that it would ease. With the *Guarda-Costa* vessel wrecked and her fellow not yet even up to her, they had no more to fear from Spanish action (nor recognition or suspicion of identity), but the piping gale grew ever stronger and the seas grew worse. After Taylor's news, the pumps were manned in earnest, and a bucket chain was organised. The captain and his officers had all run down below to see the damage, but Gunning, signally, had declined to budge. He was not drinking, despite the fact that they all were, but he had a long clay in his mouth and was smiling round it when the news was brought. At which he bit the stem off.

The situation on the orlop had been terrifying. Hugg and Tilley had got men with lanterns and were clearing lumber to locate a source, but the deck was running water like a river under ground. The ship was rolling violently, with great walls of water slopping from one side to the other, meeting amidships, throwing up great gouts. In the light of smoking lamps, Will could see white gushes driving through the seams, growing and contracting as the timbers worked. Round their feet and knees it foamed and bubbled, some fresh from outside, some mixed with thrown-up bilge filth, rank and vile.

"You bastard," Bentley heard the captain saying to himself, of John Gunning, there was not a doubt. "You filthy, lousy, lying *bastard!*"

Hugg and Tilley, then Bosun Jem, all pointed out danger points, all shook their heads in blank dismay at any way of stopping it. Holt said to Will, digging with a fid he'd taken from a rack, "She's rotten, Will. She's fucking rotten. She's a sieve."

The ship had one main chain pump, which hoisted buckets in continuity from deep down in the bilge up to the deck. It was run by manhandles, each long enough to take three sailors side by side. Working at top effort, it would wear a man down in fifteen minutes or so, when other men would leap on to keep momentum up. With this pump manned, the water coming in was beating them with ease, so after consultations, pails, scoops, bailers, and buckets were all broken out from stores, and teams of men put on to using them. At con, John Gunning—still maintaining a stiffish smile—issued commands to ease and trim the sail-plan to avoid the worst of the battering the tired hull was getting from the sea. And in the cabin, Slack Dickie, like a man condemned to hell, sat poring over charts of the Jamaica coast and wondering where the hell his ship might be exactly, and where was best to hit.

By morning, it was clear that all was lost for *Biter,* if not yet for the hope of saving treasure. No need for constant sounding of the hold: the water could be seen down the companionways. It was slopping to an awful rhythm, as she rolled more sluggishly with her increased weight and depth. Each time she rolled, it slopped and ran, and rushed down to the low side, and with each roll she went further and took more time for the reverse. Then the water had to climb, hold her leaden on the balance point, then begin the awful rush to the new low. The feeling that she would not stop, but just continue till she rolled right over, became an enormous strain, almost unbearable.

By morning also, something else was clear. Jamaica was quite visible, white strands, green undergrowth and jungle, purple, brooding hills. Kaye, who could hardly bear to talk to Gunning, had nonetheless to huddle on the poop with him, lend him the spyglass, listen to him smugly make prognostications. Gunning, a man become quite happy with himself again, allowed, with apparent pleasure, that he was not certain where they would hit, but thought he knew within a mile or five. With luck, he said, they would rest the ship on sand, not far off a beach where they could make shelter in some safety, and sail round to Port Royal in the boats and bring back hulls and men to lift and carry off the booty. When Kaye objected, acidly, to that pirate term, Big Jack laughed delightedly. With luck, he also said, there were no Maroon bands living in the area. Otherwise— more loud laughter—they would all be dead.

Insist he did, however, that they would make the beach before the *Biter*'s rotten bottom planking kissed goodbye to her sides. The beach would be long and shelving, he further promised—as it mostly was along this part of coast—and they would beach inside the strongest of the surf. She would be swept, quite possibly, by long rolling Carib seas, but she would be high enough to take no mortal damage, and the lifting of her precious cargo would be like eating cake. Kaye, because he had to, because the desire to was almost as concrete as his very bones, believed him. As they came closer, Will and Sam could smell the need and lust off him, the sheer, crushing desire to get his treasure on the beach and safe. When they had reached a mile off-shore, when it looked as though Jack Gunning had been completely right, Kaye fell from time to time to whimpering, letting out small sounds of anxiety and delight, which he was unaware of. And all the time Jack Gunning smiled his sober, drunken smile.

Their luck ran out a quarter mile from land. The sea had eased, the wind had eased, and anxious scanning of the shoreline revealed no black runaways preparing fiendish death for them. Despite Gunning's promises and contempt, attempts had been made to bring some of the "booty" up from the hold, to make it easier to recover if *Biter* went underwater rather than resting on the beach, but the holds themselves were under many, many feet—and raising heavy weights brought added instability. For the last long time their progress had got slower, and it had been mooted that they must fill the boats with silver to ferry it to shore in case the brig just did not make it in that far. But there was another problem, on top of inundation of the hold, and instability, and Gunning's acid mockery. Few of the men could swim, and there would be no spare room for anything at all. Even Slack Dickie, it was thought, would not have brass neck enough to save the shekels and not men. Even at best, some would have to hold on ropes or drown.

And then the ship began to go, and Taylor took a sounding with the lead, and only hit the bottom when he'd reached almost sixteen fathoms—one hundred feet. A hundred feet of water so clear it looked as if a child could touch the bottom with a finger. As he sang out, the boats were launched from off the deck, and gouts of water burst up from the hatches.

Slack Dickie, standing on the poop, looked like a man whose heart had given out. Four hundred yards or less, and underneath his feet riches beyond most men's belief. The chance to rise, to stand alone, to show the world, and men, and father what he was made of, what he could make of life. Sixteen fathoms. More than ninety feet. He could not believe it. It was beyond his grasp. Sam swore afterwards that he had heard a strangled sob. But maybe it was Gunning, stifling a laugh.

TWENTY-EIGHT

In the next minutes, a strange silence fell. Boatloads of men, dozens of heads bobbing in the clear, lovely, friendly water. When the main truck disappeared below the surface, chests, planks, baulks, and lumber came bursting up, and then subsided. Sam thought of his captain, who had climbed into a boat like a whipped dog, but who had oddly taken care to bring Black Bob out of the cabin to sit beside him in the sternsheets. He thought of Kaye and wondered why he felt so sorry for him.

Sorrow for themselves felt more appropriate for some of the seamen. Land was but a gentle pull away, and even those whose fate it was to be dragged in the water on long lines, or cling to the gunwales if they could not float at all, did not find the sea a problem when they realised there were no sharks or likelihood of waterghoulies lurking in the depths. The beach looked friendly, but beyond the beach was . . . what? A sailor at sea is a giant. A sailor in port is a terror and a threat. But here were rolling sands, strange trees and undergrowth, and—doubtless—serpents and spiders and savages and beasts with bloody fangs. Port Royal, they had heard of that, they had seen it, damn nearly got their claws in it, and in its drink and women. But where was it now? How long a march, on bare feet made for decks, not loam and sand and rocks and spiky undergrowth? Would there be retribution for the things they'd done? There would be no reward, for certain, as they had no gold to give the King and Admiralty. Would they be blamed for losing it?

Sam also wondered, idly, as they slid across the glossy swells towards the shimmering sand, if any blame could be attached to them, but it did not strike as likely, when all was said. They had gone on their illegal expedition with the Navy's blessing, Captain One-leg Shearing had sent them open-eyed, and his first requirement—that the *Santa* should be certainly destroyed before the *Guarda-Costa* found her or any other evidence—had surely been fulfilled. Could they be disgraced? Court-martialled? Lose their commissions, even? He could not see what for. They had set out from England to aid the Squadron, but their bottom had dropped out. Who was responsible? Slack Dickie, in reality—there was little doubt of that—but his tracks were truly covered and his hands were clean. The Admiralty had decided on the purchase, and no doubt chosen or agreed to the men who had done the checks and surveys. Gunning had hinted that Kaye had had dealings with some murky Navy Office clerk, that money had changed hands, and Kaye was still deep in the fellow's debt. Well, God help him then, and curse him for a greedy fool, to boot. He doubted, though, if Dickie were so slack that he would not have cleared himself of blame or any taint or route to it.

Dick Kaye, sweating in the sternsheets, the black boy by his side, felt sorrier than anyone, but only for himself. In his eyes it was an overwhelming tragedy. He had lost nothing, as a fact, but as he saw it he had lost everything. Ruin. Debts. Failure. That was what he'd ended up with; those were the jewels he had plucked from out the flames. He had looked to end up in the clear, a rich man and a triumph in his own right. He caught Gunning's sardonic face, and Gunning winked at him. He said something, which Slack Dickie, luckily for his wrung-out soul, could not hear.

Jack Gunning had said this: "I wonder where your Scotchmen are, Capting. Be funny, wouldn't it, if they hove up on shore with all their ill-got gains? That would be a cause for jest, now wouldn't it?" Jack Ashdown, squatting down beside him on the bottom planks, did hear, and allowed himself a private little smile. He had left these shores with those three awful men, and he would bet his life that they'd got back as well as he; they were indestructible. He had already sworn, inside his head and soul, that he'd survive this "homecoming" and would strive like very heaven to see that they should not.

Will, in another boat, thought of the silver momentarily, regretting that his friend Sam could not be rich and his own family eased of cash constraint. He knew no man would ever see the treasure again, though, and moreover, did not care. He thought of Deb, and felt his heart rejoice. He knew where she was, at least not many miles away, on a plantation near Port Royal. He would find her out, and see her very soon. He thought of her, with a small, secret, sentimental smile, as his Spithead Nymph. He had lost her, and he had found her, still alive.

But Deborah Tomelty, though still alive indeed, was a Spithead Nymph no more, nor ever would be. She was seated in a clearing, by a freezing rill that splashed down from the mountains, her ears full of water music and the shrieks of vivid birds. Her feet were bleeding, her clothes were torn, and her heart—like Will Bentley's—was full of hope. There were eleven of them, fugitives from Alf Sutton's, including Mabel and her little son, and all of them were hungry and afraid. They had tried to tell her what they faced, but Deb would not allow herself to fully understand it.

She was a fugitive; she knew that. She was an outcast from the white society on the island, and she would probably be hunted. Some blacks, some runaways, some Maroons, would help her and her fellows, and some would track them down to kill or capture them.

Mabel smiled at her, and offered her a piece of fruit Deb did not recognise. She tasted: it was good. Deb smiled.

She would never, ever, be a Spithead Nymph